The Flapper, the Scientist, and the Saboteur

THE FLAPPER, THE SCIENTIST,
AND THE SABOTEUR

a novel

Charlene Bell Dietz

QUILL MARK PRESS · ALBUQUERQUE

LIBRARY OF CONGRESS CONTROL NUMBER: 2016939696

Dietz, Charlene Bell
The flapper, the scientist, and the saboteur: An Inkydance book-club mystery /
Charlene Bell Dietz.—First Edition.
ISBN 978-1-945212-50-5 (hardcover)
ISBN 978-1-945212-51-2 (paperback)
ISBN 978-1-945212-52-9 (electronic)

1. Roaring Twenties—Fiction 2. Science Institute—Fiction 3. Murder—Fiction
4. Economic Espionage—Fiction 5. Multigenerational—Fiction 6. Mystery—Fiction

 Quill Mark Press
933 San Mateo NE, Suite 500–159
Albuquerque, NM 87108

AUTHOR'S NOTE: My inventive twists, my errors, my stubbornness, are my own and must not reflect negatively on the expert advice from those who've given me counsel. Please remember, the characters in this book lived only in my imagination, and all events and places are fiction or used fictitiously, except of course, when they're not.

BOOK DESIGN BY LILA SANCHEZ

DEDICATED TO THE MEMORY OF THESE DEAR WOMEN

(Aunt) Margaret Graham Cassidy—role model for life's passion.
Billie Graham Bell—role model for life's goodness.
My Aunts—angels who comfort.

ACKNOWLEDGMENTS

Often authors debate whether to include acknowledgments or not to those who touched the shaping of their story. After all, it's the author who spent all those hours writing and rewriting. It's the author who looped and tied those ideas into a compelling plot. It's a laborious task to sit at the computer long hours, to hide away from distractions in order to create other worlds, to endure the rather lonely process of putting thoughts down day after day. Yet, the creation of a well-written novel needs other hands, minds, and even inspiration.

Any book you see on the shelf at your favorite bookstore or advertised on Amazon didn't get there because the author worked in a vacuum. I'm filled with gratitude when I think of all the unselfish people who guided me down this path, especially my spouse, Michael Dietz Sr., who coaxed me to step forward and not to amble.

Peter Gelfan showed me writing is a journey of love. He taught me the craft and encouraged me to have fun with my imaginary gang.

Reni Browne and **Shannon Roberts** kept my voices true and sharpened my story.

Paula Munier, Andrea Hurst, and **Michael Neff** proved valuable mentors in Monterey.

Cheryl Eckart: pushed my ignition button, turning my ideas into stories.

My Writing Group: patience ears, exacting tongues, and encouragement from **Patricia Wood, Margaret Tessler, Joan Taitte, Mary Blanchard, Dianne Flaherty, Annie Kyle, Betsy Ross Lackmann, Jan McConahy.**

Karla Greth Smith: my resident sociologist.

Michael Dietz II: my resident firefighter.

K. Doug Greth: my resident biologist and techy.

C. Eric Greth: my resident remodeler and co-architect for planning out life goals.

Tamii Abraham Greth: showed Beth how to deal with a demolished kitchen.

Sue Hettema: companion world traveler, first proof reader, policeman making my characters behave, and head cheerleader.

Kevin Greth: my resident pharmacist.

Ed Mims: expert authority on all things criminal.

Mary Ann Domina: beta reader.

Marlene Kurban: long-distance, beta reader.

James Ayers: beta reader with a professional eye.

Debra Faulkner: Brown Palace Hotel Historian and tour guide par excellence.

Lovelace Respiratory Research Institute: inspiration.

Family and friends: those who unknowingly loaned me the use of their names.

NOTE: Did you know? Authors are ecstatic when readers tell their friends about books they've enjoyed and then write book reviews on Amazon.

The FBI seeks your help in safeguarding our nation's secrets!
Our nation's secrets are in jeopardy, the same secrets that make
your company profitable.

—FBI

No human thing is of serious importance.

—PLATO

1

Die, old lady, please die. Tears filled Beth's eyes.
She turned away, swallowed hard, then said, "You only want a hamburger
with a bun and nothing else. Is that what you said?"

The late afternoon sun filled her parents' bedroom with shadows. Beth
let her purse drop to the floor and clicked on the antique table lamp. The
cold grays of the room changed into a buttery glow—full of old cigarette
smoke.

"That's right, dear." Aunt Kathleen kicked off her slippers and padded
across the Oriental rug toward the unmade bed, then she climbed under the
top sheet.

Aunt Kathleen said something else, but Beth's concentration for small
talk was gone. She couldn't stop worrying about her research lab.

What went wrong this morning? Her panic started with disbelief. Teri,
her assistant, stood in the doorway of the inner lab saying something about
Beth's lab animals. Then disbelief turned to terror when she discovered her
multiple sclerosis research hanging on the verge of ruin. Who, or what, had
invaded her lab?

Beth prided herself in controlling her emotions, but now anger bubbled
out. This afternoon's emergency trip to Valley View, and now still being

here tonight with her aunt, her resentment sprung to the surface when she least expected it, completely disorienting her.

She needed to be at the institute, protecting her MS research. The ache in her throat grew. Beth knew the etiology of MS hid within a synergy created by key issues and underlying T cells and immune responses. Revealing the cause of extensive demyelination of the central nervous system would lead to a cure. *Too many are suffering. . . .*

She shouldn't be here playing nursemaid.

Stop it. She owed this to her aunt, a small favor for a huge debt.

Her aunt fumbled with the covers.

"Aunt Kathleen, the nutrition in a hamburger isn't much help to you. The emergency-room doctor said you should eat more—" Her aunt waved her off and continued struggling with the blanket. Beth helped her tug up the cover.

"I hate the word *aunt*, child, and I don't need any goddamned help."

Beth stiffened, but she smoothed the bedding over her aunt anyway.

Had the heat lamps saved any of the mice? How many lived? Had this morning's damage taken her past the point of no return? No matter. She'd find a way to work around it. She wouldn't let this research fail.

Her aunt reached for a pack of Pall Malls on the bedside table. Her tousled hair and baby-bird skin seemed to melt into the white linen pillowcase.

"Don't you even want mustard?" No fast-food restaurant served plain hamburgers—not without a wait. Sorrow encompassed her, weighed her down. She picked up Kathleen's jacket from the floor and hung it in the closet.

"I don't understand," Kathleen took a puff before continuing, "how people can garbage up their hamburgers with so much junk."

Stale cigarette smoke stung Beth's eyes. The room smelled like an old saloon.

Hey, everybody, raise your hand. Do you prefer pickles to cigarettes?

"On second thought, I do like onions." Kathleen's bony fingers clutched a matchbook along with her cigarette. "Some thinly sliced onions would be splendid."

"I might not be back before the woman we hired gets here." Beth squared the collection of magazines. "You won't have to get up. I made her a key."

"Frankly, dear, I don't want her here."

"You liked her this afternoon." Beth frowned. "The nurse liked her, too. Remember the woman's great sense of humor?" The hospital had given Beth several phone numbers of caregivers. Kathleen settled for Mrs. Harrison, a hefty woman with brassy dyed hair and two-hundred pounds of steel muscle. She looked like a mama lioness ready to protect her cubs.

"I'm capable of taking care of myself." Kathleen stubbed out her cigarette.

Beth shrugged. Kathleen talked tough but it was all a façade. The smoke curling from her aunt's cigarette had more stamina than she did.

How do you care for someone like that?

"To hell with the hospital. I've never seen people so upset over a few bruises." Kathleen waved her cigarette. "For God's sake, I only tripped." A red cinder fell onto the lace bedspread.

Beth gasped and swiped it away. Oblivious, Kathleen struggled to balance her cigarette on top of the other butts in the ashtray.

"Aren't you worried you'll torch this house?" Beth swiped the spot again, but a small hole with dark edges remained on the heirloom cover. Her grandmother had handed it down to her mother. Beth's throat closed.

"I'll leave that worry to you." Kathleen tucked a few strands of white hair behind her ear.

"When we talked at the hospital about your care," Beth said, "you told me—"

"I know what I said, child. Call and get rid of her."

"I won't be calling her. I won't leave you unattended. Besides, you'd be depriving this woman of her livelihood. Her husband died last year. She's scratching around for any work she can find."

"Dammit, Beth, I don't want a stranger in this house."

But you're the stranger in this house.

She barely knew her aunt. Her family, for the most part, pretended the woman didn't exist. But then this caustic old lady had rushed in and taken over the care of Beth's dying mother. A lump began to form in her throat. Even considering her tainted research, today's trip to Valley View wouldn't begin to cover her gratitude to this aunt.

Kathleen lit a second cigarette, then turned and looked at the one still smoldering in the ashtray. "Oh, hell." She stubbed the other one out.

Slow hormonal heat started deep in Beth's chest and bloomed on her skin, leaving a wake of perspiration. She slid out of her herringbone jacket and cracked the window. It would be spring soon. Damp pine smells mingled with the stale, smoky air. She craved the clean air of her lab.

Was she kidding herself? Was her research even salvageable?

Kathleen said something. Beth turned from the window.

"Wouldn't that be best? Think of the money I'd save. My housekeeper comes on Friday." She managed to sit a bit straighter. "You could stay in your old room until she gets here."

All of this—everything—irritated Beth. She once loved this dusty-blue wallpaper with its pale-pink flowers, but now it looked as tired as she felt.

But then to stay down the hallway in her old room. . . . After a day like today she craved her childhood treasures. She'd find sanctuary under her favorite comforter. Maybe she could take it back to Denver with her, but she couldn't stay here. She needed to be at the institute first thing in the morning.

"I wish I could, but I can't play hooky any longer."

"Nonsense, nothing's that important. Besides, didn't you tell me you work in a library? If people can't check out a book they won't die, will they?"

"Kathleen, I'm not a librarian. I'm a researcher, and I do documentation for other scientists." She slammed the window shut. "I need to finish up here and get home."

"Well, I hope you aren't one of those who spend their days working with rats." Kathleen touched Beth's wrist. "You're wearing my sister's watch. That's sweet."

Beth wanted to explain why she couldn't stay, but how could she? She didn't even understand what had happened in her lab.

"We're only talking about a few days, Beth. I don't know much about you except for what my sister shared, and you know Mary didn't talk much."

"She said plenty when I dug a tunnel under her garden or climbed on the roof. Kathleen, the timing's wrong. I'm vying for an important position, and now I'm worried some jerk may have sabotaged my research this morning."

"Interesting. Do you suppose it's because someone wants that important position?" Kathleen raised one eyebrow. "I'm quite good at solving mysteries. When I lived in Chicago crime permeated everything, such a dangerous and exciting place. Once when—"

"Thanks for the invite, but I have to go." *Was* there a connection between the promotion and the dead mice?

"Mary used to say, 'Beth's always on the go. I wish she'd slow down.' I think she found you a bit difficult."

"What would my father say?" She didn't mean to sound snippy. She missed him.

"See, child, I don't know you at all."

"I'll come and stay for a few days when you're feeling better. You can tell me about crime in Chicago." She fought back a groan. Her to-do list seemed to keep growing.

"Oh, for heaven's sake." Her aunt blew out a smoke ring. "Call Howard and tell him you're staying the night."

"Howard wouldn't care." She picked up her aunt's pearl-colored satin robe and slid her fingers over the soft material. "His name is Harold, and he's a worrier."

"I know, I know, a library unlike any other. I took a speed-reading class in high school, did I tell you that? You should bring me a mystery to read, one of those page-turners."

"It's a media-resource center." Beth's temple throbbed. "It's not a library, unless you like to read journals about rats and rocks."

Her aunt scowled. Beth folded the robe and placed it on the foot of the bed.

"Everything's arranged with Mrs. Harrison." Beth patted her aunt's arm. "She's quite capable—"

"Mrs. Harrison can go to hell." Kathleen jerked her arm away. "If you can't stay, then go. I'm fine. I've taken care of myself all my life." She fumbled around for something. "I certainly don't need babysitting now."

"Until you're more stable on your feet I need to know you're safe." Beth's jaw tightened. "I'm surprised you didn't break something." She emptied the ashtray into a small copper wastebasket, grabbed a tissue, wiped up the overflow off the nightstand, and glanced at her aunt.

"Beth—"

"And we should get to know each other, but for now, think of this as a vacation—you won't have to go up and down those stairs." She threw the tissue into the wastebasket.

Kathleen's Lhasa apso, Saucy, bounded into the room, dragging her leash. She dropped it and gave a joyous yip. Bits of red food stuck to her whiskers. She leapt onto the foot of the bed, circled three times, and plopped down. Her feathery tail swept back and forth.

Beth pulled out another tissue and wiped the food from the dog's fuzzy face. She sighed. She'd forgotten that the dog needed to be walked before she left. Beth would be driving back to Denver in the dark by the time she'd finished all the dog care and dinner buying.

Kathleen's eyes narrowed.

"Go home, girl." She turned her head away from Beth.

"Kathleen." She tossed the tissue away. "I'm not ditching this obligation—"

"Go!" Kathleen's eyes now blazed at her. "I refuse to be your *obligation*."

"I didn't mean it that way."

"I damn well think you did."

"Before she died, I told mother—"

"I don't care what the fuck you promised her." Kathleen closed her eyes. "Leave me alone."

Beth's face burned. She grabbed an empty glass and filled it from the bathroom faucet. She picked up a magazine-subscription card off the carpet, placed it on the nightstand, then thunked the glass down.

Kathleen studied her matchbook cover.

Beth snapped Saucy's leash to her collar. The shaggy dog hopped off the bed and lunged toward the door.

Kathleen stared at Beth, and then she flicked the matchbook to the floor.

Was this woman really related to my mother?

Beth managed to slip her jacket on with one arm. With her free hand, she picked the matchbook up and dropped it next to the water glass.

"Are you always like this?" Kathleen glowered at her.

Beth stopped in the doorway. "Like what?"

Kathleen waved her cigarette in the air. "Never mind."

In 1994, the president of the software firm Ellery Systems reported to FBI Denver the theft of source codes that had been developed for the emerging "information superhighway." This led to an early economic espionage case.

—DENVER DIVISION, FBI, APRIL 2011

Page 1: The goal of this guide is to promote the humane care of animals used in biomedical and behavioral research, teaching, and testing; the basic objective is to provide information that will enhance animal well-being. . . .

—GUIDE FOR THE CARE AND USE OF
LABORATORY ANIMALS, NRC, 1996

2

Early the next morning, Beth unlocked the door to the institute's atrium. Huge windows, cultivated plants, and her footsteps echoing off the polished tile floor erased her dark mood from the night before. She passed her Research Resource Center office and took the stairs to her lab on the second floor.

Last night, with Harold asleep next to her, she imagined some rather impossible ways to save her research. What had made sense in the gray hours of the morning now seemed silly. In her laboratory's outer office she donned protective clothing before pushing open the animal-room door.

A slight breeze brushed her bare forehead and her muscles relaxed. The Laminar Flow was on, exerting enough air pressure to keep foreign pathogens out of the animal room. *Did it malfunction yesterday?* Muted light, slight movements from the nesting units, and a faint, musky smell brought the comfort she craved after being in Kathleen's smoke-filled bedroom. She counted each of the units with their little inhabitants. Only those nearest the door were missing.

What was that?

She heard a soft shuffle, like someone making a sound not meant to be heard. Her muscles tensed. She scanned the room, listened, but the only noise she could identify came from the rustle of her tiny charges in their bedding. She didn't move.

Was someone in her outer lab?

She held her breath listening for the slightest noise. Nothing.

She peeked back through into the other room. Nothing.

She laughed, a short, breathy burst at her suspicious self. Then she stopped. *Nothing* was funny. Her mice had died because something or someone had invaded her inner lab. She drew in a deep breath and stood straighter.

Beth's gaze swept beyond the two rows of units housing the mice, to the polished counter tops, and then to the gleaming stainless-steel surgical area. She bristled at her dead mice and her outdated microscope and the faded, green paint on the scuffed walls. She couldn't let this world-class, private research facility deteriorate into nothingness solely because of benign neglect. Her head churned with thoughts about her research. Her animals' deaths weren't an accident.

She examined each mouse and checked Teri's data in the daily log book. All the surviving animals remained in good health. When she locked her lab's outer door and headed toward the main staircase the elevator doors opened.

"You." Borstell, a stout, square man in a starched lab coat, stepped out and shoved an accusing finger at her. "Stop interfering in my research."

She expected his wrath when she'd reported him to their boss.

"I can't be silent about blatant disregard for institute rules." She towered over him, but he'd be insulted if she kicked off her heels. "You know this place operates on highly ethical principles. We're all expected to manage our projects within institute guidelines—"

"I'm on probation now because of you."

"The CEO makes those decisions. I don't. If you want, I'd be happy to sit and discuss—"

He pivoted and strode down the hallway. If he had agreed, she would have talked with him about the incident. She drew her cheeks in and stared at his back.

Who knew what went on inside his strange mind?

She shrugged and took the stairway leading down to the atrium.

Her heels clicked on each marble step. Halfway down she heard voices and could see Nancy, the institute's receptionist who was also her secretary, talking with someone. After a few more steps Beth could see her good friend, Joe Hammer, the lead researcher on their macaque project. Nancy and Joe were deep in conversation.

When Joe noticed Beth, he motioned her toward her office in the Research Resource Center. He looked more than ready to retire today.

"Ms. Armstrong?" Nancy held up a note. She and Joe stopped. "There's a message from some bakery ready to deliver six dozen stale bagels. I'm sorry, but they insisted it wasn't a mistake. I can call them back if it's an error."

"A bagel bash, Nancy, I've been waiting for this." She grinned at the confused look on Nancy's face. "Don't worry, I'll take care of it."

Beth unlocked her door and snapped on the lights.

Joe slid into a chair and scooted it up to the long, oak table.

This wasn't like him—so serious.

He glanced around the large, windowless room lined with honey oak–colored bookcases, a matching desk, and metal file cabinets. And there stood her blasted outdated copy machine. Asking Orin over and over for a new one didn't seem to help. *Was Joe searching for the right words? He'd never had trouble before saying whatever was on his mind.*

She sighed, took a seat across from Joe, and waited.

"Terrible events yesterday." He spoke in his usual slow, methodical way. "Teri gave me the particulars."

"She's the best lab tech in this whole place."

"Your nude mice, how many died?"

"Four units." She squeezed her hands together and sat straighter.

"And the rest?"

"Naked but happy."

"Teri mentioned their bedding was damp." He paused, looked at her, then added, "Did you notice?"

"We wore gloves. I don't know how the bedding could be damp." She visualized each of the units from yesterday. "Now that I think about it, the material did look darker in places. Guess all I cared about was saving the mice." Yesterday's bitter helplessness still chafed.

"Seems Teri noticed the wet bedding when she cleaned those empty units." He rubbed his balding head.

"Teri wouldn't spill water and leave it. She knows athymic mice can't tolerate damp or cold. Who else has been in my lab?"

"Don't you keep your door locked?" His eyes met hers.

"Of course. I'll sort it out." She looked away. . . . Wet bedding? She glanced toward the ceiling. An emergency shower room on the third floor was directly above her lab. "Anybody check the ceiling for leaks?"

He opened his mouth in surprise then shook his head.

Beth jumped up and pressed the intercom on her desk phone.

"Nancy, have Wayne run up to my lab, put on protective clothing, and check the ceiling for leaks." She would go herself, but she knew it couldn't really be the ceiling. Water would be everywhere. Wayne knew how to suit up, and she trusted him.

"If it's not a leak," Joe said, "don't be too hard on Teri."

"It's not Teri. If it is a leak, Orin needs to brace himself for the full force of my wrath. He's the CEO for Pete's sake. He has to put some money back into this facility." She sighed. "Now tell me what's happening with the macaques. Nancy said Wayne's refusing to clean their room."

"They throw feces at him." Joe's loose fist hid his mouth, but the crinkles around his eyes gave his mirth away.

"They're bored." She stared at him, then slapped her pen onto the desktop and slumped into her desk chair.

Joe leaned forward in his chair and cleared his throat.

"You need to know," he began, his voice expressionless and low, "our nonhuman-primate conference scheduled with Gordy has been postponed. I hate being the one to add to your . . . mood."

"Gordy told me he'd cleared his calendar for us. Is he sick?" Compared to Joe's soft voice, hers sounded sharp.

Cornering the institute's zoologist for a simple meeting shouldn't be this difficult. But he also served as a co-researcher for Denver University's research department. She stuffed her frustration and started flipping calendar pages.

"Gordy specifically said we'd meet tomorrow afternoon. Why is he always overbooked?"

"Can't blame anyone this time." Joe rubbed his chin.

"You're serious? What does he find more important than discussing our in-captivity macaque-breeding program?"

"Death."

Beth stopped swiping pages and looked up.

"When he unlocked the lab to his DU research area early yesterday morning, he found his co-researcher dead." Joe tented his index fingers. "He has to spend a few more hours with law enforcement answering questions."

"Good grief, he's not a suspect is he?"

Joe stretched and looked like he needed to escape somewhere with his fishing rod. "Take a deep breath, Beth. He's not even a person of interest. They're questioning him because of his knowledge about what drugs might have been available in their lab."

"They think this researcher overdosed? Was he a young college student?"

"All this makes me tired. They don't think it was an overdose. The man's religious beliefs didn't allow him to ingest anything stimulating, not even caffeine."

"Murder?" The unlikely word surprised her when it slipped from her mouth.

"Don't know." Joe glanced at her. "They only suspected his body might be full of some toxic chemical because he's young and had access."

"So they haven't actually found any substances yet? They're guessing?" Again, she grounded herself by pressing her palms tight.

"Gordy wondered if it could have been a fatal dose of ketamine."

She froze. *No public displays of emotion.*

"Did he have high blood pressure?" Usually, ketamine wasn't fatal and was valued for many reasons, mainly amnesia, but it often raised the heart rate. Often scientists used Rompun with ketamine in animals. Unfortunately, ketamine had gained a recent reputation as a date-rape drug.

Neither found anything to say to the other. She had ketamine in her lab, as Joe did, and she figured Gordy had ketamine in his lab, too. Her mind flicked back to her mice. Her jaw tightened.

The phone on her desk rang. Wayne assured her there were no leaks.

"Joe, this happening, and with my mice dying—"

"Don't even. There's not a connection."

"Something tells me you're wrong. My mice were murdered in this research facility, then a person is murdered at another research—"

"Stop right there."

"Dead scientist, dead research mice isn't a coincidence." Beth kept her voice even.

"We'll know when the autopsy and the lab reports are in." Joe stood.

Beth perched on the corner of her desk with her lips pulled in tight.

"Don't get yourself in a twist." He shook his head and moved toward the door.

Her damaged research . . . she was definitely on edge. Now with this death, the death of an associate . . .

She stood and walked with Joe into the atrium.

"Ms. Armstrong," Nancy called to her from the reception desk, shuffling notes. "Here's a thank-you for recommending that new brand of solution, and another for information you found on the red algae in Florida. And Teri left to pick up supplies."

"Super. Now I need the number for that bakery."

Back in her office, she scheduled the bagel delivery for one o'clock. As she stepped out of the RRC, their main custodian, Wayne, sprinted toward her.

"Hey, Ms. Armstrong, I checked for those ceiling leaks real good."

"Thank you, Wayne. Can I borrow you for a minute?" She turned to Nancy. "We'll be over in Joe's area."

"You have another special project for me?" he asked as they walked.

"Let's find out what's happening with the macaques."

He stopped.

"I don't want to be insubordinate, but I hate that place. They jump up and down and screech and holler whenever I'm in there."

"What do you do?" She took him by the elbow and steered him down the hallway toward the macaque wing.

"I smile real big." He showed her a toothy grin. "And I pick up their toys and hand them back."

They saw Joe in the corridor near the macaque room. When she and Wayne caught up with him, Beth glanced through the window at the non-human primates. Bagels wouldn't cure their boredom—these animals needed an enhanced environment.

"I want Wayne to assist you," she said, "to do a little rapport building."

"By doing what?" Joe leaned against the wall.

"At one o'clock Wayne will help you distribute bagels."

"We're giving the nonhuman primates bagels?" Joe shoved his hands in his pockets.

"Every day, with cream cheese and coffee. They don't like jam."

"Is she serious, Mr. Hammer?" Wayne said.

"Don't you think that's extreme?" Joe leaned away from the wall.

"They're tough and chewy. Hard-rubber canine Kongs don't hold their attention, but stale bagels present a real challenge. I watched a young female with one. Next week the bakery will bring another batch."

"Still, Ms. Armstrong, I don't want to go in there." Wayne stepped away from the door.

"Keep your mouth shut." Joe touched Wayne's shoulder. "You'll be fine."

"Are these bagels a secret?" Wayne's eyes opened wide.

"Wayne, when you smile, or open your mouth, they think you're threatening them," Beth said. "Don't show your teeth."

Beth hurried back to the RRC. She had questions to ask the building engineer about the heating and cooling mechanisms in her lab. All those pipes were old. She'd find some logical explanation for her mice dying.

"Ms. Armstrong?" Nancy called as she passed. "Your husband's on the phone."

What on earth? He'd only called her at work a dozen times over the years. The last time he called was when her mother died.

She closed her door, sat on the corner of her desk, inhaled, and put the phone to her ear.

"Harold?"

"Hate to bother you, but it's your aunt. She's upset."

"She called you at work?" Why couldn't Beth ever reach him there?

"You have to find someone else to stay with her."

"There's nothing wrong with Mrs. Harrison." Beth massaged the back of her neck. "Kathleen knows that or she wouldn't have called you, she'd have called me."

"Can't you get rid of her?" Harold's stubborn streak was speaking.

"Like have somebody rub her out?" She couldn't help her smirk.

Silence.

"A joke, Harold."

Silence.

"I'll check on her, Harold. Okay?"

"What if that woman's abusing her?"

Beth closed her eyes.

"Mrs. Harrison comes highly recommended. I checked her references." She waited. "Hello? Are you there?"

"It does happen, more than most people think."

"We'll talk when I get home." The dull ache of an oncoming migraine started deep under her skull. "Besides, Harold, no one could get away with abusing Kathleen."

An Ellery programmer who was a Chinese national had transferred the code to another Chinese national, quit his job, and tried to sell the code to a company called Beijing Machinery for $500,000.

—DENVER DIVISION, FBI, APRIL 2011

One of the symptoms of an approaching nervous breakdown is the belief that one's work is terribly important.

—BERTRAND RUSSELL

3

The alarm clock. No, the phone. Beth rolled over to Harold's side of the king-size bed. She pushed hair out of her eyes, leaned over him, and grabbed the receiver.

"Hello?" Her voice sounded hoarse with sleep.

"Ms. Armstrong? This is Mrs. Harrison. We got a problem."

Harold lifted his head, his hand resting on her thigh, and he mumbled something in her ear. She turned away to concentrate.

"Kathleen?"

"I'm calling from the hospital. There's been a fire at the house."

Beth sat up.

"Fire?" The red cinder on the bedspread, the overflowing ashtray . . . "Are you two okay?"

"Not burned, but I'm worried about Ms. Kathleen. She's not looking good. What do you want me to do?"

"What does the doctor say?" She held her breath.

"The smoke—her lungs are full of it."

"And the house?" She hated to imagine.

"I think it's bad. I came right here to the hospital with your aunt."

Beth braced herself. "What about Saucy?"

[14]

"That dog's a fast runner—neighbors took it in. You need to get here, Ms. Armstrong."

"I'll hurry." Beth handed the phone to Harold, who hung it up.

"What's the trouble?"

"Seems Kathleen started a fire. She's in the hospital—smoke inhalation." Beth kicked away the covers and swung her long legs out of bed. "I have to get to Valley View."

She looked at her watch. *Too early to call Teri.*

She slipped into panties and a bra, pulled on a pair of jeans, and slid a burgundy turtleneck over her head. Then she swept a brush through her fawn-colored hair and felt thankful that she looked fine even without her usual makeup. She'd hoped to keep her relationship with Kathleen in the background, but she certainly didn't want anything like this.

Harold tossed back the sheet and blanket. His feet hit the floor. His head of thick salt-and-pepper hair stuck out in all directions. A small strip of gauze was taped to his inner forearm.

She touched the wound. "What happened?"

"Scraped some skin—no big deal—Ted's Harley. He wants all of us to take a spin up to Evergreen for lunch some weekend."

"Mine's buried under dust in the garage." She wished she could find extra time. If Ted and the group wanted to lunch with her they'd have to eat in the science institute's cafeteria.

"When will you be home?" he said.

"Better go ahead and have dinner without me."

He glanced away. "I'll call Laura and Ted and cancel."

"Oh crap—our surprise date." She twisted her face into an apology.

Their special thing, something Harold started doing for her years ago. Except this time he'd invited her best friend and her husband. She disliked disappointing him by missing his surprise evening, but his recent tendency to miss work made their disappointments in each other reciprocal.

"Teri doesn't know I won't be in. Would you call her at work this morning and let her know?"

"I'd rather go to Valley View with you." He pulled on his khakis.

"No sense both of us wasting a day." Harold would make everything too complicated.

"You have no idea what you're facing. Let me run interference for you."

"I'm tough, Harold."

"No shit." He grinned. "Come on, I'd like some time alone with you. I'll be your chauffeur."

She found a softer look, but she knew his real motive.

"Kathleen annoyed the daylights out of you at Mother's funeral, remember? Besides, I have no idea what's going on or how long I need to be gone, and you shouldn't call in to work again, right? Do you even have sick days left?" She slung her purse over her shoulder. "If you handle Laura and Ted, I'll deal with this." She needed to go.

"Have you thought about one of those new wireless phones? Might be handy if you're bouncing back and forth from Valley View," he said.

"Pay phones work fine. I'll call if I'm not coming home tonight. Don't forget to let Teri know."

"You can't dismiss technology. Last month IBM's Deep Blue whipped the world chess champion." He touched her arm then drew her in close. She started to resist, but then she surprised herself, snuggling closer to enjoy a few seconds of comfort wrapped in his warmth.

"I have to scoot." She pulled away.

"Wait." He went over and took a business-sized envelope out of the top dresser drawer. "Something for you."

The envelope seemed paper-heavy in her palm. She slipped a fingernail under the flap, but he put his hand on hers.

"Later—when you're not in such a hurry."

"You know I can't stand not knowing. . . ." She raised her eyebrows. He didn't remove his hand. Beth stuffed her curiosity and slipped the envelope in the front pocket of her hooded sweatshirt. She studied him for a moment, then she slid both arms around his neck and kissed him goodbye before she headed off, in the dark, to Valley View.

The morning sky, streaked with pastel colors, elevated her mood a little when Beth crested the ridge above Valley View. She drove down into the town and past the boarded-up Grand Theater. Main Street's pink granite and white sandstone buildings usually triggered a touch of nostalgia, but this morning they looked small-town fatigued in the morning haze.

Haze? She'd never even seen fog in Valley View.

Beth drove into the hospital parking lot, parked, and stared at the brick building. Her thoughts weighed her down. She rested her forehead on the steering wheel for a moment, then she slipped her hand over the cold door handle and pulled it open. *Relax. Mother isn't in there this time.*

She stopped at the information desk. Kathleen was undergoing pulmonary lung function tests for the next hour. She found a pay phone, called Nancy, told her she wouldn't be in, and then asked to be connected to Teri.

"How are the mice? Anything unusual?"

"Don't worry, everything's fine. Your husband called and said you were back in Valley View. How's your aunt?"

"Not sure yet. I'll call you later. Wait, Teri, even if you're only going next door for supplies, would you please keep the outer lab door locked, as well as the inner lab door?" Teri assured her she would.

Disinfectant tickled Beth's nose. A cart of glass containers clattered somewhere around the corner. She longed for the familiar smells, sounds, and routine of the institute. She pushed through the front doors and out into the cool morning air.

Back in her car, she drove down Main Street, then Ninth Street, and finally turned at the corner of Greenwood Avenue. Elm trees guarded the grassy areas behind the curbs of the wide street where she'd learned to ride her bike. Smoke hung heavy in the cool morning air.

Beth could smell the smoldering debris, breathing in what she knew must be minute incinerated particles of her childhood.

Yellow barricades forced her to park a block away. Her muscles tightened. She climbed out of her Taurus, broke into a jog, then froze. Blackened brick fireplaces jutted up from heaps of charred wood. Travertine front steps led nowhere.

"Oh—my—God. Nooo . . ." She couldn't breathe.

Her Madame Alexander doll collection, her grandmother's china, all the family photographs, the stained-glass window on the stairway landing that scattered colors from the afternoon sun around the downstairs rooms—all gone.

This wasn't a fire, it was total devastation. The only thing left was the black-and-white scene everyone would see on the news tonight.

Her family home had graced this corner years before her parents moved to Valley View. A long time ago she had struggled to negotiate the grand oak staircase with toddler legs—each stair a step for a giant. She had descended that same staircase years later with a large bouquet of gardenias and stephanotis cradled in her arms, fearful she'd trip on the lace that edged the hem of her wedding dress. But she'd kept her gaze riveted on Harold.

It all hurt.

Her mother's trampled flowerbeds oozed wet, gray ash from deep boot prints. The muddy lawn would never recover. Huge black hoses stretched from the corner hydrant and the fire truck. A fireman blasted water on a smoking mound. Acrid smoke turned white as it rose into the morning air.

The painful lump in the back of her throat grew. The bridge of her nose tingled, the way it always did before she cried. A hundred thoughts raced through her mind. She caught her breath and leaned against the rough bark of a nearby elm.

"Damn you, Kathleen." Wetness trickled down her cheeks.

A policeman stood near some of the firefighters, along with a few neighbors in bathrobes and slippers, talking quietly.

Beth waited until the neighbors left, then she wiped her eyes and marched over to the police officer.

"Excuse me." The words emerged hollow and shaky.

"Beth Craig—rather, Beth Armstrong." The officer put his hand on her shoulder. "I'm sorry about your home."

She chewed the inside of her lip. She didn't know what to think, what to say.

"Ms. Armstrong, I know how hard this must be," he said. "These old turn-of-the-century homes weren't built like houses today. Once a fire starts, it flashes up inside the walls like a tinderbox."

"Did you save anything?"

He looked at his feet. She glanced at the blackened timbers and knew they couldn't have.

She stepped closer and turned something large and black over with her foot. Ash floated up—crumbled wood, her white tennis shoe now black.

Something caught her eye. She knelt down and lightly touched, then poked the wet ash. Only a tiny ember glowed deep under a jumble of charred debris. Her fingers closed over one of the warm pieces of fire-checkered wood. Beth studied the blackened chunk of her home for a moment, then pressed it to her cheek and closed her eyes.

Someone touched her shoulder and said something—the police officer. She replaced the bit of wood, then stood and wiped her palms on her jeans, leaving white, ashy streaks.

"Officer?" Her voice hesitated. "Have you talked with my aunt?"

"Only the housekeeper." He reached for his notepad. "A Mrs. Harrison. Wonder if that's Pete Harrison's wife. . . ."

"Most likely," the fireman said.

What did Beth know about her aunt? No one in the family seemed to like her. Kathleen had surprised her when she offered to take care of Beth's mother. She'd been even more surprised when her mother agreed.

How old was Kathleen? Beth's temples throbbed. There was no one left to ask—Beth's brother and sister wouldn't know any more than she did.

"What happens next?" Beth's voice sounded far away.

"You're lucky your aunt lived through this if she fell asleep while smoking." The officer glanced at the firefighter. They both shook their heads and then started recalling other cases of death by bed and cigarette.

She longed for her father. He'd always comforted her, always understood her anger. *Come into my study, Sugarplum, let's talk.* As for her mother? *Beth Craig, how on earth could you have let something like this happen?* That's what she would say, even if Sarah and Bobby stood there with lighter fluid and matches in their hands. *Now go to your room.*

Her room. All her keepsakes, all her treasures were in *that* room. If only—

Wait. Kathleen—she didn't have a room either.

She closed her eyes and sucked in a deep breath. Smoke wafted into her nose and filled her lungs. She coughed. She couldn't stop.

The men looked at her. She turned her back and dabbed her eyes with a tissue. She needed to stop feeling and to start thinking.

What about Bobby? Kathleen would love California—pleasant winters, lots of sunshine. Her brother loved dogs. But his sweet wife battled multiple sclerosis. She could never ask Bobby and Winifred to take Kathleen on.

Sarah loved people. Last Beth heard, her sister was somewhere in northern Italy bicycling the countryside. Forget Sarah.

There must be lots of places, skilled places that care for the elderly. Beth felt hot, hot as those damned cinders on the ground. She stuffed her feelings somewhere deep within.

She needed a plan. Fast.

Ellery Systems was a leading information systems/software products engineering services company based in Boulder, Colorado. . . . In a case spanning 1988–1995, Ellery lost everything with a few keystrokes.

—MAGNAN, CIA, APRIL 2007

The number of oldest old is rising. People age 85 and over are now the fastest growing portion of many national populations.

—NATIONAL INSTITUTES OF HEALTH

4

Beth pulled into the hospital parking lot and slammed her car door. She marched inside and past the elevator, taking the stairs two at a time. Would it have made a difference if she'd spent the night, one last night, in her own room?

Stop it. No one gets do-overs.

She shoved open the door to room 209 and bumped into Mrs. Harrison. Beth stood in her path.

"Where's Kathleen?"

Mrs. Harrison pulled her out into the hall.

"I can handle most anything," she said, "but I sure can't handle your aunt."

"I know. She's . . ." What? Difficult? Crazy?

"That woman yells at me." Mrs. Harrison pulled a handkerchief out of her shirt pocket. "She told me not to boss her, then with some ugly words she told me to get out of the house."

"But you stayed, right?"

"I do what I'm paid to do." Mrs. Harrison pushed blackened strands of frizzy hair off her forehead. "I never once left that house."

"It was her smoking, wasn't it?"

"Well, Jesus as my witness, I sure didn't start it. I let myself in, yahooed up the stairs—I didn't want to scare her—and that little dog came down snarling all the way, ears back, showing her teeth. I feared I'd be ripped to pieces, so I swung my handbag, yelling shoo, scat, and kept my valise in front of me, you know, to keep her away."

"Good grief, did she bite you?" She held her breath. How could she forget that Saucy would never let a stranger near Kathleen?

"She would have, yes sirree." Mrs. Harrison wiped streaks of soot from her forehead. "But then Ms. Kathleen appeared at the top of the stairs and called the dog's name in that raspy voice of hers. The furry devil turned and ran back up as fast as she'd come down." Mrs. Harrison tucked the hanky back into her shirt pocket.

Kathleen, out of bed by herself?

"I trudged up those stairs. Lordy, I've never seen so many steps in my life. I could hardly breathe." She patted her ample bosom. "When I got to the top, Ms. Kathleen and that dog were back in the bedroom. Ms. Kathleen tucked in as nice as could be in her own bed, smoothing out the blankets, and the yippy dog up there with her, keeping those little beady eyes on me. That's when Ms. Kathleen hollered at me. She kept on bawling me out. Finally, I hollered right back."

Beth should have spent the night.

"No disrespect," Mrs. Harrison said, "but lordy, lordy, she's nasty. The words she uses."

"She had a book of matches on her nightstand," Beth said. "Do you remember?"

"Indeed I do. Ms. Kathleen held them in her hand and played with them the whole time we talked. She stared right into my eyes, and all the time she argued with me. She thought she could scare me."

"Mrs. Harrison, is it possible . . ." She lowered her voice. "What did Kathleen say before the fire started?"

"I figured since she only wanted to yell, I wouldn't stay." Mrs. Harrison tugged down on her bra through her dress.

"You said you didn't leave."

"I only went to the guest room—by yester evening I was plum tuckered out, so I nodded off in that chair by the guest-room window. Her yappy dog woke me up, jumped right up in my lap."

"You weren't in her room when the fire started?"

"Wasn't I supposed to sleep in the guest room? You didn't tell me to stay in her room all the time."

Beth looked away.

"How was I to know what was going to happen? Until that dog was in my face I didn't know the house was on fire."

"Was Kathleen in her bedroom or someplace else?"

"I saw the smoke pouring from her room, so I scooped her up out of that bed and carried her downstairs and out onto the lawn, with that dog barking and yapping all the way."

The police officer was right. Kathleen fell asleep with a cigarette. Beth snuffed out a preposterous image of her aunt lurking in the attic near a trunk of old clothes with a lighted match. Still her aunt was an incendiary menace, sleeping with a cigarette. *Totally unnecessary. Totally infuriating.*

"Missy, don't you go thinking I had anything to do with this." Mrs. Harrison stared at her with squinty eyes.

"Of course not, I was thinking—"

"I've given my statement to the police. I'm going home. You're starting to scare me like your aunt." The big woman turned and shuffled down the corridor.

"Wait—wait a minute," she called. "You saved my aunt's life. I'll send you a check—"

Mrs. Harrison waved her hand behind her but didn't turn around.

Beth opened the door to room 209. Her mind roiled with anger until she saw Kathleen. The woman on the bed looked so still and pale, she wondered why they hadn't pulled the sheet over her face. Beth stood transfixed until she saw the slight rhythmic rise and fall of Kathleen's chest.

Kathleen, her snowy hair still damp from a bath, wore a clean hospital gown. She had a clip on her finger and a cannula in her nostrils hooked to an oxygen inlet.

The room smelled like a campfire.

Beth leaned against the windowsill. Haze still lingered over Main Street. She needed to call the insurance company—

"Dear, is that you?" Kathleen's voice came out in a low rasp.

Beth turned.

"I'm so sorry," Kathleen said. "I know there were things you needed to do today. I'd feel fine if they'd take all these gadgets off me." She coughed once. "Would you get my cigarettes, please?"

"You . . . what? Your . . ." Unspoken words piled up and caught in Beth's throat.

"I hate those rules about smoking." Kathleen raised her head, looking around. "How do they come up with such nonsense?" She reached for her soot-covered robe draped over the chair beside her and fumbled in the pocket. "Never mind, they're here. Come closer so I can see your face. The light's behind you. It hurts my eyes."

Beth lunged to the bed, snatched the cigarettes, crushed them, then flung the pack into the wastebasket. She bent close to her aunt and inhaled deeply.

"Beth, what in the world—"

"I don't know you, but I know people like you. You seriously need help."

"What on earth are you fretting about?"

"Fretting? Not me, I'm happy as a loon." Beth's lungs needed more air.

"Beth, I didn't start that fire."

"Now you're going to say it was Mrs. Harrison?" Beth's words filled the room. Until today, she had never yelled.

"It wasn't her." Kathleen said.

The room felt small, dark, smoky—no air. She heard her breath coming in short little bursts.

"Dear, you didn't mean to, but you started the fire."

Something snapped in Beth's brain. She shook her head. But Kathleen, with innocence etched in her wrinkled face, kept looking up at her.

"You cleaned the ashtray, child. Remember? And you tossed the contents into the wastebasket."

"Those cigarettes were out." *They had to have been. Weren't they?*

Her aunt gave a sad little smile and shook her head.

"You fell asleep with a cigarette." Beth's voice wasn't as confident as before.

"I do love figuring out mysteries." Kathleen examined her fingernail.

"I was long gone when that fire started." Beth set her jaw.

"Smolder, dear, that's the slow, delayed meaning of the word. I wasn't smoking when I went to sleep. I am sorry about all of this. Such an inconvenience for us, isn't it?"

"An *inconvenience*?"

"Does it matter, dear? These things happen. We need to pick up and go on."

Beth slumped down on the empty bed.

These things happen? Pick up and go on—without her home? Her memories? And her mice? Such an inconvenience.

"Of course you didn't mean to—"

"Stop it." Beth covered her ears. "You know I didn't do it."

She shut her eyes and saw her aunt balancing a cigarette on the overflowing ashtray, the tissues piled on top of all the old cigarettes in that

[23]

green-and-gold copper wastebasket, and that long gray ash with the tiny red cinder falling on the bedspread.

Beth felt shaky; she grabbed the pillow and squeezed it to her chest. Tears tickled the corners of her eyes. She wasn't the cause. She knew she didn't do it. She turned away so Kathleen couldn't see her face. She squeezed her eyes tight and took little stitchy breaths.

"When those firemen check out that bedroom, dear, they'll see—"

Beth turned and stared at Kathleen.

"There's no bedroom." She tried to lower her voice but couldn't. "There's no house. Because you, *you burned it up.*"

She slammed the pillow down onto the foot of Kathleen's bed and stormed out of the room.

A cart filled with breakfast trays clattered by and turned in to room 209. Beth wanted to leave this place and think. She swiped at her eyes and marched to the nurses' station.

"Tell me, please, where's the doctor for the patient in 209?"

"He'll be back around three or four this afternoon. And a newspaper reporter was here when they brought Ms. McPherson in. He said he'd come—"

"Give me those papers—you know—the official ones for crazy people, or whatever it is I need to sign." Beth took a pen from her purse. She would dash back to Denver, check on her mice, and be back before the doctor made his rounds.

"Oh, honey, you must be her niece, right?" The nurse studied her, then grinned. "She told us her niece would take care of everything."

Prosecutors declined the case [against Ellery Systems], however, because evidence didn't support wire fraud—the only possible violation at that time. The case was considered key to the passage of the Economic Espionage Act of 1996.

—DENVER DIVISION, FBI, APRIL 2011

5

"I didn't expect you back until tomorrow." Teri picked up a pencil and logged the temperature and weight of a mouse she held in her other hand. "Is everything okay?"

"Thought I'd see if you needed anything, but it looks like all's under control."

"There's a message on the counter." Teri placed the mouse back in its unit and picked up another. "Mr. Wendenski wants you to stop by his lab."

"Did he say why?" Beth read the note, and then tossed it into the basket. She studied the mice in the nearest unit. They seemed fine.

"He thought you might like to see how that new solution works compared to that other bottle."

"No time today."

"And—" Teri checked the mouse's ears. "Mr. Gordon called. A coworker died, so he won't be able to meet with you and Mr. Hammer this afternoon. I told them you were in Valley View with your aunt." Teri lifted another mouse, checked it over, and then took its temperature.

"Did you find anything out about the Laminar Flow being off?"

"One of the techs guessed the custodian turned if off by mistake. But Wayne swears he didn't. He didn't even know where the switch was."

"So everything's good?"

"Mice dry." Teri shrugged. "Doors locked."

~

The Valley View doctor pulled a small light from his breast pocket and took a quick look into each of Kathleen's eyes.

"I'm sorry about your father's home, Mrs. Armstrong. He was a fine doctor, a good man. Mrs. McPherson, make sure you drink plenty of water. You have a tendency to get dehydrated." He replaced his light. "Take a good multivitamin every morning, something with potassium."

"Being here is good for her." Beth set her shopping bags on the extra bed. Whatever cuckoos' nest Kathleen ended up in, her aunt still needed clothes.

The doctor tapped the chart.

"Your aunt's recuperating quite well. I see no reason she can't go home today."

"She's still weak." Beth slipped her hand into her purse. "And she requires a psychological evaluation."

"Good God, child." Kathleen stared. "What are you talking about?"

"Remember how angry you were the other night?" Beth pulled out a small notepad.

"I see," Kathleen said. "Then you'll have your head examined too."

"Mrs. McPherson, have you been hiding that wry wit from your niece?" The doctor patted Kathleen on the shoulder, then turned to Beth. "Mrs. Armstrong, there's nothing wrong with your aunt's mind."

"I've found an appropriate place for her, but they need an exam." Beth held out the information. He ignored it.

"I'm perfectly fine," Kathleen said, "except when I'm left with half a mind to straighten out your—"

"I'm sure you'll figure something out," he said. "But someone needs to be with her until she gets her strength back. We don't want her falling again, do we?"

"But her memory—" Beth glanced at the doctor. "We can't have her starting another fire either. She'll light a cigarette, put it in the ashtray, then light another one—"

The doctor held up a hand.

"We'll worry when she doesn't remember what the cigarettes or ashtrays are for. We all forget things, Mrs. Armstrong."

"But she's frail, practically immobile. . . ." Beth's insides churned. She didn't know what to do. *First my mice, now this.*

"Dammit, maybe she'll believe us if I do an Irish jig on the bed."

The doctor chuckled then wrote the discharge order in Kathleen's file. "She'll be fine." He tucked the file under his arm and left. Beth heard his jocular greeting to the patient in the next room.

"Well, dear, I hope you've gotten all that crap out of your system." Kathleen's voice still sounded rough. "Save the receipts for your purchases. I'll pay you back."

Beth retrieved a bag off the bed and pulled out a pair of gray slacks, then held them up with an amber sweater.

"I thought, now that it's almost springtime . . ."

"How thoughtful, dear. Shoes?"

"I guessed. Same size as my mother's?" Beth rummaged through the bags and pulled out a box.

Kathleen held one up, turned it around, then slipped it on.

"Oh, I like these." She stretched her foot out and wiggled it back and forth. "We'll have such fun shopping together."

You'll be riding a van to Wal-Mart, sweetie, and I don't shop there.

She picked up two shopping bags from the other bed and handed them to Kathleen.

"Here, you'll want to look through these."

"Oooo—it almost feels like my birthday." Kathleen clasped her hands together.

"Do you need help getting dressed?" An overwhelming uneasiness settled over Beth.

"In spite of what you think, I'm perfectly capable of handling my own affairs. That includes dressing myself."

"I'll be back in a few minutes." She didn't know what to expect.

Beth went past the pay phones to the ladies' room. She pulled out a paper towel, dampened it, and pressed it to her neck, then her forehead. She opened her eyes and looked at herself in the mirror. Charcoal still smudged her cheek.

How sick *was* Kathleen? The doctor had blown it off—the medical as well as the psychological issues. Kathleen seemed gray, colorless, another wisp of smoke. And she looked old, much older than Beth's mother did before she died. Beth didn't know how to take care of sick—let alone old—people. What was she supposed to do?

She washed the smudge off and tossed the towel into the bin. One thing she did know—Kathleen needed constant care.

She went back to the phones and called Teri. Were the mice still eating and drinking? How were their temperatures now? How did their bedding look?

A tiny sigh. "They're all fine, Ms. Armstrong, I promise."

"Teri, I'm sorry. I guess I'm being a terrible bother." Her heart still hadn't made this trip to Valley View. "I'd be totally frantic if I didn't have you there. I'll be back at the institute tomorrow."

She pulled the insurance-company card from her billfold and punched in the number. Automated answering machines—weren't there real people on the other end? She couldn't concentrate. She hung up.

Beth went to the nurses' station and asked for the Colorado Springs and the Denver Yellow Pages. She'd fallen down the rabbit hole into the world of geriatrics. She flipped through the pages, made some calls, then headed back to Kathleen's room.

"I'll need a belt with these slacks," Kathleen said, "but they'll be fine."

Beth picked up the shopping bags and stuffed the remaining clothes and personal items into one of them. She picked up all the tags, pins, tissue, and cardboard and forced them down into the wastebasket.

"Ready?" Beth faced Kathleen.

"For what?"

"They've sold your bed to someone else."

"Did I tell you I had a nice chat with a newspaper man while you were shopping? I used to date several newspaper men in Chicago and Detroit. . . .

The nurse appeared with a wheelchair. Kathleen protested being pushed. She insisted there wasn't a thing wrong with her. She finally sat in the chair and complained all the way out to the curb. When she got in Beth's car, the nurse buckled Kathleen's seat belt.

"God dammit, I'm not helpless." Kathleen glared at the nurse.

Beth thanked the nurse and drove out of the parking lot.

"I'd like to stop somewhere to buy cigarettes." Kathleen pulled a tissue from her pocket and pressed it to her nose. "Oh, dammit to hell—I don't have any money."

Beth ignored her because it really wasn't her nature to strangle anyone.

"I hate being an imposition." Kathleen's voice wavered. "I hate depending on others." She turned her head and stared out her side window.

Beth heard her mumble, "Christ, I never thought I'd be in a position like this."

"Kathleen." Beth had to say something. She reached over and gave her aunt a little pat. "Let's go pick up Saucy. I'm sure she'll make you feel better." Kathleen continued to stare out the window.

They drove back to Beth's old neighborhood. When they turned the corner, Kathleen let out a loud gasp, bringing on a coughing spell.

"Oh my—I didn't expect . . . When you said the house was gone . . ." Kathleen covered her mouth with a tissue through a spate of coughing. "That beautiful house . . . this must be quite hard on you, dear. I'm so terribly sorry."

Terribly sorry felt terribly trivial. The neighborhood looked foreign without the stately three-story home.

"Wait here. I'll get Saucy."

Beth slid out of her car and slammed the door for the second time that day. A parked police car started up, pulled away from the curb, then disappeared around the corner.

The firemen were winding up their hoses, preparing to leave.

She accepted the neighbors' condolences and thanked them for looking after Saucy.

"Tyler, my five-year-old son," the neighbor said, "loves that dog. We can't have one because the backyard's not fenced."

Tyler, contrary to his frown, came skipping up the hallway holding Saucy in his arms. Saucy didn't look happy either.

His mom held the door open for them. Beth reached for Saucy.

"Can I take her to your car?" Tyler pleaded. He glanced at his mom and then added, "Please?"

Beth smiled her approval. He bounced out onto the front porch and carefully stepped down each step. Saucy wriggled and struggled, paws flailing. One of her nails nicked Tyler's cheek.

He howled. His hands flew to his face, Saucy fell to the ground, rolled onto her paws, and skittered across the lawn. Tyler darted after her, screeching Saucy's name.

Beth leapt off the porch and joined the chase.

A repetitive beep sounded from the fire truck. The truck inched backward, but Tyler only saw Saucy. Beth sickened. Saucy darted around behind the moving vehicle. Tyler's young legs strained to close those few yards between the dog and him.

The diesel engine revved. Beth bolted. Her heart pounded against her ribs, her feet flew hard, but she wasn't fast enough.

Dear God—no more tragedies.

She dove headfirst into a tackle. She and Tyler hit the wet grass together, slid through thick mud, then stopped.

The ground vibrated. She felt deafened by the roar of the truck. No air. She couldn't breathe. The truck rolled back, next to them, squishing mud around her face. It paused, the wheels turned, and the truck pulled forward, off the curb and down the street.

Beth put her ear against the boy's back. Had she knocked the wind out of him? He squirmed—then giggled. Something wet moved over her ear. She opened her eyes. Saucy's sloppy tongue licked Beth, then Tyler, then Beth again.

Beth opened the door to the backseat, and Saucy jumped from her hands, over the armrest, and into Kathleen's lap, where she snuggled down. Her swishing, feathery tail announced her contentment.

"Magnificent, dear," Kathleen clapped.

Beth was out of breath and couldn't speak. She stared back at Kathleen, then gave a nod.

"I remember running like that once when I lived in Chicago," Kathleen said. "Danger certainly motivates."

Tyler's mother insisted that Beth come into the house to wash off the mud. She refused Neosporin and a Band-Aid for her skinned arm and didn't mention the damage to her knee. She wanted to be home.

Finally, Beth slid into her car, which now smelled as if some wet animal had been cooked too long.

"A standing ovation, dear—what a performance." Kathleen fingered the dog's silky ear. "At least you still have that valuable lot."

Beth adjusted her rearview mirror.

"You poor girl, you were almost run over, and now your home is gone." Beth glanced at her.

Her aunt cuddled the dog. "My baby must be terribly confused."

Beth gripped the wheel, and the tires squealed when her car pulled away from the curb.

What would you say about your crazy sister now, Mother?

Dear Chairman Hatch; Thank you for your support of the Economic Espionage Act of 1996. The need for this law cannot be understated as it will close significant gaps in federal law, thereby protecting proprietary economic information and the health and competitiveness of the American economy.

—ATTORNEY GENERAL JANET RENO, OCTOBER 1, 1996

Apparently there is nothing that cannot happen today.

—MARK TWAIN

6

"I'm sure we'll be fine in a few days." Kathleen glanced at Beth. "Child, you were too preoccupied to hear, but would you mind buying me a carton of Pall Malls?"

"A *carton*? You want enough to set the whole town on fire?"

"You're distraught, and I do understand. I'll pay you back as soon as I get some checks."

"Absolutely not." Beth kept her eyes on the road.

"That's generous of you, but I insist—"

"Absolutely not on the smoking, Kathleen." Surely this woman didn't think life would go on as before.

"You don't understand—"

Beth flooded her mind with a field of wildflowers and a Mozart violin concerto.

"This is not the time for me to quit," Kathleen said. "I've tried many times, but there's too much going on right now—are you listening?"

Violin sounds changed into a chicken farm invaded by geese.

"I've been smoking since I was sixteen. It's my way of life. . . ."

Beth pulled onto the graveled shoulder. Her knee, wet and sticky, throbbed.

"Young lady, are you going to throw me out of your car?"

Beth looked at her—actually saw this woman sitting next to her. She studied Kathleen. It was time to end this circus.

"You're a strong-willed woman, Kathleen." She stared at her aunt. "I'll help in any way I can, but you are not going to be smoking anymore." More composed, she moved back onto the highway. Harpsichord music glided back into her head.

Beth glanced over. Kathleen, silent, stroked Saucy's fur. What would happen to Saucy if Kathleen wasn't around? Her stomach felt unsettled. A bigger question—what happens to the pets of the elderly when they die?

"Did you know my sister had no idea what type of work you do?"

Beth bit her tongue. Was her aunt being antagonistic or congenial? Beth had made special time with her mother last fall, told her all about her work to take her mind off what lay ahead. Sadness crept over her.

"What will Howard think about Saucy, dear?"

"Harold." Her knee didn't feel the warmth of blood anymore. "Why do you ask?"

"This is Colorado Springs," Kathleen said. "We're headed to Denver, then?"

Beth turned onto Academy Boulevard.

"Colorado Springs is an attractive place to live." Good grief, Beth now sounded like a real-estate agent. "Great four-seasoned climate—"

"Have we passed the Broadmoor Hotel? I stayed there with a friend a long time ago."

"Behind us, back up on that mountain." Beth remembered the elegant linen-and-crystal dining room well. "That's where Harold surprised me with an engagement ring at dinner."

"Exceptionally romantic. Such a lovely place. . . . We're not on the highway anymore, are we?"

Beth pulled onto a wide street with a strip mall on one side and lawn on the other. She slowed, turned, then drove uphill through an open wrought-iron gate set in a high red-brick wall.

"You can stop right here." Kathleen sat up straight and held Saucy tight. "Dammit, didn't you hear the doctor—"

"It's okay, Kathleen. This isn't what you think."

Several red-brick buildings with white trim faced a manicured courtyard. Beth drove up to the central building and parked in front of the glass doors.

A man appeared, pushing a wheelchair. A woman walked along beside him.

"Beth—"

"Saucy can stay with you here." Beth opened her door.

The man held Kathleen's car door open.

The woman took Kathleen's elbow. Kathleen held tight to Saucy and ignored her.

"Beth, don't do this to me." Her words came low and firm.

"You'll live in luxury." Beth's muscles tightened. She had to convince her. "This assisted-living home is highly rated."

"You found one that didn't require a psychiatric exam."

"Psychiatric exam?" The man shook his head, grinning wide. "Only thing anyone's crazy about here is the chef's food."

"You'll be in the medical wing until you're back on your feet," the woman said.

"God dammit, there's nothing wrong with me."

The two caregivers exchanged looks.

"There's a vacant apartment," the woman said. "One bedroom, a living room, and a kitchenette. It's in this building. Shall we go look?"

"Why?" Kathleen said. "Haven't you seen it?"

"Kathleen, please." Beth bent over to face her. "Let's at least look. You might actually like it. From what mother said your assets can easily cover this."

Kathleen's lips tightened into a thin, hard line. Beth's face grew hot. What had she done? Kathleen glared at her.

"I'm not a goddamned research project."

"Excuse me?"

"You keep those animals at the institute in cages, I assume?" Kathleen's eyes weren't only angry, they looked hurt.

"That's a specious argument. This isn't like that."

"Bullshit." Her chin quivered. "We both know what type of place this is." Kathleen's voice dropped an octave. "They'll tuck Saucy away in some noisy kennel and I'll quietly be encouraged to hurry up and die."

The woman leaned close to Kathleen.

"We're not—"

"I'm sorry, dear. I didn't mean to insult you. This establishment looks attractive and well kept. But we all know the type of population you garner, and I wouldn't fit." She tossed back her hair from her eyes and turned toward Beth. "Hell, Beth, I don't even own a walker."

"I'm sorry we inconvenienced you." Beth shook her head, slid back into the car, started the engine, and drove down the drive.

"To think, your mother was the one who used to drag home all the strays she could find—even ratty little children like those Peckinpahs." She sighed. "My sister would be quite pleased with you about all of this, don't you think?"

Beth gripped the wheel and bit her tongue. Mozart and wildflowers wouldn't help here.

"Why in God's name do you insist I be in a place like that?"

"You're unsteady on your feet, you have an awful cough, and you don't drive."

"I took care of your dying mother all winter. I can take care of myself."

"You've been in the emergency room twice in one week." Earlier this winter, Kathleen's cheeks showed a bit of color. Now she looked ashen.

Kathleen sat in silence.

"As for that assisted-living place?" Beth said. "I thought, based on your current needs—"

"My needs? Those are a bed, a bathroom, and a little food. Doesn't sound like much to me—I'll be perfectly fine at the hotel with cigarettes and room service. What's troubling is that you planned this without saying *one* word to me."

"I thought you'd pitch a fit, but if you saw the place first you might actually find it appealing." Beth needed to quit gritting her teeth.

"I'm sure it's perfectly appealing if you've nothing better to do than sit around, drink Maalox, and wait for your clock to quit ticking."

"My home isn't set up for medical issues—"

"I told you, I plan to live in a hotel."

"I'm not taking you to a hotel. Who'd watch over you?"

"The doctor said I'll be fine in a couple of days." She jutted her chin out. "I'll not stay where I'm not wanted."

Beth flushed. What about her gratitude for all the care Kathleen had given her mother? She sighed and stuffed her anger. She couldn't do a thing about the house fire.

"Kathleen, self-determination and self-reliance are two different things."

"My God, girl, I totally supported myself in a large city. How many sixteen-year-olds could do that?"

"My grandparents were always there, they wouldn't have let you suffer."

"You didn't know them very well."

"The point is that neither of us are teenagers anymore." Beth, keeping one hand on the steering wheel, tugged at her jeans where they were stuck to the dried blood on her knee. "We don't have the same physical stamina, and every year it declines."

"Surviving in Chicago was more of an intellectual challenge."

"I've read about Chicago back then. You must have been a clever teen." Beth glanced at her sullen aunt. "Let's not argue, Kathleen. The fire, and today with Tyler and Saucy . . . it scared me. I can't run as fast as I used to, and I bet my balance isn't what it was a few years ago."

"I manage quite well on my own."

"And you *will* be on your own in our home, during the day. I'll leave you my work number and have your breakfast and lunch organized. We'll talk about a hotel or apartment later."

"I feel like we're in a business meeting." She scratched Saucy's ears. "You're quite angry."

"More like frustrated. I shouldn't be away from the institute, and Harold and I aren't used to having houseguests."

"Shouldn't you stop and call him?"

"He'll be fine with it." She treasured Harold's amiable disposition.

"You make decisions affecting him without discussing them?" Kathleen cleared her throat. "What kind of marriage is that?"

"Mother said you were never married. Sorry, no credibility there."

"And I suspect," Kathleen said, "Mary is the reason you keep things to yourself."

"You didn't like my mother?"

"It's complicated." She looked away.

"Blame your father." Beth moved into the fast lane.

Kathleen stared at her.

"For keeping things to myself," Beth said. "Grandfather used to lecture us about public displays of emotion."

"A convenient excuse," Kathleen huffed. "You're an introvert—a bit subversive too. How can people trust you when you don't show emotions? Dear, seriously, people don't have a clue what you're thinking if you're always an ice woman."

"Subversive introvert? An ice woman?" Her mother always complained about her being too loud, not using her inside voice, and being far to friendly with strangers. "Why are you harassing me?"

"*Har-ESS*, dear. Not *har-ASS*."

Perhaps Beth could have her committed even if she didn't intentionally set fires. She glanced at her aunt. Kathleen wore a different expression, not harsh, but more like she'd swallowed something pleasant.

"Dear, I have an idea."

"Well, I'm fresh out of them." And she was. She'd mentally examined every angle possible, but none explained the spilled water that had caused the death of her mice. She stiffened. What if Teri *was* to blame? Had she piled their bedding so high it touched the drinking tubes? Her temples throbbed. She knew these thoughts weren't right. Teri was never careless.

"Leave me the number for the insurance company." Kathleen sounded like they'd come from some afternoon tea. "I'll do the follow-up phone calls for you."

"Thanks, but I'll need to make them my new best friends." The thought of Kathleen courting the insurance company unnerved her.

"You have work on your mind. I'm quite good at getting to the bottom of things."

Work . . . until her dead mice, she'd found it a place of solace. And her home tasks were now doubled with Kathleen and Saucy.

"I suspect the insurance company will ask questions that only I can answer. But thanks."

"Do you have problems accepting help?" Kathleen said.

"I think independence runs in our family." Beth stole a look at her. "You told me you didn't need help, remember?"

"Still, that's no reason to refuse a hand."

Beth felt a sharp pang of apprehension. What if Kathleen *had* set their house on fire? Silly. She relaxed knowing Kathleen had no cigarettes.

The trip home seemed hours longer than usual because of heavy traffic. Harold's SUV sat parked under the streetlamp. What was that about? She pushed her remote-control button and the garage door slid open. Her headlights flooded their large garage, revealing sawhorses, lumber, the table saw. . . .

What in the devil?

Harold stood waiting in the kitchen doorway, his face full of emotion. She winced when she stepped out—her knee. . . . Saucy darted past him, snuffling around for her food bowl.

"She's going to be a disappointed dog," Kathleen said. "Hello, Howard."

"I'm Harold."

Beth thought she'd scream. She threaded her way through the construction clutter, past Harold, and into the kitchen. Beth froze. She couldn't breathe.

"Harold—"

"Wait, you'll love it."

He gave her a one-arm squeeze as she surveyed torn-up floors, counters covered in dust, cabinets hanging open.

"I know things are a mess right now," he said, "but that center island you've always wanted? I'll move the refrigerator over there, and the oven—"

"Jesus Christ, Harold." Kathleen choked back a cough. "You've certainly been a busy boy. Beth dear, do you have something Saucy might like for her dinner?"

"Holy crap!" Both Beth's knees felt like Jell-O.

"In a few weeks this will be—"

"You've—you've . . ." Beth's internal thermostat bubbled over. "This'll be the same as the deck, the utility room, our closet shelves—It's too much, Harold, *too much*."

Any second now, she'd melt away, sag into nothingness. She forced herself to look at his face.

He stood there, slumped, as if he'd lost his best friend.

"I'm—Harold, don't. . . ." He looked so wounded. "I'm—*surprised*. You didn't tell me." Beth tried to picture her kitchen functional again. She couldn't.

"Any little thing will do for Saucy," Kathleen said.

Beth stepped over stacks of lumber. Boxes of something blocked the refrigerator door. Harold hurried over and moved a couple of them.

"How much of the house burned?" He picked up another and set it down a few feet away.

"Every last goddamned inch of it." Kathleen's voice sounded tired.

Beth searched the kitchen for something to feed Saucy, but Harold stopped her. He placed his hands on her shoulders.

"Are you going to be all right?" He looked into her eyes. "When you told me about the fire, I figured—well, I thought the kitchen of your dreams might help. Of course it doesn't replace what you've lost."

"Do you mind if I have a seat?" Kathleen was using three fingers on the table to steady herself. "I'm quite tired."

Harold scooted the last box aside, then took Kathleen's arm and escorted her to the living room.

"Would you like a drink?" He raised an eyebrow then gave Beth a silly grin.

Beth fixed Saucy a paper plate of leftover meatloaf. A few minutes later, Harold appeared in the kitchen, asking where she kept the rum.

"Your aunt's lucky it's almost spring," he said when Beth joined them. "She only brought some of her winter clothes when she came to take care of your mother."

"Everything else is safely stored in Chicago," Kathleen said. "Tomorrow, Harold will look into having it shipped here for me. He's such a dear."

The FBI Director has designated espionage as the FBI's number two priority—second only to terrorism.

—FBI, AUGUST 2010

7

Beth unlocked her RRC office door and found three files on her desk. Nancy, competent and dedicated, must have come in early this morning. The files could wait. She called the bedding supplier and told their quality-control person about her mice dying because of the wetness. They insisted athymic mice wouldn't push bedding close enough to the drinking tubes to cause wicking if the tubes had been installed properly. It had to be human error.

She called her homeowner's insurance company. They needed information from the official report of the Valley View Police and the Fire Department. What a nightmare. When would she find time to make a trip back to Valley View?

She forced herself to pull one of the folders from the stack of three and then opened its corresponding file on her computer.

Nancy rapped on her doorjamb.

"Your aunt phoned. She said her call was urgent. I told her I'd give you the message as soon as you hung up."

"I'm sorry about these personal messages, Nancy."

"It's no problem." She shrugged and left.

What had Kathleen said? She had called Beth an introvert. Nonsense. Efficient and busy is all.

Was Kathleen one of those alarmist personalities, a person who thrived on drama? Beth's hand hovered over the phone before she dialed.

"Hope the coffee was strong enough for you," Beth said. "What's happening there?"

"Nothing, dear, but I do know how to get around protective secretaries. When do you get home?"

"Between five and six." *What now?*

"I thought maybe you could you take me to a bank to get some checks ordered, but the banks will be closed by then."

"Some stores have banks that stay open later." Beth relaxed. "We'll go right after dinner."

"One does need money to survive."

"Are you feeling up to going out?" Beth knew she shouldn't have asked.

"There's nothing wrong with me."

"Guess that's a yes." Beth hung up and started adding data into the computer from one of the folders on her desk.

A few minutes after one o'clock Teri came through her doorway.

"We need to sort this lab problem out." Beth motioned her to a chair.

"Every time I think about it—" Teri's pale cheeks and neck glowed with blotchy red patches.

"How deep was the bedding layered?"

"I set it up exactly as it says on the instructions." She smoothed down her lab coat, not looking at Beth. Her voice came out quiet. "You've watched me. I never let it get close to the drinking tubes."

"Hey." Beth reached over and touched her. "I'm covering all aspects. I know how competent you are. Relax."

"Will the numbers work?" Teri looked fit, like a college tennis player.

"Maybe, if we don't lose more—even if I called in favors, I couldn't get a new shipment in time."

When Teri left to go to a meeting for technicians, Beth started reviewing the previous month's research protocols. She'd lost track of time when the phone interrupted her.

"Ms. Armstrong, it's happened again." Teri's voice trembled. "The mice—"

Beth ignored her damaged knee and raced to the stairway. She paused to throw on protective clothing before she dashed into the lab. Damn, no air flow on her exposed cheek.

"Get the live ones and put them in dry cages under heat lamps." Beth picked one up and shoved it at Teri. "Hurry—"

"But it won't be enough—" Teri's words came out in sobs.

"Doesn't matter, we have to try." Bile rose in Beth's throat.

Teri positioned heat lamps and flicked them on.

"Their bedding's soaked again." Beth picked up one of the mice and stroked it with her finger. "The drinking tubes—the bedding's touching them—Laminar Flow is off." *Human caused.*

After they'd finished what they could do, they returned to the outer lab.

"I checked them all at six-thirty this morning," Teri said.

"How long were you gone?" Beth kept her voice low. She struggled to remove her gloves.

"I knew you'd check them this morning before you went to your office. I picked up supplies from the warehouse, inventoried the storeroom, met with you after lunch, then there was that technician's meeting. . . ." Teri's voice cracked. She removed her protective clothing.

Beth tugged off her mask, pulled away the rest of her disposable clothes, and tossed everything in the waste container.

Teri washed her hands. Beth could see her eyes were wet and red.

Beth dialed the CEO.

"Hello, Beth," Orin said. "How's your day?"

"There's a problem in my lab." Beth paused, caught her breath, then took the plunge. "Some of my mice died two days ago, you might have heard, and now more have died, from hypothermia."

"Wasn't your tech trained on—"

"Teri didn't have anything to do with this." Her voice flared. "Have you authorized anyone to come into my lab?"

"Of course not. Don't jump to conclusions. How many died?"

"I've lost several dozen or more."

"Athymic mice are expensive." A pause. "What about your study?"

"Forty would let me squeak by, but now I'm at twenty and even that number is headed down."

"What a shame. Well, see what you can do. When you find out what happened, let me know." He hung up.

That was it? She turned back and looked at Teri. None of this made sense. Her knee felt warm and wet.

Teri looked down. "You're going to fire me, aren't you?"

"You're not at fault." But how could Beth even protect her own position?

Her research, her dreams for the institute—all tied up together—she couldn't let it all end like this.

"I'm no longer the primary researcher on any project." She swallowed hard. " A new order for mice wouldn't be processed or shipped in time.

We've got to keep these alive and I need to find more to replace the other ones." Beth choked up saying these next words. "If there aren't enough mice I won't need a technician."

She looked around. What was happening? She spotted a yellow legal pad on the counter. There was no writing on the pad except for a phone number at the top written with Teri's carefully penned printing. She started to dismiss it, but then Beth saw something else. There were indentations on it from something written on the previous sheet.

She turned the pad sideways. Someone had drawn the layout of her lab.

"Did you draw this?"

Teri leaned over, frowned, and shook her head.

Had Orin had those damaged ceiling tiles inspected and forgotten to let her know?

"Do you need this number?" Beth held it out.

"Not anymore."

"Get all the equipment cleaned—fresh bedding and water in each unit. We'll see if we can make this work. If not, I'll help you check other labs for another position."

Too bad it wouldn't be that easy for her.

Beth went over and scrutinized the lock on the door. No damage. She went back and examined the inner lab's door lock. It looked fine. Someone with keys had to have been in the lab, someone other than Teri. *But why?*

Her swollen knee throbbed. She decided to wait for the elevator. This whole thing sickened her—the lost animals, the lost potential from her research, her lost opportunity for a voice in governing this facility.

On the way to her office Nancy handed her a message slip.

"Your aunt called about fifteen minutes ago."

"I'm sorry—"

"Don't worry about it, Ms. Armstrong."

"Thanks. Would you please have Wayne call me?"

Nancy's phone rang. Beth heard her say, "Not yet, Mr. Borstell. I'll let you know."

Beth unlocked her door and placed the yellow legal pad and her aunt's message on the corner of her desk. Then she sat and stared at the screensaver on her monitor. Borstell was a quirky little man with an ethics problem. He shouldn't be on probation. He should be fired.

Beth buzzed Nancy again. "Did you find Wayne?"

"Someone saw him on the third floor an hour ago. I'll keep trying."

Beth wanted Mozart back in her head. She clicked the site that documented all the research animals at the institute. She scrolled through and looked for the slim chance that someone might have extra nude mice. There was Borstell's name, but his requisition held only opossums. She doubted he'd lend anything to her since she'd told Orin about Borstell's illegal requisition for his opossums.

Her phone rang.

She grabbed it. "Wayne?"

"Do I have the wrong number?" Kathleen's voice.

Beth propped her elbow on the desk and massaged her temple.

"I'm here, Kathleen."

"You sound different. Is everything all right?"

"Everything's fine."

"I was thinking—when we go to the bank, we could stop by the pet store and pick up some dog food and a bowl for Saucy. Would you mind?"

"The grocery store carries those."

"How silly of me—I'm sorry I bothered you. But are you sure you are all right?"

"I think I'm at the mercy of a full moon." Beth thought of something. "Remember you complained how I never ask for help?"

"I've never seen the point in being Superwoman."

"Would you take that package of steaks out of the freezer to thaw? They're on the left-hand side, down low." She'd pick up some nicotine candy on the way home—several packs. She could keep a couple in her purse when Kathleen claimed to have lost hers.

"Of course, dear. How fun—a cozy family dinner."

Trade secret theft has hit some of the nation's best-known companies, such as DuPont and Goodyear.

—RANDALL COLEMAN, FBI, MAY 2014

I'm extraordinarily patient, provided I get my own way.

—MARGARET THATCHER

8

White haze from cigarette smoke hung in the air when Beth came through the garage into her kitchen. Kathleen's voice spilled out from the living room.

"And there I stood asking my drunken friend what the hell she'd done with my mink." Kathleen paused for a coughing fit then said, "Guess what she said?"

Someone had forged paths between the stove, refrigerator, and sink to the cluttered kitchen table. No steaks on the counter top—only half-full Coke cans, a bottle of rum, and a mess of nails and screws. No place to set anything, not even the new loaf of bread. Beth slung the nicotine candy on top of the construction mess and stormed into the living room.

"She said she threw the goddamned thing in the lake, can you believe that?" Kathleen's laughter stopped when she saw Beth.

"Oh, lookie who's home." Kathleen lounged in the satin floor-length nightgown and robe Beth had purchased in Valley View. Harold stood. He'd loosened his necktie.

He went to Beth and kissed her cheek. Beth pulled away.

"Where did you get those cigarettes?" She glowered at him.

He hunched his shoulders, a highball glass in his hand, and wore his party-mood face.

"I suppose you smoke now too." She could see that he wasn't smoking, but she didn't know what else to say.

"Don't give him grief, child, it was my doing."

Harold winked at Beth and set his drink down. "I've been totally bewitched by this royal lady. She has enchanted me beyond all control."

He sank into his favorite chair, and Saucy jumped into his lap. Beth's face burned.

"Kathleen and I had an agreement." Her words came quick and tight.

Harold flinched.

"Doesn't an agreement require two parties, dear?" Kathleen studied her fingernail.

Jeez, her aunt felt entitled to jump into their arguments. Logic, that's what she needed. She relaxed her death grip on the new loaf of bread.

"Secondhand smoke isn't healthy for us, and Kathleen already has that nasty cough." She shifted the loaf to her other hand.

Harold touched his finger to his chin. "There was this recent study on the addiction of nicotine up in Canada, or was it in the UK?"

"Don't go giving me research junk, Harold. That's my profession. The bottom line is . . ." She flailed at the haze around her. "You know how I hate this."

"It's not humane." He paused, then frowned. "You're demanding that she stop now. Nicotine's as addictive as heroin—or is it cocaine? You don't want Kathleen to go through withdrawal, not while she's sick."

He set Saucy back on the floor. Kathleen watched them over the edge of her glass.

"She insists she's not sick." Beth's voice crackled. "This smoke, it's all through the house."

He said something to soothe her. She ignored the words. She didn't understand why he'd allow this.

He stepped toward her. She stepped back.

"We both hate cigarette smoke." She didn't want to be calmed.

He moved closer. She didn't even want him near her. *He'd allowed this. He'd sabotaged her authority. He'd undermined her.* She needed him to feel like she felt.

He held both palms up. *Damn him.*

"You've—" She backed farther away.

"But, Beth—"

"You *don't even care*."

She flung the loaf of bread at him. The second it left her hand, she felt better, then she didn't. The cellophane split. She watched the slices fly in every direction.

Saucy darted under the table.

Kathleen and Harold stared at her, their mouths open. She glared back.

The two looked at each other and erupted in whoops and chortles.

Beth's throat ached and her nose tingled. She looked at the bread, at Kathleen and Harold, and she wanted to run away.

Harold kissed her on the cheek, then collected her arsenal from the floor and furniture.

"Beth." He held up the jumble of slices and cellophane. "I think we're out of bread."

"You might," Kathleen murmured, "want to put some on your grocery list for tomorrow." Both partiers howled again with delight.

Beth pushed her hair back out of her eyes and noticed a plate of cheese cubes and saltines on the coffee table.

"We're having a drinky-poo. Harold's such a dear. He made Saucy a bed, covered some foam with his old army blanket." Kathleen stubbed out her cigarette in a Coke-can ashtray.

"Sweetie, it's your nature to care." As Harold headed into the kitchen to throw the bread away, he called back to her. "You know Kathleen's immune system is compromised."

Beth paused and considered. No one said anything until Harold returned.

"So Kathleen's bewitched you, has she?" She spoke soft. "And now you're her Knight of this Cuba Libre Round Table."

Harold glanced at Kathleen, then back at Beth.

"Here's my mandate." Beth set her jaw. "This includes you too, Kathleen."

Harold grinned and winked at Kathleen. Kathleen stared at the ceiling, taking a drag on her cigarette.

"The two of you come up with some plan for Kathleen to stop that lethal habit. When she succeeds, you, sir, paint the whole inside of this house forest green."

"Child, forest green is far too dark for these walls."

"Not at all. It'll complement my new silk draperies—in a red and black forest fire motif. Kathleen, why aren't you dressed? You wanted to go to the bank."

"There's no rush." She lit a fresh cigarette. "Harold, fix your charming wife a drink. He makes a good cuba libre, but he needs to stock up on limes."

"Don't bother," Beth said. "I need to start dinner."

"Nonsense. It's not even six." Kathleen crinkled her nose.

Beth knew her stomach would reject all food. But the resident partiers wouldn't fare well on nothing but alcohol, cheese, and crackers.

"Then maybe Harold should make us some sandwiches."

"Sit with me, dear." Kathleen patted the couch next to her. "Go on, Harold—that drink."

"I need to start thawing something, unless you've invited Julia Child to make dinner."

"You're far too businesslike about things. You're home now, relax." Kathleen put a square of cheese on a cracker and handed it to her.

Sit and eat a cracker with a chunk of cheese? And Harold, he never did anything in the kitchen—except rip and saw it up—yet there he was making drinks.

"Harold and I are having fun getting to know each other." Kathleen blew him a kiss when he came back to the living room. "Heavens, Beth, you certainly don't have much around here to munch on."

"I keep all the good stuff at the neighbors'. Keeps our weight down."

"Something go wrong today?" Harold held out the drink for her.

"Nothing I care to discuss." Beth waved the drink away.

"Why not?" Kathleen said.

"It's complicated and doesn't have anything to do with my personal life." They'd find it boring. Harold certainly preferred play over his work. She hated his half-finished projects—in the backyard, their bedroom, the utility room, and now the kitchen.

"Isn't your job part of your personal life?" Kathleen leaned forward. "How can you attend to one without affecting the other?"

"You could find another job in a heartbeat," Harold said.

"If you worked in a real library," Kathleen said, "now that would be something."

"Have you ever thought you might be happier if you gave it all up?" Harold set his drink down and reached for her. Beth pulled back and faced him.

"Happy? Even if I wanted to quit, which I don't, how could I—considering *your* work situation?"

Kathleen looked from Beth to Harold.

Beth headed toward the kitchen, then stopped and faced them.

"Do you both think I'm incompetent in my work? Do you think I'm incompetent in dealing with people? Harold, I wonder if you even think I'm incompetent in bed."

She didn't know where that last part came from. It just slipped out. She turned and flounced into the kitchen to fix their dinner.

She banged pots and dishes around while she cleared the table, made space on the counter, and listened to snatches of conversation. Saucy followed her from the refrigerator to the counter to the stove and back. The dog became adept at jumping over the toolbox.

Harold's rich voice floated in: "Kathleen, if you spent so much time at the Brown Palace why didn't you call us?"

Beth couldn't concentrate enough to hear the mumbled answer.

"Saucy!" Beth almost tripped. She stomped her foot and pointed toward the living room. The dog slinked out. Her mother never mentioned Kathleen spending time in Denver.

She assembled the tuna casserole and put it in the oven.

"Wouldn't you enjoy a drink, sweetheart?" Harold's words made her jump.

She continued tearing greens for the salad. He wanted to scrap his job, so did he expect she would feel the same about hers?

"Okaaaay, if that's the way you want it."

She heard ice clink and liquid slosh into a glass.

The phone rang. He grabbed it, his back turned toward her.

"Uh-huh . . . tomorrow? . . . I'll stop by."

He hung up. Her skin bristled, but she refused to question him.

A few seconds later, he set a fresh cuba libre beside the salad bowl. He swept her hair back, nibbled her ear, then kissed the nape of her neck.

She ignored him.

"Beth, I do love you."

"Oops, sorry." Kathleen stood in the doorway. "I thought maybe I could help."

Her aunt made her way to the table, set her drink down, and sat. Harold pulled out the chair across from Kathleen and joined her.

Beth screened out their conversation. Wayne said he hadn't touched the units or her mice, but could she believe him? She needed to talk to the building engineer again. Had a power outage tripped the circuits and caused the Laminar Flow to turn off? But wouldn't the generator have kicked in?

Rick, a lab tech, came out of one of the beagle runs this afternoon carrying a yellow notepad. Silly, everyone at the institute thrived on yellow legal pads. The bedding . . . only could be wet from human error. Who had been in her lab?

"You're rather like my dear friend Sophie," Kathleen said. "You worry all the time."

Beth set plates on the table.

"Sophie and I would be off on some grand adventure, and all she did was fuss. Dear, your style of clothes is quite off-putting, especially those colors."

"And you've made nightgowns the fashion of the day." Beth couldn't find the napkins. She settled for paper towels.

"You'd look smashing in something soft with color—turquoise, or even a deep salmon to complement those green eyes. What do you think, Harold?"

"Her green eyes complement everything she wears."

"Anyway," Kathleen said, "it would be fun to see you in something that wasn't nubby black or scratchy brown."

Beth tensed. She'd forgotten to call the Valley View Police and the Fire Department.

"Once when we were quite young—all of sixteen, actually," Kathleen said, "Sophie and I decided to apply for these jobs. We hadn't a clue what we were doing. When we walked in the office, the man who interviewed us took one look, tilted back his chair, puffed on his cheap cigar, and gave us this nasty smirk.

"He told us, 'I suppose you two think you can do this type work?' I gave him a look over my left shoulder with one of my special smiles. But Sophie . . . I thought she was going to pee her pants."

Beth plunked down three large glasses of ice water on the table.

Kathleen made a frown reserved for poison.

Beth craved chocolate.

"I said, 'I'm Miss Kathleen McPherson and this is Miss Sophia Dagget.' I slinked up to his desk—and there was Sophie clunking along behind me."

"She tells great stories, Beth." Harold said. "She reminds me of your grandfather."

Beth understood how much Harold needed her grandfather.

"I told him we were both from Minneapolis," Kathleen said, "and I slipped off my mother's lamb's-wool coat and draped it over one of my shoulders.

"'You lying little high school bitches,' he said. 'You think you can waltz in here wearing some god-awful clothes you stole from your mothers and fool me? We get fifty like you every week and only a few get hired.'" Kathleen stubbed out her cigarette. "And you'll never guess what he said next."

Beth couldn't guess. Harold kept silent, too.

"He said, 'If you dames are serious about working here, take off those dresses.'"

"Damn." Harold stamped his foot. "What type of job *was* this?"

Saucy skittered out from under his chair and into the living room.

"He said he needed to see what our bodies looked like under that ugly yardage." Kathleen glanced up at Beth. "We actually had worn our mothers' clothing. You see, dear, it's all about packaging."

Beth put the casserole on the table next to the salad. She felt Harold watching her. She went back to the sink.

"Beth always dresses professionally," Harold said. "Being a scientist, her research work's important."

She caught herself studying him. The other two filled their plates. She wiped down what counter space was left, loaded the dishwasher, and poured her untouched drink down the drain. A part had fallen off the can opener. She fiddled, trying to reassemble it.

Harold pushed back his chair, took the can-opener piece from her, and adroitly put it back in place.

"When you get a moment," he said, "would you pick out your favorite from those wood-stain samples over there?"

"Excuse me, I'm not hungry." He hadn't even worked on the kitchen since she had come back from Valley View. Construction mess and Kathleen's funny little stories—no wonder Kathleen didn't understand Beth's world. This woman lived a life of freedom from real responsibilities—even marriage.

Beth started toward the bedroom. Harold caught her arm.

"Listen, I have lots of bad days too. That's the way it is. Come on, sit, eat with us."

He was right. He used to enjoy accounting, the investment management, and being the CFO of the auto dealership. Now every workday was a bad day for Harold.

She sat and listened to their chatter. Their voices sounded miles away. She nudged her food into a circle with her fork.

"I feel so guilty." Kathleen poised her fork. "Sometimes I crave a simple tuna casserole, but tonight I didn't even raise a hand to help."

"Sweetie, Kathleen's right. You need a break. We should take some time off, go to Durango, Aspen, or the Grand Canyon."

"Harold, my dear boy," Kathleen glanced at Beth. "This is more than problems at her office. Her mother's death upset all of us."

"Even more reason for her to take care of herself." He slipped Saucy a little something under the table.

A fresh cuba libre stood next to her water glass. She picked up the tumbler and sipped—cool, rich sweetness.

Kathleen turned to her. "When did you start working?"

Beth wiped a bit of condensation from the tumbler with her finger, then looked at her aunt. The cold rum warmed her emotions.

"Why?"

"Curious."

"Right out of college, after I received my PhD."

"You aren't called doctor." Kathleen furrowed her eyebrows.

"Don't you think it sounds pretentious unless you are a medical doctor?"

"When did you marry Harold?"

"The next month." She glanced at him.

"Were you working then?"

"I—yes, why?" She set her fork down.

"Did you and Harold discuss your continuing to work after your marriage?"

"He didn't want me to, but he agreed."

Kathleen waved her hand in the air.

"For crying out loud, Harold. You married her when she was working. You knew she wanted to work. We're talking thirty years here—why are you trying to tell her what to do now?"

"I'm not—I only . . ." Harold leaned back in his chair and held up his palms up.

"You want her to stay home, and take care of the house, and wait on you?"

"Not at all."

"Oh, I think that's what it is. That's why she never settles down. She's cleaning every minute so you'll be happy."

"I don't care about the house." He put both palms on the table beside his plate and glowered at Kathleen. "Well, of course I do, but that's not what's important."

Kathleen touched his sleeve. "What is important?"

"It doesn't matter." He slumped back in his chair.

"It certainly does." Kathleen's voice was now a raspy whisper. "This is no way for the two of you to live. What's your problem here?"

Beth turned her glass, watched the ice, then took another swallow. She faced Harold. His face had lost all muscle tone. She needed him to smile.

Beth reached over and covered his hand with hers. He looked up at her. She squeezed.

"I've been thinking," Beth said. "If Ted and Laura still plan on us riding up to Evergreen for lunch, I better dust off my motorcycle."

He didn't need to know she'd not go anywhere until she knew who murdered her mice.

Good morning Chairman Whitehouse, ranking member Graham, and distinguished members of the subcommittee. I am pleased to be here with you today to discuss the Federal Bureau of Investigation's efforts to combat economic espionage and trade secret theft.

—RANDAL COLEMAN, FBI

Page 8: To implement the recommendations in this Guide effectively, an institutional animal care and use committee (IACUC) must be established to oversee and evaluate the program.

—GUIDE FOR THE CARE AND USE OF LABORATORY ANIMALS, NRC

9

Beth managed to unlock the RRC door without sloshing coffee all over her pink silk blouse. She *was* flexible—she could wear less severe clothes if she wanted to. Her mother had given her this blouse, saying it looked springlike.

Nancy wasn't at her desk. Gordy walked through the entrance and waved to her. He always impressed her as someone who could fell a tree with an ax in one hand while cradling a kitten in the other. And she considered him a friend, not merely another researcher.

"Too bad about your athymic mice." He took his mail from his box.

"I suppose everyone knows." She hated the truth in that.

"Heard you'd developed a new technique. Is that gone with the mice?"

"Don't you love entropy? That second law of thermodynamics will get you every time."

"Sorry about your chaos." He sorted his mail out on Nancy's counter top.

"But what about your DU lab worker?" She walked over to him.

"What a confusing mess. Decent man, too. Left a wife and a daughter." Gordy paused, then shook his head.

"Do they know what happened? Joe said possibly ketamine."

"He'd never take something like that." He looked at her. "It's a tough one."

"But you think it might have been ketamine, right?"

"He'd vomited, showed signs of respiratory distress, and his wife said he had a heart condition. So it might be cardiovascular. Have to wait for the autopsy report."

"Would you let me know?" She knew her voice sounded too urgent.

"Sure. Nancy—is she okay?" he said.

"Excuse me?"

"Sorry, none of my business." He picked up his mail and started back across the atrium toward the courtyard exit.

"Gordy, wait." She caught up with him. "What did you mean about Nancy?"

"You know, her son and all."

Beth raised a brow.

"The cancer thing—those treatments are rough. Catch you later." He went through the door.

How could she not have known? She unlocked her door. Everyone knew everything around here, except for her.

She found a message on her desk calendar from Nancy. Orin wanted to see her. She expected this, but his summons felt akin to the dentist chair. She picked up her notebook and pen and locked the Research Resource Center.

Nancy stood at the reception counter studying something.

"Good morning, Nancy." See, Kathleen, she wasn't an introvert, only professional. "How was your evening?"

"Not too bad, Ms. Armstrong." Nancy tilted her head, like a puppy unsure about what might happen next.

"Oh for Pete's sake, Nancy, call me Beth." Her stomach churned—Orin was waiting. "Is your son doing better?"

"Only one more round of chemo. We'll see what happens."

"Does someone need to be with him?" Now she knew why she'd never done this before. *Once it starts, there's no end.*

"Clayton's still out of work. The two of them hang all day. They were involved in bug identification when I walked through the door last night—strictly guy stuff."

"Hey, Ms. A." Hugh Wendenski's voice. "You're looking mighty spiffy today." He came up to her and pinched a ruffle. "I like that color."

She stepped back. "You picked up some sun. Does it hurt?"

"Should have seen me a few days ago."

"You've been on vacation?"

"Enjoyed a patriotic week of white sands, blue water, and red me. Hey there, Nancy, meant to give this to you on Monday." He handed her a package of coffee. "Enjoy."

"This is the best." Nancy grinned. "Thanks."

"I've been meaning to ask you," Beth said. "How is that optic-nerve experiment going?"

Hugh always looked dapper in black Florsheim shoes, silk ties, and Harris tweed jackets. She'd heard he came from a rough background—it certainly didn't show.

"Your proposal was impressive," she said.

"How's that?" He leaned closer.

She moved back another step. She considered herself tall, but he towered over her by a good seven inches. He didn't have a clue about personal boundaries, but with all he accomplished, she could forgive him that.

"Lowering ocular pressure to protect the nerve is inadequate— it's only medication for prevention. You take it a step further."

"Come on up to my lab. You'll get the full microscopic tour."

"I'll do that." She turned to Nancy. "I'll be in Mr. Stamford's office."

"Off to the boss?" Hugh said. "What's wrong?"

"Trust me, by noon you'll know all the gory details and more." With that, she hurried away. She couldn't put Orin off any longer.

When she entered Orin's outer office, Yvonne, his secretary, gave Beth a once-over.

"Mr. Stamford." Yvonne opened his door. "Mrs. Armstrong is here."

Orin stood as Beth stepped into his office. Research journals were stacked precariously on the edge of his desk. A well-cared-for orchid sunned in his north window, and an overcrowded bookcase stood next to the door.

"Sit, sit, we need to talk." He gestured toward the chairs.

"About the mice?"

"That too, but first I wanted to thank you for the way you handled that nasty business with Mr. Borstell." He sat in the matching chair. "You keep a sharp eye on these things."

"He was a bit obvious—ordering twice the number of opossums as approved?" She tilted her head. "Have you made a decision about my request?"

"Seems extravagant." He rubbed his chin.

"This institute is lagging behind. Our environments can hardly be called

[54]

enhanced. We have to do more, Orin—right now we're bordering on animal cruelty."

"Yes, well . . ." He leaned back. "How many mice did you lose?"

"Twenty-eight in all. Human error."

"You said it wasn't Teri." He furrowed his eyebrows.

"I'm certain she's not at fault. She's loyal and capable."

He paused, then said, "When's the deadline?"

"I called yesterday. There's not enough time to order more and redo the runs."

"What if the animals were already ordered and on their way?"

"You're talking about the ones for Gordy's study?" She caught her breath.

"That study was cancelled, but his cognitive one's almost finished. He can pick up your protocol and use his mice."

"You're cutting me out? But, you can't—" Her heart lurched.

"We'll still honor our commitment to the funding entity."

"I don't understand. Why not let me use his animals?"

"They're assigned to Gordy." He stood and walked behind his desk.

"That means nothing." She could feel all her muscles tightening. "I'll talk to the chairman of the Institutional Animal Care and Use Committee—"

"That's not the IACUC's function."

"Orin, why are you being unfair?" She popped to her feet. "I worked day and night writing that grant."

"We have a time constraint here." He glanced away. "We have to get this right."

"You're saying I'm not capable."

The room temperature felt a hundred and ten degrees.

"That has nothing—"

"This is *wrong*." She lowered her voice. "What's going on here, Orin? Something stinks."

"Mr. Gordon will do your research—if it's to be done at all." He picked up a journal. "Is there anything else we should discuss?"

"There's a *lot* we need to discuss."

"This subject is closed." Orin set his jaw.

"I can't believe you'd do this."

She stared at him. He shook his head.

"Then what about my chances for that promotion?"

"We promote on abilities. You know that."

"I more than meet those qualifications, and you know it." She crossed her arms and plopped back into the chair. "Did you even look at what I submitted?"

"We need an administrator who can keep grants coming and find new funding sources." He opened a bottle of pills on his desk, looked in, shook it, then closed it.

Did he only think of her as the RRC person? Did the RRC cause her to be an introvert?

Get out of my head, Kathleen.

Orin took his glasses off and set them on his desk.

"Since no new medicines can be approved until they've been tested on animals, we have to be on the lips of all the major pharmaceutical companies." Orin looked directly at her. "Finance is the lifeblood of this institution."

"But Joe and I originally set up the whole research division. Don't you want someone with leadership skills?"

"The other two applicants are strong in research experience—successful in their results."

"What if the results are there because a researcher cuts corners?"

"Do you know something I don't?"

"I'm at all the Environmental Oversight and IACUC meetings. When we discuss the protocols and do our semiannual inspections of the labs I get feelings about things."

"Come on, Beth, we can't operate on feelings. If you've discovered someone being unethical, you're obligated to tell the committee chairs—"

"Someone *killed* my mice." She jumped up and slapped her notepad against his desk. "I think it's obvious they want me out of this competition."

"That's preposterous."

"I want this position, Orin. You know how I operate. You know I'm thorough."

"Have you applied for other grants?"

"I've submitted to the lymphoma research network, I'm investigating the possible impact on municipal resources when elderly owners can't care for pets, and I'm the second on Joe's macaque projects."

"But you're not the primary scientist on any projects." He sat, picked up a file, and opened it—dismissive. "The board requires this of all candidates. It's a key part of their selection process."

"Then let me *keep* my research instead of handing it to Gordy."

She hated feeling jittery.

"The IACUC chairman said they took a calculated risk when they approved your protocol," Orin said. "What you submitted seemed logical, but your research design was out of the ordinary."

"Most CEOs would value innovation."

"Careful, Beth."

"Before I submitted the protocol, I consulted the research departments at Lilly, Abbott, and Merck—"

"For God's sake, Beth." He rubbed his head with both hands, then sank back into his chair, with his lips tight and his face crimson.

"*What?*" She stared at him. "What's wrong with that?"

"We're working to get the Economic Espionage Act passed and you announce your research to the world?"

"Those companies are rock solid—"

"You're too naïve. Billions of dollars are lost in the theft of trade secrets every year. If customers knew proprietary information was being leaked to competitors, what would happen to consumer confidence? Think how it would affect their shareholders. Some companies have even moved off-shore—competition's fierce."

"They're offshore because they're *smart*. Everyone else competes in a global market while we sit on our hands. Hasn't anyone read my proposals?" She paused to catch her breath, then shut her eyes. "Oh—of course. How silly of me. Can't compete globally because of 'corporate espionage.'"

"Beth, we have to maintain common-sense safeguards. Nondisclosure, non-compete agreements, even protected passwords—"

"All the more reason for me to do my own research—I'm the one that knows it best."

"Gordy hasn't had any accidents. You've had two in a week."

"Those were not accidents. *Not* accidents, Orin."

She lowered her voice.

"I'm telling you, *someone killed my mice.* There's something wrong here—something terribly wrong—and *you don't care.*"

"That does it." Orin took her by the elbow and forced her toward the door. "Get some fresh air, and for God's sake get a hold of yourself."

If the US were to adopt an "intelligence-for-profit" approach, it would be sending potentially antagonistic signals to its allies and all of the other members of the international community. Still the problem of other countries using this approach remains.

—BURTON, CIA (JUNE 2013)

10

Beth hurried back to the RRC. The smell of rich coffee greeted her. She picked up her mug, now squeaky clean.

"Nancy, thanks." She held it up. "Is Mr. Gordon in?"

"He ran over to DU, should be back within the hour." She handed Beth a message slip. "Your aunt called."

Beth glanced at the note and stuffed it in her pocket. Kathleen could wait.

"I need to talk with him." She opened a drawer in her file cabinet. If he wanted the administrative position, would Orin give him an edge?

His current research file would tell her more. She thumbed through the files: E, F, G, and H—where was Gordon?

"There's something else, Ms. Armstrong."

Beth's files couldn't be misplaced. These files were her responsibility and were the heart of all research funding. She started back through the index tabs.

"Ms. Armstrong?"

"Sorry, Nancy—give me a minute." She wiped her hands on her skirt and started through each name again. There—Gordon's file was stuck in the Js.

She never misfiled.

"Ms. Armstrong, is something the matter?"

"It's Beth, please. Did you do any filing for me while I was gone?"

"I wouldn't do that."

"Was there anyone in my—never mind." The cabinet was locked. She and Nancy had the only keys. She looked over at Nancy. "Did my aunt say what she wanted?"

"She insisted on talking to you, but I didn't want to interrupt your conference if it wasn't an emergency. There's something else, Ms. Armstrong—"

"Why won't you call me Beth?" Cultivating friendships should not be this exasperating.

"Because you're my superior." Nancy flushed. "I'm not sure how to bring this up. I know you've had a rough time these last few months, your mom and all."

Beth closed the file cabinet and focused on Nancy. Her panic over Gordy's file could have waited.

"According to someone who's a good friend of Mr. Stamford's secretary, Yvonne— Well, when he taught hydrology at a university in another state, he left because of problems with female students not dressing appropriately. They—well, came on to him."

"I don't understand where you're going with this." Beth couldn't visualize voluptuous college girls ripping off their sweaters for Orin.

Nancy straightened a few pens on the desk, glanced around the office, then looked at her.

Beth's blouse—that's what this was about.

"Good grief, Nancy, I only wanted a softer look. I'm sure I'm not showing cleavage—I'm positive I'm not. Am I?"

Did Orin question her professionalism? Was that the reason he'd pulled her research out from under her? Yvonne certainly gave her the look.

Nancy shrugged. "A bit, if you lean forward enough." She straightened a pile of folders, then headed toward the door.

"Thanks." Heat flooded Beth's face. "And for the coffee, too."

She'd changed into the blouse as a last-minute impulse. She picked up the phone and called home. After the fifth ring, she hung up. She spent the next hour thumbing through Gordy's folder.

"Hey." Gordy stuck his head around the corner of the doorway.

"I've been reading about your latest research."

"It's almost wrapped up. Pay attention to your protein intake."

"Significant findings? Have you talked to Orin?"

"Got a note from him."

"Think you'll do it?"

"Grants fall from the sky, no need to sweat blood and ink over it." He glanced at her and then quickly looked away—her blouse or her research? His face and arms were deeply tanned, not sunburned like Hugh's.

She picked up the coffee pot, paused, then held it out toward him.

He shook his head. "Caffeine overload."

"Did you see the autopsy report on your coworker yet?" She refilled her mug.

"Doesn't make sense. It was ketamine. Must have been giving himself injections."

"Do you believe that?" She sipped. "His religion and all?"

"What else can I believe. He had a heart condition. The combination is deadly."

"What if someone else injected him?" She put her mug down and stared at him.

"Why would they? He still had his wallet, credit cards, money, watch. There's no motive."

"Someone killed my mice right after that." She held her breath.

He twisted up one side of his mouth, so she turned away and picked up her mug.

"Heard about your bagel bash for the macaques," he said. "It's their social activity that's linked to their well-being."

She went to the file cabinet, careful not to lean over, and took out the folder containing her research information.

"You can make copies on the machine over there. I track all paper changes, so I can't let you have the original, but I'll move it over to your folder as soon as I get a chance." She held out the document for him, but he ignored it.

"Who's handing out the bagels?"

She frowned; a strange question. "Joe, Wayne, and Joe's tech. Why?"

"Tell them to wear heavy gloves."

"We're well aware of Weigler's 1992 study and the human-mortality rates. Besides, our macaques aren't rhesus, they're cynomolgus."

"Still don't like it," he said. "Rhesus get the bad publicity, but we haven't studied what other zoonotic diseases lurk in your nonhuman primates. Bet we'll find some bad stuff down the road."

A chill raced through her body.

Gordy turned on the copier, picked up her documents, and started flipping through the pages.

She pressed the button on her phone and told Nancy to get Joe on the line. When she finished her conversation with him about the gloves, Gordy held up one of her file pages.

"Thought you'd be mad over this."

Why would he care how she felt? Her mug clunked too loud on the desk.

"Tons of work goes into these projects." He checked the lights on the copier. "I'd be pissed if it were my research."

"Public displays of emotion aren't my style." She took a sip of Nancy's coffee. "But you're right. I'm furious."

"So what happened? Infection? Systemic assault? Latex?"

"Hypothermia from wet bedding." She rubbed the back of her neck for a moment. She couldn't believe he didn't know. Everyone else did. He spent too much time at DU.

"Teri?"

"Everyone picks on the poor girl. She's the best."

He was staring at her. Was it the blouse again? *Dammit, Kathleen.* She inhaled the strong coffee's aroma.

She asked, "How well do you know Wayne?" But then Wayne was so dedicated.

"He's okay, why?"

"Then tell me what you know about that supervisory position." She watched his face.

"Don't tell me Wayne's applying."

He hadn't answered her question. "Do you know who is?"

"Don't care about those things." Gordy fed paper through the copier. "Not my style."

"You're qualified."

"On overload with plans to take another path. You?"

"When do you think you'll start on mine?"

"Orin stamped rush on it, but I promised Dan I'd take over his research. I'll have a tech do the initial set-up and prep work. I have to go back to DU for a few more days—start my actual trials right after."

"What's happening with Dan?" She sorted through her mail.

"His wife's on complete bed rest. Twins aren't due for two more months."

She paused. A flicker of excitement caught her. "I know the intricacies of his aging research from our IACUC committee." She set her mail down. "Let me do it."

"Why volunteer for more work?" He removed his copies from the machine and placed the originals back in the manila folder.

"I'd be the primary biologist."

"Aha." He handed her back her documents. "You were going to showcase your mice project for the new supervisory position."

"I'm not giving up. Let me ask Orin before you talk to Dan, okay?"

"Run up to my lab around four-thirty. We can discuss this." He held the copies up.

"It's all thoroughly documented. You won't have questions."

"You could see my space," he said. "I may need to make some changes."

"Don't you dare," she said. "Besides, I'm hoping to get out of here on time for once."

After he left, she logged on to her computer. How would she get all that secondhand smoke out of her home? She picked up the phone, dialed again—no answer.

Would the phone still ring if the house had burned?

Don't be silly. Kathleen was probably out with Saucy.

One of these evenings, she needed to get Kathleen away from Harold and liquor, and off to a bank.

She selected one of the folders Nancy left on the desk. She held her breath. Was her mind playing tricks on her? Hadn't Marion Shaw finished her research with those rabbits a couple of weeks ago?

Beth flipped to the last page in Marion's file, ready to record the researcher's results into her computer. Once entered, the institute would bill the company who had contracted with Marion. She pulled up Marion Shaw's file on the computer screen and scrolled to the data page. She stared at the screen. Her eyes opened wide, then her mouth.

Someone had already entered Marion Shaw's final data.

Competition among businesses is good, but among countries it is not necessary. Indeed, government involvement in commercial competition can be dangerous. If they cannot compete, companies can reduce their size or go out of business, but countries cannot.

—BURTON, CIA, JUNE 2013

11

Beth decided to stop at a hardware store before going home. When she struggled through the kitchen door with her heavy box, the house still smelled of cigarettes, but it also smelled of food.

Cartons of Chinese takeout sat on the counter along with drywall tape, a crowbar, coffee mugs, and two rum bottles—one empty. The cupboard where she stored her coffee mugs held a mess of electrical wiring. Harold's renovations seemed endless.

The partiers' voices sang out louder than usual from the living room. They quieted when she entered.

Harold rushed to her side to take the heavy box. He set it on the floor.

"Thanks for your artful pursuit of our dinner, Prince Valiant." Beth turned to Kathleen. "I tried to return your call today but didn't get an answer."

"From knight to prince." He kissed her cheek, then bent to read the label on the box. "But you have to thank your aunt."

Kathleen took a long sip of her drink, leaned back, and looked at Harold. She was wearing her gray slacks from Valley View but now with a scarlet sweater.

"Chinese food at the dial of a phone—clever and thoughtful," Beth said.

"My dear child, I keep telling you I'm not helpless."

"She went out today." Harold pulled his pocketknife out and started opening the box. "Went to the bank, went shopping—"

"Sure she did. You gave her money, she drove your car."

"I'm not stupid, Beth—I called a taxi." Kathleen blew a smoke ring. "He was the nicest driver. He waited for me at the bank, and my God, it took forever. I promised him a nice big tip for his lost time."

"But the fire—you don't have identification."

"Colorado Front Range called my bank in Chicago, and the insurance company, and—I don't know—did all sorts of verifications." She dropped ash on the white carpet.

"That's . . . impossible."

"Not if you know the chairman of their board of directors. They're mailing me a MasterCard."

Harold now plucked packing debris from the box.

"She knows lots of people," he said.

"Treated me like royalty." Kathleen surveyed the room, apparently concealing a grin. "Do you have an ATM card? Stands for Automatic Teller Machine—you enter your code and get your money. Dwayne was so patient while I did all my shopping."

"Dwayne?"

"The young cab driver—said to call him anytime, even gave me his phone number. Now then, how was your day?" Kathleen helped herself to cashews from one of Beth's china bowls. A plate with a round of brie and some fancy crackers sat on the coffee table along with some spilled liquid.

Beth wiped up the liquid with a couple of tissues and left to throw them away.

"Your aunt's been telling great stories about Chicago," Harold called after her. He pulled the large component from the box, which scattered more packing material over the carpet.

Beth returned with a dishtowel.

"For God's sake, don't you ever relax?" Kathleen patted the couch next to her. "Every evening you find something to fuss about."

Beth picked up the cheese tray and wiped the table. Then she slipped a coaster under Kathleen's drink.

"Now." Beth sat. "What should we talk about? We could talk about the effect of water on fine wood—"

"Behold, an air purifier." Harold looked around the smoky room, then grinned at Beth. He stuffed some of the packing material into the empty box and stood. "Man, what a job."

He knelt down again and put the remaining packing debris back into the carton.

Beth knitted her brow.

He finished and stood. "My neck is killing me."

"What's wrong?" Why was opening this box a big deal?

"Arrgh." He rubbed his neck, then placed both hands on each side of his head and slowly turned it side to side.

With each turn they heard a sickening crunch.

"Christ!" Kathleen knocked over her drink.

"Harold?" *His cervical spine—what on Earth?*

The women jumped to their feet.

Beth grabbed him. "Are you all right?"

He stared at them with wide-open eyes of shock. *He'd never complained of neck problems before.*

"Harold? Oh—Harold—" Her breath caught.

He opened his mouth. Between his teeth he held crunched packing bubbles.

Kathleen let out a howl of laughter. Harold joined her. Beth watched the two, then a giggle slipped out. He used to do these playful things all the time.

"Come on, love, join us," Harold steered Beth toward the couch. "You don't have to fix dinner. Would you like a glass of wine or a cuba libre?"

"Oh . . . what the—" His silliness brought back memories of youthful days filled with comfort. "Wine, please."

She cleaned up Kathleen's spilled drink while Harold dashed off and returned with fresh ones.

He poured, she sipped, and they watched her.

Kathleen wasn't the only one who could tell a story. Beth sank back in the chair and held up her glass. She never talked about her work. But after today . . .

"Here's to mice that live, secure computers, and a boss who gives a flying . . . ." She sighed. "Never mind."

"I'd say she had a bad day," Kathleen said. "What do you think, Harold?"

He stared at Beth.

"Well, child, I'm all ears."

Harold slipped into his chair but kept his eyes on Beth.

She started with her sabotaged lab that had resulted in the separate mice disasters.

"God, I love a good mystery." Kathleen hugged herself.

"My money," Harold tapped his temple, "is on the custodian. I bet he loves those *darling* nude mice."

Kathleen howled with laughter, then calmed herself by taking a large swallow of her cuba libre.

"You're wrong, my good man." She cleared her throat. "From Beth's description of her tech, I'd place my money on her perky little derrière."

"Cute doesn't preclude reliable, Kathleen." Beth sipped her wine. "And Teri would never let something like this happen once, much less twice."

"Dear, she's an underling. If she gets rid of you she can take over your position."

"Good grief, you both flunk as super sleuths. Wayne's a decent guy and Teri has to finish her degree."

"No matter, dear. You'll uncover who this desperado is in no time."

"Your aunt's figured you out." Harold patted her damaged knee.

Beth winced but kept silent.

"We both know you can't stand messes," he said. "You'll clean this one up fast."

Kathleen winked and raised her glass to Harold. Beth pulled her cheeks in, and then decided to tell them about her interview with Orin.

"Why did Stamford give away your research?" Harold leaned in and place his elbow on his knee.

"That's a puzzle." Beth paused, then said, "Orin doesn't understand what's needed for long-term success."

"And what *is* needed?" Harold picked up Saucy.

"Everything's outdated—building space, equipment, animal habitats. . . ."

"Have you pointed this out to him?" Kathleen asked.

"He knows how I feel. It's the board I have to convince. Which is why I need that promotion—and giving away my research cuts me right out of the competition." She looked at Harold. "I've found another project. But if Orin wants me disqualified he won't approve it."

"Those mice dying had to be an accident," Harold said.

"*Two* accidents? In one week?" Beth wanted to break something.

Kathleen sighed. "She's right, Harold."

"There's more." Beth glowered at Harold

Now Kathleen leaned forward.

"I'm the one who enters *all* the researchers' hard-copy data into the institute's computer. I track every file, and when each one is finished, I notify the billing department. Today I found data that I needed to enter, already entered. Someone's hacked into my computer."

"Easy fix—get your password changed." Harold offered her the dish of cashews.

"Wrong, Superman." She ignored the nuts. "The IT guy refused to do it."

"Don't ever take the word *no* from a mere underling, dear. Harold and I might see things from a different perspective, we often don't agree, but you're not alone here." She touched Harold's hand. "But Beth, you have to make people say *yes* to you."

"What's the IT guy's reason?" Harold said.

Beth took sip of her wine and looked away before she answered.

"Gavin says he doesn't have time, he's overloaded."

"That's bunk," Harold shook his head. "It's no big deal to change a password."

"He insists my computer is secure so it's a waste of time to do busywork on a whim."

"Hell, Beth," Kathleen said. "This isn't some whim. Don't let him bully you."

"Is changing passwords on par with changing diapers?" Beth sipped her wine.

"Enough." Kathleen swiped the air with her cigarette. "We're getting bogged down. Have I told you the story of Sophie's disappearance?"

"I relinquish the floor to your mystery." Beth settled back and swirled her wine.

"Sophie became tangled up with the wrong crowd. We all warned her, but you could say she was looking for love in all those wrong places."

"Ha." Harold glanced at Beth. "Been there, done that."

"Are you still?" Beth set her teeth and gave him the squinty eye.

He slipped Saucy a cashew.

"One day Sophie didn't show up for work. We thought we'd find her body washed up on the shores of Lake Michigan.

"Then one night Ed and Max, he was a policeman, grabbed me from the middle of a performance. A canary matching Sophie's description was singing at a hotel over in Cicero. Max didn't want to rush in there looking for one of the big guy's dames. But Sophie wasn't one of *those* girls."

"Are you making this up?" Harold stopped stroking Saucy's ears.

It sounded like something out of a movie, but Kathleen's face told otherwise.

"I was still in my dance costume, so Max thought I could slip in unnoticed." Kathleen grinned. "Now how fine was that? Two big-muscle men hide in the car while I go and get my brains blown out."

"Did my grandparents know you were an entertainer?" Beth pictured herself with cropped hair, long pearls, and a life of pure fun. "My parents would have a cow."

"I didn't want to be in that neighborhood alone, day or night." Kathleen spoke low.

"Why would your friends put you at risk?" Beth cringed. That sounded like her mother.

"They found a guy named Sullie to be my escort. But Max said we had to be careful because Sullie played both sides, which can get a person a ticket to the bottom of the river."

Beth and Harold looked at each other, then burst out laughing.

"Child, what's so funny?"

"Go on, we'll be quiet—honest."

"Sullie was waiting on the corner where they let me off. We sauntered along as if we were doing the town. We all agreed, if it was Sophie, we wouldn't do anything, and Max insisted we leave right after her number. She wouldn't be able to see us because of the stage lights."

Beth could feel the cold night air, the rush of adrenaline.

"Sullie was a handsome guy, tall, well dressed—I'd been expecting some smarmy weasel. We entered the hotel, went down a few steps, and he knocked on a paneled wall. When a window opened he said, 'Deuce of Clubs.' The panels hid a door that opened into a huge room, packed with people. The band was incredibly loud—trumpets blasting.

"By the time we made our way through the room, the band started up a softer number. When our drinks arrived, a buxom blonde pranced up to the microphone in a low-cut black number with gold beads. I glanced at Sullie and shook my head. It wasn't Sophie.

"He set some bills on the table, then motioned for me to drink up. And that's when I saw Hymie—a sadistic creep—with a redheaded floozy on his arm. She's the one who caught my attention." Kathleen paused. "I knew she was wearing Sophie's mink."

Beth's eyes widened.

"How can you tell one mink from another?" Harold fed Saucy another cashew.

"That's what Sullie said. But I'd worn Sophie's coat shortly before she went missing. She had a shit fit because my cigarette burned a hole in the sleeve. I walked by but couldn't get a good view. Hymie and the girl moved on to an empty table, where Hymie helped remove her coat, and then he slid it over the back of her chair.

"I darted over and said, 'Excuse me, don't I know you?'

"Hymie, playing a gentleman, straightened up. 'Naw, I don't think so.'

"'I was talking to your lovely escort. I could swear we've met before. Didn't we audition together a few years back?'

"She gave me a blank stare.

"'Well, it doesn't matter now, does it?' I said, and I picked up the sleeve of the coat. 'We'll do anything to get one of these North Side minks, right?' Hymie said something like, 'Hey, that ain't no North Side coat. I gave that to her myself. We don't like nothing from North Side and that includes you, you North Side charity case.'

"Sullie, who'd been right behind me the whole time, came to the rescue. 'Don't talk to my girl like that if you want to live. Come on, Sweetheart, let's get out of here.' He grabbed my arm, told me I didn't know what I was messing with in there, dragged me up the stairs, and practically pushed me out of the hotel."

"Was it Sophie's coat?" Harold was on the edge of his seat.

"The sleeve was burned," she said. "But that doesn't matter now. What do you plan to do about your research, dear?"

Beth's stiffened. She looked at both of them.

"We guessed you were miserable," he said. "Let Orin Stamford handle this."

"I should talk with Nancy." She stared at the reflections in her wine. "She might know something."

"Should you even trust your secretary?" Kathleen said.

"She's completely trustworthy."

"Your boss needs to—" Harold's voice pushed her words aside.

"She needs more evidence," Kathleen touched Harold.

"Beth shouldn't be the one to get it." Harold leaned away and set his jaw.

"Nonsense, my fine man. Her boss obviously doesn't believe her. Beth will bring all truths to light."

"Kathleen, you can't encourage this. What if Beth puts herself in danger?"

Saucy put her ears back, hopped off Harold's lap, and curled up under his chair.

Beth felt almost calm after her crappy day. Amazing what a little evening chardonnay could do when she nestled down and listened to others fight her battles.

The reality is that the vulnerability of the Department of Defense— and of the nation—to offensive information warfare attack is largely a self-created problem.

—SCIENCE BOARD TASK FORCE ON INFORMATION WARFARE-DEFENSE, CIA, NOVEMBER 1996

12

Nancy wouldn't arrive for five more minutes. Beth slipped an unmarked envelope under the edge of the reception calendar.

"A surreptitious note?" Gordy's voice startled her.

"Nancy's the sole breadwinner for her family on a secretarial salary," she said. "Cross your heart, don't snitch on me."

"You've checked with Orin about Dan's assignment?"

"He said he wanted to talk to Dan before he made his decision," she said. "I'm betting he'll nix it."

"Why would you think that?"

"Never mind." She turned toward her office.

"Cheer up—He called Dan and told me you're in." He sprinted up the stairs whistling *Heigh-ho, heigh-ho, it's off to work we go.*

What the . . . Why did Orin tell him? Beth strode to her office but stopped in the doorway and stared, not believing what she saw. Three files were on her desk. Nancy never left files out overnight.

Beth needed a brain refill—a top-off of solutions for unexplained events. She slid into the desk chair. These files on her desk made no sense. Gordy knowing about Orin's decision wasn't professional. If some scientist wanted her out of the promotion race, then killing her mice and messing with her computer would have done it. Still, receiving Dan's opossum study put her back in the race.

Yesterday Orin gave the research department a lecture about corporate espionage. He seemed sure that President Clinton would sign the Economic Espionage Act into law this fall. She could consider that angle, but how would that fit with dead mice, files entered into her computer, and now errant files on her desk?

She left the RRC and locked the door behind her.

At the elevator, she pushed the up button and waited. The door dinged opened. As she stepped inside, she heard someone running. Hugh Wendenski loped up and thrust his hand in right before the door closed.

He held his finger over the floor numbers and raised an eyebrow.

"Four—thanks for driving," she said.

"My lab or the tech department? Bet you're going to talk with Gavin? What's wrong with your leg?"

"Football. Tackled a six-year-old."

"Heard you're taking over Dan's research."

"How—I can't believe this. I just found out myself. Who told you?"

"Gordy and I had a beer after work." He winked at her. "No one has secrets around here."

"I shouldn't be the last to know." She put on a carefree look even though she felt a wee bit murderous toward Mr. Gordon.

"Take a second and come look." He escorted her through his immaculate office and into his lab and showed her the electron microscope. His excitement spilled over, contagious, as he gave her a brief synopsis on his optic-nerve study.

As they left through his office, he stopped, grabbed a ceramic pin from his bookcase, and handed it to her.

"What's this?" She studied the brownish-green tree frog with disk-shaped toes.

"Picked it up a few years back during one of my vacations. Take it. Consider it a thank-you for all the contacts you've made for me on the Internet."

"It's lovely, but . . ."

"Come on, Beth." He held it close to her jacket. "You can't think it would look good on me."

～

The IT guy, Gavin, held a brick-shaped wireless phone to one ear. Beth didn't see the point of cell phones, except for emergencies. She'd never had emergencies until Kathleen came along.

He clicked off and beckoned her.

"I'm planning to switch your Internet access over from dial-up to cable when I get back from LA—big technology conference."

"Cable? Super, but now I need some technical advice. Convince me my computer's secure."

He shook his head in a *give it up* look.

"Seriously, I have good reason to think someone inside the research department has hacked into my RRC computer."

"Not without your password." He positioned his needle-nose pliers.

"What are those wires?" She pointed to the tangled cables on his work-table. He explained each one as he worked.

"Guess being electrocuted isn't a biggy on your list."

He grinned until her next statement.

"Take me off the network."

"Nope." He pointed to a list on his corkboard. "Orin's doing. 'All scientists will be connected to the Institute's Scientific Researchers' Network at all times.'"

"I get hard copies of everything they do. If they need references or information from the Internet, I'll put my findings in their mailbox."

"Sorry, I covet my paycheck."

She folded her arms.

He stared back at her.

"What?" he said.

"I need to be sure no one can mess with the data in my computer."

"I told you—"

She cleared a tangle of cables off a chair, pulled the chair over to Gavin's table, and sat.

"You're going to sit there and watch me work?"

"Consider me your new roommate."

He groaned.

"Or change my password."

"Man—okay, I'll change your password, okay?"

When she returned to her office, Beth walked around her desk and studied the back of her computer. She identified the power cord, printer cable, and speaker wires. The gray one connected to the phone jack was her modem. There was another cord, thicker, that ran along the floor and into a small hole in the wall—this must be the BNC network cable. She twisted it. It turned but didn't do anything. Silly, it must unscrew. It didn't. What type of connector was this?

She mulled the pros and cons of having the network. She could work around the inconvenience. She only needed the modem to connect to the Internet. How could she disable this connection to the network?

She yanked the network cable. Nothing.

She took out her industrial-strength scissors and considered Gavin's explanations with the possibility of electrical currents. She examined where the cord disappeared into the wall. She saw no electrical connections.

She snipped.

The scissors sliced through the cable's plastic coating.

She snipped again, this time with muscle behind it. The cord resisted, then yielded, leaving the cable dangling, impotent, from her computer.

As she settled behind her desk, she realized she hadn't received even one of Kathleen's annoying daily calls.

Beth picked up the phone and dialed home. After four rings she was about to hang up when she heard Kathleen's voice.

"Armstrong residence."

"I thought I'd check on your day."

"Why, is something wrong?"

"I—no, everything's fine." Beth waited.

Silence.

"Do you need me to pick up anything on the way home?"

"Not tonight."

"Are you okay?"

"Perfectly." More silence.

"Call me if you need anything then."

"I will, dear."

The dial tone sounded.

What in the world is she—?

"Coffee break time." Gordy stuck his head around the doorframe. "I'm buying, but the blend of the day is Cafeteria-Weak."

"That's as good as it usually gets around here." She stepped outside, locked her door, and told Nancy where to find them.

"I feel special," Beth said. "Why the treat?"

"Two reasons." He touched her shoulder to guide her through the doorway. "Hugh said I needed to apologize to you. Plus, I need to know how proficient you are if I'm the new foster dad for your protocol."

[73]

"Apology accepted, but shove your interview, Mr. Gordon."

In the cafeteria they sat at a table next to the bank of windows. She studied him as they sipped.

"Joe said you're quite the adventurer." That could explain his cocoa-brown tan.

"Only in the line of duty," he said. "Working with the institute and in conjunction with DU keeps me on the go."

"Your research is the reason you travel?"

"Partly." He leaned back, keeping his eyes on her face.

"How'd you land a position like that?"

"Probably because of who I know, who I am, and who knows me."

"I'd love to hear about it." She caught a reflection of herself in the window. The flattened, washed-out image made her look imbedded in the institute.

"Another time," Gordy said. "Dan's conflicted, you know."

"Giving someone your research hurts."

Gordy raised a brow.

"I'll talk with him," Beth said. "How did Orin react?"

"He seemed preoccupied but thought Dan should stay with his wife."

Shouldn't Orin be pleased she had a new shot at promotion?

"I've been reading your protocol," he said. "You said I wouldn't have questions, but I do."

"Questions or concerns?"

"Both."

Damn him.

He took a final sip. "Can't understand why we haven't had coffee before."

She picked up her cup and stood.

"Because I had no idea, Mr. Gordon, if you could meet my standards."

Despite the comprehensive outreach efforts undertaken by the FBI, Companies which discover misappropriations of their trade secrets . . . sometimes attempt to address the issue through private negotiations or civil litigation, rather than alert law enforcement.

—COLEMAN, FBI, MAY 2014

13

Beth arrived home and opened the door to the smell of something wonderful.

Harold, wearing an apron, greeted her with a kiss on the cheek.

"Wait till you see what Kathleen's cooked up." Kathleen stood at the stove, oblivious to the construction clutter, stirring something that smelled rich, making Beth's mouth water.

Kathleen wiped her hands and turned off the stove. Harold escorted Beth to her place at the dining-room table and handed her a linen napkin. Kathleen brought in a serving dish of fluffy mashed potatoes.

"Light the candles, Harold, while I set the rest of this on the table."

Harold lit the candles and poured the wine. Kathleen invited Beth to help herself to tender beef in a dark-brown gravy.

"It's called Flemish Ragout." Her aunt sat back and watched their faces. "It's beer that makes the sauce so rich."

"Kathleen told me gravy is only used as a meat sauce in polite society, but who likes naked potatoes?" Harold drowned them.

In the glow of the candles, Beth could almost forget the clutter in the kitchen.

"I feel like we're celebrating," she said.

Kathleen sipped her wine. "No matter how awful our worlds may be, we all have something in our hearts to treasure."

"You're not eating?" Beth frowned.

"Seems whenever I create a big meal I lose my appetite."

Beth put her fork on her plate and leaned toward Kathleen.

"I had no idea you could cook like this. Everything's perfect—you're a first-class gourmet chef."

"Now there's a compliment." Kathleen picked up her fork and took a small bite.

"She's right," Harold held up his glass in a mock toast. "You've created a masterpiece."

"And here's what I do with compliments," Kathleen said. "I save them all in this little special place, and on a night when I'm in bed and feeling lonely or sad, I take them out one by one, polish them until they shine, and enjoy them all over again."

Beth considered those words before saying, "Something happened today, but I don't know if it's a compliment or not."

The two stopped eating and looked at her.

"When Orin gave away my research, I figured he'd lost confidence in me, or he didn't want me to be promoted. But now he's giving me a second chance."

Kathleen held her glass up, and they all clinked. Harold beamed.

"That ranks as a compliment," he said.

"Why did he take me off my research in the first place?" She smoothed a wrinkle from the tablecloth.

"He may be covering something up, dear."

Harold shook his head. "It was probably some financial thing."

"Athymic mice aren't cheap. But when I told him, he acted like he didn't care."

"Maybe he knew about your mice before you did." Kathleen took another bite.

Harold glanced at Kathleen. "That's crazy."

Beth shrugged. "Then why would he approve me as the primary researcher on this new project?"

"What will you be doing?" Kathleen leaned back and sipped her wine.

"It's about aging." She looked at Harold, then Kathleen. They seemed interested. "Two scientists in the 1980s, Austad and Zimmer, discovered that opossums in Venezuela only lived a couple of years. But the opossums on an island five miles from Georgia were living almost twice as long. The Venezuelan opossums showed dramatic aging within a few months."

Harold leaned forward. "What were the variables?"

"Appears to be predators. They believed the Venezuelan jaguars feeding on opossums created a fast-forward time line. Those dinner-buffet opossums had to hurry up and mature by breakfast and deliver offspring by lunch, so by the time the jaguars rolled around for dinner, the opossums' offspring had secured their species' future."

"That's an interesting analogy." Kathleen pulled out her matchbook and cigarettes.

"Don't buy it," Harold said. "Risk from predators can't explain rapid aging."

"It does if all your nutrients go into maturation and gestation rather than tissue repair."

"Sounds like it's all tied up with a ribbon." Kathleen took a puff. "Where does your research come in?"

"Right this minute the world's oldest known living person is a woman in France. She's a hundred and twenty-one." Beth thought a moment. "Think about a predator-free opossum environment and diet. Can diet be manipulated to further improve genetic longevity?"

Harold turned to Kathleen.

"She's something, isn't she?" He grinned. "I've heard about this French woman, Jeanne Calment or something. She's smoked for over a hundred years."

"And you call this a lethal habit." Kathleen blew a smoke ring. "Maybe this *is* some financial thing with Orin."

"See, there you have it." Harold set his empty wine glass aside.

"If it is," Beth said, "I suspect it's something illegal. Remember I told you someone's been into my computer files? No one's authorized to do that."

"What can you do about it?" Kathleen said.

"I forced the IT guy to change my password."

"Passwords aren't the only way to hack into someone's computer, you know." He slipped Saucy a tiny scrap of meat. He looked up and caught Beth's eye.

"I disconnected my computer from the network." She smirked. "No one at the institute will hack into it now."

"Your boss probably believes the lab disasters are mistakes," Harold said.

"Bullshit. He wouldn't give her another project if he thought she was careless."

"Maybe." He pointed at Kathleen. "Don't go making this into something bigger than it is. Whatever it is, she should let her boss handle it."

"Harold, please put that finger away. I don't know where it's been."

Beth inhaled. Kathleen stubbed out her cigarette.

"Beth's not going to solve anything by turning it over to Orin."

"But she's required to follow procedures."

"Even if her boss is involved?" Kathleen pulled out another cigarette.

"He must be," Beth said. "Why else would he act the way he has?"

"She's right," Kathleen said.

"What do you expect her to do?" Harold pushed his chair back. "Orin Stamford needs to be the one to handle this. I don't believe any of this sabotage crap, but right now we're only talking about dead mice. If this does happen to be something criminal then what if it's taken to another level?"

Harold left the table and poured rum and Coke into tumblers and added lime wedges.

"Harold, you're being paranoid." Beth frowned. "And you make it sound like I've bungled the whole thing."

"You'd rather I didn't give a shit?"

"Of course not." Beth dabbed her lips with her napkin. "But if it's Orin I'm in trouble, because I'm the financial gatekeeper for the researchers."

"What's your evidence?" He set one of the cuba libres next to Kathleen's wine glass and another at Beth's place.

"My dear boy, if it is Orin, the worst he'll do is slap a few hands and ask stupid questions that cover his tracks."

"Don't you care about her safety?" He went back for his tumbler.

"I'm saying she needs to operate more covertly. Watch other scientists, ask pointed questions. . . ." Beth studied the two. They were arguing over who had her best interests at heart.

"You'd love it if she gave up and quit work." Kathleen jutted her chin toward Harold.

"What the hell's that supposed to mean?"

"It means I don't believe you care about her career."

"Give it up, woman, I'm not looking for a housewife."

Beth shook her head, stood, and started collecting empty plates. Saucy followed her to the kitchen. Why such a heated argument now? When they talked about all of this last night, it made a great evening.

Kathleen mumbled something.

And both of their arguments seemed right. Her position could be in jeopardy whether she did or didn't tell Orin. But she couldn't dump all that unrelated information on someone else to figure out.

She turned off the water.

"That's irresponsible." Harold was nearly shouting. "And stop encouraging her."

She cringed. *Harold, Harold.*

"And you, my man, are a son of a bitch." Kathleen stalked off to the guest room and slammed the door.

"Harold?" Beth stood in the dining-room doorway.

"She's wrong." He squeezed past her and picked up the can opener. "What's with that woman?"

"I don't like you two fighting." She hadn't liked them partying either. Until now, Harold never even pulled his own plate out of the cupboard, yet tonight he'd helped Kathleen make dinner.

"You know," He fiddled with the aged can opener, "If you did want to quit, we could work something out."

She flushed. Why did he keep saying that? *Just because he hates his job doesn't mean she . . .*

The doorbell chimed.

Beth hurried into the hallway.

Kathleen brushed past her carrying a new purse, some shopping bags, and the large sack from Valley View.

"That's for me." She swished out, slamming the door. Saucy tore into the hallway in a yip-fit.

"Where's she going?" Harold came up behind Beth.

She grabbed Saucy's collar and opened the door in time to see a taxi pull away from the curb.

"She called Dwayne."

"Dwayne who?"

"Remember? The cab driver."

"But she doesn't have anywhere to go." He stepped out on the porch and stared out into the chilly night. "You think she's running off with him?"

"She's a frail old lady and you've driven her away." Her heart sank. *She* hadn't exactly given Kathleen the open-arms welcome package.

Harold stared at the door. "If she's not back in an hour I'll look for her."

Kathleen's rushing off bothered Beth—not only her own part in it, but some feeling she couldn't put her finger on. This was more than worrying about Kathleen these past days, or Kathleen's argument with Harold. Her aunt gave her new ideas to consider, and she made her home different—full of an undefined energy.

Dwayne—the cab driver—he'd taken Kathleen to the bank. He knew she had money.

Beth grabbed her keys off the counter.

"You won't find her," Harold said. "She'll call in a while."

"She too stubborn," Beth said. "And you underestimate my imagination."

On a daily basis, however, personnel in DoD and in the rest of the IC freely, and, more than likely, inadvertently, give more information away via the computer (e-mail and web pages), phone, fax, garbage, or any other number of methods.

—MAGNAN, CIA, APRIL 2007

If I had my life to live again, I'd make the same mistakes, only sooner.

—TALLULAH BANKHEAD

14

Sweat trickled between her breasts. Beth turned the air-conditioner knob to high. The banks would all be closed, but was there a place nearby that might draw Kathleen? Something about Colorado . . . Colorado United? Front Range . . . downtown somewhere. Broadway, Lawrence, Laramier? Why hadn't she paid attention?

She left Colorado Boulevard, turned onto the freeway, took the Broadway/Lincoln exit ramp, and drove into the heart of Denver. She flipped the AC knob to heat.

The Brown Palace—old, elegant, an exciting past. It was close to Kathleen's bank, and she'd mentioned it to Harold.

Beth found a spot to park and hurried inside to the house phone.

"Please ring Ms. Kathleen McPherson's room."

"One moment please."

While she waited, she studied the seven stories of grillwork—two were supposed to be upside down—and the stained-glass ceiling above the atrium. There were floors above and around the skylight, an innovative design for 1892.

"I'm sorry," the receptionist said. "We have no one named McPherson registered. Could the room be under a different name?"

"Please check *Macpherson*." They had misfiled. Beth knew she'd find Kathleen here.

No luck.

Were any shops open near Kathleen's bank? She headed toward the main doorway, then stopped. The bar.

She walked into the Ship's Tavern but turned around and left a minute later. Too loud, too light, too many families. She went back to the atrium and headed left to the Palace Arms restaurant, which shared an entrance hall with the Churchill Bar.

Her eyes stung from cigar smoke. Sure enough, there was Kathleen, sitting at the bar with two men in business suits, her cigarette held high in one hand and a drink in the other, having a jolly good time.

Beth went in.

"Kathleen, we were worried—"

"Excuse me, gentlemen, my niece is here to check on me." Kathleen scowled. "I'm fine, dear. Shouldn't you be home cleaning?"

"Harold and I—"

"Don't talk to me about that bastard." She whirled around, sending a wave of rum and Coke sloshing over her glass's edge.

"You know he cares about you, Kathleen."

The dark-eyed man raised his eyebrow. The blond man knuckled his friend on the shoulder and grinned.

"Go ahead, enjoy your drink," Beth said. "I'll wait over here."

"And I'll do whatever I damned well please." Kathleen nodded to the men at the bar. "Then Moran's guys took the mink coats right off the back of the trucks and gave them to the newspaper reporters."

She stared at her aunt.

"And you know what the reporters did with the coats, don't you?"

They chuckled, assuring her they did. The blond man slid over to Beth and put an arm around her.

"Come on, join us."

Beth removed his hand. Kathleen took a drag of her cigarette and gazed at the liquor bottles behind the bar.

"I won't go without you." Beth stood strong.

"My sister had no right making me an albatross around your neck." She flicked her ash in the proximity of the ashtray. "Besides, I'm having a good time here with Mr. Archuleta and Mr. Parker. You can go with a good conscience."

"Join us." The blond man said again. "I'll buy the next round."

Beth always kept control. So why was her world now unmanageable? The bridge of her nose tingled. The frustrations, sadness, months of pent-up grief, some of it slipped out. She wiped moisture off her cheeks with the back of her hand.

Kathleen slid off the bar seat, winked at the two men, downed her drink, picked up her purse and shopping bags, and linked her arm in Beth's.

"Let's go sit at that table over there—more comfortable." She stopped, turned back toward the bar, and called, "Anthony, my dear man, would you bring us fresh cuba libres, please? Oh, and some more of those nuts."

She guided Beth to one of the leather chairs.

"I'm not sitting here." Beth felt around for a tissue.

"Why?"

"Because—" But she sank into the smooth softness of the maroon leather chair.

"There's no *because*. Trust me."

"Harold thought you'd run off with the cabbie."

"That man has a unique sense of humor." Kathleen crinkled her brows together.

Beth patted her pocket, found a few tissues, and blew her nose.

"Why did you marry him, dear? Never mind, I suspect it was lust. He does radiate charm and vitality. But it's hard to imagine your being lustful or even passionate. You aren't much of a divergent thinker, are you?"

Had Beth received three insults in a row?

"Now don't jump up to leave," Kathleen said. "If you do, I might not stop you. Besides, I can tell you'd much rather be here with me than home with him right now."

Beth would storm out, but, no, she didn't like drama.

"This work-before-pleasure thing—total nonsense. We do need to find you some appropriate clothes, dear. You can't go around hinting at cleavage one day and hiding under turtlenecks the next. You have a good figure, you need to learn how to package it."

"I work in a research institute, not a strip club." Beth checked her watch.

"I'm surprised that watch still runs after all these years," Kathleen said. "Your wearing it would please my sister."

"Do you know who gave it to her?" Her mother had removed it from the original box and slipped it on Beth's wrist the day she left for the University of Colorado.

"I wasn't around, dear. I wouldn't know."

Anthony set their drinks on the table. "I'll run a tab, Ms. McPherson."

"I need to call Harold. He'll be worried."

"Why *did* you marry him?"

"We love each other."

Kathleen scoffed. "Then tell me, what's the problem between the two of you?"

"Don't you think that might be none of your business?" Beth glanced away.

"Probably, but if I only stick to my business, life would be rather boring, don't you think?"

Beth worked to keep her face neutral.

"You're angry with him," Kathleen said. "Is it because he's wrecked your kitchen?"

"Not at all. By the end of the month I'm sure the rest of the house will match it, too."

"You think he's lazy?"

"He's not lazy—" Beth stirred her drink. "But he's not interested in working."

"Was he before you married?"

"He was an honor-roll student with plenty of time to womanize."

"Now that's interesting. Was this high school behavior, college behavior, or current behavior?"

"It started in high school. Currently? I don't know." She sighed. "He gets these calls—I found a phone number on a receipt for some construction purchase . . . from a Rachel."

A little "Ha!" from her aunt. No wonder. Here Beth was, the so-called introvert, spilling personal stuff all over the place.

"Did you ask him about it, dear?"

"He says Rachel asked for his help on a project. This wasn't the first time I've found something like that."

"And you don't believe him?"

"He tells me he's doing a project for some friend or other, and I know he loves that kind of work. But then he tore apart our closet, and he hasn't finished the shelf unit he designed for the utility room, and now the kitchen. . . ." Beth took a swallow of her cuba libre.

"And you don't understand why he makes time for others' needs and not yours."

She hadn't thought of that.

"You think he's sleeping around?"

"He loves building and sex." She sipped again. "'Will saw for sex.'"

"To be fair, dear, I see him terribly devoted to you. Have you considered that he's telling the truth, and doing something for someone else is a reward in itself? I don't buy that he's having affairs."

"Sometimes he's not in his office and no one knows where he is." A spot of condensation from her glass pooled on the dark-wood table.

"Do you question him?"

"He says he's at a friend's house, helping them."

"Time to put that aside, Beth."

"I shouldn't care if he's screwing around?"

"You don't know that he is, dear. And there are worse things than infidelity."

"Like what? Using your fork to scratch your eye? Can we talk about something else?"

Kathleen took a long draw from her cigarette and blew a perfect smoke ring. They both watched it until it dissipated.

"There's a tunnel," her aunt said, "that runs from under that other bar in this hotel to a building across the street."

"Because of the severe winters?" Beth watched the two businessmen leave.

"Hardly. I'll bet it's cemented up now."

Beth studied the painting by the bar.

"You don't believe me." Her aunt gave a closed-mouth chuckle from deep down. "I see it in your face."

"Where did the tunnel go?"

"Across the street. There's a brick building, the one with the cupola on top—you know the one?"

"The old girls' school back in the 1890s."

"There used to be a gentleman's smoking club next to the other bar. And next to *that*—"

"You're not going to tell me businessmen went from the bar over to the girls' school."

"The girls' school closed. The building changed hands. Then Prohibition came along. Beside the smoking club was a discreet stairway that led to the basement."

Beth's eyes widened. "To the tunnel?"

"If you had the right connections, you could gamble and buy alcohol in that building." Kathleen looked around. "If you were staying here, you could tell your wife to enjoy her shopping while you sat there in the gentlemen's area and enjoyed your tea and cigar. The waiters could use the tunnel to bring you some unusually strong tea indeed—from the other side of the street." She sat back and took a sip of her drink.

"I have a feeling there's more," Beth said.

"There were certain ladies—if a gentleman wanted some hanky-panky. He could slip down the stairs and be back before his wife paid for her new hat."

Did this woman make up one story after another?

"Infidelity's a symptom, dear. It's the disease that's the problem."

Beth glared at her. Kathleen waved a hand.

"Relax, you can call him later. It'll do him good to have a wife who's unpredictable."

"I don't play games."

"Nonsense, we all do. But you need to play the right ones."

Beth frowned. A twinge of something inside stirred.

"I suppose you're right." Beth held up her glass. "Here's to unpredictable me. He sure won't guess where we are or what we're doing right now."

"Poor Harold." Kathleen shook her head. "He loves you, but for some reason you don't believe it. Neither of you know how precious this thing is—you have to cultivate love or it dies. I don't think you even know what true love is."

"I wouldn't have married a man I didn't love."

"Probably not, but Harold's love runs deep. Yours—frankly, I don't see it. I suspect you take care of his physical needs, but do you nurture his emotional world?"

"I've never cheated on him." Kathleen was right. She *didn't* feel it.

"Surely you don't think you can measure love—his or yours—with that flimsy yardstick."

"As if you could even guess what goes on in my marriage." Beth took a large swallow of her drink.

"You don't understand what you're doing, Beth."

"You think *I'm* responsible for all this?"

"What I know is a different side of life. A person has to know what isn't to know what is."

Beth glanced away. "That doesn't make sense."

"Years ago my heart belonged to one man, a man I couldn't have. Martin."

Beth didn't know what to expect. A flutter down deep made her anxious. She took a swallow of her drink, mostly for something to do.

Kathleen stared at the glowing tip of her cigarette.

"You've confused me." Beth's words were soft. The drink made her tongue tingle. It warmed her throat.

"We had such good times together, you can't even imagine—no matter what, we found much to laugh about." Kathleen straightened, stubbed out the cigarette, and pushed errant white hair behind an ear. "In the winter of 1928, right before I left Chicago, my dear friend Ed came to my apartment to talk me out of going to Detroit. He sat there on the edge of the windowsill and watched me fold clothes and begged me to stay. I kept packing clothes in this big, old trunk.

"At one point he realized he wasn't going to change my mind. Guess he gave up. He decided we might as well enjoy a good-bye drink. Actually, he fixed us quite a few of those good-byes while I sorted and packed. God, I had so many beautiful clothes.

"He complained about my counter top being sticky. I was getting over a bad cold—did you know a tablespoon of honey mixed with whisky helps soothe coughs? Guess some of the honey spilled."

Beth knew *spilled* meant *all over everything in sight.*

"Ed couldn't leave well enough alone. He asked me about Martin. I was folding my teal beaded dress—I loved that dress. I wonder what happened to it? Anyway, I didn't want to talk about it. No matter how much he loved me, Martin wouldn't leave his wife. So I told him Brandy and I needed a career change."

"You dated a married man, and you want to give *me* relationship advice?"

"Ed kept pushing me. 'You don't even have a job there, Detroit's a tough town. That Canadian whiskey's piped right under that lake. I hear there are turf wars all the time.' On and on.

"So silly—I couldn't believe a word of it. I mean, a pipe under the lake. How could they do that? And the turf wars couldn't be any worse than the ones in Chicago.

"Ed said Brandy and I were running away because we were afraid. He kept me on the verge of tears. But then I looked at him . . . and I started giggling. The toilet tissues for my cough that I'd dropped on the floor were stuck to the undersides of his shoes."

Kathleen squeezed the triangle of lime into her glass, chuckling softly.

"It was the honey. Beth, I felt so goddamned lousy over everything. Ed sat there on my vanity stool, pulling bit after bit of tissue off his soles. The tissue stuck to his fingers, and when he picked up his drink and downed it the tissue stuck to his glass and everything he touched."

Kathleen was back in that apartment, still with Ed as she chuckled now and reached for another cigarette.

"And here's the thing, dear. He looked up at me. I remember so clearly. A smile spread over his face and he couldn't help himself. The two of us laughed until we hurt."

"It's ... well ..." Beth sighed. "I rush home from work to fix dinner. I keep our house spotless. Outside of work, Harold is my life. I *do* love him."

"Love is wanting the other person to be happy, dear. If you love someone, be passionate about it. If things go wrong, be there for each other. If you're having fun, then for God's sake let yourself go. When was the last time the two of you did something for the joy of being with each other?"

Last month? Before then? She couldn't remember.

"Ed and I laughed and joked all the time. He even came to see me in Detroit once." Kathleen stared into the distance. "That was the biggest joke of all, but it wasn't funny."

Beth looked down. Somehow, her glass had refilled itself. She took a sip.

"We pretended to be in love," Kathleen said. "A rebound for me because my own true love was off at sea somewhere."

"Was this Martin? Your own true love?"

"I want to go to the ladies' room, but I need to set you straight."

She looked serious. Beth waited.

"That night in Detroit, Ed and I were both drunk out of our minds. We pretended we were together, to irritate Brandy. After the hockey game, our playacting not only convinced Brandy and her date, we convinced ourselves. Mitch knew a Justice of the Peace who'd give us a license and marry us that night."

"Holy cow—you *married* this Ed guy? Even though you loved someone else who was out at sea?"

"Up to the marriage vows, it was one big practical joke." Kathleen rolled and unrolled a corner of the cocktail napkin. "I think the joke was on me. When we sobered up, Ed headed back to Chicago and I stayed on in Detroit." Kathleen's words were now almost inaudible. Beth strained to hear. "Several months after we were married, Ed died of a heart attack."

Ash fell from Kathleen's cigarette.

"Being the next of kin to speak, I went to the reading of the will. Ed left everything to me. I told the lawyer to sign it all over to Ed's daughter from his first marriage."

"Why?"

"Because I wasn't entitled to it. Actually, she insisted I keep some of the stocks, bank stocks mostly. They didn't seem promising at the time—the crash, you know—I accepted them." Kathleen again stared at the glowing tip of her cigarette. "She took me to his house afterward. All the years I knew him, I was never in his home. In almost every room there were huge photos of me. His daughter told me I was Ed's true love." Kathleen pressed a tissue to her lips, then to her eyes. "I didn't know. I didn't know."

Beth felt the sadness, sadness for her. What could she say to a story like that?

"I'm sorry." She reached out to touch her arm, but Kathleen shrugged her off.

"What on earth do you want out of life, child? You have a beautiful home, a devoted husband, an exciting career. Why aren't you happy?" She shook her head. "I have no patience with fools who treat love casually."

Her aunt stood, briefly placed three fingers on the table to steady herself, then headed toward the ladies' room.

Beth slipped out of her chair and followed. Why *wasn't* she happy?

She pushed the door open and waited until Kathleen emerged from a stall, went to a sink, and washed her hands. When she looked around for the paper towels Beth handed her one.

"Harold and I do seem to be at odds with each other."

"I doubt you were at odds when you married. What happened?"

Beth held the door open for her and they walked back to their table.

"We came from the same hometown," Beth said. "All the girls in high school were dying to date him. We both ended up in graduate school at CU. He made me laugh. We liked the same things. We both wanted careers—his in business, mine in science. But he wanted children—I didn't."

"What about love?"

"I told you, I loved him. And I know he loved me—loves me. But now he doesn't seem to want to work, and that scares me."

"Why?"

"We can't live on my salary. In a few more years, he could have a great retirement pension. I can't let him give that up."

"Don't you trust his judgment?"

They stared at each other. Beth finished her drink and stood.

"They'll be closing the bar in a few minutes," she said.

Her aunt sat perfectly still.

"Come on, let's go home."

"You go on, dear. I *am* home."

A federal jury convicted three defendants in the DuPont case . . .
of 20 charges, including economic espionage and theft of trade
secrets. Liew and Maegerle stole trade secrets from DuPont and
sold the information to state-owned companies in China.

—RANDALL COLEMAN, FBI, MAY 2014

15

Harold met Beth at the door.

"You scared me. I called the police, the hospitals—"

"I could use a hospital right now." She wanted a shower, aspirin, and bed. "Splitting headache."

"Where's Kathleen?"

The floor moved.

"Shhh—not so loud, okay?" She put her finger gently to his lips. "I found her, she's all right."

"I've been worried—do you know how many murders are committed in this city? Gangs, carjackings—"

"I may throw up." His timing—he needed to work on that.

"You should have called me." He followed her into the bathroom. She turned on the shower, kicked off her heels, and started taking off her clothes. He watched for a moment.

"Where is she?"

"Staying at the Brown Palace. Would you give me a few minutes?"

He closed the door behind him as she stepped into the shower. The hot water beating on her neck helped. She shampooed her hair, rinsed, dried herself, then combed her hair and slipped into her robe. She took two aspirins from the medicine chest, downed them with a huge glass of water, and climbed into bed.

~

Saucy lunged at her face, licking and yipping. Gray light spread across her bedroom window.

"Harold?" She threw back the covers.

Beth let Saucy out into the backyard, then went into the kitchen and moved a can of unopened varnish so she could make coffee. Harold wasn't home but the morning paper lay open on the kitchen table, next to a large box of screws.

The coffeemaker gurgled and sputtered out steam. She grabbed the paper, turned to the rental section, found a pencil by the phone, and started circling ads.

Saucy yipped to come inside as Harold walked through the front door.

"Feeling better?" He handed her a box of donuts. "Thought some sugar would help." He took one with white frosting and colored sprinkles.

Sweet fried things, ugh.

She was about to push the box away, then stopped. Hadn't Kathleen said something about humor?

"I need a napkin." He licked his fingers. "You're not eating any?"

"Didn't you notice? Guess I'm too fast."

He cocked his head. "Don't get it."

"I ate half the box when you weren't looking." She grinned. "See all the little holes?"

He rolled his eyes. "Thought you liked donuts." He took a large bite.

She selected one, broke off a small piece, and nibbled on it while he looked for the napkins.

"You were too drunk last night to be driving." He tore off two sections of paper towel and handed her a piece.

She put the rest of the donut on it and found two clean mugs.

"Did the two of you figure out what to do about your institute mystery?"

Knots tightened in her shoulders and neck.

"All I'm saying," he said, "is you know how Kathleen loves a good story. Don't let her make this into something elephantine, okay?"

She thought for a moment.

"Well, let me see. I guess my animals died for no reason, I forgot the alphabet and misfiled everything in my cabinet, then I forgot I'd already entered data into the computer—oh, and I guess my secretary has Alzheimer's too, because she gave me a file she'd already given me."

She filled the mugs with her back toward him.

"Sweetie, listen." He massaged her shoulders. "Let's look for some logical answers. These incidents aren't even related. Please don't let Kathleen talk you into something risky—"

"You're blaming this on Kathleen?" She turned and folded her arms. "Someone, somehow, sabotaged my research."

"Beth—"

"Let me finish. The institute is a part of who I am, and now something isn't right. I can't ignore it. I'm the one who has to decide what I'm going to do next. I'm sorry you're still angry with Kathleen, but this is my decision."

"Can we take this one step at a time?" He picked up his mug and went back to the table.

She leaned against the counter.

"You say it isn't Teri—could those water tubes have malfunctioned?"

She stared at him, then slid into the chair next to him. She hadn't thought about that.

"I'll check," she said. "I don't believe they could but—I don't know."

"Your files have only been out of order this one time, and it was only one file. It could be a slip-up. If it happens again we'll come up with another idea."

"What about information already entered in my computer? This whole thing feels off, Harold."

He put his elbow on the table and rested his chin on the back of his hand.

"Brainstorming here. Have you checked with the scientists who have labs next to yours? Could they've seen something?"

"There's a broom closet with cleaning supplies, a supply room with office supplies, a small closet with an electrical panel, the elevator, and the main stairway with huge glass windows. That's all you can see from my doorway."

"Not much help then." He grimaced.

"Only our main custodian, Wayne, is around on a regular basis." She pictured him making his nightly rounds. "He'd be the first to tell me if he saw anything unusual. Thanks for the suggestions. Even if they don't work, it helps trigger other possibilities in my mind."

"Anything in particular?"

"Something will click. I need to check with the billing department about the computer data in question."

"We're good then?" He raised an eyebrow.

She touched his cheek, then sipped her coffee. "What do you remember about Kathleen before she slammed into our lives?"

"She intimidated you, and you didn't know anything about her. What happened last night? Is she sick?"

"She's fine—actually I think she loves being at the Brown Palace. What I don't know about her is more telling than what I do know. My grandparents wouldn't discuss her. When we were together for family dinners, everyone acted strange if her name came up."

"I enjoyed dinners at your grandparents, the way the family sat around the table and talked long after dessert." Harold picked up an envelope and handed it to her. "Forgot to give you this."

It was from the insurance company. Which reminded her—he'd given her another envelope awhile back. Where had she put it?

"Once, she visited my grandparents when I was still in grade school. Before dinner, my mother asked me to show Kathleen some of my dance steps—tap and ballet." She read the letter.

"Ah, Little Miss Twinkle Toes." He picked up his tape measure, measured the front and depth of the refrigerator, then started jotting something down and drew a diagram. "I think we need to exchange our refrigerator for one of those small office coolers. You won't mind, will you?"

"If you take away my refrigerator, I'll burn *this* house down," she said. "After Kathleen watched me dance she told me to concentrate on ballet or tap, that if I spread my skills too thin I wouldn't be good enough at either. Like I cared? I was only six for Pete's sake. At the time, I wondered who she was and what made her such an expert. Her bluntness scared me. The atmosphere during that visit—no one breathed the whole time."

She pushed herself away from the table and stood.

"Why isn't she coming home?" Harold said. "She knows how much I care, doesn't she?"

"She does, but she doesn't want to. She wants to be independent and smoke without guilt. That's my bet." Beth placed the letter on the desk by the phone.

"What did the insurance company say?"

"It's a questionnaire, something about the fire department's investigation. They want repairs on the house over the last ten years—dragging their feet. I guess if someone's negligence caused the fire they won't pay."

Harold found more things to measure.

"When I asked my mother if Kathleen was ever married, I thought she'd have a coronary. Last night I found out Kathleen was. I wonder why it was such a taboo subject."

He shrugged. "For your information—I do plan to finish the kitchen."

"Will you have to take more time off work?" She bit her lip, wishing she hadn't said that. "Would you do me a favor? My secretary's husband's unemployed. He worked for a small company that redesigns office spaces and sells modular units and furniture. Because he doesn't have basic construction experience, they couldn't keep him on as a salesperson."

"Send him over—if he doesn't mind working evenings or even weekends. Hell, we're always home—we never go anywhere."

She moved close, feeling guilty.

"I promise sometime this summer we'll go wherever you want." She slid her fingertips into the back of his jeans waistband.

"I can think of somewhere I'd like to go right now."

"It's been a while, hasn't it? We'll do something special tonight." Kathleen was right—it was time to quit treating love so casually.

He hugged her and said, "By the way, did Kathleen tell you about her life in Chicago?"

"Not much." She pulled away, sat, and studied the list of apartments. If she planned her route carefully, she could save about an hour of driving time.

He jotted numbers down. "She owned a mink coat. How do you think that happened?"

That tape measure—how big was this kitchen island going to be, anyway?

"She told me. Well, not exactly, but she worked in the entertainment business as a choreographer." Beth watched him write some numbers, then move on to the oven.

"I think I might know why your parents and grandparents wouldn't talk about her."

"Why?"

"She embarrassed them."

She set the pencil down. "In what way?"

"You know." He raised his eyebrow, looking lecherous.

"You don't believe that."

"That's the only thing that makes sense, isn't it?" He measured some more. "That old lady used to be a hot young babe turning tricks."

"That's a mean thing to say." She stared at him.

"Think about what she's told us."

"You're still angry about that spat." She picked up a small strip of paint colors and studied them.

He mumbled something, then said, "You're the one that's out of character."

"And you're the one out of line." She slapped down the color strip.

"Beth, you left her at that hotel."

"She refused to come home."

"Because Kathleen thinks you don't like her. Most of the time you barely tolerate her."

"I do like her. You can't help liking her. It's the cigarette thing, Harold. The air purifier helps, but . . ." She put her mug in the dishwasher and leaned against the counter.

"Would you stay someplace you weren't wanted?" He kept his voice low, but he sounded intense. "She needs us, Beth."

"I begged her to come home. And we actually talked, for a long time. We talked about her life, and our life, and life in general. I want her here too."

He looked at her, then approval spread across his face.

"Good for you." Then his face grew dark. "But she's alone at some hotel."

"The Brown Palace isn't *some* hotel."

"And she'll spend the rest of her life there?"

"Of course not."

She walked over, took the tape measure out of his hand, and set it on the counter. She draped her arms over his shoulders and looked into his eyes.

"Kathleen's a special person," she said. "You've become close friends. And you're right about how I acted around her, certainly not as patient or pleasant as I should have been. But the last few nights, especially last night— we've talked, we've shared things, we actually had a good time together." She looked away. "And now I wish she'd come home. But she won't. And that tells me more than I care to know about how I've treated her."

He pulled her close. "This hasn't been an easy year."

She leaned against him for a long moment before he released her and picked up the tape measure.

"I'm off to find her an apartment." She folded the paper, leaving the circled parts visible, and waved it at him.

"Better make it close by—check the Cherry Hills area. You won't want to drive all over town when she needs you."

"If she needs me I'll be there."

"I'll call her," he said. "She'll change her mind. She's not ready to live by herself."

"Come on, Harold. She thinks she's totally independent."

"And you believe her?"

"Regardless of what you and I think, Kathleen's in charge."

Kudos should go to several commands within DoD that have begun filtering the information they post.

—MAGNAN, CIA, APRIL 2007

16

Kathleen and Beth checked out high-rise apartments, garden apartments, duplex apartments. None of them even came close to meeting the two women's standards.

"One more place," Beth said. She turned into the Cherry Hills neighborhood. "Harold suggested it."

"Lookie there—" Kathleen pointed to a low, sprawling complex nestled between tall spruce trees with areas cultivated, promising spring flowers. "My new home."

"You haven't seen it yet."

"If Harold likes the neighborhood, then this is where I'll live."

Kathleen sat in the car and smoked. Beth found someone to show her the vacant apartments.

"You'll love it," she said when she returned to the car. "There's one with Queen Anne living-room furniture, a four-poster bed in the bedroom, and an off-the-side kitchen—"

"I've had quite enough tromping through apartments," Kathleen said. "I'll see the place after we go pick up my household goods. Did you sign the rental agreement?"

"Kathleen, you haven't even looked at it."

"You've seen it, and evidently like it—how much?" She pulled out her new checkbook.

Kathleen selected bed linens and towels at a nearby strip mall. Next she and Beth purchased other necessities.

"Now, let's go see my new home."

"Shall we pick up Harold? He'll want to see the apartment. We'll order in some dinner."

"Not tonight. When one's exhausted, one should make one's own bed and lie in it." She laughed. "And dear, that's exactly what I'm going to do. First I'll fix some crackers and cheese, then I plan to stay in bed and read for the foreseeable future."

～

Monday morning at seven-thirty, Beth sat at her desk and stared at one of the tube feeders for her mice. As far as she could tell, there was nothing wrong with it. She'd had the building-maintenance supervisor check the Laminar Flow system again, but he insisted it was in perfect order—someone must have switched it off.

She headed for her new lab, where Dan waited for her. He tossed his protocol on the desk and crossed his arms. He looked like he hadn't slept.

"My opossums weren't eating this morning—emesis, but only a few of them vomited. I started running some blood studies."

He showed her the lab. Thirty minutes later she took over and sent him to take care of his wife. By mid afternoon, she'd finished most of the diagnostic tests but would have to wait for some of the results. Meanwhile, she was determined that the animals, sick or not, would get round-the-clock attention.

She called Teri, who said her parasitology class was about to host a seminar—she could watch the lab tonight but then wouldn't be available for the rest of the week. When Teri arrived Beth reviewed the instruction sheet she'd prepared, then she went back to the RRC.

She picked up the yellow legal pad—the one she'd found in her lab—and walked down the hall to Orin's office.

"Yvonne, may I speak with Mr. Stamford, please?"

"Impossible." The secretary flipped through her scheduling calendar without looking up. "I can fit you in tomorrow, check back." Her phone buzzed. "Today isn't a good day for that, Gavin, he's confirming speakers for the hydrology conference."

As Beth turned to leave she heard Yvonne say to Gavin, "Come down in thirty minutes. I'll work you in."

Beth frowned and went over to Joe's building.

He was locking the door to the macaques' space. Gavin was now up on a ladder poking his head through removed ceiling tiles.

"Need to talk with you," she said to Joe. "In private."

Once in his office Beth held up the yellow legal pad.

"Did you leave this in my lab?"

"Why would I?"

"If it wasn't you, then Orin or someone made a drawing of my lab before my mice died." She showed him the indentations. "Look at how carefully all the electrical devices are recorded."

He frowned, squinting at the indentations.

"Joe, didn't you lose some opossums a couple of years ago?"

"Lazy lab tech contaminated their food by mistake."

"How was it contaminated?" She sat.

"Some chemical used to poison rodents. They ended up with massive diarrhea and died from internal bleeding."

"Are you sure?"

He looked at her. "I may be old, but my memory's excellent."

"What if it wasn't your lab tech—wasn't a mistake?"

He set the legal pad on the desk and sighed.

"Come on, Joe, help me out. Would there have been a reason for killing your opossums?"

"Beth, the guy was unreliable."

"Which could easily have been part of the plan."

Joe leaned back and looked at the ceiling.

"I fired him on the spot." He turned his gaze back to Beth. "Some other research lab came up with a similar investigation a few weeks later. Talk about frustration."

"Can you remember anything else like this happening to other researchers here?"

"Nothing that blatant. We've had almost no animal accidents since then, except for yours."

"You were at Orin's lecture on corporate espionage."

He started laughing.

"Joe, I'm serious. That other research lab had something to do with your opossums."

"They wouldn't know what we're working on. How would they gain access?"

"Do you know the name of the company?"

"I have it written down somewhere. I'll have to look."

She stared at him.

"What's wrong?" he said.

"If someone like Abbott, Merck, or Lilly beat me at my research, I'd sure remember."

A knife sliced through her insides. Joe was her best friend at the institute. He'd helped get her hired.

"It was some dinky research lab in the Caribbean." He studied her. "Don't start getting all paranoid, Beth. It doesn't become you."

"Here's something that does makes me paranoid, Joe." She stood, ready to leave.

He waited.

"With your opossums, my mice, and Gordy's associate dying, I do have to wonder. This morning Dan found some of his opossums anorexic, nauseated. The food has to be analyzed, but I don't think it's the food, and in the meantime I need to keep them nourished and hydrated. Teri's spending this afternoon and tonight with them. Tomorrow I'll find out how comfortable Dan's lab cot is." She nodded and headed back to the atrium.

The IT guy was back in the atrium, standing at the top of a ladder and poking around behind another ceiling tile, this one above Nancy's desk. She'd scooted her chair to the side and kept glancing overhead.

Beth told Nancy she'd be in Gordy's office and took the stairs.

The door was open. Gordy stood by the window, studying some yellow liquid in a stopper bottle. She couldn't see the look on his face because of the backlight. His dark hair caught the sunlight.

"Hate to interrupt . . ."

"You're not."

"You're busy."

"Have a seat." He pointed to his desk chair, then sat on the corner of the desk. "What's up?"

"I need a zoologist. Would you slip down to my lab this afternoon? I'm dealing with a problem, but I don't want it broadcasted."

He fixed his gaze on her eyes. She felt unnerved.

His phone rang. He answered, then passed it to her.

"Harold?"

"I'm at Kathleen's apartment."

"Is she all right?"

"I woke her up," he said. "Other than that—"

"Her phone isn't connected." Beth half-turned from Gordy. "How can you call me?"

"She can make outgoing calls. Beth, she needs someone here, someone to take care of her."

She glanced at Gordy. He stood over by the window studying the liquid in the beaker and making notes, then held it back up to catch the sunlight.

"If she's the same as yesterday, she's okay." She swallowed. "After tonight I'm trapped in my lab for the rest of the week."

"Doesn't it bother you that she won't get out of bed?"

"It didn't until now. How does she seem?" She'd never known of anyone staying in bed for days to read.

"What if she's—"

"Harold." She looked toward Gordy, then lowered her voice. "I can't let my lab animals die."

"Can't you find someone else?"

"There's no round-the-clock care for them unless I do it."

An idea. She shoved it away, but it sprang back. Her mind filled with oboe and bassoon sounds, fighting her pros and cons. Inside she groaned.

"Harold, you think she's pretty much okay. What about you?"

"I'm fine."

"I mean . . . would you take care of Kathleen?"

"Not sure how that would work. It's a one-bedroom apartment with a Queen Anne couch, and I'm over six-one."

"You don't have to spend the night—go over first thing in the mornings, make her toast or something, let Saucy out. . . ." Her head ached. She rubbed her temple.

"No problem. I could dash over midmorning and afternoon too."

"You don't have to do that but be ready to help if she calls." He never wanted to go to work anymore anyway.

"It's not a problem." His voice even had a lilt. "I'll tell her I'm her new nursemaid."

"Are you sure? I know it's a lot."

"Something different, might be fun. We'll be fine."

Their future—what had she done?

Economic espionage is (1) whoever knowingly performs targeting or acquisition of trade secrets to (2) knowingly benefit any foreign government, foreign instrumentality, or foreign agent.

—FBI, AUGUST 2010

17

"One zoologist reporting for duty." Gordy strolled into her lab and peeked into one of the opossum's cages. "What's so secret?"

"Prudent is a better word, considering everyone knew about my new research before I did."

"You called me here to chew me out?"

"I need you to be discreet, that's all."

She told him about the sick opossums.

"Do you have your blood-sample results?" he asked.

"Vitamin D overdose. We caught it in time."

"Give me samples of their food. I'll test it."

"It's not the food." She almost smirked. "This study's blind, three groups getting different nutrients. Each group has sick opossums."

"And all your food, no matter what the nutrients, comes from the same manufacturer?" He hunched his shoulders with his palms up.

"Right." She sighed. "I'll use food from a different source until they've recovered."

"You said only some from each group were sick?"

"That's another reason I don't think it's the food."

He looked serious. "Puts your research on hold for a few days, doesn't it?"

"But at least none have died." She looked at her calendar. *Yet.*

When she returned to her RRC, she found a short stack of folders on her desk. They could wait.

She accessed the Internet and searched for "1994 lowering human metabolic rate."

There it was—a laboratory in Puerto Rico had announced their success in lowering core body temperature. She skimmed through the rest of the article—it was definitely Joe's study, same protocols.

She picked up the phone to call Joe, then dropped the receiver back in its cradle. Joe knew all this.

Harold and Kathleen would have a circus with this story.

She looked at Nancy's stack of folders. Charlie Perea's folder lay on top. *What the—?*

She checked each page—she *knew* she'd entered this data last week. She compared the numbers in the folder with what was entered in her computer. They didn't match.

She jumped up and checked the lock on her file cabinet. There weren't even scratches on the chrome. But then—what about that misplaced Gordy file? Someone had misfiled it, and it sure as hell wasn't her.

She picked up Charlie's folder, walked over to the reception desk, and waited for Nancy to hang up the phone.

Please call the billing department and see if they've started the billing process with this protocol. She held up Charlie's folder. "Also, can you tell me what am I to do with it?"

Nancy took it from her.

"Was it in the group I set on your desk?"

"Do you keep a list of folders and who gives them to you?"

"I never have. Either a member of the IACUC hands me something or a researcher gives me a folder to be documented." She flipped through it. "No corrections are flagged. I don't know anything about this one."

Beth took the folder back.

"From now on, make a running list of the folders you put on my desk."

She started toward her office, then turned back.

"Nancy? Please put that list out of sight. And keep this between the two of us, okay?"

Beth sat at her computer and skipped to the pages flagged in George Anderson's protocol. An investigation of electrocardiographic changes in animals exposed to their specific aerosols, the project brought the institute enormous funding from an international petroleum company.

A chorus of flutes trilled in her head. The study clearly showed the petroleum company's products to be nontoxic. The petroleum company—and Orin—would be pleased.

She set Anderson's file aside and picked up Charlie's folder again.

The flute music died.

The numbers in his file or the numbers in her computer—which were real? Had someone accessed her computer or was someone slipping these folders in with the rest of her workload to get her to change the data she'd already entered? But to even get the folders they'd have to have access to Nancy's or her filing cabinet.

No wonder people had migraines.

"I'm perplexed," she said when Joe showed up at her door.

"Always ready to help."

She showed him the petroleum company's folder and the matching data in her computer.

"Looks like good science to me," he said.

"Right, but look at this."

She opened Charlie's folder, then pulled up the corresponding file on her computer.

"You've entered the wrong analysis."

She shook her head. "I think someone wants me to change the numbers in my computer."

"How's that work?" he said. "As soon as you started entering data, you'd see the numbers were already there."

"I change numbers all the time. If someone finds a problem, makes a correction, I don't sit in judgment about it. But I'm guessing they don't know that Nancy flags the files that need corrections."

"They'd need access to your files too." He walked over to the filing cabinet and fingered the chrome push lock. "Doesn't look like anyone jimmied this."

"Correct, Sherlock."

He stroked his chin. "You think whoever did this has a key?"

"You know who has a set of keys for everything in the institute." She stared at him.

Joe shut the door.

"You can't say anything about Orin unless you're sure."

"Okay, I'm not *sure* sure, but think for a minute. Some of these numbers are impressive, some aren't." She watched Joe's face. "Showing grant providers what they want to see makes the institute profitable. And finance *is* the lifeblood of this organization, remember?"

"Beth . . ." He paced the office. "If you're wrong, think what'll happen. And what about that administrative position?"

"That position is all but yours," she said. Joe was everyone's senior in time and experience. He shook his head.

"Joe, the board will listen to you long before me."

"Too old—looking forward to retirement. Besides, we had an agreement." He tapped his head, then pointed his finger at her. "You get that position and you can turn this place into what it needs to be—what we know it should be."

After Joe left, Nancy knocked and entered.

"The billing department told me they have a week's lag time before they bill to allow for possible adjustments. They do have Charles Perea's in their queue to be billed in two days."

Beth looked at her calendar.

"And, Ms. Armstrong, I've received a strange message—some farmer's co-op outside of Greeley?" She handed Beth a note.

"Greeley?" She took the paper from Nancy, read it, then read it again. *Orin must have approved the request for corncribs.* A minuet filled her head.

"This is great news, Nancy, thanks." Nancy shrugged and went back to her desk.

Beth's celebration screeched to a halt. Why would Orin approve her project if he was the one who tampered with her files? This didn't fit—especially since he dismissed the project as too extravagant.

She called Harold and told him she'd be late getting home.

"We're eating dinner at Kathleen's," he said. "Any idea what time?"

"About an hour."

"What's up?"

"Lots of things going on."

"Care to share?" His voice carried undertones of stress. She at least owed him some explanation.

"Some files don't match the data in my computer. I want to check it out."

"Who else has access to those files?"

"There's a good question. I'll find out." She found herself smiling. "Thanks, Harold."

Economic espionage and theft of trade secrets represent the largest growth area among the traditional espionage cases overseen by CD's (Counterintelligence Division) counterespionage section.

—RANDALL COLEMAN, FBI, MAY 2014

18

She left the institute and drove to the nearest Army surplus store. The owner was locking up. Her best smiles and Kathleen-like cooing managed to convince the owner to reopen his store.

She bought a flashlight, a small can of pepper spray, and a pair of night-vision goggles with batteries. He rang up the sale and put everything in a bag.

"Make sure you only use the goggles in the dark," he said. "Bright lights could damage them."

She drove back to the institute and parked on the far side of the building. Almost everyone had gone for the night.

She let herself in with her keys and crossed the lobby.

The night custodian left a dim bank of lights on, enough for her to make her way to the RRC. She slipped in, locked the door behind her, flicked on the flashlight, and pulled her other purchase out of the sack. She dropped the pepper spray in her purse and trashed the shopping bag.

Beth assembled the night-vision goggles. She slipped them over her eyes and turned the switch. Amazing—everything showed up perfectly clear in science-fiction green.

The filing cabinets along the wall with the row of bookcases in front of them created a small aisle. If she pulled a chair over to block the entrance to the aisle, and then knelt behind it, she could see the whole office. Anyone entering her office this time of night would want to use a flashlight. She wouldn't be noticed.

She settled in to wait.

Fifty minutes later she felt her calf cramping up. This whole bizarre idea only wasted time and was proving less than stupid. She should be at Kathleen's by now. She stood, removed her shoe, and massaged a cramp.

The lock on the door clicked.

She froze.

Someone opened the door, backlit by the hall lights outside. She held her breath.

The florescent overhead lights blazed on, blinding her. She jerked, gasped, and knocked over the chair. Before she could think, Orin was in her face.

"What's wrong with you?" he yelled. "Are you insane?"

She whipped off the goggles.

"Hey, Mr. Stamford." The IT guy appeared in the doorway. "Nothing in the conference room. Hi, Ms. Armstrong."

"Gavin," Orin said, "I suspect you'll find the cause of the downed network somewhere in this office."

Gavin sauntered in and looked behind the computer.

"You're a genius, boss. The cable's cut—why would anyone do that?"

She exhaled. Gavin's network was one of those blasted serial connections—the whole network must have gone down the moment she cut the cord.

Orin took a firm grip on her bicep and dragged her to the conference room, leaving Gavin to replace the cable.

"Here's my problem," he said. "I need you to finish Dan's research, but my first impulse is to send you packing. You've been someone I could rely on, Beth. Joe values you too. But these last few days—"

"You have to let me explain—" She gripped the back of a chair.

"I know you're upset I gave your research to Mr. Gordon—"

"This isn't about my research. It's about the survival of this institute." The room was stifling. She needed oxygen.

"You downed the network." His face was bright red. "That's hardly professional."

"Orin, please. Something is seriously wrong here. Why don't you understand?" Her voice cracked. "Don't you *care*?"

"You're on probation for the next sixty days." He rubbed his temples. "The slightest provocation and you're gone. Is that clear?"

"We could be one of the leading institutes in the country." She lowered her voice. "Someone's sabotaging our work. Whoever it is, they know we're on the cutting edge."

Now he was listening.

"I thought someone ruined my research because they didn't want me to get that supervisory position, but it's bigger than that." She gave him a hard look. "I'm not the only one whose job is in jeopardy. You should be worried too."

His jaw ground back and forth for a second. He motioned for her to sit. Beth pulled up a chair.

"My mice died because someone pushed the bedding up to the drinking tubes. The water wicked down and dampened the floor of each unit. My Laminar Flow was off too."

"Teri—"

"Absolutely not. She and Joe were desperate to save the mice."

"I had security check your locks." He sat. "No sign of tampering."

"Someone was in my lab. They left a yellow legal pad on my counter—"

He slapped his thigh. "You have any idea how many legal pads are floating around this place?"

"Except this one had indentations on it where someone had pressed too hard. They sketched my lab in detail—the units, the sink, all the electrical switches. I can show you."

He rubbed a hand over his face. "Why bother? Why not go in and kill the mice?"

"The Laminar Flow. The switch is hard to find. Someone marked its location, wanted to make sure this looked like a lazy lab tech." She needed to keep her voice calm. "That someone also has keys to my office and my filing cabinet."

"How—"

"Some of my files were out of order." Her calmness flew off somewhere. "Folders are on my desk that shouldn't be there and research numbers have been changed."

"What?" He half stood, then collapsed back into the chair. "Are you sure you didn't—"

"You of all people know I'm *not* careless." She glared at him.

He put his head in his hands.

"This morning Dan found some of his opossums sick," she said. "They need constant supervision. I think it's related, but maybe not. But I'm not taking chances."

"Say I believe you—I'm not saying I do, but if I did—why should I worry about my position? You've been the target of all these incidents."

"If research data is being manipulated, you're facing a huge problem."

"A corporate nightmare . . ." He leaned forward. "What about computer security?"

"I don't know," she said. "That's why I cut my cable. I couldn't trust anyone."

He shook his head.

"You knocked everyone off the network. That's valuable time and money lost. I can't let that go without a consequence."

She kept her mouth shut.

"I'll talk to the custodians," he said. "They should be more vigilant, make frequent checks on the RRC after hours. I'll make sure none of my keys are missing, and you do the same." He looked thoughtful. "Is there anyone here with a grudge against you?"

"Borstell?"

"I'll call him in, see what he has to say. And I'll increase the perimeter security for a few weeks."

"What about installing some of those security-type cameras?"

"Too costly, but not if this continues."

"Orin, you must believe what I'm telling you."

He stood and put his hand on her shoulder.

"I'll admit you *may* be onto something." He studied the conference room for a moment. "Be sensible, Beth. Keep me informed. No more Halloween stunts, and two months' probation."

As the FBI's economic espionage caseload is growing, so is the percentage of cases attributed to an insider threat, meaning that, individuals currently (or formerly) trusted as employees and contractors are a growing part of the problem.

—C. FRANK FIGLIUZZI, FBI, JUNE 2012

In the past, living alone in older age often was equated with social isolation or family abandonment. However, research in many cultural settings shows that older people, even those living alone, prefer to be in their own homes and communities.

—NIH

19

Saucy barked and leapt in circles when Beth entered Kathleen's apartment. Harold stood in the one-butt kitchen, his suit coat and tie thrown over the back of a chair and a dishtowel tucked apron-like in his belt.

"Come see." He grabbed her hand and led her to the stove.

"You're a chef now?"

"Kathleen's described every step of the process."

He pointed to buttered English muffins on a cookie sheet topped by Canadian bacon. A carton of eggs sat on the counter with a cut lemon. A double boiler simmered on the stove top.

"Eggs Benedict? Wow—where's Kathleen?"

"In bed. Go talk to her, I'll bring our dinner in there."

Beth found Kathleen upright in bed with a pen, solving a crossword puzzle.

"Hello, dear." She looked over the top of her drugstore reading glasses. "My, you look like you've had a long day. Harold's been holding off dinner for you."

"His café is now open." Beth gave her aunt a peck on her cheek. "Glad to see you have some color in your face."

"Well, it is rather warm in here, don't you think?" Kathleen wrinkled her nose. "I've decided that if one's done all the things in life that I've done, one should be entitled to remain in bed and do nothing if they so please. And I so please."

"Beth?" Harold called.

"I'll be right back." Beth returned to the kitchen.

"Would you mind giving this to Kathleen?" He handed her a cuba libre. "I've made one for you too."

"Should she be drinking?"

"She's fine, she doesn't feel like doing anything. After you give her that, would you come back and get two of those small tables so we can eat with her?"

If Kathleen was fine, why did Harold think she needed a nursemaid?

She brought Kathleen her drink, fetched the folding tables, then set out napkins and silverware. By the time she finished Harold was ready to serve his masterpiece.

Kathleen waved a couple of fingers.

"Now, tell us about your custodian, your technician, and your felonious boss."

"Believe it or not, there's even more going on now." Beth cut into her muffin, took a bite, opened her eyes wide, and ginned at Harold. They stared at her, waiting.

She took another bite, savored it, set her fork on her plate, and wiped her hands.

"I'll start with Joe's opossums and the Puerto Rico research."

She filled them in on Joe's experiment, her own opossums falling ill, and the confusing file numbers. She glanced at Harold. She didn't want another fight—she'd keep her failed after-hours adventure to herself.

"Joe's wrong," she said. "I'm not being paranoid."

"That *was* two years ago," Harold said. "I don't know if . . . wait a minute. Is that why you wanted twenty-four-hour supervision for your opossums?"

"I only learned about the Puerto Rico thing this afternoon." Why did she feel defensive? Because her mice were killed, and probably that DU researcher too. "And they're sick. I need to keep an eye on them. I'm not about to risk losing another project."

"Did anyone from your facility leave in the last few years?" Kathleen said. "Maybe someone went to work for that Puerto Rico pharmaceutical lab?"

"Guess I should find out." Beth sighed. "But there's still the computer files."

"With so much on your mind it's easy to make typos," Harold said.

"My dear man, you have to give Beth a little more credit."

"All I'm saying is everything she sees is suspect."

"You know she's quite meticulous." Kathleen gave him a teacher's eye. "She's dealing with a serious situation here."

"Hey," he said, "did you hear up in Canada they stopped using opossums in research?"

"You dear boy, where do you get all this information?"

"I can't believe that." Beth smirked.

"It's true. They couldn't complete their studies."

"Why?" Kathleen glanced at Beth.

"Their opossums kept falling asleep."

Kathleen howled. Beth closed her eyes and set her lips.

"Dear, did you check with the scientist whose numbers didn't match?"

"Hold the paper up to the light," Harold said, "see if it's been doctored."

"Anyone can print the basic forms off," Beth said. "Someone can print the form out, enter new data, slip that form into the existing file, then discard the original."

Harold looked frustrated. "Maybe you should leave this alone for a while."

"Suppose she does nothing," her aunt said, "and gets accused of negligence down the line?"

Beth focused on her eggs.

"Then she damned well better have a sit-down with her boss."

"Don't get testy with me." Kathleen sat up straight.

"I'm sorry," Harold said. "I worry."

The two of them chattered while Beth fought a slow slide down the hill of exhaustion. Then she realized they were talking to her.

". . . unusually late tonight." Harold said. "Is everything okay?"

She hesitated. Her heart skipped.

Kathleen raised a brow. "That struggle behind your face tells me this wasn't one of your shining days."

"Not exactly." She bumped her knife off her plate. "My office files . . . I had to find out who kept putting them on my desk." She retrieved her knife. "I bought some night-vision goggles."

"No way." Harold jumped up.

Beth loved his childish behavior.

"I hope you brought them home, dear, because it looks like Harold wants to play with them."

"I decided to hide in my office to see who might show up. Goofy, I know."

Harold groaned and plopped back down.

"I realized how ridiculous that was. I decided I'd leave, but then I heard someone's key in my lock.

"It was Orin." Kathleen sat up straight. "He had the keys. Wasn't it? You were wrong all along, Harold."

"I hate this," Harold closed his eyes.

"POW! The bank of overhead lights popped on." Beth suppressed a giggle. "I was blinded. I yelped, knocked over the chair, and the intruder let out this unearthly sound that probably scared both of us."

"Good God, girl." Kathleen dropped ashes all over. "You were still wearing the goggles?"

"Imagine what I must have looked like. He wasn't expecting anyone in there in the dark, and there I am, yelping, crashing around, and looking like a space creature."

Beth gasped to get enough breath to continue.

"Damn." Harold could barely talk. "What'd he do?"

"I know the meaning of 'climbing the walls' because that's what the man did. He clawed at the walls like Spiderman."

"Now he'll be madder than tangled snakes, Beth," Harold said.

"My calf cramped." Beth picked up her fork. "I'd kicked off my shoe—had to limp all the way to the conference room wearing only one heel."

"Splendid work." Kathleen applauded. "You have your culprit."

"We're both wrong, Kathleen. He was only helping Gavin because of the failed network." Beth enjoyed another bite.

"Orin wouldn't need to hack the network or your computer," Harold said.

"I thought someone had, so I cut the cable."

"You did *what*?" Harold said. "You downed the network?"

"Now I'm on probation." She ate the last bite of English muffin. Cold but still good. "Two months."

Kathleen glared at her. Harold couldn't seem to find words.

"I thought that would be a sure way to . . ."

"To get yourself fired for damaging company property?" Kathleen smashed her cigarette butt in the ashtray.

"I needed to make sure no one messed with my computer."

"Damn right, but be a grown-up about it, for God's sake." Kathleen climbed out of bed and headed for the bathroom.

Beth glanced at Harold.

"She's right," he said.

"I know . . . now." She sucked in a long breath, then let it out.

"You're tired." He chuckled low in his chest as if he was aware of some great insight only he was privileged to know. He drew her in and cradled her for a moment. "Go on home."

"Aren't you coming?"

"I should clean up the kitchen."

He'd spilled flour on the counter and the floor and used way too many pans and cooking utensils. Until tonight, he never cooked, and he never did dishes.

"I'll help."

～

The next morning, between sips of coffee, Beth ticked off items on her to-do list while Harold slathered blackberry jam on his toast.

"Remember last April," he said, "that Mesa Verde trip I suggested? Do you think we could take time this year?"

"Probably." She looked up from her list. "But what about Kathleen?"

"If you don't want to travel tell me."

"I want go to Mesa Verde," she said. "There's lots of places—Chaco Canyon, Padre Island, and I'm dying to go to the Galapagos. You know that's been on the top of my list since college."

"Mesa Verde's much closer. Forget it."

"Harold." She looked at him. "I'm sorry." She touched his hand. He didn't look at her. "We will go somewhere, I promise—soon. But right now I feel like an overbooked airplane flight."

"I'm know." His eyes met hers. "I only wanted some time together, alone, the two of us, maybe even a playdate."

Playdate was his term for bedroom fun, but not necessarily in their bedroom.

"Once I wrap up this opossum study we'll go somewhere." She squeezed his hand. "And I promise we'll have lots of fun."

He nudged her overnight case toward her. "You go on to work. I'll stop by Kathleen's, let Saucy out."

"She seemed fine last night." Beth sipped the last of her coffee.

"I told you, she needs us."

"Harold, I know you enjoy your drinking buddy, and you're also being kind because you know I have to stay at the institute." She stood and zipped her overnight case. "You care about Kathleen. But this feels like you're avoiding your work."

"Don't we all get what we need this way?"

"You want your own business, but look around. You aren't the least bit diligent about time schedules."

"You can't discount the motivation factor." His look caught her, and she stared back.

"Still, you started that patio two years ago." This wasn't how she wanted the conversation to go. "Kathleen and I both enjoyed your dinner last night. You surprised me with your zest for cooking."

Beth folded the morning newspaper, then patted her pockets.

"Maybe your new goggles will help you find your keys."

His face etched a picture of seriousness until he winked.

She grinned back at him and shrugged.

"Car keys on the counter," he said, "by the toaster, behind the sander. While you're at it pick your favorite floor tile." He'd sanded all the cupboards at some point.

"What do you think about this one?" She waved a tile. "It looks like sandstone."

"Sold. That one is yours. I'll might even get you more. Now you get to point to your favorite sink photo."

She pointed to a double, stainless steel one. She almost believed he'd finish this project.

Her insurance questionnaire laid next to the sink photos. "Would you mind mailing this for me?"

He nodded and held up his toast. "Don't you think you should have some breakfast?"

"I've lost my appetite."

"Orin won't fire you," he said, "assuming you don't scare the hell out of him again."

She tucked her to-do list into a pocket.

"I'll be home Sunday, earlier if the opossums recover."

"Beth, I'm going to miss you."

She picked up her overnight bag and went to him.

He sat there with the tiniest smidgen of blackberry jam on his cheek. She wiped it off with her forefinger and leaned over to kiss him good-bye—then stopped.

"If someone cooked the institution's books, how could I find out?"

"I don't see—"

"Come on, help me with this."

"First you'd need the financial records, or maybe only the annual financial statement. Who does the auditing? If they're reputable the books are probably fine."

"Could the annual financial statement be all right and something still be wrong with the finances?"

"If you aren't looking for something specific you'll never find anything." He frowned. "Leave it alone, Beth. Please."

"Bet it's easier than hiding in my office." She held up a finger. "Harold, you're the answer. You're the accountant. You can come to the institute some evening and help me."

"Nope."

"Why not?"

"Count me out, detective lady. No way in hell I'm going to get cussed out by Kathleen."

Yuan Li, a former research chemist with a global pharmaceutical company, pleaded guilty in January 2012 to stealing her employer's trade secrets and making them available for sale through Abby Pharmatech, Inc. Li was a 50% partner in Abby.

—FBI, MAY 2011

I believe a scientist looking at a nonscientific problem is just as dumb as the next guy.

—RICHARD FEYMAN

20

"It's Beth." She heard Harold's voice when she turned her key and opened Kathleen's door. He rushed over and escorted her in. Saucy twirled around, then pawed at Beth until she bent down and scratched under her chin.

"Delightful, come close, dear." Kathleen patted a chair. "Sit next to me."

"We've eaten, but I can fix you something," Harold said.

"And tell us how your opossums are." Kathleen's eyes sparkled.

Beth gave her a thumbs up. "The research continues."

"Wonderful. Here, have some smoked oysters."

"Did you get all of your in-bed reading finished?" Beth put an oyster on a cracker and nibbled at it.

"One can do nothing for only so long." Kathleen dug for her cigarettes.

Harold placed a cuba libre next to Beth, then sat. Saucy jumped into his lap.

"Do you think your opossums are safe?" he said.

"Tonight's Wayne's shift, and Teri said she'd be in later. I've asked him to keep close watch on my lab." She didn't want a drink. "He lives and breathes his work—more diligent than the rest of our custodial staff put together."

"Harold and I did worry about you being there at night."

"You shouldn't." Beth pushed the lime into her glass. "And Teri's excited about being back too." She hugged herself. "When everything's going well at the institute, there's nothing better."

Harold seemed to have found something interesting in the bottom of his glass.

"What's wrong?" Beth looked at him, then Kathleen.

"It's about his promotion, dear."

"Excuse me?" Familiar internal heat started in her chest and crawled up her neck. "You two talked about this?"

"He's miserable." Her aunt picked up her cigarette pack and took one out.

"Haven't you ever wanted security?" Beth said. "It's not a dirty word."

"Your financial security isn't the issue here."

"Kathleen." He reached for her glass. "Not now. I'm tired of the whole argument."

"You can't drop this."

He retreated to the kitchen.

"Kathleen, am I missing something?"

"Have you seen your kitchen?"

"I came straight from the lab." She stuffed her anger.

"I think you'll find your husband is an artist, not an accountant."

"Harold's a skilled businessman." She glared at Kathleen. "He could be the top CFO of three dealerships."

"Is this trophy collection? If so, you're like your grandfather."

"You're not making any sense." Beth nudged her glass away.

"Your grandfather used to say, 'Fools' names and fools' faces are always seen in public places.'"

"Ladies, you've completely lost me." He had more ice.

"Your grandfather cared how things would look to others." Kathleen waved her cigarette. "'Think about your heritage.' Or when he was three sheets to the wind he would drone on and on about how 'the blue blood of kings' flowed in my veins. What a bunch of bullshit."

"Why are you bothering to tell me this?"

"Once when Sophie and I called home to let our parents know we were in Chicago, and that we had auditioned for a—"

"They didn't know where you were?" Beth couldn't imagine.

"My father was so incensed he hung up on me."

Harold put fresh ice in Beth's drink, but her mind went to a young Kathleen. Kathleen once said she had auditioned for something when she was sixteen. How would a sixteen-year-old Kathleen cope in a strange city after her parents rejected her—like they abandoned her.

"The point is, Beth, if I had stayed in school and then gone to college, I would have ended up as an English literature teacher, and my body would be found under some chalk-dusty desk, dead from boredom. He would have been quite proud of me, and he'd boast to all the grandchildren about what a fine specimen of womanhood I'd become."

"I'll make this simple." Beth shoved her glass away and glanced up at Kathleen. "Reliable employment helps pay the bills."

"My dear child, that job isn't what makes him happy. Sometimes our hearts break at the choices we have to make."

"Responsible choices."

"I'm talking about both of you, dear." She took a sip of her cuba libre. "If you don't follow your dreams you die a slow death day by day."

"Here's to happiness." Harold was back with Saucy. "We find it wherever we can, don't we? Kathleen's happy with her cigarettes and Saucy at her feet, Beth's happy when she slaves away at the institute, and I'm happy when I'm anywhere in the world but that damned office."

Beth stared at him. What he'd said distanced him from her and their home. Or did she have it backwards?

"You're in a fuss, dear. It's not about security."

"Fill me in," Harold said. "I sure don't understand what this fuss is about if it isn't about me being in power and making a mint of money."

"Go on, Harold." Kathleen held her glass up toward him.

"It's . . . what's the point of it all? We have our house, we have investments, what else do we need, Beth?"

She flushed. This sound too simple.

"I only know what you *don't* want," he said. "Outside of us wanting to travel—rather, me wanting to travel."

"I'd love to travel." He knew that.

"But nothing's a priority unless it's work related. It's rather admirable how devoted you are to your work. I wish I could muster up that sort of dedication."

"Harold can't work at that dealership any longer." Kathleen stubbed out her cigarette.

"This is something Harold and I need to work out together." Beth stood. "I'm going home to take a shower."

Harold scratched Saucy's ears.

"His new boss is an idiot." Kathleen lit a new one.

"Everyone works with idiots." Beth suspected this team had sidelined her.

"Drop it, Kathleen." Harold placed Saucy on the floor. "The lady gets a tad grouchy when she's hungry and tired."

His defeated look and submissive remark hurt more than if he'd lashed out. She felt out of balance, out of tune. He took the glasses into the kitchen and rinsed them. His new leaving behavior.

Kathleen played with a silver lighter. Beth guessed that Harold had bought it for her.

But then they *hadn't* ganged up on her. Kathleen had only voiced her opinion. Beth looked at Harold and then at Kathleen. *Sometimes there is no fault; things just happen.*

"Sometimes I feel as if you both conspire against me. But if you hadn't agreed to this arrangement here, I couldn't have protected my research." They both watched her, waiting while she searched for words. "You gave me a chance to stay in the running for that administrative position. I'm more grateful to you both than you know."

Beth went over to where Harold stood and looked up into his face.

"You both knew how important this was to me. Tonight I—I have no excuse for my bad behavior. Kathleen, make a list if you need some things. I'll stop by tomorrow. Harold, let's go home. We need to talk."

~

After her shower, Beth stood in her robe in front of the mirror and brushed her hair.

"You're glowing." Harold came up behind and put his arms around her. "Want to see your new kitchen?"

"Someone told me it's a work of art." She walked down the hall.

He followed her. She flipped on the lights and gasped.

Her kitchen sparkled with granite counter tops, fresh paint and stain, a tiled floor, and a new refrigerator with an ice machine. How she'd coveted an ice maker.

She pulled open a door in the center aisle and found her mixer. On the side of the cabinet where she'd kept her coffee mugs was a built-in can opener.

"I'm speechless."

Harold's eyes sparkled.

"Here, let me show you." He spent the next few minutes pointing out features.

She stood there in awe. Her minimum expectations were wrong. She stood with a huge hole in her, uncertain how to fill it. *And with what?*

He touched a small drawer in the aisle.

"Open, my lady."

"What treasure's stored here, sir?" She carefully pulled it open.

Harold's laughter filled the room as she looked inside at the stack of paper napkins.

"I haven't seen these since Kathleen came." Tears slipped down her cheeks. She composed herself. "No more paper towels intruding into napkin jobs."

She took one and dabbed her eyes. He stood there, his eyes taking all of her in.

"It's more wonderful than I could have dreamed." She went to him, put her arms on his shoulders, and searched his eyes for answers to questions she didn't know how to ask.

"You've been through a lot this year," he said. "I wanted this to be special."

He deserved more from her—much more.

"How you could have finished this so quickly? It's impossible."

"After the electrician, the plumber, and the counter-top guy, Clayton and Nathan took up my deadline challenge." He grinned. She must have looked puzzled. "Your secretary's husband and son, remember? Nathan's hair's starting to grow back. He's a quick learner, that kid. Told him I'd hire him in a minute."

She stiffened. "You've decided to start your own business then?"

"A figure of speech."

She didn't much like herself.

"This remodeling, building—it's your passion." She paused. "It's this that makes you happy."

"I can't stop my mind from imagining and designing things." He stepped back. "It's frustrating when I can't turn my designs into realities."

She gestured toward the kitchen.

"If I weren't in your life, this would be your work."

"Do you expect an answer?" He looked around the room. "I obviously don't know how to make you happy."

She stepped close to him, touched him, moved her head to get him to look at her.

"I've had my way too long."

He studied the corner of the counter top, rubbed it with his thumb.

"I have no idea what you put up with at work." She thought for a few moments. "You tell me bits and pieces, but you always give me the happy side of life."

"I wish I could go to the office with a smile on my face," he said. "It used to be easy, but when the owner died—now his son makes it all impossible."

A headache started at the back of her neck.

"Harold, people get sick if they're subjected to stress over long periods. Their immune systems break down."

The muscles in his face seemed tight.

"I have way too much say in how you live your life," she said.

"Family members all have a say in what other family members do."

His blue eyes fastened on hers. She couldn't think.

His face flushed and turned hard.

"Goddamn boss kid, he's going to have me do something that goes against my principles, what I value. The financial—crap, I'm the one responsible." Harold's voice quivered, a low baritone with no music. "I know it's coming."

She slipped her arms around his neck. After a few seconds, he buried his head in her hair and held her close.

She arched back so she could say what she needed to his face.

"I've deprived you of so much, and you still keep on giving." Her next words were barely audible. "It's way past time for you to quit."

Five individuals and five companies were commissioned by these PRC [People's Republic of China] state-owned enterprises collaborate in an effort to take DuPont's technology to the PRC and build competing titanium dioxide plants, which would undercut DuPont's revenues and business.

—C. FRANK FIGLIUZZI, FBI, JUNE 2012

21

All night the wind whipped in from the west, pushing cold air down the east face of the mountains and into the city. Its wail kept Beth awake long after Harold fell asleep, his arms still around her.

Early-morning rain started to fall. She slipped out of bed, stopped, and listened to him make his sleepy motorboat noises. She didn't understand what to feel about anything—she only knew she needed some forgiveness from her aunt.

She went to the living room and pulled open the drapes. The cold drizzle had driven off even the die-hard weekend joggers.

She stopped at the Tattered Bookstore because Kathleen considered no gift finer than a good book. Beth let Saucy out, made coffee, toasted two English muffins, and placed the items on a tray. She carried it all into the bedroom and woke her aunt.

"Harold and I always thought we'd retire early, then see the world." Beth picked at her muffin. "Now he'll have no retirement plan, no health insurance—unless he goes on mine. And I can't see him taking time off for years."

"You dear girl." Kathleen clasped her hands together like a child presented with an ice-cream cone. "You finally understood. The two of you talked."

"I need to ask you something."

Her aunt flipped her palms up in readiness.

"You left home to follow your dreams. Did it surprise you that your father acted so selfishly?"

"Selfishness was a family trait."

She thought of her grandfather in his hat and tie and remembered his laugh. It sounded like a chuckle deep in his throat. Other memories glided in and slipped out.

"He did insist on his own way," Beth said.

"I loved Chicago and Detroit, dear."

"Detroit's a rough place."

Kathleen glanced up and burst out laughing.

"But what if he'd turned you loose?"

"At my tender age? Never." Kathleen drew a long inhale of smoke. "And Sophie did make a mess of her life there. She hung around the wrong people."

"Was this before she disappeared?"

"She showed up at the Friars Inn one afternoon, where Brandy rehearsed—"

"And Brandy was a singer?"

"And danced. I was the choreographer. Sophie came in with a black eye, so I gave the dancers a break. The next thing I knew, Brandy and Sophie were gone."

Beth loved the transformation of her aunt's face. Kathleen lived these stories.

"When they came back, Brandy was soaking wet and freezing, and she wasn't wearing her mink. She ended up with a terrible cough for weeks."

Kathleen settled back and ran her hand over Saucy's back.

"Kathleen, you can't leave me hanging like this."

"Sorry, dear. Sophie was going to throw herself in the lake because Hymie was a classic loser. When Brandy tried to stop her, Sophie pushed her away and Brandy fell in the water. Sophie managed to fish her out, but she decided Brandy's soaked mink coat looked like some drowned mammal. She threw it back." Kathleen lapsed into a coughing fit.

Beth thought for a second.

"Didn't you tell Harold a friend threw your coat in the lake?"

"The point is Sophie refused to follow advice. If my father could even guess what all we did—" Her cough started up again.

"Did you ever reconcile?"

"A strange turn of events caused him to reach a level somewhat above tolerance years later."

"Was it important to you," Beth paused, "to have a man in your life?"

Kathleen raised her brows.

"Beth, men make life fun. The way they think, the way they treat a lady—men have always been important in my life. Why do you ask? This isn't about your grandfather."

"In a way. Grandfather and Father aren't in my life anymore." She sipped her coffee and thought. "I haven't had much experience with men, only Harold. You said I needed to know what isn't to know what is, remember?"

"You're not thinking of leaving Harold?"

"I'm only curious. What attracted you to the men in your life?"

"Different things." Kathleen took another drag on her cigarette. "Always a good sense of humor. I want people around me who make me laugh, and who I can make laugh. But more than that, never entertain being with someone who doesn't respect you or what you believe in. That's not to say you can't disagree, but the disagreement has to be founded on mutual respect. My one true love, he shines high above all the others."

"What was he like—other than being fun?"

"Martin was a true gentleman," she said. "Intelligent, knowledgeable about the world, loved Shakespeare and practical jokes, and I don't know where he got his strange sense of humor." She stopped and chuckled. "I'm somewhat surprised at the similarities he shared with my father." She looked at her left hand and touched her ringless finger. "I miss Martin." She looked away.

"You okay?" Beth touched her arm.

Kathleen remained silent.

"Do you want to tell me?"

She shook her head, lit another cigarette.

"Then tell me about living on your own," Beth said. "Was it difficult?"

"Good God, what a question." She picked up her spoon, took some orange marmalade out of the jar, and spread it on one half of her muffin.

"So it *was* hard."

"Whatever gave you that idea?"

"Because you haven't answered my question."

Her aunt stared at her for a moment, took a bite, then wiped her mouth with the napkin.

"I suppose if one didn't have money one might find it difficult."

"You'd need a lot of money for a carefree life like that."

Kathleen scoffed. "Who said anything about carefree? I worked hard, had to get up and be at my physical, charming best six days a week. I had to be creative, invent new dance moves, design costumes, synchronize music, and deal with left-footed stumbling kids who never should have been hired."

"Were you lonely?"

"I doubt if I've ever been lonely my entire life. Probably the opposite."

Beth bit her lip.

"Why do you think I insisted on this apartment? Sometimes I don't want to talk." She struck her lighter a few times and held it to a cigarette. "There's no way anyone can *think* if their mouth is yapping and their ears are flapping—I made that up."

The conversation wrapped Beth in comfort.

"I love my private, quiet space. It's good for the soul." Kathleen stared off into some distant time. "But I needed my friends too."

"Your stories . . . they sound like one grand adventure after another."

"It was a different world then. Prohibition, war looming, the stock-market crash—damn. If you didn't laugh, take some risks, you'd die from depression."

"I crave aloneness sometimes. That's why I didn't mind staying at the institute those nights," Beth said. "Speaking of the institute, I'd love to know what you think about the messed up files on my computer. Why would *anyone* change data to look worse than the original numbers?"

Kathleen took a minute to answer.

"They did that? Did they make an error the first time?"

"I don't think so. Nancy flags them to show me where the researchers made their corrections. These files didn't have flags."

"Maybe she forgot?"

"Nancy never forgets."

"Who did you think would be in your office the other night?"

"I didn't know." Her breath caught. Could she have been in danger?

"You don't have a suspect?"

"There's one scientist who dislikes me. I caught him doing something unethical."

"You need to check the broom closets." Kathleen blew a smoke ring. "That's much more fun."

"May I use your phone? I need to call a coworker." She bent over, pecked her aunt on the cheek, slipped the sack of new books next to her pillow, and removed the breakfast tray. "When you're feeling better we'll go shopping."

"Shopping? I'll treat you to lunch. Pick someplace fancy."

∾

Beth left Kathleen as the drizzle turned into a downpour. She pulled to the curb, braced herself, then dashed to Gordy's porch and knocked on the door. It opened almost immediately.

"I made ice tea," he said. "Want some?"

"I have errands, but I have a few minutes. . . ." She ran her fingers through her damp hair and followed him into the kitchen. "I read your message. What's so important?"

"A call from a friend has me psyched," he said. "What do you know about Ecuador?"

"The equator runs through it." She hated quizzes.

"More, give me more."

She sighed. "It's west of Columbia and Venezuela. Quito is the capital. They control the Galapagos Islands—"

"Bingo."

The Galapagos Islands—where she wanted to go more than any place in the whole world.

"That's where you get your winter tan?"

"I ski," he said.

"Not in short-sleeve shirts."

He handed her a glass of tea, then sat on the corner stool.

"I'm going there after the first of the year."

"You're joking." She studied him. "To the Charles Darwin Research Center?"

"Great plan, isn't it?" He couldn't hide his excitement.

"That's . . . Gordy. How did—they're rather closed to outsiders. How did you get this position?"

"I have a friend who knows a scientist emeritus at the Smithsonian's Zoo who serves on the Galapagos Conservancy board. My friend hooked me up. Need to fill out some papers." He beamed. "After I'm settled, I'll find you a spot too."

Living in campsites, studying life on hundreds of small islands. . . . Her stomach fluttered. She glanced away.

"What?" he said.

"I—I can't think about that, Gordy."

"Come on, I know you're not happy at the institute. In a few years the government of Ecuador might tighten the regulation on research, travel, and even who can live in the islands. Now's the time."

"I'm not leaving." She didn't even know much about Gordy. She wasn't about to run off with anyone who lived on the edge of some slippery unknown world.

"You still think there's some sort of conspiracy?"

"Orin asked if someone had a grudge."

"Borstell."

She huffed and sat back. "Does everyone know?"

"He's not quiet about how he feels about you, Beth."

"Well, there we have it."

"No way, he's okay." He went to the cupboard and found a box of Oreos.

"What makes you say that?"

"The guy's smart, but he's an idiot at the same time. He'll come up with a brilliant idea then screw it up. You saw." He opened the bag, offered her a cookie, and ate one when she declined. "He's your typical absent-minded professor, not the kind of guy to kill someone's research animals."

"Where did he work before?"

"Some private research company." He popped another cookie in his mouth, chewed, and thought for a moment. "I think it was in Puerto Rico."

~

Harold met her at the door and helped carry in the grocery bags. He dug around in one and pulled out a box of chocolate-mint cookies.

"I'm starving." He held the box up and grinned.

"I'm not your mother. Help yourself."

"You know my weakness." He opened the box.

She told him about her visits with Kathleen and Gordy as she stacked canned goods in the cupboard.

"Kathleen's astute when it comes to relationships," he said.

"Our relationship?" She opened the fridge.

"Sometimes."

That wasn't a topic she cared to discuss.

"Gordy said Borstell wouldn't have killed my mice."

"What do you think?" He ate another cookie.

"He worked for a pharmaceutical company in Puerto Rico. Remember Joe's opossums?"

"Beth, a thought, but could this Gordy guy be misdirecting you?"

"Certainly not." But then she hadn't ever considered something like that. She saw Harold watching her. She managed a weak-looking smirk with a shrug. Her mind went back to Gordy. Why had he refused to tell her where he went this winter, and he *did* have that copper tan, and he *could* have lied about the Galapagos, and he could be planning to disappear with a ton of stolen institute secrets.

She liked Gordy, a lot. She trusted him. But now he had her research. Was she a fool?

She dropped the bacon on the counter and slumped into a chair.

"Are you okay?"

She couldn't answer.

Harold took a glass out of the cupboard, poured her some milk, and handed her a cookie.

Eating and crying weren't compatible. She sipped her milk.

"What's going through that incredible mind of yours?" He went over to the drawer and returned with a napkin for her.

She took it, dabbed her eyes, then focused on him. She'd forgotten how much she liked mint cookies, and his looks—looks that would last. Strong clean features, thick hair, deep-set eyes that never completely hid his feelings.

"Hey, I'm here for you."

"This is so maddening." She picked up his hand and held it to her cheek. "Outside of you and Kathleen I don't know who to trust.

Shalin Jhaveri gave trade secrets to a person he believed was an investor willing to finance a business venture in India, and confirmed that the information he had taken from his employer was everything he needed to start the business.

—FBI, MAY 2011

22

On Sunday, Harold played golf all day. She decided to fight corporate spying with what she did best, some first-class research snooping.

That evening Beth picked up Kathleen to meet Harold for dinner at the Suds and Under.

"I had coffee with the paleontologist at the Museum of Natural History this afternoon," she said when Harold slipped into the booth next to her. "Mr. Gordon is no longer under my magnifying glass."

"Oh goody." Kathleen picked up her menu. "You've found more suspects."

"Afraid not. Gordy didn't make my list until yesterday, but now I've crossed him off. Seems the paleontologist met *Doctor* Gordon in Hawaii. I suspect that's where he acquires his tan."

"What in the hell is the museum's paleontologist doing in Hawaii?" Harold said. "You can't have fossils *and* erupting volcanoes with flowing lava."

"Gordy's a zoologist. He used modern-day bird remains to lecture on prehistoric avian life because most fossils in Hawaii were obliterated by volcanic action."

Her brilliant, modest Dr. Gordon was someone she could trust.

"You're back to your boss?" Kathleen said. "Or Mad Scientist Borstell?"

"I still think these are isolated events," Harold said.

"Borstell's number one." Beth studied her dinner choices. "But a researcher I respect doesn't think he'd do it, and anyway two doesn't make much of a list."

"Have you figured out what's corrupting your computer data?" Harold said.

"I can't shake the idea that it has something to do with proprietary information theft by an insider. It's becoming a real security risk—insidious because companies rarely report it."

Harold picked up his menu. "The auto industry guards their new model designs like secret weapons."

"I did turn up a new tidbit." She put her menu aside. "That Puerto Rico company was founded by one Roberto Sheering in 1990. Borstell worked there before he came to the institute. But then Sheering's company in Puerto Rico disappeared."

"You mean all records of it?" Kathleen said. "What year?"

"Recently, 1994 to 1995. There's no more information—except that Roberto Sheering attended a Chicago conference last year and was listed as the owner of a company in Guatemala."

"It could be cheaper to run a company in Guatemala than Puerto Rico." Harold put his menu on top of Beth's. "If he ran into government interference, the press of money in an official's palm would take care of that."

"Their major products," Beth said, "are probably other companies' intellectual properties."

"Seems like this Roberto Sheering's a dastardly man, dear. What will you do next?"

"Stop right there," Harold said. "That question always gets us into an argument."

"No arguments tonight." Kathleen patted his hand. "We're having too much fun."

He signaled the waitress and they gave their orders.

"I have another question," Beth said, "but it's not related to the institute."

"What's bothering you?" Kathleen stubbed out a cigarette.

"At the library, I decided to look up the quote on the back of my watch. *For where thou art, there is the world itself.* It's from Shakespeare's *Henry VI*, part two, act three. Grandfather loved Shakespeare. Why didn't mother simply tell me he was the one who gave it to her?"

"Well, there's no answer for that one, is there?" Kathleen gave Beth a soft look then turned to Harold. "Now, tell me about your exciting new decision."

Harold lit up. "I'll hand in my letter this Monday, effective in two weeks."

Beth dug a pleasant look out from somewhere.

"And will you work from an office or your home?" Kathleen sipped her drink.

"I'll have to check out the various tax advantages. I hadn't given it a lot of thought until now."

Beth felt everything agreeable slide away.

"There's always way too much paper work," Kathleen said. "How long have you wanted to do this?"

"Since the owner died and left his sleazy son in charge."

"About three years," Beth said.

"You must be wild with excitement."

"I didn't think it would ever happen." He glanced at Beth. "I have some ideas I'm researching."

"Harold," Beth said, "when someone wants something bad enough, they think about it regardless. We're ready to plunge our financial well-being into this, and you're saying you haven't made *any* plans?"

"I did find out some things today that'll help," he said.

"Playing golf?" She changed her tone. "Oh, networking . . . networking's good."

"Give me some time, okay?"

"Of course he hasn't set his plans in concrete yet," Kathleen said. "We haven't even launched this grand endeavor in style."

She waved at the waitress, who rushed over with pen poised.

"Please bring us three glasses and your best champagne," Kathleen said. "We're celebrating."

Harold beamed.

Beth sagged against the back of the plastic booth and watched Kathleen orchestrate their lives.

During a social gathering held in 1970 at a commercial establishment in the New York City vicinity, one Sergey Viktorovich Petrov (fictitious name), a Russian citizen, happened to strike up a casual conversation with an individual employed as an engineer with the Grumman Aerospace Corporation.

—FBI, MAY 2010

23

After they'd dropped Kathleen off and were home, Beth and Harold sat up and talked for a while.

"Mr. Johns worked out of his garage," she said. "I hope you're not planning to do that." She stretched and yawned.

"You're talking forty years ago. I doubt if the City of Denver would be agreeable."

"Still, if you plan to work from home—"

"Our neighbors might object, don't you think?" He sat forward and rested his arms on his knees. "Not to mention there are zoning laws."

"And I can't see you making a go of it if you don't hire a few more people." Inspiration struck. "What about Nancy's husband?"

"He doesn't have a license."

"Still—"

"Beth." He held up a hand. "I'm on top of this. You don't need to lead me through the process."

The old can opener—how many times had he taken it out of her hands and fixed it, as if she couldn't manage by herself. Was that how he felt now?

"Of course. I know."

No matter what she said, the conversation looped around into a nose-dive.

She went to bed—the far side of the bed.

Harold started the night with his back to her, then flopped over the other way. He fluffed his pillow and turned it over. A few minutes later, he slipped an arm around her. She almost scooted away, then didn't. His warmth, his arms—her kitchen. . . . Kathleen was right. His work was masterful.

∽

The next morning, after checking her lab, Beth headed for Orin's office. He might know something about Borstell and Puerto Rico.

"Mr. Stamford is out of the office all day," Yvonne said.

Beth headed back to her office.

"Ms. Armstrong?" Nancy waved her over. "Mr. Gordon stopped by. He had to run, but he gave me an envelope for you. It's on your desk." She held up more messages.

Breathy wooden flutes, the sounds of the Galapagos, serenaded her.

"Mr. Stamford's at a hydrology conference at DU." Nancy handed her the note. "Here's another memo about the 401K meeting in the conference room at five-thirty tomorrow. Oh, and the network's back up."

"Nancy, do you have access to the financial records?"

"That's not my domain, Ms. Armstrong."

"Right, I shouldn't have asked." She'd figure it out on her own.

"What is it you're looking for?"

Beth lowered her voice. "I keep thinking about everything that's going on. It could have something to do with finances."

"That sounds ominous." Nancy whispered the last part. "What do you think is happening?"

"Wish I knew." Whispering seemed contagious. "I'm trying to figure it out."

"Hey, Ms. A." Hugh's voice. "Bet you're happy the network's back up."

She cringed but gave him a thumbs up. He turned to Nancy. "I'll be out of the building at least two hours this afternoon, a working lunch."

He trotted up the stairs. Nancy made a note.

A few months ago Orin went on a tirade because he couldn't locate one of the researchers. Beth suggested the scientists or Nancy log them in or out. Then everyone would know whenever someone left their usual work areas or even stayed after hours for more than thirty minutes. Knowing where everyone was now seemed a wonderful idea.

"Is Mr. Borstell in?" she said.

Nancy flipped a page. "He hasn't signed out."

Beth hid her satisfaction, went over, and unlocked her office door.

She picked up the envelope from Gordy and tore it open. She stared at a cartoon dinosaur struggling to get out of a tar pit. The inside message read *Keep Smiling.*

Below it he'd carefully printed, *Opossum food checked out normal. Did you check their water?*

Crap, she'd only disinfected and refilled the containers. She dropped the card in the wastebasket, then shoved Gordy and the Galapagos behind a steel vault in her mind.

She looked up to find Joe standing in her doorway, looking miserable.

"You look unhappy," he said, but he didn't look happy either.

"My opossums were sick from an overdose of vitamin D, but I can't discover the source. Too many unknowns happening around here, and please don't call me paranoid."

"I'm the paranoid one."

"Never." She beckoned to him. "Come on in."

He plopped down at the long table. She waited for him to speak.

"We announced that our final trials were scheduled for Friday." He shook his head. "Then Friday morning a few of the macaques had diarrhea."

"You postponed the blood draw?"

"Yep. I came back Friday night to check." He looked up. "The log we keep all the pre-documentation in and the earlier blood draws was gone."

"Disappeared? You checked with your tech?"

"You name it, I did it." He sighed. "When I came in Saturday morning the log was back on the counter. I'm losing my mind."

"Are the macaques okay?"

"They're fine, but the physical research is technically convoluted now."

Beth jumped up and went to the door. She beckoned to him.

"Nancy, were there researchers in the building Friday night?"

Nancy picked up the sign-in notebook.

"Mr. Hammer, you came in at seven-thirty and left a few minutes after eight. Mr. Gordon stayed at his lab at the University of Denver, and you, Ms. Armstrong, were here most of Friday evening. Mr. Borstell did lab work here until nine on Friday. That's it."

"Thanks." She led Joe away and said, "There you have it."

"But—"

"Do you know why they had diarrhea?"

"Could be a number of things."

"You need to talk to Orin." She knew he'd listen to Joe. "He's not in today, but leave him a message. Let him know this is urgent."

~

When Beth arrived at Kathleen's apartment, her aunt called to her from the bedroom.

"You'd make a great campaign poster for the library: *Books in Bed*." Beth moved a stack of books off the chair and sat. "You feeling okay?"

"I think I might have a slight bladder infection. It saps my energy."

"Blood?"

"A touch."

The front door opened, then shut.

"Where is everyone?" Harold called. He and Saucy entered the bedroom.

"Thank you for those books," Kathleen said. "And the deli sandwich made a delicious lunch."

"Cuba libres in the boudoir, madams?"

"Not tonight," Beth said. "Kathleen, I wish you'd consider moving back in with us."

"I second that," Harold said. "Let's celebrate. I'll be right back." Saucy followed.

"It's a work night for me," Beth said, "and you have an infection." She heard the clink of ice on glass in the kitchen.

"Nonsense, child. Alcohol fights infection. It's what the doctor would order."

"Only topically." She went to the door. "None for me, Harold."

"You're not going to start being like that again, are you?" Kathleen said.

"It's—"

"Don't go giving me excuses." Saucy bounded in and yipped at Kathleen. "You're no fun when you . . ." She fumbled in the sheets, pulled out a sack of doggy treats, and gave one to the dog.

Harold returned and handed Kathleen a tumbler.

"Made you a light one, okay?"

"Tell your wife alcohol fights infection. She doesn't believe me."

"She's the scientist." He pulled a chair up. "Seriously, Kathleen, come home with us."

[135]

"Your grandfather told me a story once about some distant relatives, three cousins, who left home to seek their fortune in the California Gold Rush. Did he tell you this one, dear?"

"None about the Gold Rush."

"They decided to get on a boat and sail from Maryland to California. They agreed on equal shares of whatever they found, and if anyone died the survivors would bring their body back to be buried in Maryland soil. They packed their gear, a barrel of rum, and playing cards." She sipped her drink. "One of them did die, before they even made it to California. Guess what they did with the body?"

"Broke their promise and dumped it at sea?" Harold said.

"Ships didn't have freezers then." Beth grimaced. "This could be ugly."

"They stuffed their cousin in the rum barrel. Ruined their rum, but all was not lost—they used the barrel as a card table."

Kathleen and Harold did their howling laughter thing.

"I'm still making you a doctor's appointment tomorrow," Beth said.

~

Beth jotted down the time and address, closed the phone book, then called Kathleen.

Several rings later, a groggy voice answered.

"Are you okay?"

"Never before coffee."

"I've made you a doctor's appointment," Beth said.

"That's not necessary. Give me a few days."

"In a few days the infection could spread to your kidneys."

"I'll call a cab. What's the address?"

"Nice try. I'll pick you up at three-fifteen."

~

Kathleen came out of the doctor's office into the waiting room. "Well, that was certainly interesting."

"Here, let me help you." Beth held Kathleen's purse while the woman fumbled with her sweater. Once Kathleen mastered the art of both arms in the right sleeves, Beth gave her back her purse.

"It's a bit chilly, isn't it?" Kathleen opened her purse and took out her cigarettes. "They don't let you smoke in there." Kathleen nodded back toward the office. "Did you know he was black?"

"The doctor?"

"I asked him if he was from India. He's from Wisconsin."

"Does that bother you?" The weight of this discussion exhausted her. She grabbed her aunt's elbow.

"Watch the curb here."

"It doesn't bother me. Is he your doctor?"

"I picked him from a list. My doctor won't take new patients. I'll make you an appointment with a different doctor if you want."

"He's quite all right. I've never been to a black doctor before. It surprised me."

Beth unlocked the car doors, helped Kathleen in, and cracked her driver's window.

"What did he say?"

"We chatted about the Caribbean, this lovely cove on St. John. There was a map of the BVI on his wall."

"Why are you talking about the BVI?"

"British Virgin Islands. You and Harold simply must go there. You take a taxi from the main city on St. Thomas to Red Hook, then catch a ferry to St. John. Trunk Bay, that's the name of the place. The turquoise water is crystal clear and warm—we danced on the sand until the sun—"

"Kathleen," Beth said. "What about your urine test?"

"I didn't have one. The beach is pure white with palms all around, and you and Harold would love it."

"But there's blood in your urine."

"He asked me to give them a sample, but I refused."

"He let you get away with that?"

"It's a bladder infection."

"How can he diagnose what's wrong if—"

"It's quite common. He said I needed to get some potassium tablets when I get my prescription filled." Kathleen fumbled in her purse and brought out a tissue.

"What's the prescription for?"

"An antibiotic." She dabbed at her nose. "On second thought, let's skip the potassium—we'll buy some more bananas."

"Is that it?" Beth's knuckles were white on the steering wheel. "Anything else?"

"Not a thing, dear."

Beth picked up the groceries and the prescription, took Kathleen home, then sped back to the institute. She was too late for the 401K meeting.

Headlights flicked off her windshield. She pulled behind the building as an institute van turned the wrong way down the long exit drive. Who would have one of the vans out this late?

She parked, turned off her lights, and waited.

Someone drove to a rear door, got out, and went in. She started to turn the key in her ignition but stopped as the man came out and passed under the security light hung by a side door.

Borstell.

A few seconds later, he rounded the corner. She waited, then slowly drove to the front of the building.

There were quite a few cars in the lot. Did he drive away? What type of car? Did he go inside?

She parked, slipped out, and made her way between two sedans. One of the car doors opened, blocking her path. Borstell popped out.

She jumped back.

"Are you stalking me?" He said.

"Excuse me?"

He was only a dozen feet away. She slid her hand into her purse.

"You drove around that building, spying on me."

"Isn't it rather late for you to be at work?" she said.

Borstell slammed his door and strode toward her, his jaw clenched.

"You're a first-class bitch, you know that?"

"Back off." She whipped the pepper spray can out of her purse, held her arm straight out, and aimed at his face. Her finger hovered over the button.

Borstell's eyes widened, then his gaze shifted to something behind her.

"I left the van behind the building," he said. "Put the keys in your box."

An old trick. She scoffed.

"Heard something." This came from an unfamiliar voice. "Everything okay here?"

She glanced over her shoulder. It was the new security guard, wearing a rumpled uniform and a large shiny badge.

"It's nothing," Borstell said.

She tucked the pepper spray back in her purse.

"Nothing at all," Beth said.

The guard looked from one to the other. After a minute, Borstell slid back into his driver's seat.

"Then I'm off to the south wing," the guard said.

Borstell climbed into his car, revved the engine, and scorched the tires as he peeled out toward the other side of the institute.

Had he been in her office? Beth hesitated. She was already here. She might as well check her desk. It would only take a few seconds. She'd see if someone left more folders.

Petrov went on, explaining that in the meantime he was preparing his doctoral thesis. In this regard he wished to obtain some engineering data about the F-15 aircraft.

—FBI, MAY 2010

24

When Beth snapped on her office overhead lights she saw three folders on her desk. *Confidential folders.*

Borstell might have driven around to the back lot and entered through one of those doors. But did he have time? Not likely. She scanned the room. Someone could be crouched behind a filing cabinet. Her office suddenly felt cold.

She backed out, snapped off the lights, and relocked the door.

Should she call security? The security guard didn't impress her. Three folders seemed too flimsy a reason. She should go back in the RRC and check. *Don't be stupid.* She could use Nancy's phone to call the phone on her desk. But what would she do if someone answered? Or worse, ran out?

A paper drinking cup was on the floor by Nancy's counter. She picked it up and peered inside—remnants of a milkshake? She moved around the desk to throw it away.

She jumped and squealed.

Wayne, the custodian, sat slumped on the floor, leaning against the counter. She dropped the cup and bent over him. His eyes were glassy and unfocused. She felt for a pulse. His breathing was labored, shallow—sporadic. His left leg twitched.

She'd seen symptoms like this before when lab animals recovered from ketamine.

She rubbed Wayne's hands and arms. At low dosages animals might remain awake; at high dosages they could slip into a coma, or die like Gordy's lab partner.

Beth grabbed Nancy's phone and dialed 911, then Joe.

"I'm at the institute," she said. "Please hurry, I don't want to explain over the phone."

She wiggled Wayne's shoes to increase circulation in his legs. The custodian stirred, rolled his head from side to side. Wayne's keys hung on his belt.

Ketamine caused memory loss.

"Wayne? Can you hear me? Wayne. Answer me."

She wet a paper towel and pressed it to his forehead. He moaned. She patted his cheeks and massaged his hands. He mumbled something.

Orin wouldn't need to drug Wayne—he didn't need Wayne's keys nor permission to come and go as he pleased.

She kept talking and working with Wayne.

Joe tapped on the front door.

"He's almost conscious now." She let him in. "But I can't understand him."

"Who?"

"Wayne, I think he's been drugged. He's behind the counter."

The custodian wobbled to his feet. Joe helped him to Nancy's chair.

The emergency medical team arrived along with a police car. They flashed their credentials and checked Wayne's vital signs while Officer Chavez asked him what he remembered.

"Whoa, don't know." He rubbed his face. "I was working, like usual."

One of the EMTs listened to his heart and took his blood pressure.

"Is this yours?" The officer pointed to the paper cup.

"Milkshake," Wayne said. "They're made with real ice cream."

"You realize you ended up on the floor after you drank this?" Officer Chavez wrote in his notebook.

"Don't remember that."

The EMT shined a small flashlight in Wayne's eyes and mouth.

"You're saying this wasn't the cause?" Chavez donned gloves and picked up the container.

"I think maybe there's something in these pineapple-orange ones that I'm allergic to or something."

"How's that?"

"Last time I drank a pineapple-orange one I didn't feel good afterward, sort of like now. I might throw up."

"Have you ended up on the floor before?"

"Not sure." Wayne rubbed the top of his head. "Having a hard time remembering."

"If it's the milkshakes, why do you keep drinking them?" Chavez wagged his pencil at Wayne.

"Been drinking them for months, mostly chocolate, strawberry, vanilla. No problem."

"How often do you get the pineapple-orange shakes?" Chavez said.

"Not often. I don't much like them."

"But you keep drinking them?" Chavez sighed. "Never mind, where do you get them?"

"From the Dairy Queen, probably."

"What do you mean, probably?"

"Ms. Sterling leaves them for me."

"Nancy Sterling," Beth said, "is our receptionist."

But wait, aren't Dairy Queen and other chains zealous with branding? Someone had poured this milkshake into a generic cup. Something else was off—not a lie, exactly, but a misperception?

"Yeah, nice of her, isn't it?" Wayne said.

"How often does she leave you milkshakes?" The officer wrote notes.

"She leaves me one or two some weeks, then she skips some weeks."

"Do you drink them down right away?" Beth asked. "Or do you leave them here on the counter while you work?"

"They're not that big. I drink them all at once. I have lots of work to do."

"I'll take this down to the lab." Chavez slipped the cup into a plastic bag while Beth wiped up the small puddle on the floor with one of the wet paper towels.

The medical team started to pack up their gear.

"How's he doing?" Joe said.

They said the custodian's pulse rate and blood pressure were elevated, but outside of that he seemed fine. The hospital would do a complete examination.

"Naw, I hate going to the hospital," Wayne said. "I had an uncle die in the emergency room last year."

"We think you should go," Joe said.

"I'm dizzy." He looked at his Timex. "I need to get back to work."

Chavez stopped him. "We'll contact you at this number if we have more questions."

Beth looked at Joe and then the officer.

"We'd like to talk to you for a few minutes. Joe, Mr. Hammer, can take Wayne to the workroom, let him lie down on his cot."

Beth took Officer Chavez into her office and told him everything, about Borstell, the mice, and the break-ins. Joe joined them and added what he knew. The officer wrote it down but asked several times for evidence—tampered locks, numbers doctored, whatever they could produce. Which was nothing.

When they finished, he stood.

"I don't see how this all fits together," Chavez said.

"Officer Chavez," Beth said, "Ms. Sterling wouldn't leave work to buy milkshakes then come back here to leave them for Wayne. And she wouldn't have a clue how to get ketamine or how to use it. I want to ask Wayne another question."

"Well, I'll be honest," Officer Chavez said, "I think it's a lot more likely your custodian's been hitting his own stash a bit too hard." He opened her door.

Wayne was back in the atrium preparing to mop.

"Wayne," Beth said, "I know she likes you, but what makes you think Ms. Sterling bought the milkshakes?"

"She left me a note."

He pulled a folded piece of paper out of his pocket and handed it to her. Officer Chavez took the note. Beth looked over his shoulder.

Wayne, Thank you for keeping the institute clean. Mrs. Sterling

"It's been printed off a computer," she said. "But Nancy, no matter what, always initials and dates everything."

When Joe and Beth were alone in her office, Joe slumped into a chair and shook his head.

"You're thinking about who did this." She was too.

"Must be Borstell." He put his face in his hands. "But I can't believe it's him."

"And I don't see how it can be him."

"Why not?" Joe lowered his hands.

"I saw him drive up to the institute. Why would he do this, leave, then come back?"

"Maybe he's working with someone."

She gave a heavy sigh. "I don't know why Orin hired him."

"The guy's a Yale graduate with degrees from physics to physiology."

"He's dishonest."

"Disagree. Forgot to send his second protocol to request those additional opossums to the IACUC committee."

"Why would he check out the van in the middle of the night?"

He shrugged.

She jumped up and walked into the atrium. Joe followed.

At the counter, Beth opened the sign-out notebook and ran her finger down to the last entry. Joe leaned over and read what Nancy had logged.

"Our new Denver International Airport is too far for efficient taxi service," Beth said. "Borstell must have offered to pick up Orin's keynote speaker in one of the vans."

"He needs brownie points."

"After tonight," she said, "I don't see how Orin or Borstell could be behind this."

"Got to file a report." He pointed at her.

"Joe, if word gets out about someone killing animals and manipulating protocol results, the institute's reputation will be destroyed. You and I have worked too hard to make this into a world-class facility."

"We aren't in power. Have to turn all of this over to Orin."

"Orin doesn't feel this same dedication." She glanced around the atrium. "He's too busy taking everyone's mental temperature and tucking us all in. He doesn't see there's no roof over our heads."

∽

Her kitchen smelled of bacon—burned bacon. Harold stood by the stove with his back to her, fanning a pan with a dishtowel.

"I cooked them over low heat, but they turned dark. Take a look."

The pan was filled with blackened strips swimming in grease. He held one up on a fork.

"It came from outer space."

"Certainly crisp, I'd say." She nudged him and put the pan in the sink. "What were your plans?"

"BLTs. Thought while the bacon cooked I could slice tomatoes, wash the lettuce, and put it all together when you walked in the door. Kathleen told me it'd be easy."

"Does she feel better?"

"I stopped by her place a few minutes ago. Here, she asked me to give this to you."

He handed her a small envelope. Beth pulled out the square, white piece of paper.

She paused a moment, studying it. Something familiar, Kathleen's handwriting was identical to her mother's. Except Kathleen's had a hint of an extra flourish on each capital letter. She read it, a thank-you note for taking such good care of her.

"Kathleen said you left a few hours ago," Harold said.

"I stopped by the institute."

"This late?"

"It's not *that* late." She pulled her brows in and looked at him.

"Who's Hammer?"

"Joe?" He couldn't be jealous of Joe.

"He called about two minutes ago. Said he thought of something after he left. He wants you to call him. He handed her the number. Or he'll meet you early tomorrow morning in your office."

"I'll see him in the morning." She shook her head, cleaned the pan, and pulled some fresh bacon strips out of the refrigerator.

"Something wrong?"

She glanced at him. "You're perceptive."

"You act surprised."

"I shouldn't be, considering." She remembered the things he did to break tension, the packing bubbles between his teeth, the silly jokes, or the surprise dates timed to get her over down moments.

"I'll listen if you want to talk," he said.

"You won't like it."

"Try me."

She began with the Borstell incident. While she talked, she turned the bacon. When it reached a deep golden brown, she started searching around.

"What do you need?"

"Now I haven't a clue where the paper towels are."

"To your left, on a horizontal spindle under the bottom of that cupboard's fascia."

"Clever." She drained the bacon.

"Borstell's your problem?" His brows pulled together.

"We've decided it probably isn't him because of the timing."

"We?" He started slicing tomatoes.

"Joe and I."

"What about Orin?"

"He's off the list too."

"Do you want to tell me why?"

She sighed. He'd been quiet about the pepper spray. But this was sure to upset him. Still, he deserved to know.

She told him about Wayne.

He set the knife down on the cutting board.

"Damn." He shook his head. "The police didn't do much for you, did they?"

She knew why she loved him.

"I figured it can't be Borstell, unless he's working with someone else."

"Maybe he's still working for that offshore company?"

She was enjoying this.

"You're smarter than you look, cowboy."

"Don't own hats or boots."

She took a soapy dishcloth and wiped the counter where they'd been working.

"If it's corporate espionage," she said, "they'll turn our information over to someone else. Did you know there's a whole underworld that deals with voice-activated imaging devices, tiny microphones you can fit in your shoes—some real James Bond stuff."

"Next you'll want an Aston Martin."

The phone rang. She answered it.

"Dear, I know I'm taking up too much of your time."

"Thanks for your note. Do you feel better?"

"As a matter of fact I do. The reason I called—should I take these tablets with or without food?"

"With. I'll see you after work. Oh, Kathleen? Rum and Coke doesn't count as food."

Her aunt grumbled something, said good-bye, and hung up.

Harold hummed *Zip-a-dee-doo-dah, zip-a-dee-day. My, oh my, what a wonderful day. Plenty of sunshine* . . . and emptied the dishwasher. She watched him for a minute.

"Why are you piling the dishes all over the counter top?"

"I thought maybe you'd want to rearrange the cupboards now that the kitchen is different."

She tilted her head.

"I can tell you're up to something."

"What I'm up to is a dinner for my lady. That's the way to a woman's heart."

"You've swapped your genders."

She watched him. He washed off the lettuce and carefully placed each piece on paper towels to drain.

"Okay," she said. "Not that I don't appreciate it, you've been wonderful, but why this, why now?" She waved her hand at the bacon, the kitchen, the dishes.

"Did Kathleen tell you why she ran away from home?" he said.

This man's conversation never went in a straight line anymore. Not surprising, considering how much time he spent with Kathleen.

"She fought with my mother and grandparents all the time."

He opened a new loaf of bread and put two slices on two plates. He reached for the lettuce and started assembling the sandwiches.

"She told me when things went wrong, her parents blamed her," he said. "She knew she was intelligent, talented, capable, but nobody seemed to see it, or appreciate her."

"You think I might run away?" The Galapagos—a chance to do research there was a once-in-a-lifetime opportunity. And Gordy . . . She felt blood rush to her cheeks.

He held her shoulders and looked into her eyes.

"I suspect you're feeling unappreciated. And since you've been through so much, I'll forgive you for dismissing our playdate."

What could she say?

"It's fine. You're busy, stressed—"

"We'll eat later." She took his hand.

As she led him out of the kitchen, the phone rang. They stopped and stared at each other. He dropped her hand, went to answer the call, and listened for a minute.

"What did you eat? No, that won't do it. We'll see you in a few minutes."

He hung up.

"Need to make our sandwiches and one more. All Kathleen's eaten are a couple of crackers, and she can't open her pill bottle."

Ironically, Petrov, who worked as a Russian-English translator at the UN, remained silent during his court appearance, indicating that he did not understand the English language!

—FBI, MAY 2010

25

Joe stuck his head in Beth's office.

"Those files on your desk last night?" he said. "They might tell us something."

"Richard's, Gene's, and Hugh's." She handed them over. "None of their results have been entered yet—they all seem okay."

"Who's in your periscope now?" He glanced through a folder.

"Whoever it is, I bet they're worried I'm on to them. They misfiled some of my folders so I'd be concerned about my memory." A seasick wave of nausea splashed over her. "This person, or persons, knows too much about me—thinks I'm too busy caring for my aunt and worrying about my research to pay attention to the rest of my job."

"And we know nothing."

She tapped the files. "What do you know about the rest of these researchers?"

"Hugh Wendenski's hot after that promotion—he's been joking that everyone needs to be nice to him because he'll be their supervisor next month." He flipped through the folders again. "George Anderson's file isn't here."

"He's a contender?" She jotted Hugh's and George's initials on her notepad.

"He is, but more reserved about it."

"If someone wanted to get to my files they'd have to wait until Nancy and Wayne weren't around. But if Nancy was gone and Wayne was drugged, there'd be free access to everything. I bet the researcher at DU was drugged—"

"Don't go there, Beth." He held up his hand. "You need to tell Orin about Wayne."

"He so loves getting exciting news from me." Why couldn't Joe see the connection?

She walked with Joe out to the atrium and then headed for Nancy's desk.

"Nancy, would you see if Mr. Stamford is back? It's urgent, and I need to check your private list of files."

Beth took it back to her office. Only Richard's and Gene's names were on the list. But she had three folders.

Richard's study on brevitoxins was great. Red algae was a nuisance and a health hazard to swimmers, but it also impacted the environment because it affected sea life.

Gene's study involved a nasal-spray application. The efficacy of a nasal spray over the absorption of tablets in the GI track indicated improvement, but his research didn't show it to the degree she would have expected.

She picked up Hugh's folder—the only one not on Nancy's list.

Hugh's preliminary study of glaucoma, before he started on the optic-nerve experiment, seemed impressive.

She took the list back to Nancy.

Nancy glanced furtively around the atrium, then slid around to the front of her desk.

"You asked me about the financial records?" she whispered.

Beth waited.

"A minute ago, Yvonne let me check on a requisition transaction, and that gave me access to internal documents." She handed Beth a piece of paper.

On it was a username and password.

Beth rushed back to her computer and entered the private access codes. She held her breath. The screen blinked, and then what looked like a menu page for the institute's internal affairs appeared.

She didn't know much about accounting, but the financial documents seemed in order. Payroll, revenue, general expenses, building mainte-nance . . .

Pausing at a file labeled Analysis of Revenue Production, Beth clicked it open. It showed two main sections, environmental and biological. She clicked on one and found it loaded with data. Her stomach tightened. This would take a large chunk of time. She copied the file onto her hard drive and saved it under a new name, Alternative Rodent Food.

Jeez, she felt jittery. How could any of this be connected to her corrupted files or the animal deaths? And Wayne—Orin needed to know. She went back to Nancy.

"Nancy, you're the best." She handed her the username and password. "You can destroy this now. What about Mr. Stamford?"

"Yvonne said he couldn't be reached by phone."

Beth should tell him face-to-face, but what choice did she have? She wrote a note, sealed it, and gave it to Nancy.

"Top priority. Will you see that Yvonne gets it to him immediately?" She saw Hugh march in through the side door. His face was hard as stone.

"Ms. A., I need to talk with you."

She waited.

"Are you doing renovations to kennels in Building D?"

"You seem angry."

"They're reserved for *my* new beagles."

"That can't be right." She frowned. "I've waited months for those kennels."

"Terminate the order, will you?" His face flushed dark crimson.

Nancy stopped working and looked up.

"Hugh, Orin did sanction it—"

"That's a lie." His hand sliced the air between them. Beth moved back. "He approved my request over six months ago."

"Concrete pourers are coming tomorrow," she said. "Materials are already on the way—"

"You ruined your research, now you want to fuck up mine too?"

His nose was inches from hers. She kept her voice low.

"Come on, Hugh, let's talk. We'll find an alternative—"

"Screw the alternative." He threw his hands out, turned, and stormed down the hall toward Orin's office.

She stared after him and took a long, shaky breath.

"I think he might be mad when he finds out Mr. Stamford isn't in," Nancy said.

"I've never seen him like that." As furious as she was about her mice, she'd at least maintained a professional façade.

"I used to think he was Mr. Smiley." Nancy glanced around. "That only lasted a few months. I bet he didn't submit anything to Mr. Stamford."

Beth returned to her office, locked the door, then brought up the file: Alternative Rodent Food. She started with the environmental documentation.

Richard's brevitoxin protocol didn't have a revenue amount because she hadn't entered the results yet. The document had been initiated about a month prior. That made sense—keeping track of where the revenue came from, which projects brought in more funding.

She scrolled through pages and came to a listing of scientists. Next to each name was a percentage.

She scanned the list several times. Richard Graphy's name topped the previous month's list with his environmental studies, George Anderson's came in third. On the biological side, Hugh's medical studies placed in the top three. Gordy's and Joe's names were in the top ten percent. Beth's was in a different category because lab research was only part of her job description.

Wait. This wasn't tracking *projects*, it was tracking *researchers*—who made the most money for the institute.

Would Orin fire the low producers? Damn, he didn't care at all about the research, only its financial revenue. Her disappointment destroyed her concentration.

Does someone know about this? Is this why someone wanted her data files changed?

She exited the screen. She stood to go tell Joe. She sat back. She couldn't tell anyone about this, not even Joe. He'd want to know how she discovered the information. She stared at her desktop then picked up the Greeley corncrib letter and studied it. The dirt work for the corncribs had started early that morning.

She pushed herself away from her desk, gathered her purse, and locked the office. A brisk walk, fresh air, then she'd check on her dirt work and say hello to the goats.

Later Beth made the unpleasant trip to Hugh's office. She knocked on Hugh's doorjamb and peeked into the lab. He stood at the sink with his back to her.

"Come on in." He put the piece of glassware on a towel to dry.

"About Building D," she said. "I thought you were through with the beagle research."

"My new order isn't due for another month. Think I might cancel the project though."

"I don't want you angry over this."

"A mix-up." He shrugged. "Hey, will your lab tech need a home after she's finished with your project?"

"I didn't know your tech left." *Did he lie, too?* "Thought I saw him sketching out the beagle runs the other day."

"He's here, but I have another project coming up—overlaps my current one." Hugh wiped his hands and faced her. "Teri's more experienced."

"I'll ask." She glanced at her watch and backed toward the door. "Talk to you later."

She went downstairs and signed out. This whole institute needed a large dose of Valium.

She needed a dose of Kathleen.

Sergey Aleynikov worked as a computer programmer for a
Wall Street company. During his last few days at that company,
he transferred 32 megabytes of proprietary computer codes—
a theft that could have cost his employer millions of dollars.

—FBI, MAY 2011

26

When Beth arrived, Kathleen opened a bottle of wine. As she filled her aunt in on Wayne and the spiked milkshake, the wine level in the bottle plunged.

"I should go home," Beth said after a while.

"Stay and eat dinner with me." She looked into Beth's eyes. "Is something else heavy on your mind, dear?"

Beth told her about Hugh's flash of anger and his no-big-deal attitude afterward.

"When you've lived as long as I have, you see every type." Kathleen toyed with her lighter. "Stable, unstable, in between. Harold's most stable. But this Hugh person? Sounds like mood swings. Sophie was like that—she'd be excited and happy one moment, then almost suicidal the next."

"Bipolar?"

"I suppose it fits." She put out her cigarette. "I wonder about the wisdom of slapping a label on everything, like it gives a person permission to be dysfunctional."

Beth ran her fingers over Saucy's ears, so silky.

"Borstell seemed to be the culprit because he's furious with me." She held her fingers still. "And Hugh was chewing razor blades that ended up like cotton candy."

"How's your cure for aging?"

"Excuse me?"

"Your animal study on aging—have you found a cure yet?"

"I'd be drowning in dough if I had." Beth ruffled Saucy's fur. "It isn't a cure, it's an attempt to increase longevity with better nutrition. We'll probably be finished in a couple of weeks. With everything going on, I'm fortunate to have Teri."

"Those clues are right in front of you. Pay attention to details."

"My intuition's on vacation."

"Then open another bottle of wine. Sophie had no intuition at all. Did I tell you about the time she disappeared right out from under our noses?"

"This was after you had how many cuba libres?"

Kathleen made a lopsided smile. She watched Beth pour more wine.

Beth grinned at her. "I do want to hear, okay?"

"We convinced Sophie that Hymie would keep beating her until—well, we had to get her out of Chicago. Mac took her to the train station. He was this big ex-cop, six feet tall and weighed two-fifty at least. They stood in line to buy Sophie's ticket."

"How did she get hooked up with Hymie-the-creep anyway?"

"Listen, dear. Mac bought the ticket, but when he turned around to give it to her, she was gone."

I'm guessing she didn't go to the ladies' room." Beth put the cork back in the bottle, wiped up a drip of wine, and put her wine glass in the dishwasher.

"He searched there—everywhere, actually. Now, what do you think happened?"

"Hymie was an alien, and he teleported her?" She sat.

"You sound like your husband. Hymie had several guys, taller than Sophie and dressed like nuns. We figured they surrounded her to make sure no one could see, held chloroform to her nose, slipped a habit over her head, then dragged her off. Mac was so intent on getting her ticket he forgot to focus on keeping her next to him. No one pays attention to what's going on around them while they're in a hurry to pay for something. And no one ever pays attention to nuns."

"You're worried about my safety?"

"I'm saying that some things deserve more attention than others."

Beth gave her aunt a peck on the cheek and stood to leave.

"I got it. Make it a habit to watch out for nuns."

~

Harold caught her in front of the opened freezer.

"Looking for something?"

"Only the truth." She closed the door and buttoned her shirt with one hand.

He raised an eyebrow. "Okay, what *were* you doing?"

"A feeble attempt to cool off."

"You're miserable? I mean hot flashes and such?"

"They come and go." Did he suspect she used them to dodge intimacy? "Hope you didn't mind dinner at Suds and Under. I figured you'd enjoy pool with your buddies while I was with Kathleen."

"There was an article on hormone-replacement therapy in the company's newsletter," he said. "Talked about all the pros and cons, some studies they did in Canada."

"Do you think it might help?"

"You're the researcher."

"I'll look into it." She was exhausted. "Do you hear bedtime calling?"

"Maybe we could do something this weekend," he said. "The two of us. I could get us tickets to the melodrama?"

"I can't be out of touch with Teri for a whole weekend."

"What are you doing tomorrow night?"

"The usual—work, errands, check on Kathleen."

"The weather's great," he said. "Want to go on a short hike, eat in the park? Or we could have dinner out?"

"I . . ." She caught the building disappointment in his face. "Sure, let's do an early dinner."

"This is a surprise date." He held her hand and fingered her wedding rings.

"Can't be, we both know about it."

"It's been so long since we've done this, I'm surprised."

~

The phone rang at three-thirty. Beth turned on the light before she answered.

"Hello?"

"Dear, I've seem to have a problem. Could you come over?"

"Give me five."

Beth climbed over Harold, hung up the phone, and went to the closet.

"What's wrong?" He raised up on one elbow.

"Don't know."

"Want me to drive you?"

"No sense both of us losing sleep. I'll call if it's important." She dressed, pulled out her car keys, and left.

"Kathleen?" Saucy met her at the door. The apartment lights were all on. "I'm in the bedroom."

Kathleen, in bed, appeared so pale she blended in with the pillows.

"Is it the bladder infection?"

"I still have some blood, but only a tiny bit," she said. "Maybe that's normal for a bad bladder infection."

"Kathleen, put on your robe. Let's check this out."

"Do you think something's wrong?"

"I'm no doctor, but blood signals something isn't right." She held out Kathleen's robe and found her slippers.

"Hold my arm." Kathleen sighed. "God, I hate to bother you this time of night."

Beth stuck out her foot to block Saucy at the door, then locked it. Kathleen held Beth's elbow on the way to the car.

"I guess the antibiotics haven't worked yet," Kathleen said, lighting a cigarette as soon as her seat belt was fastened. "Maybe it takes more time."

That bottle of wine—Beth hadn't thought about how alcohol affected antibiotics.

"Oh hell." Kathleen twisted this way and that. "My cigarette—think it went down between the seats."

Beth pulled over to the side of the road, jumped out, ran, and jerked the passenger's door open. The cigarette glowed on the floor next to Kathleen's slipper. Beth threw it on the ground and scrunched it out with her heel.

"I should have called a cab." Kathleen pulled her robe snug. "That's what I'd do if you weren't available." She was quiet for a few moments. "I try to be independent. It's getting harder because you make everything easy."

They pulled up to the ER entrance.

"Let's go," Beth said.

"I'm sorry to be such bother. I hate this."

"Kathleen, you're not a bother."

～

The emergency room was crowded. Beth found a place for Kathleen and went to the window to sign in. The nurse checked Kathleen's Medicare card, then scanned the waiting room.

Beth pointed her out.

"Is she in pain?"

"She'd never tell me if she is."

"Let's bring her back, take a look. They'll settle her in, then I'll call you."

"I'll go move my car."

Beth returned and tried to read a magazine, but she couldn't concentrate.

Surely the doctor told Kathleen not to drink with her antibiotics. And the pill bottle carried a whole list of warnings. Silly, Kathleen wouldn't bother to read them. Did she even take the pills on schedule?

Beth should have thought about the conflict with alcohol, should have monitored Kathleen's medicine intake. She couldn't cut out alcohol entirely because Kathleen would throw a fit.

What if she made cuba libres with lots of Coke and put a splash of rum on top? Would her aunt notice?

She glanced at the wall clock and went to the triage window.

"I checked my aunt in a half hour ago. Is it all right if I go back now?"

The nurse consulted her monitor and gave directions to Kathleen's room.

The hallway behind the waiting-room door was a different world. Medical teams in green scrubs rushed in and out of cubicles and rooms with rolling carts and bed linens.

Beth found the second door to the left ajar. She pushed it open.

"May I come in?"

"I have to wait here until the doctor can see me." Kathleen lay in bed wearing a flower-print hospital gown.

"Ms. McPherson?" A woman's voice from the doorway. "I'm Dr. Morris." She shook Kathleen's hand.

"What seems to be the problem?" she said.

"Not much. I'm rather weak, and I have to urinate a lot."

"Kathleen, you said you pass blood in your urine," Beth said.

"Are you related to Ms. McPherson?"

"I'm her niece."

"How long has this been going on?" Dr. Morris asked Kathleen.

"A couple of months now, but I did go see a doctor. He prescribed an antibiotic, said it would take care of a bladder infection."

"Dr. Morris, the other doctor didn't do tests," Beth said. "He took Kathleen's word for what she thought was wrong."

"I know the nurse did this, but I want to check it again." Dr. Morris put the blood pressure cuff on Kathleen and held her arm level with her heart.

"Would you mind if I smoked a cigarette?"

"No one's allowed to smoke here. How many a day?"

"If you tell me cigarettes make me sick, I won't believe you. You doctors would blame ingrown toenails on smoking."

Dr. Morris turned to Beth. "I need to examine your aunt. There's a chair in the hallway. When we're finished you can come back in."

Beth left and closed the door. She found the chair and spent another fifteen minutes watching people until Dr. Morris called her back into the room.

"I need to order some tests. We've talked, and the most efficient way to do this is to admit your aunt. They'll move her to a room in a few minutes. After she's settled you can come back and stay with her if you like, or you can go home and see her later in the morning."

"I'm well taken care of," Kathleen said. "Get some sleep."

"What are these tests?"

"I've called in the urologist, Dr. Goodlough. Whenever there's blood in the urine we need to rule out tumors. He'll schedule a cystoscopy. It'll give him a visual look into the bladder. Ms. McPherson may need to spend at least one or two more nights in the hospital. In the meantime, I'm calling the pharmacy to place her on a different antibiotic. We don't want to battle infections."

Kathleen looked nervous—because she needed a cigarette? No, more like a frightened bird. A twinge of that fear slid through Beth.

Dr. Morris looked at her notes.

"I probably won't see you again. Dr. Goodlough will stop by your room this morning when he's making his rounds. If you have other questions, he'll be able to answer them."

"See, Beth? I'm fine. Go home."

"I'm not going to leave you."

"Go home. I'm tired. If you're here I won't sleep."

"But—"

Her aunt pointed a finger at the door.

"I'll check on Saucy and be back later." Beth straightened the top sheet and pulled the thin blanket over Kathleen. She looked around for something else to do.

There must be something.

"If you're all right by tonight, Harold's asked me to go out with him," Beth said. "Dinner somewhere—you know, a date."

"For heaven's sake, please remember to enjoy yourself, dear."

Beth left. She couldn't shake the image of Kathleen—she looked as fragile as she had that night in Valley View.

No one ever said why she fell. Everyone assumes old people fall. What if that wasn't true? What if Kathleen was sick even then?

Remind employees that reporting security concerns is vital to protecting your company's intellectual property, its reputation, its financial well-being, and its future. They are protecting their own jobs. Remind them that if they see something, to say something.

—FBI, MAY 2011

27

Beth slept for a few more hours until Saucy woke her. After breakfast, Beth hurried to the institute to check on her lab and tell Nancy that she'd be at the hospital for part of the day, but Nancy wasn't there. She wrote out the hospital number, her aunt's name, and put the note on Nancy's calendar. Then she drove back to the hospital.

How accurate would Kathleen's version of her medical issues be? It was time to finagle a few minutes with her doctor.

"I'm Kathleen McPherson 's niece." She'd found the fatherly-looking doctor at the nurses' station. "Could you explain to me what's happening?"

"She has a tumor in her bladder. We can't say whether it's malignant or not at this time, but I'll be doing a transurethral biopsy. That's inserting an instrument into the bladder, then taking a sample of the tumor."

Tumor? Cold stabbed deep inside. *But he's going to do something—that's always good, isn't it?*

"Will you know if it's cancerous right away?"

"I'll do a resection—remove it, unless it's too invasive. We'll get the lab results later."

"If it's not cancer?"

"When she recovers from the anesthesia, and when all her body functions are normal, she'll be released."

"But . . ." She couldn't help it, "What if it *is* cancer?"

"We'll take it one step at a time." He looked at his watch. "She's a heavy smoker, that isn't good, but we'll see. I need to get some lab work on her before surgery. Any other questions?"

This didn't sound quite so ominous. Having options—that was good. Beth walked down the hall to Kathleen's room.

"Don't fuss, I'm fine." Kathleen waved Beth away as she tried to fluff the pillows.

"You look uncomfortable. Don't you think if I propped another pillow behind your shoulders you would—"

"How's Saucy?"

"She seemed upset so I brought her to our house."

"I have to go to the lab in a few minutes. Come with me and tell me about your work."

Beth pulled a chair up to the bed.

"I dread Orin's reaction about what happened to Wayne. The police being there . . . He's mad at me already."

"Good God, girl, you haven't told him?"

"He's been away. I sent him a note, and I'll talk to him. But I need to be here."

A few minutes later a nurse came in with a wheelchair. Kathleen snatched her purse from the bedside drawer and tucked it under the blanket on her lap.

The three of them made their way down the busy hallway.

When they reached the lab's double doors, the nurse pushed the wheelchair through and told the intern to buzz the nurses' station when they were finished.

"All right." The intern looked at Kathleen, then scanned his clipboard. "I need to ask some questions before we start." He sat on a stool, propped one foot on the rung, and pulled out his pen. "Please tell me your name and the day of the week."

"My name's Ms. McPherson and it's Wednesday. My God, man, I'm not stupid." Kathleen reached in her purse.

"I'm sorry, Ms. McPherson, it's standard practice. We're required to assess how alert you are." The intern wrote something on his chart and, without looking up, said, "You're not allowed to light up in here. You might as well put those back in your purse."

"I don't much like you, you know." Kathleen slid the pack back into the depths of her bag.

"Let me take your blood pressure."

"First you treat me like I'm stupid, then you insult me by not letting me smoke, and after that you take my blood pressure? What the hell do you think your blood pressure would be?"

He put the cuff on her right arm, pumped the bulb, watched the dial, and made another note on the chart. Then he held her wrist and took her pulse.

"Now I'm going to put this on the end of your finger to check your oxygen levels. It won't hurt."

"I know that—I told you I'm not stupid."

Beth stood in the far corner of the room.

"Could you tell me the results, please?" Kathleen said.

"She might be more comfortable if we gave her some oxygen."

"Don't expect me to drag one of those tanks behind me," Kathleen waved his words away.

He studied her then said, "I suggest while you're here, Kathleen—"

"Ms. McPherson, if you don't mind. You're too young to be a doctor anyway."

"Ms. McPherson, you mustn't smoke."

"What does that have to do with anything?" She ran her fingers through her hair and gave it a flip, then glared at him.

"I assume Dr. Goodlough told you that if you continue to smoke after the surgery, and if the tumor we remove *is* malignant, the cancer might come back?"

"Nobody ever tells me anything." Kathleen pushed the blanket aside and smoothed her hospital gown's hem. "Besides, that's a bunch of nonsense."

He pulled out a tongue depressor. "Open please."

"I always wonder what the hell doctors are looking for when they do that." But she opened her mouth. He stuck the depressor in, looked, then threw it away.

"Is her oxygen level low?" Beth asked.

"We'll give her oxygen at night and during the day if she wants." He wrote on her chart while he spoke. "I'm sure the blood work will tell us we need to get some nutrients in her too. Dr. Goodlough will have the results of these tests before her surgery."

"God, I love it when everyone talks about me as if I'm not here." Kathleen blew her nose and looked around for a place to put the tissue. Not finding one, she put it back in her purse.

"All right, the tech will draw blood. The nurse will be in to get your signature and take you to your room. Good day, ladies." He opened the door.

"Oh, doctor?" Kathleen said.

"Yes?"

"Do you know what they call a medical student who graduates at the bottom of his class?"

"Excuse me?"

"*Doctor.* You have a good day." Kathleen looked at Beth. She winked, then started to cough, grabbed the tissue from her purse, and covered her mouth.

Beth knelt in front of her.

"You told me that when we get in a tough situation, we need to face things head on." Her voice shook as she gently took Kathleen's face in her hands. "I think you'll be all right, but like you always do, we'll handle this head on."

"Don't you dare lecture me." Kathleen glowered at her. "You need to clean up some of your own unfinished business."

"Ouch. I'll see you before surgery." She gave her aunt a firm squeeze.

Unfinished business indeed. Where should she start?

~

Beth's mail stood neatly stacked on her desk, but Nancy wasn't there. Had she taken the day off?

Beth sorted through the envelopes and found a blue one from Gordy. She ripped it open. His card pictured two cartoon dinosaurs laughing at a tiny furry rodent, while a third dinosaur puzzled about the start of a snowfall. He'd written words in bold print on the inside.

It doesn't snow in the Galapagos.

His card triggered sounds of floating notes from piccolos accompanied by breathy Ecuadorian wooden flutes.

She tossed her imagination in the wastebasket along with the card.

She trashed the junk mail, then flipped through a few catalogues. A medical journal caught her attention. She ran her finger down the index. Barcelona would host a convention this fall. She turned to the section and skimmed through the papers to be presented. Her breath quickened. There was one on multiple sclerosis. "Multiple Sclerosis: Genetic via Viral."

No! That was *her* research—she jumped up and slammed the journal on her desk. Those bastards stole it. *Genetic versus viral could be expected, but not via!* She couldn't breathe—she needed oxygen. She headed toward the door, then darted back to her desk and snatched up the magazine again. She thumbed through the pages, and there it was. She took a deep inhale and read the blurb carefully. The presenter was a scientist from Tikal Research Laboratories. Scientist? Hell no. He was a damned thief.

She dropped the journal back on her desk and rushed out into the sunshine. She stood blinking at a more sane world, a fresh-smelling, soon-to-be-green world now awakening to spring.

She strode back behind the main buildings toward the kennels. A cement truck rumbled past and stopped next to two workmen with shovels. They gave instructions and the truck moved into position beside kennel Building D.

Beth's frustrations turned into fascination, and then a certain type of thrill as she watched them make something important from not much of anything.

"Why are there circular areas at the end of these three outside runs?" Hugh's voice, right behind her, made her flinch. She took a half step away.

The kennel buildings were long rectangles with prep rooms at one end that opened to inside center aisles. Eight kennel runs projected from each side of the building's aisle, and these inside runs all had dog doors that opened into outside runs.

"I need it for the structures that we'll be attaching to these chain link fences," she said.

The workmen spread and smoothed the concrete with shovels and floats. Another cement truck appeared down the drive.

"What're you building?" Hugh sounded pleasant.

"You don't need these runs, do you?" She wondered if she should have even brought it up. "Some other ones might become empty soon."

"What? Oh, don't worry about it. I'm curious, that's all."

"When it's finished and cured, they'll bolt corncribs down in the new concrete." She pointed to the specific spots. "Then they'll weld them to the chain link runs. I need to find some large, dead trees for the middle of each of corncrib—about eighteen feet high."

"I get it—an enhanced nonhuman-primate habitat."

"I can't wait to watch the macaques play and climb and socialize."

"Let me help you with those trees," he said. "My cousin in Ft. Collins runs a landscape business."

"Hugh, about yesterday—" She never could leave well enough alone.

"I'll give him a call." He sauntered down the path toward the main building. She watched in disbelief, and she would have doubted that whole anger episode of his except that Nancy had witnessed the outburst too.

Beth headed back, pushed through the institute's glass doors, and found Joe with Orin. They looked up as she entered.

"Let's go to the RRC, where it's private," Orin said. They sat at her table, and she told him about Wayne and the 911 responders. As she spoke, Orin turned various shades of red.

"I made it quite clear that I don't want this institution all over the news," he said, "unless there was something felonious. If the police charge Wayne with illegal drug possession, there'll be a huge investigation into the security of our pharmaceuticals."

Joe stopped him. "They won't."

"Orin," Beth said, "the bigger question—the question you need to ask—is what's going on here?"

She picked up the medical journal, turned it to the convention announcement, and handed it to him.

"You still think someone doctored information?" He glanced at the announcement.

Joe nodded at Beth. "I think she's onto something here."

She leaned over Orin's shoulder and pointed out the MS panel.

"What the—?"

He shoved the Barcelona information over to Joe, who glanced at it and looked up at her.

"Damn. *Your* research."

Both men were silent.

"Now about these folders left overnight on my desk . . ."

While she explained, Orin leaned back in his chair and shut his eyes. His face glowed red and little veins popped out. She glanced at Joe.

"Orin," she said, "do you want me to call—"

"I'd like to say if you called anyone else I'd fire you," he said, "but you've uncovered something important."

He sat a few minutes longer, then breathed in and straightened.

"What time is it?"

Joe said, "One-thirty."

"Do you believe all of these files were changed?" He pointed to her stack.

"Probably only the two medical-pharmaceutical ones," she said. "The others might have been left in the stack to divert suspicion. It almost worked."

"So George's petroleum and now Richard's red-algae research numbers seemed all right." He tapped his finger on the desk.

"Can you think why someone would want to doctor numbers to show statistically deficient results?" Her heart pounded in her ears. Of course he knew of a reason. If the scientists knew he was tracking their earnings, they'd want the best numbers. She reconsidered. This wasn't true. Those untouched environmental studies would be a part of the same competition.

Orin's jaw worked back and forth. "I've been losing sleep because of a foreign medical-research company."

"The one Borstell came from?" She pressed her hands together, hard.

"That one no longer exists."

"It didn't concern you that he came from some offshore, shutdown place?"

"What's your point?" Orin glared at her.

Joe touched her shoulder. "He came with good recommendations."

Beth scoffed.

"So which research company bothers you now?" She straightened her stack of files.

"This one." Orin held up the Barcellona call to convention. "It's suddenly quite prosperous. They've won contracts I thought were ours."

"Now I understand," Beth jumped up. "Not only is information being leaked, but the doctoring of files could make us look incompetent, or maybe unethical, to the big-boy pharmaceuticals. My mice were killed to slow us down." Her heart raced. "They could steal my research model, and still have time to publish their own results."

"That's a large chunk to digest," Joe said.

"I know what I'm talking about." Beth held both their attentions. "Puerto Rico Research, the company that shut down, was owned by Roberto Sheering. Sheering is now the CEO of Tikal Research, located—guess where?"

"Close to Lake Tikal in Guatemala." Orin looked at the journal again. "I didn't know—he has some other person's name out front." He stood. "I'm increasing security. I'll have cameras installed next week. Tikal won't get any more of our business."

"But who's feeding them information from this institute?" Bile slid into her throat.

Joe shook his head. "What do you want us to do?"

"Nothing yet." Orin stood. "I'll take this to the board. They don't like surprises any more than I do." The bright red returned to his face. "For some reason, I don't think any of this will solve our dilemma." He stormed out.

"Beth, this is a tough one," Joe said after Orin left. "I think he's more troubled than he's letting on. Even though he knows you're right, you're bugging the hell out of him."

"Think he wants to kill this annoying messenger?" Her stomach—nausea?

He shrugged. "Orin's always liked you—"

"But he hasn't been his usual sedate, in-control self lately."

She walked Joe to her door, and when she opened it she found a Post-it note from Hugh stuck to the doorjamb about the dead trees—with his home phone number.

The Office of the National Counterintelligence Executive, using estimates from academic literature, has estimated losses from economic espionage to be in the tens or even hundreds of billions of dollars annually to the American economy.

—RANDALL COLEMAN, FBI, MAY, 2014

28

Beth arrived at the hospital to find Kathleen tucked beneath fresh sheets with a thin blanket. The head of the bed was raised. Kathleen seemed to study the trees outside the window.

"Tell me what you need from home." Beth set a bouquet of flowers on the shelf. "Some crossword puzzles? A magazine? A book?"

"Those flowers are lovely." Kathleen fiddled with the bandage that covered the IV stuck in the back of her hand. "Shouldn't you be at work?"

Beth sat on the brown, plastic-covered chair and wondered about the toxicity of hospital disinfectants.

"Dear, Dr. Goodlough scheduled a full day of doctoring. Not even a single round of golf."

Compared to how Kathleen had looked that morning and knowing what she was about to go through, her mood didn't match. She seemed almost chipper.

"We'll both be happier," Beth said, "when you're back home."

"You don't need to sit here and wait."

"I thought you understood the inner me," Beth said. "Don't you know I *want* to be here?"

She missed the look on Kathleen's face because a tapping sound caused her to glance toward the door. A nurse entered, holding up a chart.

"Ms. McPherson? The doctor ordered a sedative before you go into surgery." She handed Kathleen a small paper cup with a white pill.

Kathleen popped the pill into her mouth and took a sip of water.

"A whole glass, Kathleen," Beth said.

"I never drink a whole glass of anything unless there's rum in it." She took another couple of sips. "Besides, I'm not supposed to eat or drink anything before surgery."

"Feisty woman you, you still have spark."

"Frankly, I'm scared shitless. Surgery's a new experience for me."

She lay back on the pillows. Beth stared at the traffic in the hallway.

"You've drifted someplace else, dear. Is this about work?"

Beth blinked. "Sorry, Kathleen. I can't stand it when things aren't clear to me."

"Your marriage?"

"My marriage seems way too important to you."

"Maybe I'm envious. Harold's quite well read, certainly attractive, and rather funny."

Beth didn't respond.

"Hello? You're quiet again. He's proud of you, you know."

They must make hospital chairs uncomfortable on purpose. She should clear her mind, focus on the moment.

"I've wondered . . ." Beth said. "You found your one true love, but you never married him. Why?"

The expression on Kathleen's face—she looked like someone had run over Saucy.

"Oh, Kathleen—I shouldn't have asked."

"Martin loved me with all his heart." Kathleen didn't look up.

"But why didn't he leave his wife?" She knew she should stop, but something didn't make sense. "I don't see how any woman could compete with your wit and intelligence."

"Child, you'll be happier when you stop being judgmental."

"If I were that much in love with someone else, Harold would be history."

"What if you found a reason that made staying with Harold more important than your love for this other person?"

Beth thought for a minute. "I can't imagine what it would be."

Kathleen closed her eyes.

"Martin had this villa up on the hillside of St. Thomas. I lived there for six months. One morning I asked his cook if I could help her prepare for my afternoon bridge party, hoping to pump her for information about his marriage. I thought the cook and I were friends and she might let something slip."

"You *are* clever."

"When people think they're being clever, they often aren't. This rather hurt, because I took great pride in my ability to solve mysteries." Kathleen opened her eyes. "She made it quite clear I was prying. Apparently our little friendship was only from my point of view. I learned then about an invisible boundary between staff and employer that's impossible to cross."

Kathleen's eyes closed again, her hands folded on top of the sheet.

"You're tired."

Kathleen opened her eyes and stared straight at her.

"Before I tell you, take inventory. What have you known all along about Harold? I'm not talking about your vague suspicions or his wanting to quit the dealership. What do you know about his true character?"

Beth had never thought about him in those terms.

"Martin's wife desired a certain Arabian stallion," Kathleen said. "She loved fancy horse-foot work, now it's called dressage. So Martin bought the horse for her as a wedding gift. One afternoon her horse took a jump but stumbled—a terrible fall. The horse broke his leg. They put the horse down, but his wife's spinal injury caused her to lose the use of both her legs." Kathleen looked away. "She and Martin had been married exactly one month."

Beth stared at the trees for moment before she said, "A most honorable man."

~

She waited until Kathleen came out of surgery, then called Harold. They'd meet at the Evening Grosbeak at seven.

When the maître d' escorted her to their table, Harold stood, eyes sparkling. Her choice this morning to wear his favorite periwinkle silk dress under a dark suit jacket felt right for tonight. She'd slipped the jacket off and left it in her car.

"How's Kathleen?" he said.

"Lucid and comfortable." Beth sat. "I wish I knew how serious this was."

"Any problems driving over here?" He took his place.

She shook her head, her lips tight.

"Not knowing about Kathleen is tearing you up, isn't it?"

"There's that. But I'm not sure I want to know."

"It's more than that," he said. "You want to keep her in our lives."

She pressed her hands together. She couldn't speak. He reached over and put his hands over hers. His empathy made her feel more vulnerable.

"What's happening at work?" he asked.

She turned her palms to his, squeezed his hands, and let go.

"Please don't tell me," he said, "that you're spending another week of nights sleeping at the institute."

"You worry too much." She looked around the room, avoiding his eyes.

"Maybe, but I know something is wrong."

"For the first time in my career, being good isn't good enough. If we don't do something soon, our clients will drift away to more modern institutes. Some of them already have."

"And you know how to fix it?"

"Aren't you hungry?" She opened her menu.

Watching him ask the waiter about the specials, it occurred to her that if a stranger saw him, Harold would look impressive—distinguished even. She'd never thought of him like that.

When he finished, he said, "It's more than Kathleen. You've discovered something upsetting at work."

"If you don't go ballistic, okay?" She waited. He kept silent. "My research design's been stolen and will be showcased at a convention this fall in Barcelona. And the institute's financial department is secretly tracking the percentages of revenue generated by each scientist."

"And you're ready to run away." His eyes held hers.

"Even if I could, I wouldn't."

"Tell me." He reached across the table again. "Why is this administrative position so damned important?"

"Orin and the board are shortsighted. They're only interested in a quick fix, not a long-term solution. If the foundation only knew. But Joe and I are stymied—we're not administrators. We have no voice."

The waiter brought their salmon and refilled their water glasses.

"What would they do differently if they listened to you or Joe?"

"The whole plant needs to be enlarged—we have researchers fighting over space. All the animal habitats must be enhanced. Some key diagnostic equipment is out of date. We'll never compete in a global market if something doesn't change." She ignored her salmon.

"The institute does pay good dividends to investors," he said. "Guess it's all short-term financial return—not smart."

She studied Harold.

"We're close to being a prototype for the rest of the world," she said. "The one intelligent thing Orin's done was to create this new administrative position—I *know* I'm the best person for this job."

"I wish I could help, but I won't nose around in their financial records."

"You watched over Kathleen, letting me take care of my new project. That was big, Harold. Remember the other night?" She took a bite.

"Which one?"

"When you were about to burn the house down with your cooking."

"The bacon . . ." He swirled his wine for a second. She sipped hers, looking over her glass rim at him.

"I've thought about that night—being in the kitchen with you, joking, cooking."

"Me too," he said.

"I know you were disappointed when Kathleen called us at *that* moment. But . . ." She set her wine glass down. "I felt disappointed too." She placed a hand on his thigh.

"Here's to a promising evening where neither of us ends up disappointed." He held up his glass.

She winked.

"We haven't talked about you." she said. "What's happening in the world of construction?"

"I need to finish a certain project," he said. "Then I'll start the process of getting the LLC from the state and move on from there."

"I can't wait to see."

"The documents from the state?"

"The project."

"It's not one of ours. Something I committed to finish for a friend."

Program by program, economic sector by economic sector, we have based critical functions on inadequately protected telecomputing services.

—SCIENCE BOARD TASK FORCE ON INFORMATION WARFARE-DEFENSE, CIA, NOVEMBER 1996

29

Nancy, phone to her ear, held up a stack of mail as Beth approached.

Beth thumbed through it on her way to her office, then hung her suit jacket over the back of her chair. The warm spring day created a fresh energy in her. She'd stopped by the hospital, but Kathleen had been asleep.

Her phone buzzed. "Ms. Armstrong, there's a man here from some farm cooperative outside of Greeley who says he has a truckload of—"

"My corncribs are here." They were a week early. She darted back to the atrium.

"This is Mr. Franklin from Western States Co-op," Nancy said. "He needs to know where you want the corncribs."

"Great to meet you, Mr. Franklin. I didn't expect you this soon. "Beth stuck out her hand, and he shook it. She glanced through the double doors and saw a long flatbed truck loaded with materials.

"We're headed to the Springs to pick up supplies. Didn't make much sense coming through with an empty truck with your shipment there waiting to be delivered. Hope this isn't inconvenient."

"Not at all." But it was. The concrete pads in Building D needed time to cure before they could install metal structures. She visualized the kennel area and searched her mind for a place to store the cribs out of everyone's way.

"Then if you don't mind signing these papers and telling me where to put them, we'll head on down the road."

Nancy handed her a pen while Beth studied the billing receipt. Everything looked in order. She scribbled her name on the line indicated, then handed the pen back to Nancy. Her delight bubbled out in grins. This small accomplishment would make a huge difference for their nonhuman-primate charges.

"Mr. Franklin, I need you to drive out the exit." Beth gestured toward the direction. "That dirt road right outside the chain link fence circles around to the back of the property. Follow it all the way to the south side, and I'll meet you at an entrance gate behind the kennels." That old road and gate didn't get much use since those ancillary buildings had been completed.

Nancy fingered through her assortment of keys.

"Got it." She waved the gate key in the air.

Beth thanked her, then rushed out along the walkway toward the kennels. When she came to Building C, she left the walk for a weedy dirt path and made her way between the dog runs. Colonies of serenading, exuberant beagles begged expected treats from her.

The southwest fence and gate were set a distance behind and away from the kennels. Months ago, the institute had staked out a small plot of this land for a new IT center and printing department combo. The foundation decided to branch out and publish scientific bulletins and white papers. She wondered if they'd ever start construction on that building. But then, considering the sorry neglect of everything, it was no surprise that nothing happened.

She stepped out into the open field behind the kennel and a flare of annoyance stopped her.

Tumbleweeds barricaded the locked entrance in the south fence. She hated them—the scourge of the West. They settled everywhere, where nothing else cared to be.

Beth had to deal with it, so she waded through dormant prairie grasses mingled with tinges of new yellow-green shoots and listened to the nattering conversations of the goats on the far side of the beagle compound. Those goats could clean up this weed problem fast. Bad idea. The goats were on a special diet. Beth glanced up in time to dodge a spiky stalk left from last fall's dead sunflowers.

At the gate, she quickly pulled each weedy ball of stickery nuisance away by its tiny rootstalk and tossed it aside. Beth continued until she reached the padlock and inserted the key.

The low rumble of the truck came from somewhere near the west fence corner. She turned the key and pulled at the lock. What a surprise—the rusty thing opened. The truck labored up the rutted road. Kicking more tumbleweeds out of the way, she shoved one side of the gate and then the other back against the fence. Tiny pieces of vegetative debris clung to her clothing. She picked at it until the truck turned into the property.

Her hands and legs itched, but still Beth couldn't help grinning. Her almost-completed construction project made her want to dance and sing for all those isolated macaques. The men positioned the truck, unloaded and stacked the materials where she indicated against the back wall of a kennel, and then drove away in a cloud of dust.

When the truck cleared the gate on it's way out, and after the dust settled, Beth pulled each gate back to its closed position. She tugged the chain around to hook the padlock in place and froze. *Why?* She didn't believe in those creepy feelings people talk about when they think they are being watched. It must have been a sound like a twig snapping. Hair standing on end, chills on the back of the neck—those things had no logical explanation. Maybe the crunching of dry grasses put her on alert. She felt certain someone *was* watching her.

What then? She stood straight, breathed deep, and whirled around. He stood back between two of the kennel buildings, watching. When their eyes met, Hugh called out to her.

"Not interested in those dead trees?"

"On the contrary." She turned back and snapped the lock shut before facing him again. "Today, dead trees are my greatest passion."

He moved forward a few feet, and then he leaned against the corner of one of the buildings. She wandered toward the kennels on the dirt track made by the truck. She couldn't wait to check out the corncrib panels.

"I left a note. I know you saw it." His voice reeked acid.

"I've been out on personal matters until a few minutes ago. Who do I contact?"

"Do you seriously think I carry contact numbers with me?" His tone sounded pleasant, but his face seem to consume the sunlight.

"Then leave it with Nancy, please." She walked the length of the neatly stacked panels, studying them.

"The number's at my condo." He touched her arm. "Stop by tonight after work? I'll fix you a cold one, we can chat."

"Not a good idea." She eased away from him, knelt, and poked at the panels. The way they were bundled with metal straps and paper, she couldn't tell much.

"Tomorrow night?"

She straightened up and looked at him. "What's the problem with bringing it to work tomorrow?"

"Thought we could talk in a more relaxed atmosphere."

"I have to sit with a sick aunt at the hospital." *Well, that sounded phony.* But there was no way she'd be alone with him after his tantrum the other day. She gave him a dismissive shrug and savored the pleasant, spring air on her walk back to the main building.

Beth stopped at Nancy's desk. "You were gone yesterday. Is everything all right?"

"Nathan's doctor wanted him to take more blood tests. We should have the results tomorrow on the last chemo."

"Harold's quite fond of Nathan." Beth scanned Nancy's face. She couldn't imagine how any mother could deal with the awful possibilities. "Our best thoughts to all of you."

Nancy glanced at her, then blinked and looked down at a collection of papers.

"There's paper work in that stack from me." Beth leaned over and pulled out a couple. "Here, I've turned in requisitions for a change of locks on our file cabinets, my office, and my lab. And here's another one to repair the outside locks on all those kennel buildings. If anyone asks, tell them I said someone's bound to find themselves locked in sooner or later—they should have been replaced long ago."

Nancy didn't look up. Beth sighed. She didn't know how to take away Nancy's worries.

"I'll be in Joe's office for a few minutes."

When she got there, Joe and a tech were in with the nonhuman primates. Both wore long-sleeved shirts, face masks, and heavy gloves. A few minutes later, the two came out and joined her in the hallway.

"Rick, I thought you worked for Hugh," she said.

"He's between animal projects." Rick pulled off the gloves and put them in a cubby marked with his name. Then he peeled off the heavy shirt and hung it on the hook next to the cubby. "He lets me help out where I can. College money, you know."

"I saw those floor plans you drew for one of the beagle buildings."

Over a short-sleeved shirt, he wore an army-green long-tailed shirt with metal buttons. Either the factory or he had cut the sleeves off. Letters and numbers were stamped in black over the breast pocket.

"Renovations—had to get the dimensions." His hand pushed the outer shirt aside where he rested his fingers on a case attached to his belt.

"Do you like working with the macaques?"

"It's not too bad—they sure like those bagels. Is that all, Mr. Hammer? It's time to give the goats that special food and some water."

"Sure. Thanks for your help."

"Oh, Rick?" Beth said. "How can you do those drawings when all the doors are locked?"

"Aw, Mr. Wendenski has a key for everything." He waved. "Later."

She turned and raised her brows at Joe. He held open his office door, then closed it behind them. Rick seemed like a good kid. She admired his work ethic, his motivation to continue his college education. She didn't like Hugh's influence on him.

"Joe, do you think that was one of those new cell phones attached to Rick's belt?"

"Didn't notice."

"It was rectangular and gray. What would he need a cell phone for?" Even she didn't have one.

"You've solved the notepad mystery, then." Joe squinted at her.

She sat, grinning. "And I bet the Wayne mystery, too."

"Interesting," Joe said. "Why would Hugh need floor plans of the different kennels? They're all the same, aren't they?"

"Remember the Laminar Flow switch in my lab? The drawing focused as much on the electrical system as it did the floor plan. That lowest bidder who won the electrical contract six months ago did several repairs out in the kennels too. Go out there in the dark and go into any one of those kennels and try to find those working light switches."

"And why keep drugging Wayne after he made copies of those keys?"

"It's not the keys," she said. "It's being able to steal research without being seen."

"Can't accuse Hugh of being a corporate spy based on some kid bragging." Joe leaned back in his chair, staring at her.

She stared back. Joe picked up his pen and rolled it between his thumb and forefinger, then set it down.

"I think you have to let Orin and the board deal with this."

"Hugh will be putting his feet up in some Lake Tikal summer home by the time they agree to do something." She burned inside, but she continued to give him an icy glare.

He leaned forward and said, "We don't know anything for sure."

"*I'll* continue to deal with this, Joe, because no one else cares to." She pushed up out of her chair.

"You shouldn't get involved." He stood too.

"I am involved. My mice died. My reputation is on the line because data been doctored." She fumed but refused to raise her voice. "You've given excuses for Borstell, you want me to back out where Hugh's concerned, and you want me to turn this over to someone else."

He held his hands up, palms toward her. She didn't want a truce. She wanted answers.

"Who then?" She wanted him to feel frustrated, too. "Who do *you* think is at the root of all this?"

"Your facts are circumstantial. They'll get you in trouble—especially when you jump to conclusions." He looked away. "You're on probation, remember?"

"Jeez." Beth shook her head. "Let's ignore everything and hope it goes away."

"Orin should be the one dealing with this, not you." Joe touched her shoulder. "Besides, his paycheck is larger."

"Evidently his job description doesn't cover sabotage. There's something else." The sharp edges of resentment scratched inside her. "Even though we're best buddies, don't smother me. Please? You're annoying when you try to protect me."

We have created a target-rich environment, and US industry has
sold globally much of the generic technology that can be used to
strike these targets.

—SCIENCE BOARD TASK FORCE ON INFORMATION WARFARE-
DEFENSE, CIA, NOVEMBER 1996

30

Kathleen shuffled down the hallway dragging her
IV. She held the back of her hospital gown shut with her other hand. Beth
knew what her aunt thought of this little activity.

"Hi." She showed Kathleen a stuffed, Saucy-like dog.

Kathleen's face didn't change, but she did managed a low, "Hello, dear."

"How much longer do you have to walk?"

"I'm headed back now. Shit—I don't walk this much at home."

"What did the doctor say?" Beth helped her back into bed.

"Maybe he got it all, maybe he didn't."

Beth should make an appointment to talk with the doctor herself. She
tucked Kathleen into bed, moved her water glass closer, and set the dog
between her flower vase and a new bouquet.

"An admirer?"

"Your neighbors, Laura and Ted."

"Laura and I've been friends forever—since grade school. She always
asks about you."

Kathleen feigned an in-depth study of the trees.

"I have something to tell you," Beth said. "Something I've not told anyone
else except Harold, and even he doesn't know how I got the information."

That caught her aunt's attention. How this woman loved secrets. Her eyes brightened as Beth told her about the Alternative Rodent Food file.

"What do you think Orin's up to?" Kathleen asked.

"He might be planning personnel cuts, keeping the best revenue producers, and firing everyone else."

"Bastard. I know nothing about science, but this is a good example of why you have to know what isn't to know what is." Kathleen pressed the button that moved the head of her bed. She raised it higher, then lower, then higher. She let go of it with a flip of her hand. "If you only see what appears to be good, you'll end up being blind to reality."

"Poor results," Beth said, "force researchers to go back and rethink." Was Orin creating a culture that allowed no errors?

Her aunt sipped some water from a straw, then pulled the straw out of the glass and flung it toward the wastebasket. She missed. She slapped the glass down on the bedside tray and glared at nothing.

"I have another problem," Beth said.

Kathleen seem to sit straighter and study Beth's face.

"Someone else may know about this comparison study. That might be why the files are being put on my desk. But then Orin says another company might want the numbers changed for their own competitive financial gain. I don't know if this is about personal gain for someone at the institute, or someone at the institute being a spy for another research lab."

"That's a dilemma." Kathleen raised the head of her bed a bit more. "You can't know who's responsible until you know their motive."

Beth picked the straw off the floor and dropped it in the wastebasket.

"Competition enters into everything, dear. Including relationships."

"I never compete with anyone," Beth said. "Only myself. When someone else wins something, I cheer them on."

"You're an idealist. Harold brought some jelly beans. Are there any left?"

On the nightstand were two magazines and a small, white sack. She looked inside and handed the sack to her aunt.

"Lucky me, a handful," Kathleen said. "I'll share."

Beth took a few.

"Mary and I were always at each other's throats," Kathleen said.

"You were older than my mother by—what? Four, five years? You wouldn't have much in common at that age."

"We had one thing in common, and it defined who we became."

"My grandparents?"

"They drove us apart."

"Oh, come on, they wouldn't play favorites." Beth laughed.

"I don't find it one bit funny." Kathleen took another jelly bean, looked at it, saw it was black, and dropped it back into the sack.

"I'm shocked you'd think they had favorites."

"When I was sixteen," Kathleen said, "your mother decided society wasn't fair. She was about eleven at the time. She pestered me with different school projects, usually helping herself to anything she wanted of mine to complete her endeavors. I'd grit my teeth and not complain until the month she decided we needed to open our home to the world and feed the hungry."

She handed Beth the jelly-bean bag—only black ones remained.

"Can't imagine my grandparents letting that happen."

"Then you don't have much of an imagination, dear."

"I'm hooked. Tell me."

"We went to different schools, but we walked home every day for lunch. I opened the door one day and heard all this chattering coming from the dining room. You can't imagine my surprise when I saw seven ratty little ragamuffins sitting around our dining-room table." She chuckled. "Now it's actually funny—and to think I've been mad about this for years."

"Guess you aren't sixteen anymore."

"They were the Peckinpah children, from another neighborhood but they went to Mary's school. She kept bringing them home, every day for at least a whole week. I bet Louisa was pulling out her hair."

"Louisa?"

"Our cook. She set the table with a white-linen cloth and used the company china, crystal, and silver. She waited on them like they were mother's guild friends."

Kathleen fell into a fit of giggles, and Beth followed.

"I complained, and complained. The last thing I wanted to do was have lunch with a bunch of dirty, noisy kids. Mother sided with Mary, so I quit going home for lunch. I ate in restaurants." She stared into space. "Of course, those children weren't the least bit dirty. But now I'm never able to pass some poor soul on the street without slipping them a few bills."

Beth had known that her mother opened her arms to anyone in need. Why wasn't she more like that?

"Once, when we were quite young, Sophie, Brandy, and I had to compete." Kathleen sighed. "No one could touch Sophie with that voice of hers."

"Did you have to compete against each other?"

"Brandy's skills were acting and dancing—now, that was tough competition—but I'm talking about an audition."

"Were you nervous?"

"Not in the least. When Sophie finished hers, everyone hung on to her, followed her everywhere—she was a true canary. Afterward I saw Brandy standing alone in an empty hallway outside those audition rooms, watching Sophie disappear down the stairs with her entourage."

Beth pictured Kathleen standing there.

"Sophie snagged a primo gig, but her beautiful voice took her to the South Side."

"What about you and Brandy?"

"Oh, we crossed the street and drank a milkshake. God, I wish I had a cigarette."

"If Sophie went to the South Side, where did you and Brandy work?"

"The Friars' Club—I *loved* it, danced there for years. That's where I learned to do choreography. Friars' became like home." Kathleen shook herself out of the past. "Did I tell you I can go home tomorrow?"

"Are you sure you feel well enough—"

"Child, don't start that again. What's that pin on your jacket lapel? Come closer."

Beth went over to the bed and touched the brownish-green frog pin Hugh had given her. She'd forgotten she'd put it on that morning.

"Why, it's a coqui frog from Puerto Rico. I didn't know you'd been there."

"I . . . haven't. Are you sure it's Puerto Rican?"

"They're the cutest little frogs." Her aunt clasped her hands. "Most of them look brown because they're almost translucent. You can't believe the noise that comes from such tiny things."

Companies also need to educate their employees about some of the warning signs of insider threat. . . . working odd hours without authorization; taking home company proprietary information; and installing personal software . . . short trips to foreign countries . . . living beyond his or her means.

—RANDALL COLEMAN, FBI, MAY 2014

31

Beth skipped breakfast and stopped at the hospital before she went to the institute. She wanted to verify Kathleen's declaration that she could go home. Beth caught the doctor making rounds. He ushered her into a small conference room off the nurses' station.

"My aunt says she can go home." Beth slipped into a chair.

"Ah, yes. Well . . ." He sat, opened a folder, and studied it for a moment. "She should go home. It would be good for her to get out of here for a while."

He stared at the file.

Cold crawled into her and that little room with no windows. It had slinked across the floor, climbed the oak table, and slipped into her fears. It turned her into an ice statue—rigid and still. She waited. His eyes stayed downcast on the file. Was he reading or selecting words?

"The surgery went well as far as removal of the main tumor."

She held her breath.

"When some of the tumor is imbedded deeply in the bladder wall there's a chance of cells being dispersed to other organs and parts of the body." He paused. "I'm afraid that's what's happened."

Her heart thudded against her ribs. She wanted out of this room.

"You're saying—" She swallowed hard. "The tumor was malignant and—and—it's metastasized." Under the table she pressed her palms tightly together.

He nodded.

White noise filled her head. Pressure—she couldn't think, the corners of the room became dark and moved toward her. The non-noise deafened her. She leaned forward and forced herself to inhale deep and willed her muscles to relax.

"Are you all right?" He touched her arm.

She swallowed. Why hadn't she known?

"Your aunt is feeling well today. She may continue feeling fine for quite a while. We have no way of predicting."

The scrape of his chair on the linoleum floor, her chair's broken-down seat pad, the smells of disinfectants—these were her realities. They were all around her, but *his* words were fiction. They had to be.

. . . for quite a while, the doctor's words. She let these words sink into her mind until she could find her voice.

"If she can go home, should she have someone with her?"

Her guest room waited. Harold would be pleased to have her back.

"If she chooses, but she's fine for now." He stood, straightened the file, then tucked it next to his ribs.

"Treatment? What's next? Radiation, chemo—"

He looked away for a moment.

"You're not saying there's no treatment." Beth's heart tumbled.

"At this stage," he glanced down at the file, "it's all through her system. Anything we give her would make her feel weak, and sick, and the chance of it extending her life even a few months just isn't there."

"But—there has to be something."

"If she were my aunt, I would let her enjoy her life."

She didn't hear what else he said—something about some assistance if she needed it. She remembered shaking his hand again and agreeing to something inane as he left—but there had to be something, anything.

A nurse poked her head in the door. "Sorry. Thought the room was empty."

Beth stepped into the hallway. Lights, noise, people doing . . . what? Busy with life. Did any of it matter? She'd forgotten to ask the doctor if Kathleen knew. She went to the nurses' station.

When one looked up she said, "Could you tell me when my aunt will be discharged?"

The nurse picked up a clipboard and turned some pages.

"Later this afternoon."

Beth couldn't respond. She walked down the hall beyond Kathleen's room to the window at the end of the hallway. She stared beyond the panes, but her brain saw nothing. After a few seconds, she forced her face to relax and waited for her stomach to settle before she turned back toward Kathleen's room.

Kathleen pushed her tray away and turned her cheek up for a kiss.

"How are you this morning?" Beth kept her voice strong.

"Splendid. I get to leave this place."

"Why do you have to stay until the afternoon?" She should have asked the nurse.

"Something about a liver-function test. Don't you need to go to work?" Her aunt settled back with her coffee.

"Come home." Beth swallowed. "We don't care about the smoke."

"Beth, I feel quite well, especially since they took all those tubes out of me." She held up her hand. "I'm going back to my place with Saucy. I miss her and I don't want to be smothered."

"I'll be back after lunch." She wouldn't fight. "I'll bring clothes."

~

She entered the institute's atrium an hour late.

"Have you gotten Nathan's test results yet?" she asked Nancy.

"Not yet. How's your aunt?"

Without thinking, Beth told her.

Nancy touched her arm and handed her a box of tissues.

"We learned that the kindest thing we could do for Nathan was to treat him like he was the picture of health," she said. "Even though we were dying from fear on the inside."

"That's so counterintuitive." Beth swiped at her eyes with a tissue. "But, you're right." Beth struggled to keep her voice from quivering. "You're a treasure."

Air refused to flow through her lungs. She hurried away and pushed open the outside doors into the sunshine. She wanted breaths of clean Rocky Mountain–scented air. What a joke. The daytime carbon emissions from the traffic and the smells from the surrounding city obliterated any wild nature smells. Someone opened the door behind her. She glanced back and saw Rick carrying a steel bucket. He hesitated, stared at her for a second, then continued outside.

[185]

"Hi, Rick. Off to the goats to give them special food?"

"Yeah." He put his head down and loped off toward the kennels.

Beth felt uneasy. True, he was a kid of few words, but his response didn't hold a hint of friendliness. Was he offended with her questions about the notepad?

Who knew how teens thought? They always appeared so moody—ups and downs. Probably from sitting around and listening to their hormones change. She certainly didn't want to be responsible for a fit of youthful depression. Next time, she'd make a point of letting him know how much she thought of his diligence here.

She forced herself back inside and headed to Joe's office.

She tapped on Joe's door. "May I come in?"

He looked up from a clipboard.

"You don't look happy. What's up?"

"Learned something interesting last night." She told him about Hugh's coqui frog.

"Maybe he vacations there," he said.

"Remember his scorched sunburn a few weeks ago?" She fiddled with a lone paper clip on the corner of his desk. She looked up and saw him staring at her. "What?"

"You're supposed to say, 'He's the spy. Arrest him and haul him off in chains.'"

"You're supposed to be the devil's advocate." She glanced at the paper clip.

"You're rarely this down," he said. "What's going on, Beth?"

"Life." She flipped the paper clip onto his desk blotter. "Joe, what should I do? I wish I knew more about Hugh. What do you know?"

"What everyone else knows—excellent researcher, fairly happy person, kind to everyone, enjoys expensive clothes, drives a fancy car, lives in an upscale neighborhood."

"A Mercedes, isn't it? He's asked me to come to his place to have a 'cold one.'" She stood. "Guess he's not married."

"I don't know if he has been, but I don't think he is now." Joe stood. "Doesn't he know you're married?"

"He does." Beth explained the dead-tree information.

"You're going to need those dead trees soon. I went out and looked at your little project yesterday."

"Where does Hugh get money for all his fancy stuff?" She went to his door.

"Don't know. Good point."

She closed the office door quietly, leaving him to his thoughts.

When she entered her office the smell of coffee greeted her. That was Nancy. She poured herself a cup and sipped pure comfort, rich, bold, and hot.

She walked out into the atrium with her cup.

"This is the best coffee, Nancy. Where do you get it?"

"Enjoy it while it lasts." She pulled the almost-empty bag from under her counter and handed it to Beth. "Mr. Wendenski brings it to me when he comes back from vacation."

Beth remembered Hugh handing her this coffee. She unrolled the top of the bag.

Product of Guatemala.

Beth's internal temperature skyrocketed. She regained control and pasted on a professional look.

"Hugh's kind to bring you this, and you're generous to share it with me."

That pin from Puerto Rico. The coffee from Guatemala. Angry heat burned away all traces of pleasantness. *Mr. Wendenski has a key for everything.*

Beth left her cup on Nancy's counter and charged up the stairway. She'd confront Hugh, make him—what? She was almost to the second floor when she heard the elevator ding open down below in the atrium.

She leaned over the rail to see who was getting out. Hugh, briefcase in hand, strode over and said something to Nancy. Nancy handed him the sign-out book. He wrote, then glanced over at the steaming cup of coffee. He said something to Nancy, nodding toward the coffee cup. She responded, and he turned his head toward the stairway. His eyes moved up the stairs and locked on Beth's. She glared back. She wouldn't look away. But then she couldn't because the ice forming within made her rigid.

He spun away and strode out the front door.

She watched through the large windows until he stepped out into the parking lot and disappeared from view.

～

Beth entered Kathleen's room with an array of colorful shopping bags. Kathleen straightened, her face bright.

"You went shopping—how fun."

The two of them sorted through the sacks. Kathleen's delight spilled over and caught the attention of a passing nurse. The three of them evaluated everything from the dainty matching underwear to the turquoise silk blouse and black slacks.

Beth placed a long, silver chain necklace around her aunt's neck. The nurse held up a mirror.

"I thought it would go well with the turquoise."

Kathleen touched it. Her eyes sparkled.

"I'll go sign you out while you get dressed," Beth said.

On the drive to Kathleen's apartment, her aunt fingered the necklace, commenting on Beth's shopping. Beth parked, and then held her arm out to Kathleen as they made their way to her door. Saucy greeted them with leaps and yips, then bounded into Kathleen's lap the minute she sat in her chair.

"Oh my, what a welcome, my fuzzy-faced one." She reached for her cigarettes as Beth opened a can of soup.

"She missed you," Beth said. "I should have dressed her in a red bow."

"I do hope Harold knows I'm home. He always stops by my room after work."

"I called. He knows. We'll come over this evening."

"Dear, not tonight. I think I'll read for a while, then sleep. I'm not hungry. What's today?"

"Friday."

"Well then." She took a long draw from her cigarette. "If either of you have time tomorrow, why don't you stop by? I'm sure I'll feel more up to things by then."

"This is the most activity you've had in a couple of days." She set a bowl of mushroom soup with crackers next to Kathleen.

"You don't need to stay, dear."

"I thought you'd enjoy company."

"We can talk tomorrow."

"I'll stop by to check on you a little later." Beth folded her arms. "You may be as stubborn as your father, but he was also my grandfather."

Beth went to a nearby drugstore and used the pay phone. Yvonne refused to give her Orin's home phone number, so she called Nancy for his mailing address.

She bought a box of white note cards and wrote down everything she wanted him to know about the coqui frog pin, the coffee, the notepad, and Rick's comment about Hugh's keys. She sealed the card in the envelope, put a stamp on it, and slipped it into the mailbox. Orin wouldn't be at the institute over the weekend, but now, according to his zip code, he'd have the information at home by tomorrow morning.

She stood in the fading light next to the large blue spruce tree by the mailbox. The setting sun warmed the tree's trunk. Last year's grasses beyond the shade of its branches showed new patches of green. Spring always seemed to take forever to arrive. Why did she feel so exhausted?

She wanted to be comforted . . . to be with Harold.

Being aware of potential issues, exercising good judgment, and conducting discrete inquiries will help you ascertain if there is a spy in your midst. However, if you believe one of your employees is a spy or is stealing company trade secrets, do not alert the person to the fact that he/she is under suspicion, but seek assistance from trained counterintelligence experts—such as the FBI.

—FBI, MAY 2011

32

Harold's car wasn't in the driveway. The house seemed different. She stood and gazed around the living room. Someone had vacuumed and straightened all the books and newspapers.

But everything inside her felt upside down.

She drove back to Kathleen's apartment and found Kathleen tucked into bed with several pillows behind her head, a book in her hands, chocolates on the nightstand, and her cigarettes nearby. Saucy did her exuberant so-happy-you're-here dance. Beth gave Kathleen a kiss on the cheek and left to find Harold.

Harold's car was parked beside the Suds and Under building, but the only vacant space for her car was at the far end of the lot close to the street.

Inside, her eyes took a few minutes to adjust. She didn't need to search the room or the booths—she knew where he'd be.

A hostess with thin legs, denim shorts, and a too-tight T-shirt asked if she wanted to sit at the bar or in the dining area.

"Dining, but I need to find someone first."

She checked the pool tables in the back and spotted him at the first one. He talked and laughed as he lined up his shot. She waved at him, then eased into a booth where she could watch.

"Want some dinner?" the skinny waitress asked.

"Do you mind if I sit here and wait? I'll take a glass of white wine—your house one will do." She set her keys on the table, took her mirror from her purse, and dabbed on lip gloss. She looked more than exhausted.

"We have great subs with homemade fries." The chirpy woman pulled out an order pad and poised her pencil.

"I might later." She put her lip gloss back in her purse and fluffed her hair. Harold seemed to be enjoying himself. What would she say to him?

"Here you go, some water too. Anything else?"

"I'll see what my husband wants."

"Which one is he?"

"He's in the gray shirt with the sleeves rolled up," Beth said with a nod toward the pool tables.

"Oh, I know him. Good looker, always polite. Rachel and the girls think he's a honey." With that she flew off to take care of another booth.

Beth sat stone still. Harold did have a healthy sexual appetite, and she didn't always encourage him as much as he wanted. As much as *she* wanted, for that matter.

For a second she felt sick.

She forced herself to study the black-and-white photos of submarines that lined the walls over the booths. She wanted to dive deep with them. Why? Something symbolic? Kathleen would know.

"How long have you been here?" Harold's baritone voice.

She slid over to make room for him, then held up her untouched wine.

"Hospitals can do that, can't they? Take longer than you think, I mean." He settled in next to her. "I'm surprised Kathleen wanted to be alone tonight."

"I know she appreciates your chocolates. You're thoughtful, Harold." She looked down at the Formica tabletop. She had no more words.

He waited, then put his arm around her and bent in close.

"Can you tell me?"

"The doctor said . . . Oh, Harold—" Her voice cracked.

"Damn."

"There's nothing more they can do," she whispered in short little breaths. "It's metastasized."

She wished she hadn't said it—the words gave it a physical form. A lump swelled in her throat.

"She'll want us to forge ahead like everything's fine." He put one arm around her. "We can't be giving her *that* look, Beth."

His thoughtfulness made her feel fragile.

"Do you want to eat or go home?" He gave her a gentle squeeze.

"Honestly?" She felt numb. "I want to go home."

Harold scooted out of the booth and put ten dollars on the table. Beth picked up her purse and followed.

"Where'd you park?" he said as they stepped outside.

"You don't need to walk me to my car."

"It's dark—"

"I can take care of myself." She didn't like her tone. "I'm sorry, I'll see you at home."

"Beth, I can't have you—"

"Can't have me what?" Why did he do this? If he kept this up, she feared she'd start feeling jumpy, too.

His eyes swept through the packed parking lot before meeting her stare.

"Beth, I worry my ass off every time you leave the house. I can't live this way."

"And *you* order me around every time you start worrying. I can't live *that* way."

He sighed, then gave her a peck on the cheek and left.

Beth walked to her car and opened her purse—no keys. *Dammit.* She put her mirror, lip gloss, brush, wallet, pen, pocket calendar, pepper spray, and breath mints on her car hood, then dug around in the bottom of her handbag. The keys weren't there. She patted her pockets—nothing. *Where in the—*

Her muscles felt heavy and molasses slogged her brain. She did need to eat. It was late, but it couldn't be that late. She must have overlooked the keys. She started back through the items, then stopped. She remembered— the keys were lying on the table in the restaurant. She shoved everything into her handbag and dashed back inside.

The booth was still empty. The wine and money sat untouched, and there were her keys. A wave of relief flooded through her. She reached across to snatch them—and felt hands on her waist.

"Well, well. If it isn't the queen of the RRC."

She whirled around, but Hugh Wendenski shoved her into the booth and slid in beside her, blocking her exit.

"Here, sit and finish your wine." His words and his actions activated some sort of protective armor within her. Wouldn't he ever understand personal space?

"Hi, Hugh." She was imprisoned in the booth by Hugh's large frame. Beth fought an urge to shove him. She didn't want to trigger his explosive temper.

Heat flared somewhere deep inside and sneaked upward into her neck and cheeks.

He looked around the bar, tapping the table with his index finger. "You said you weren't available tonight."

"It's been a strange day." She shrugged, but inside she boiled.

"Administrators need to be dependable." His eyes pivoted back to pierce into hers. "Can't let little personal problems interfere."

"Going to your home to talk about trees has nothing to do with that supervisory position." She scanned the room, keeping her anger from surfacing. "Orin values my work."

Beth searched for a face she might recognize. Someone she might signal.

"He values producers of quality research. Let's drink to that." He held his finger up to the busy waitress. He pulled her wine glass over.

As in top scientist according to skewed data? This egotistical jerk must be the corporate spy. She could best him at this phony conversation.

"Thanks again for that frog pin." She touched the base of her wine glass. "Where'd you find it?" Would he lie?

"Puerto Rico. Used to scuba in the Caribbean. You like it, huh?"

"You don't scuba dive anymore, or do you go somewhere else?"

"Belize. Much better because of the barrier reef. Do you dive?"

"Snorkel, but someday." She wished she hadn't said that.

"There's a great school on one of the streets off Colfax. I'll introduce you to the guys there." He scooted closer to her. She smelled beer and onions.

"That coffee you give Nancy is delicious." She bet he'd lie. "Where do you get it?"

"Guatemala. Good, huh? I can bring you some next time I'm down that way." He put his arm over the seat behind her. "Great to see you relax some and enjoy the evening with me."

"I only came back for my keys, Hugh. I have to go."

The skinny waitress appeared with a mug of beer. *He must be a regular here.*

"Do you want me to run a tab?" The woman looked at Hugh.

"Sounds good," he said. "We've got lots of time and lots to talk about."

"I don't," Beth said. "You'll have to excuse me, Hugh."

The waitress disappeared between groups of boisterous customers. The Friday night crowd increased, and their noisy chatter escalated.

"I thought you wanted to know about those dead trees."

"Great. Do you have those phone numbers?" She plastered on her biggest smile.

He shook his head and gazed around the stuffy room.

"Guess we're finished here, then. Now excuse me, I have to go home." She nudged him on the arm with her palm. He didn't move. Beth pushed harder. He didn't look at her and held like a rock. She lost control and shoved him as hard as she could, then instantly regretted it. Beth wouldn't win this game.

He looked down at her hand and then glared into her eyes.

"Hugh, let me out." She kept her voice firm and low.

"You sure ask a lot of questions. Why?"

"I'm interested in things." She figured Harold's anxiety would be over the roof about now. "It's late—my husband will be worried."

"I prefer you quit asking my technician questions." His hard voice came out low. His face was too close. "Do not ask him questions. Get it? Or you'll be responsible for getting him fired."

"Hugh," her voice was now firm, "if you fire Rick, don't put that on me." He'd chewed Rick out. That's why Rick shunned her today. She clenched her teeth and added, "He's responsible and diligent. His termination will be totally your decision."

"Ha, no wonder Borstell calls you a bitch."

He sipped his beer, then set it down and stared out across the room. His voice wasn't a whisper, but his words sounded secretive.

"The institute's a large facility, all those corridors and storage rooms. Bet sometimes you think you're being watched." He lifted his mug and took another slow sip. "Do you check to see who's behind you? If not, you better, because, little lady, you're in way over your head."

His onion breath used up all her air.

"Beth?" Harold's voice, calling her name from somewhere near.

She looked around, searching for him. He pushed through the crowd toward their booth.

"Harold." She glanced at Hugh. "I forgot my keys. Hugh wanted to talk, but we're finished."

"Don't believe we've met." Harold held out his hand.

Hugh stood and shook Harold's hand.

"Harold Armstrong, Beth's husband."

"Hugh Wendenski—scientist at the institute."

Beth squeezed out of the booth, grateful for Hugh's habits of civility.

"I'll see you at home, Harold."

～

Harold walked in the door a few minutes after she did. She put her arms around his neck.

"I was so relieved to get away from that man."

"You looked exceptionally cozy." He removed her arms from around his neck, went to the sink, and held a glass under the water. His solemn face bothered her.

She sidled up next to him. "He invades other's personal space. It's quite annoying. I told him I needed to go, but he ignored me." She found herself talking to his back. "When he pushed me in and sat, I was actually trapped. Then he wouldn't let me out. The only choices I had seemed rather ugly."

She didn't like Harold this way, so somber. Still, the news about Kathleen cut deep. He had to be struggling with it too.

He studied her, and she watched his shoulders relax.

"I thought your car had problems. Didn't expect to find you with a man."

"Good grief, Harold, I didn't want to be there with him. Hugh's made the top of my list, and you timed your appearance perfectly."

"Have you eaten anything?"

"I'll fix us something," She took two plates out of the cupboard. Her neck prickled. He *knew* she hadn't eaten.

"I bought stuff from the deli." He pulled the kitchen chair out and pointed at her. "My turn."

"What a treat." She obeyed. "Only half a sandwich for me."

While he made the sandwiches, she filled him in on Hugh's connection with Puerto Rico and Guatemala, then about what he'd said in the Suds and Under. She left out the part about his name calling and threats.

"So he's the one."

"He certainly has the cash in his pockets to buy luxury items." Harold's interest revived her. "Did you see his silk shirt and Harris tweed jacket tonight? And he has help. He loans his tech out to other scientists, then has the tech draw floor plans of all the labs and kennel runs. I'm sure Rick, that's his tech, reports other information he hears back to Hugh." She stood. "I'll be right back."

She walked into the study, pulled down the world atlas from the shelf, and turned to Central America. There was the tiny country of Belize on the Atlantic coast with Guatemala along its west border. Guatemala also wrapped around the southern border of Belize and shared a small part of the ocean coastline.

She returned to the kitchen. Harold gave her a quizzical look, then set a half sandwich and a glass of milk at her place.

"Needed a geography refresher." She sat, and Harold joined her.

"Does Orin know what you know?"

"He won't until he reads the note I sent him." She picked at her sandwich.

"You weren't safe tonight. Makes me crazy."

"Come on, Harold, I don't need a bodyguard."

He hadn't touched his sandwich, so she took a bite of hers.

"You're too naïve, Beth."

"How can I convince you?" she said. "If I were a man—"

"In other words, you don't actually need me?" He stared across the table at her.

"Not to protect me I don't."

"Seems I did tonight. You work with that guy—he sees you every day." He looked away. "What if he figures out you're onto him, Beth?"

Beth watched him work his jaw back and forth for a moment.

"Thanks for straightening up the living room." She touched his hand.

Silence. She patted his hand.

"Harold, every time I come home I see countless ways in which Kathleen has changed our lives. She was right about your needing to quit."

"You're seething inside because you think I have no business plan."

"Let's not—"

"I'm working it out. But I have so many questions. . . ." He rubbed his forehead. "Should I start out alone, or hire someone else? If I hire someone I have to pay workers' comp, payroll taxes, offer benefits."

"Can we table this for now?" She picked up her glass and went to the sink.

"What if I can't afford full-time help? Who would want only part-time work?"

"Now I *am* worried." She rinsed the glass, filled it with water, then turned toward him. "You've done this so long for free you might not let yourself turn it into a real business."

Science is organized knowledge. Wisdom is organized life.

—IMMANUEL KANT

33

Kathleen stepped out of her bedroom dressed in black slacks and wearing her new turquoise blouse and silver necklace. The smoky haze in the apartment told Beth that her aunt was making up for lost time.

No matter. Beth studied her. She seemed fairly stable on her feet.

Saucy pawed at Beth until she knelt and hugged the dog.

"Harold stopped by at some ungodly hour this morning," Kathleen's voice sounded stronger. "I enjoy his visits, but doesn't he understand how early it is?"

Beth pointed at the large trunk next to the Queen Anne sofa and raised a brow.

"One of my trunks from Chicago arrived. I'll go through it later."

"Then the other trunks are on their way. Aren't you excited?" Her aunt's face even held a touch of color. Relief flooded over Beth.

"I'm not much for excavating museums." Kathleen eyed her trunk. "We should go to Grady's for lunch."

"How do you know about these places?" Beth pulled out her car keys and, on the way, delighted Kathleen with the previous night's adventure at the Suds and Under.

"Dear, that's Grady's over there." Kathleen pointed. "You didn't put mascara on your bottom lashes today. Good. It weighs them down."

And nothing was wrong with her aunt's mind, either.

She drove Kathleen up to the door, found a place to park, and walked back. When she arrived, Kathleen, already seated, was carrying on an animated conversation with the silver-haired maître d'.

He pulled out Beth's chair.

"If you'll excuse me, Ms. McPherson, I need to check on a gathering in our garden room. Let me know if there's anything I might do to make your luncheon more enjoyable." He left.

"Making a date?" Beth tucked her lips together and picked up her menu.

"I couldn't find my lighter, so he brought me matches. You don't mind sitting back here, do you? One never has to wait for a table in the smoking section." Kathleen set her menu aside. "What do you think you'll have?"

"Probably a salad." If Kathleen stopped smoking she'd get more oxygen in her blood, then the cancer . . .

"God, you're not one of those. Have a filet mignon with me and a glass of Pinot Noir." Kathleen wiggled a finger at the busboy. "Tell our waiter we're ready to order." Of course she did the ordering, and of course she ordered the filets. "Now, tell me more about your mystery."

Even if Beth could do the impossible, get Kathleen to quit smoking, it was too late now. Did Kathleen know she knew? Did Kathleen even know?

Beth started with Hugh's various connections to Puerto Rico and Guatemala.

Kathleen watched as the waiter poured a little wine in her glass. She sipped and nodded approval.

"Did your boss know about those trips Hugh took?"

"His secretary approves all the leaves." Beth shrugged. "She wouldn't care where the staff vacations."

"What if Hugh and your boss are together in this conspiracy?"

"Orin does neglect the physical plant, as if he doesn't care."

"Could he be planning to move on?" Kathleen paused, then said, "Perhaps their dead-of-the-night activities are more profitable."

"But then, why was he tracking the researchers' successes?" The wine felt warm on the back of Beth's tongue. Her internal temperature spiked when she thought of how tight Orin's relationship was with Hugh—his top producer.

"I don't like your boss—that money-over-quality thing."

Yet Orin approved Beth's primate-enhancement project, lectured them to guard against corporate espionage, and voiced concern about her computer data being corrupted.

"How many times have you heard, 'follow the money'?" Kathleen raised her eyebrows.

"I never thought Orin would put finances over necessities." Beth needed to stuff her doubt. "Orin's always showed compassion. That tracking business must be a directive from higher up."

"It's all smoke and mirrors anyway." Kathleen stubbed out her cigarette.

"Excuse me?"

"Things are never as they seem, dear," she said. "It's a basic principal of life. Most people don't understand and are blindsided by the simplest matters."

The waiter brought their food, filled their glasses, and disappeared back to wherever waiters go. Kathleen cut into her filet, took a tiny bite, and pronounced it delicious.

Things are never as they seem?

"When I was nine," Beth said, "I found part of a torn note written by my mother."

"Part? Must not have mattered much." Kathleen coughed a couple of times.

"I found it in an old armchair up in our attic. I used to look for coins in crevices under cushions. The note was to you."

"How do you know?"

"Because it started out, *My dearest sister.*"

Kathleen's steak was virtually untouched.

"Then it went on, word for word: *Father said never put anything private in writing, but what I'm about to ask you is most confidential.*"

She studied her aunt's face. No reaction.

"Excellent wine, don't you think?" Kathleen held up her glass.

"What was that note about?"

"You should have asked my sister."

"You're telling me you don't know?"

"If she tore it up, it wasn't important. And if she decided not to send it, then how could I know? Why do you cling to such trivia?"

"It *was* important." Beth put her fork down. "When I showed her that note, she had a fit. You know my mother—she never raised her voice. She tore that paper into a billion bits, threw it in the trash, and gave me a lecture about minding my own business."

"Such a long time ago . . . Memories have a tendency to—"

"I remember the words exactly." Beth rested her wrists on the table's edge. "*Don't put anything private in writing.* I think about that every time I write something."

Was she being too forceful? But, with Kathleen's health, if she didn't get some answers now . . .

"For Christ's sake, Chicago's miles from Louviers. I don't know what your parents did or didn't do."

Kathleen coughed hard for a few minutes. Beth handed her some tissues.

"What does Louviers have to do with this?"

"You said you found the note when you lived in Louviers."

"I was two years old when we moved to Valley View from Louviers. " She flushed. "I couldn't even read."

"Isn't this the perfect filet?" Kathleen prodded it with her fork.

"You know, Kathleen, most families look out for each other, keep in touch. Why didn't you?"

"Dear." She examined the women at the next table and exhaled. "Sometimes we think we want to know the truth, but we don't. Like the day your grandfather decided to go to a Chinese restaurant where I was having lunch."

Beth knew she'd not get her answer.

"The owner came over to me and said that my father had reserved a table and would be there in seconds. He suggested I leave by the back door."

"Why?"

"I was sixteen and having lunch with Father's best friend." She gave Beth her over-the-shoulder look. "Learn to leave things alone, dear. You don't want to ruin your feel-good notions about our family."

The waiter refilled Kathleen's wine glass and looked at Beth. She shook her head.

"You've barely touched it," Kathleen said.

"I'm driving."

"Nonsense, one glass won't hurt. We'll walk around and do some shopping—that'll give it time to wear off."

"Do you feel well enough?"

"There you go again." She flipped her fingers up. "We're meeting Harold at my place this evening. He's bringing dinner."

Beth's stomach tightened. The three of them needed her storytelling evening ritual.

Kathleen reached in her purse and pulled out her cigarettes along with her silver lighter. Her eyes met Beth's.

"My, it must have been in my purse the whole time." She shrugged. "I've been thinking, your outfit needs jewelry. Someone dear to me gave me a Peruvian silver and amethyst choker. It's rather chunky—absolutely perfect for you because you're tall." She lit her cigarette. "Hell, I'll never wear it again."

I haven't failed. I've found 10,000 ways that don't work.

—THOMAS EDISON

34

When Harold arrived he made cuba libres.

"Did I ever tell you about the time Sophie disappeared?"

"Did she disappear twice?" Beth put some kalamata olives in a dish and set out a few other snacks.

"I received a cryptic note that looked like an SOS. from Sophie." Kathleen seemed shaky when she went to the chair and sat. "Brandy and I weren't sure. It was after midnight. We took a cab to the Metropolitan Hotel and paid the cabbie double to wait for us at the side door."

"Your best friend goes missing." Harold studied the ceiling. "You don't know who sent this note." He stared at her. "Then you and a friend run off to some hotel at night in a city rife with violence?"

Beth cut Harold a *tread-easy* look.

He added, "Sounds exciting."

"You would have loved it." Kathleen's eyes sparkled. "We didn't know the person, and we didn't even have a plan. I went to the night clerk and asked if there was a message for Mr. Johnson. I'd made up the name, so of course there wasn't. I told the clerk to buzz us when the message came in. Brandy and I sauntered to the elevators and punched in the floor above the one the note had said."

"Why the floor above?" Beth sat forward.

"Because they thrived on taking risks." Harold took an olive.

"My dear boy, if you keep your life risk free, then it isn't much of a life."

"Got it," Beth said, "the next floor gave you time to plan." Beth shot Harold an evil-teacher look.

"We discovered a laundry room on that floor." Kathleen fingered her silver necklace." I found a maid's uniform in the laundry hamper. Couldn't do anything about my purple-and-green dance heels though. And Brandy actually lifted the master key off the maid's cart."

Kathleen paused.

"Can I get you something?" Beth asked. Her aunt's face now had no color.

"Seymour was in charge of watching Sophie." Kathleen leaned toward Harold. "Seymour—a big brute. Can you believe *Seymour* for a gangster's name?"

A violent coughing spell interrupted the story. Beth was sure her aunt would choke from lack of air. She looked at Harold. He stood—he didn't know what to do either.

She took a box of tissues to Kathleen and knelt down beside her. Saucy watched.

When she stopped coughing, Kathleen wiped her mouth, then took another tissue and wiped her eyes.

"We told him the big boss up in the penthouse wanted to see him." Kathleen paused to breath. "He left like his ass was on fire. It only took us seconds to snatch Sophie and cart her down to the cab. Excuse me for a moment."

She left the room. Beth gripped Harold's hand. A minute later Kathleen called out.

"Beth, dear. I have a problem. Would you please come?"

Kathleen leaned on the bathroom wall, trembling. When Beth put her arm around her to guide her to the bed, she glanced down at the toilet. The bowl was full of blood.

"Harold?" Beth kept her voice strong. "Dial 9-1-1. We need an ambulance."

～

In the emergency room, the doctor said Kathleen's bladder surgery should have stopped the bleeding. Since it hadn't, they'd keep her in the hospital until it was under control.

By Sunday afternoon, some pink had returned to Kathleen's cheeks. Beth handed her a box of chocolates.

Kathleen picked at the cellophane. Beth took it, removed the outer wrap, and handed the box of candy back to Kathleen. Beth sank onto the ugly brown chair. It sighed.

Kathleen picked out a dark oval chocolate. She bit into it and showed Beth.

When Beth was a young girl everyone wanted the chocolate-covered chocolate cream. Kathleen held out the box. Beth shook her head.

"Kathleen, why did my mother and my grandparents act as if you didn't exist? Why didn't we get to know you before Mother died?"

Kathleen looked away and stared at the IV drip.

"Harold says they were embarrassed because you were an entertainer."

"That's much ado about nothing."

"Jeez," Beth threw her hands up.

Her aunt glared at her.

"Shakespeare quotes." Beth shook her head. "Grandfather, after several martinis, loved to quote Shakespeare."

"I watched the same performance growing up." Kathleen nibbled for a moment. "He had a marvelous memory." She wiped her fingers on a tissue, then picked up the box of candy and studied the contents again. She pushed her thumb through the bottom of one, put it back, selected another, and repeated the thumb trick.

Beth remembered seeing her grandmother do the same thing. As a girl, Beth always checked the bottoms. She wasn't about to eat a chocolate punctured by someone's thumb.

"Something disturbing happened Friday night at the Suds and Under. I didn't tell Harold."

Kathleen set the box down.

"I asked Hugh lots of questions. He surprised me by answering truthfully. I wonder why."

"You know better than anyone else. Partial truths hide secrets."

"He kept me imprisoned in that booth." Beth's face burned. "Wouldn't let me out."

Kathleen's piercing look stole Beth's evasiveness.

"Hugh blamed me." Beth sighed. "Said I'd be the reason for his lab tech getting fired."

Kathleen flicked her hand. How did Kathleen know there was more?

"Okay. He threatened me." Beth breathed the words.

Kathleen studied her.

"He said I was in over my head, that I should remember the institute's a big place, and he inferred that someone was watching me." Her words made her edgy.

"Is Hugh dangerous?"

"He's a braggart, full of hot air. Probably not dangerous." Beth reached over and held Kathleen's hand. "But your story last night about Seymour—you minimized the danger, didn't you?"

"You need to take his threats seriously." Kathleen squeezed Beth's hand, then passed her the candy box.

Beth picked a dark chocolate. The sickening sweetness of artificial peach flooded her mouth.

"Dear, I didn't know you liked those fruit ones. Go ahead, have them all."

Beth giggled. "I still don't understand why the family didn't keep in touch with you."

"Who knows?"

"Why is it you can ask me questions, but when I ask, you won't answer me?"

Kathleen found a dark-chocolate caramel and waved it under Beth's nose. Then she put the caramel back.

Beth could see her as a girl, teasing her younger sister.

"This will help." Kathleen smoothed her blanket. "Do you remember going through your grandparents' photo albums?"

"They had photo albums?"

"Once, but they took all the photos out of the albums and kept them in a box."

"I found that box and looked through it," Beth said. "But I didn't see pictures of you, and I only saw a few of my mother."

"And why do you think that was?"

"Now you're asking me my own question."

"What did you see when they were mad?"

"Good grief." Beth stared at the ceiling, shaking her head. "It was a comedy show. Once, when my grandfather argued with my grandmother and their quarrel escalated, he announced he was leaving her. He stomped off to their bedroom and packed his leather suitcase. I was horrified—then he came down the stairs without missing a beat and said to Grandmother, 'Dear, would you please be so kind as to call me a cab?'"

Kathleen nodded in slow motion.

"Then you can picture them alone," her words were soft, "in their matching wingback chairs in front of the hearth. Each takes a photo from an album and evaluates if it should be put in the box or in the fire."

"They burned our history?" Beth couldn't believe it. But why else would there be no pictures of her aunt? "They were furious at you for running away, weren't they?"

"Sums their personalities up rather well."

"What did my mother do that made them angry?"

"Can't help you there."

They both watched each other.

Kathleen knew. And Beth knew that Kathleen knew she knew.

Chi Mak admitted that he was sent to the United States in 1978 in order to obtain employment in the defense industry with the goal of stealing US defense secrets, which he did for over 20 years.

—FBI, MAY 2011

35

A substitute receptionist stood at Nancy's desk. Beth introduced herself. The receptionist said that she didn't know why Nancy was out, and she gave Beth her messages.

"Please find out why Ms. Sterling is absent, and may I borrow a pen? If you receive a call from the hospital, or from either my husband or my aunt, be sure I'm notified." Beth wrote Kathleen's and Harold's names on the paper and gave the receptionist a brief explanation of why this was important.

Beth went to her office and called Orin's secretary for an appointment. She heard pages flipping.

"You can see him before he leaves." Yvonne sounded harried. "Wait five minutes."

"Yvonne, Orin's lucky to have you as his secretary. You're quite professional in protecting his schedule."

Beth should have told Yvonne this years ago. She studied her messages. Gordy marked his priority—with red ink. She pushed in his number.

"I have unbelievable news," he said. "Come over tonight."

"About your most excellent Galapagos adventure?"

"It is." His words were packed full of emotion. "I need to see you in person. If I wasn't trapped here at DU, I'd be in your office right now."

"Fair enough, but you'll have to tell me over the phone. My aunt's sick."

She waited. No response.

"Okay," she said. "I have a question for you. What do you know about Hugh?"

"He's an okay guy. Why?"

"What do you mean by okay?"

"First Borstell, now Hugh?" Gordy's tone carried a sharp edge.

"I have my reasons. Indulge me."

"Hugh's had his problems, but he's got his act together now. Listen, I have to see you—"

"Exactly what type of problems did he have?" Beth held her breath.

"I don't know, a two-bit run-in with the law when he was a teen. I get the sense you're upset with me."

"Did you know him before he came to the institute?"

"He was hired right out of college from the Midwest somewhere."

Midwest? Roberto Sheering went to a pharmaceutical college in upper Michigan before he started those disreputable companies in Puerto Rico and Guatemala. She pulled her lips in. Joe would give her his evil eye. The Midwest was a broad generalization.

"Beth, listen. I need your help with something." Gordy sounded exasperated.

"How's your DU project?" If he'd finished, he'd be starting on hers. But given what she read about the Barcelona convention, it was probably too late.

"I should have it wrapped up by late this afternoon. I think the project turned out well."

She waited.

"Here's the deal," he said. "I received a letter with some forms. They want me to come to the islands as soon as I can—a temporary position until they sort out the paper work for the permanent position. I'll shut things down here and be gone by the beginning of next week, but I have to get this paper work turned in."

Did she hear this right?

"Gordy, what about my research?"

"I've got it covered."

"How can you go to the islands and still do justice to my study?"

"I had a beer with Hugh on Friday after work. He said he'd be happy to take it on if Orin approves."

A beer. Friday night. Hugh. She stared at the receiver for a moment, speechless, then hung up.

When her roiling brain settled down, Beth called the hospital and asked them to let her aunt know she'd stop by later that afternoon. She hurried to Orin's office and started to sit in one of the two straight-back reception chairs, but Yvonne held up a finger for her to stop. She opened Orin's door and announced Beth's presence. He stood by his desk gathering papers, putting them into his briefcase.

"I appreciate your meeting with me—"

"I studied the note you sent this last weekend. Quite distressing." He snapped his briefcase shut. "I've told Yvonne to schedule you for a longer session."

"Have you talked with Dr. Gordon about my research?"

"Look, Beth, I'm rather busy right now." He walked her back into Yvonne's area. "Yvonne, please call Frank and tell him I'm ready to go to the finance meeting. I'll meet him at the car."

"Gordy's not available to do my research." Beth struggled to keep her voice down. "Even though it's probably too late anyway."

He stopped and turned back toward Beth. "Yvonne, fit her in as soon as you can." Beth watched him leave and fought the bitter taste rising in her mouth.

Yvonne checked her calendar. Orin would be out all day. Even though they agreed on a time tomorrow morning, Beth's internal molecules were now jumping beans. She couldn't concentrate. She needed to do something physical. She rushed out to Building D to do a visual check on her construction.

Soon they would assemble the corncribs and weld them into place. Then the macaques could play in their new home. Her heart sang.

Jarrod came out of Building B and admired the progress with her.

"How's your beagle study going, Jarrod?" Being outside, watching this construction, calmed her.

"Doing great."

"When are your final trials scheduled?" She heard heavy earth-moving equipment somewhere nearby.

"A couple more weeks."

"Always an exciting time, right?" This information felt important . . . like she should do something with it. She headed back to the main building.

Back in her office, Beth sorted through envelopes. She opened a dark brown one. Finally, she read the lab report on Wayne's milkshake. She'd been right—the residue in the cup did contain traces of ketamine.

So much for Hugh being a suspect. She mentally crossed him off her list because he wouldn't have a need for ketamine. He hadn't been doing live-animal research for months.

She turned on her computer. Or *did* Hugh have a need? She held her breath and scrolled through for Hugh's identification number. She found it and opened the controlled-substance requisition request. There—the previous month he'd ordered enough ketamine to knock out an elephant. Security at the city dump was tighter than security in this place. Controlled substances should never be requisitioned to researchers who weren't using live animals. She printed the requisition, along with a copy of his current non-animal study. She put the copies in an envelope, wrote Orin's name on it, and put the envelope in her middle desk drawer. She did the same with the call-to-convention article on the MS research. She locked her door and stepped out into the atrium.

She spotted Wayne plopping his mop in a bucket of water, wringing it out, and then swishing it around the reception counter.

"Wayne, have you seen Hugh Wendenski this afternoon?"

"Naw, he's not here much during the day anymore." He continued pushing the mop.

During the day?

"Ms. Armstrong," the receptionist said, "I'm told Ms. Sterling's with her family. . . . A celebration for her son."

"Great news." Beth grinned. "Now I need to see the sign-out book." Hugh had logged himself out for the next three days, for some conference at the Hyatt. She'd check on this.

Wayne's efforts to keep the floor shining now took him over in front of the elevator. Beth went over to him, careful not to step on the wet surface.

"Wayne, please let me into Hugh Wendenski's lab."

His puzzled look broadcast his internal conflict. He liked her, but he had rules to follow. She'd have to help him over this job-imposed boundary of not letting people have access to areas where they shouldn't be.

"I wouldn't ask you to do this, but if he's not going to be back for three more days I can't wait. Hugh borrowed a Minimitter biotransmitter from me, and I have to have it this afternoon. It's quite small." She pinched her fingers close together. "I'll probably have to look for it."

She hated lying. Wayne wouldn't know anything about these devices, which were implanted in mice. She gave him her wide-eyed look. Inside she sang a self-congratulatory song because Minimitter biotransmitter sounded so important, so official, so scientific—and best of all, he probably wouldn't remember the words.

"Sure thing." He plopped the mop into his bucket.

"Is Hugh only here at nights now?" She hurried up the stairs.

"Mostly." Wayne kept right beside her.

"Tell me, does he come in at other times?" Two flights of stairs, good for the knees.

"Around eight-thirty at night for an hour or so."

"He's attending a conference during the day. Is that why he's only here at night?"

"Don't know. He doesn't say much, just carries boxes and stuff out."

"Boxes?" She stopped him. "For the conference? Is he presenting?"

"Don't know. Do you want me to unlock his outside office door or just the lab door?"

"The lab, please."

"Want me to wait?"

"If you want. I'll need to take a minute or two to find it." Wayne hated to wait.

"Then I'd like to finish that floor." He searched through his ring of keys.

"I'll let you know when I'm through. You can dash back and lock up." She patted his arm. He unlocked the door then darted down the hall.

As soon as she stepped into the lab, her stomach started to cramp. She hated being the intruder. The slatted blinds were closed, letting in cardboard-colored sunlight.

Who's there? She whirled around and peered out the doorway to check. A white-coated researcher at the end of the hall turned a corner. *Damn.* Harold's overprotectiveness, and now Hugh's bullying—she shook it off and filled her mind with a soft Mozart concerto.

She knew which cupboard contained the controlled substances—the locked one.

Wayne wouldn't have this key. She stood on tiptoe and felt around on top of the cabinets. Beth pulled a chair over and stood on it—only dust. She opened the doors under the sink—nothing but cleaning supplies. Beth exhaled, then looked up under the sink. Nothing. Was it in his office?

She peeked out the door and checked the hallway again. Still empty. The ensemble in her head silenced. She listened. Only her heart thudded. She remembered the day he gave her the coqui frog pin. Everyone thought of him as kind, altruistic. But his threats of corridors and storage places—should she believe he was dangerous?

Beth hurried through the lab and went straight to the lab's adjoining office door. Maybe, just maybe, he left that key in his desk drawer. She turned the handle. No one ever locked these interior doors. The only light came from the lab behind her. She didn't want to turn on the overhead light. She waited until her eyes adjusted.

Good grief. Cold stabbed through her middle. What was he up to? His bookcase now stood empty, but the rest of his once-tidy office was a mess with boxes and papers scattered about. She shivered and backed away. No one here even knew this man.

She scurried down each of the two stairways, told Wayne he could now lock up, then rushed into her office. She had to do something. *What?*

Who could explain Hugh's behavior? His threats? His outburst of anger about the kennels? What was that about? She bet he hadn't ordered any beagles. Was that to delay or stop her projects? Gordy labeled him as *okay*. But Hugh either planned on clearing out of here, or his office had been ransacked by someone. Someone ransacking wouldn't steal all the books out of the bookcases. There wasn't any other explanation for the room being in such a sorry state.

That bastard probably had flight tickets to Guatemala burning a hole in his briefcase right now, that is if he hadn't already left. She couldn't let him get away with this.

If Hugh hadn't flown off yet, she'd stop him. How? What was important to him? If she knew, she could find a way. What drove him? She seethed. He'd killed her mice, making sure she wouldn't have time to recreate her experiment. Then he'd stolen her research model. Why? For money? Then there was Joe's opossum project and that Puerto Rico lab. And the other night, he had to be the one who took the logs from Joe's current project. And what he did to Wayne—drugging him. Hugh could snoop anywhere. No one would know. *What a greedy, unethical bastard.*

Hugh said he might cancel his beagle research. What a liar. He didn't care about anything here at the institute except stealing proprietary information and selling it. She remembered Jarrod's glowing face when they talked about his beagles. Now here was someone who cared.

She held her breath for a moment, then grinned and picked up her phone. She pressed in Joe's office number.

"Joe, please get Rick. Find something for him do with you in the macaque lab and make it urgent—and convincing. I'll be there in fifteen minutes."

Joe and Rick were fully suited up, wearing heavy gloves, by the time Beth arrived. Rick restrained a young macaque and smooth-talked it while Joe took its temperature.

Beth grabbed a face mask, put on the rest of the protective clothing, and opened the door.

"Hi, is one of our charges sick?"

"She's been lethargic," Joe said. "We're being cautious."

"Good idea. Did you hear the news?"

"Thanks, Rick." Joe read the thermometer and wrote down the results.

"No problem, man." He picked up the macaque. "Anything else you need me for? I got to hurry—take care of the goats."

"We're fine here." Joe glanced at Beth.

Joe pulled out the treat sack and handed it to Rick. Rick gave one to the macaque.

"So what's the news?" Joe cleaned off the examining table.

Rick headed back to the cages in the next room.

"Jarrod's log sheets for his beagles in Building B." She watched Rick take his time putting the macaque back in its cage. "You should run out to his kennel and see."

Rick fussed unnecessarily with the padlock on the cage.

"Get him to show you their blood draws for this week. You'll be surprised."

Rick clicked the lock shut and loped out of the room. Joe played his part well. He had given her what she needed.

Michael Mitchell became disgruntled and was fired from his job
due to poor performance. . . . He entered into a consulting
agreement with a rival Korean company and gave them the stolen
trade secrets.

—FBI, MAY 2011

36

"What's going on here, Beth?" Joe's voice came
from some deep, caring place.

Beth couldn't dismiss this good friend's concern by telling him some
near truths. But if she told him all she planned, he'd interfere. He'd boggle
it all. She would prove Hugh's guilt—that is, if he hadn't flown off somewhere. But Joe, like Harold, couldn't get it through his brain that she could
take care of herself. Joe stood there in his disposable lab clothing and studied her face, waiting.

She pointed toward the hall. He asked her to give him a few minutes
while he finished cleaning up. She went out, removed the paper coat and
coverings, tossed them in the bin, and then waited in the hall by his office,
watching other researchers coming and going.

After Joe locked the lab and trashed his outerwear he unlocked his
office door, motioning for her to take her usual chair. Instead, she went to
the window and back, then paced over to the window again and stood
looking out. Two researchers with heads bent toward each other in consul-
tation ambled toward the doors leading to the atrium. Across the courtyard, at the edge of the golden weed and dirt field, she could see the corner
of Kennel Building A. She caught a glimpse of a figure with lanky legs

carrying a bucket. Rick loped along past that kennel and disappeared from view. He was headed toward the goat pens. Twenty minutes ago, he'd told Joe he was in a hurry. What had delayed him?

She smirked. Rick must have spent a wee bit of time on his portable little phone talking to his master. *So Hugh's flight hadn't flown yet.*

"Beth?"

"I know Hugh's the one, and I'm going to prove it." She slipped back into the chair, working to keep her anxieties from Joe.

Joe threw his hands up and rolled his eyes.

"What's with all the eye rolling?" She'd seen too much eye rolling from everyone since her mice died. Her internal furnace stoked up an ill mood.

"Guess it is rude." Joe waited. When she didn't say anything, he said, "What's this game playing? There's nothing happening with Jarrod's beagles, right?"

"Why do you say that?" She glanced back toward the window, but from where she sat she couldn't see anything.

"You wanted to set Rick up. Too contrived to be true."

She ran her thumb back and forth along the edge of the chair arm.

"But Rick believed, didn't he?" She turned her eyes to him.

"He did. At least he seemed to."

"Joe, you said your logs were taken between the time when you left the institute and before you returned later that evening." She wanted to look out the windows, again, but not for any particular reason. Rick wouldn't have had enough time to feed and water the goats. He'd still be in their pens.

"What's so interesting out there?" Joe followed her gaze to the window. He turned back to her.

She shook her head, shifted in her chair, and continued talking.

"You don't usually come back after you leave for the day. Whoever took your logs figured that if they returned them before you showed up for work the next morning, you wouldn't know." She needed to pick her words carefully. She couldn't have him worried about her and give him an opportunity to interfere.

"Makes sense." He waited.

"Rick tells Hugh everything he knows. He even told Hugh about my questioning him. If Hugh took your log and replaced it, then how many others has he taken? If he thinks Jarrod's logs will show something statistically significant, he'll be desperate to get his hands on them."

"Hold it, Beth. You've seen Hugh's irrational temper." He started to stand.

"Oh, get off it. I'm not going to do anything risky." She settled back nonchalantly. "Before I go home tonight, I'm placing a small piece of double-sided sticky tape to the back of the clipboard holding the beagles' log sheets. When I hang it back on the nail, I'll press it against the wooden doorframe until it sticks. I'll come back around six tomorrow morning, before Jarrod signs in, to see if the clipboard is stuck to the wood or if it's hanging loose."

"That doesn't prove anything."

"Circumstantial. Rick, you, and I are the only ones who know about Jarrod's log sheets. If someone messes with them tonight, it's either us or Rick or Hugh."

She gave him a nod, then she walked back to the atrium with a sweet little clarinet ensemble playing in her head. She swiveled around at the sound of footsteps running up behind her. It was Wayne. Jeez, talk about jumpy.

"Wanted to tell you . . ." He stopped to catch his breath. "Mr. Wendenski came in right after you went over to the macaque lab. I told him he'd missed you, but not to worry because you got that thing you needed from his office. He wants to talk to you about that thing of yours he borrowed."

"You're very considerate, Wayne, but I don't have time right now. Is he still here?" Beth's heart thudded, climbing high up in her throat. *Dammit.*

"Don't know. I've been doing some things for Ms. Shaw. She asked me to look for Rick."

"He was out in the goat-pen area." Beth continued on to the atrium. Wayne strode beside her. If Hugh knew she'd been in his office, would it mess up her plans? He'd be furious.

"Naw, I searched and he's not. Rick's supposed to feed and water those goats."

"I'm sure they're fed by now. He was running late." She was running late too. She had a quarterly report due this afternoon, but her stomach told her to get some lunch.

Beth unlocked her office, pulled a few bills out of her purse, and dashed to the cafeteria. The salads contained little nutritional value with their iceberg lettuce. She selected blueberry yogurt and grabbed a napkin and a plastic spoon.

Wayne appeared at her elbow as she paid for it. He was out of breath, again.

"Ms. Armstrong, you're wanted on the phone. Ms. Sterling's substitute says it's an emergency, but she said for me to be sure and tell you that it doesn't have anything to do with your aunt."

"You're certainly running all over today for everyone, Wayne. Thanks."

"Don't mind. But if you need me, I'm on the third floor washing windows." He sprinted off.

When Beth got to the atrium, the substitute receptionist waved her over.

"Ms. Armstrong, a Mr. Smithy called twice and said it's an emergency. And earlier Hugh Wendenski was looking for you. I told him you were with Mr. Hammer. He's gone now."

"I don't know anyone named Smithy." Beth took the note and went back into her office. She decided to lock her door.

She dialed the number. After three rings she heard a recorded voice.

"Smithy here, but I'm not here now. Tell me your problem at the beep and how to reach you. I'll get on it as soon as I can."

Good grief. She hung up. What was that about?

Beth opened her yogurt, enjoyed the cool sweetness of several bites, then decided to try the number one more time. Again, only the answering machine picked up. She booted up her computer, pulled some handwritten notes out of a drawer, and waited for her log-in screen. A few minutes later the quarterly report began taking shape, causing Beth to forget about the remaining yogurt. The phone rang, startling her.

"Ms. Armstrong, this is Smithy. We've got a big mess here and you need to come over right away."

"Smithy, I don't think I know you. What do you do, and where do you work?"

"I'm head of large-equipment maintenance. My office building's at the rear of that main building across from the kennels. Listen, those contraptions you ordered, everything's all messed up."

"What contraptions?"

"You know, those metal things out by the back of Building B."

"Why would they be a problem?" She finished her yogurt. And how could this be any type of an emergency? Some people thrived on drama.

"The backhoe guy's been here all weekend digging, but now your stuff is messing everything up. They're planning to pour the cement for the floor, but we've got to get your corncribs out of the way. Would you please come out here and tell us what to do with them?"

"Smithy, if that stack is in the way, move it. Okay?" She tossed the yogurt container into her wastebasket.

"I think you need to get over here."

"I have a report due. Why can't you handle it?"

"Dang it all to heck—what'll I do now?" He let out a huge breath of air.

"Give me five. I'll be there." She couldn't imagine why this was a problem for a grown man who seemed to be adept at dealing with big equipment. She saved her work, turned off her computer, locked the office, and told the receptionist where she'd be.

Beth strode out to the kennels. When she reached them, she headed around to the rear. Holy cow, there was an excavated area, a basement, in the expansive area between the kennels and the back fence. She looked where her corncrib panels were stacked, but one of the institute's white trucks blocked her view. Not far away stood some large earth-moving equipment where several crows busied themselves. They waddled and cawed in the weeds, fluttering up, then back down. She didn't see anyone, but she could hear men talking.

The crows flew out of the weeds when she walked toward the white truck. A few seconds later, they settled back into their previous routine. Three men, all arguing, were squatted behind the institute's vehicle next to one of her corncrib panels.

"I'm Ms. Armstrong. What's the matter here?"

"We've been at war with this metal stuff of yours for over an hour now." They stood. The one in coveralls brushed dust off his knees and shoulders while he spoke.

The panels had been neatly stacked, but this afternoon they tilted in different directions. One of them, several yards away from the building, held fast under the wheel of this truck.

"I'm Smithy." This came from the coverall guy. The other two men wore slacks and button-down shirts streaked with their share of dirt. "The rear bumper snagged this thing here." Smithy pointed. "Then it pulled some of those other ones out with it, too."

Straps and wires, now a mess of spaghetti, loosely connected the whole group of panels.

"Afraid we're damaging your stuff." Smithy rubbed his arm. "That's why we need you here."

"Why drive the truck that close to the building in the first place?" She searched their faces.

"This panel wasn't up with the others. Must have slid down and off," the balding, button-down-shirt man said.

"We've been coming back and forth for several days, no problems." The slimmer one pointed to the stack. "But when we got here this afternoon, we didn't notice this one was away from the others. My fault—I backed right into it."

She couldn't figure out why the stack of panels would slide out, anywhere. They seemed so solid and secure when the co-op men stacked them.

"Like he said," the balding guy spoke, "we'd been in and out all weekend. Wanted to be sure the earthwork went according to the specs—the final inspection of the excavation is this afternoon. The cement crew starts their work tomorrow."

"I drove the truck in around that bulldozer and backhoe over there," the other one said, "and we got out and did our inspection. We climbed back in, and we were talking. I backed the truck up like I've been doing all weekend. But once I climbed in the truck I couldn't see the panel. I wasn't expecting anything to be over here."

"Smithy, what's the real problem here? Why not put it back with the others?"

"Aw, it's a total mess. Come see." He knelt in the dirt and pointed up under the truck.

She did as he did, not happy at having to kneel in the dust. She still couldn't see underneath. She sighed, went ahead and put her shoulder down on the ground, and stared up at the underbelly of the vehicle.

One of the steel straps to keep the panels secure in transport had snagged up under the wheel of the truck. Something had punctured the tire. Wire and straps were wrapped tightly around the axle. Ancillary pieces used for assembling the corncribs were caught up in the jumble, too. There were galvanized mesh straps, floor clips, lots of torn paper, and a useless door latch. Some of this twisted chaos would have to be cut away and trashed. She groaned.

"Smithy and the two of us tried to untangle all of this without doing damage," the driver said, "but it's a lost cause."

"Still have to fix that flat, too." The balding man looked at his watch.

"I've got calls to return, work stacking up all over," Smithy said.

She caught their frustration. Who knew anyone would even be back here? And who knew the board would actually fund the IT building so soon?

She slapped her dusty hands together, then she swiped off dirt and vegetation clinging to her suit.

The three men returned to the former argument about how to deal with the situation. They seemed to be rehashing and rejecting what they'd already tried.

"This is what I suggest," Beth interrupted them. They stopped and stared at her. Apparently they weren't going to object to a fresh opinion. Her face grew hot. They must be desperate if they thought she knew more about this than they did.

"All that wire and metal strapping used for packing can be snipped and disposed of. I hope you can save those galvanized mesh straps. But if you can't, cut them too. Then move this whole thing back against the building on top of those others."

Orin would never fund replacement parts. She walked over and counted each panel—one other was bent, but that wasn't a huge problem. Parts of hardware were scattered all around in the dirt. The pieces were probably packed with the panel now hanging from the back of the truck.

"We'll rig something to replace whatever is ruined." She didn't know if there was truth in what she said or not. "Go ahead and do whatever you must. I'll live with it."

She started picking up floor clips and the other small objects hidden in the dirt while she composed a plea to Orin for replacement parts. Orin wouldn't be pleasant about the cost of a new tire, either.

She spied something. What? A gray, metal box? The end of it stuck out from under one of the skewed panels. She went closer and stared for a moment, but her mind resisted identifying it. Her heart thumped hard. She didn't want it to be what she thought it was. *Rick's cell phone?*

"Smithy." Her heart raced. Was Rick still missing? She'd check with Wayne.

He came trotting over. Did she have it all wrong? Joe claimed she jumped to conclusions too easily.

"Is this yours or one of the men's?"

"My phone's racking up messages in that office over there, and those guys haven't been over here." He held it and turned it over, studying it.

"I think this belongs to one of our techs. Did you see him back here?"

"Haven't seen anyone but these two guys." He gave it back to her. "How well do these work? Maybe I should get one."

"I believe he came through here not too long ago, about noon." She didn't answer his question, because she didn't know anything about these phones.

It could belong to Gavin, the IT guy. Had he come to check on the new IT building and dropped it? She'd ask him. Or did someone else lose one? If they did, it'd be logical they'd check to see if someone had turned it in to Gavin's IT department. Or, when Rick headed to the goat pen, he might have taken this way. The heavy equipment noise might have lured him here.

When she had seen Rick from Joe's window she hadn't been able to tell which way he'd gone. Maybe he didn't stay on the sidewalk in front of the kennels as one might expect. Would he have another reason to be behind these kennels? No one could see him back here. If he wanted to make a confidential call to someone, like Hugh, this would be a perfect place. But by the time she'd seen him out Joe's window she suspected he'd already called Hugh. What else would have delayed his taking care of the goats? If he'd already phoned Hugh, then why would he need to go somewhere private, like back here?

Her head hurt from the noise growing inside. She couldn't sort this out. It wasn't her usual symphony in there; it was more of a deep vibration. This cell phone belonged to Rick. She felt sure of it. Rick had been back here. But Beth couldn't imagine anyone losing their cell phone any more than she could imagine a person misplacing a small brick. *So why don't I understand what it is I know?*

Footprints. She'd concentrate on tangible things. The recent activity here, including her hunt in the dirt for small parts, trashed any hope of seeing Rick's footprints. She wandered over to the truck.

"We've almost finished cutting, untangling, and clearing the axle," Smithy said. "Another fifteen minutes should do it. Then we'll fix that flat."

"Spinning your wheels over all my steroidal chicken-wire stuff has to make you a bit angry. Sorry."

"Frustrated, but I'm only mad at myself," the driver said.

"May I ask a favor?" She described what Rick looked like. "If he does comes back, tell him I have his phone."

The only source of knowledge is experience.

—ALBERT EINSTEIN

37

Beth entered Kathleen's room, and her breath caught. Earlier, her aunt's cheeks had been full of color. Now they looked ashen. Beth glanced at the box of chocolates—nearly empty.

"Guess you enjoyed the candy." She sat in the ugly chair to wait for the doctor.

"I love chocolate." Kathleen's voice came out flat. "But for some reason it made me nauseated."

"Me too, if I eat too much. Didn't you say the doctor comes about now?"

"You missed him." Kathleen shoved her magazine away.

"Are you going home?" She shouldn't have asked, considering Kathleen's appearance.

"The bleeding . . . they need to keep me longer. How's Saucy?"

"She misses you, but Harold keeps her entertained. What did the doctor say?"

"He said you have excellent taste in chocolates."

"Nothing like a piece of chocolate to turn a sour world sweet."

Her aunt sat straighter, pushed a lock of hair from her eyes, and waited.

"What?" Beth tilted her head.

"Child, if I'm to believe you need a piece of chocolate, I'd like to hear why?"

"It's only a general statement, Kathleen."

"You can tell that to the man on the street. To me, you tell the truth."

A dull ache entered Beth's heart. She couldn't burden Kathleen with her problems. Why couldn't she find something happy to tell her? She thought this over. Ha—anything pleasant wouldn't begin to hold Kathleen's attention. Kathleen thrived on excitement and problem solving. This woman was truly an adrenaline junkie.

"Then here's a mystery for you." Beth, too, sat straighter. "We'll call it the Cell Phone Mystery."

"Good God, what next? Don't tell me you have one of those things."

"No need for one, but I found one, and I'm guessing it belongs to a lab tech. No one knows where the tech is." Beth stared at the wilted flowers sitting on the nightstand. She should remove them.

"My dear, this sounds more like the Mystery of the Missing Lab Tech. And you thought a good deal of her. What do the police think happened?"

"The tech isn't the one from my lab. Teri's fine. This one helps my friend, Joe Hammer, with the macaques. He seems to have disappeared. Guess there are too many runaway teens to believe anything nefarious has happened to any of them. Unfortunately, today the police don't take disappearing teens seriously until a few days pass. Right now we're only talking a few hours."

"But you and others at the institute think he's missing, not a runaway?" Kathleen reached for her cigarettes, looked at the empty space where her hand fumbled for them, and then muttered, "Goddamned hospitals."

"That's another mystery. I found the cell phone, but I don't know why I would find it where I did." She decided she didn't have the energy to get up and toss the dead flowers away.

"If the lab tech didn't have a reason for being where the cell phone was, did someone steal it and leave it there?" Kathleen's cheeks now held a bit of rosiness.

"Could be. But I think the tech had a reason to go back there. He might have called someone or been waiting for a call. Can't imagine why he'd forget his phone or lose it." Until her corncribs were delivered, or the new building construction started, there wasn't any need to be back there. *And what were those crows fussing over?*

"Remember Ed, the reporter? One carefully timed phone call determined his success."

Beth settled back. Was she an adrenaline junkie too?

"Ed worked late, then he went across the street to the Tunnel. It was after midnight. He sat there at the bar enjoying his whatever when Junior-the-Slob came in complaining. You need to understand, Junior worked for Moran, and his job mandated that he increase the beer business. Seems the Tunnel didn't buy enough of his boss's beer. The bartender, Ed, and Junior were the only ones in the place when two of Capone's mobsters burst in, gunned Junior down, then left."

"Good grief." Knowing someone who knew someone who had witnessed a mob killing made it too real. "Was the Tunnel a tunnel in some basement?" Creepy. Beth didn't know much about Chicago.

"Chicago is built on top of tunnels, dear."

"And they used them as speakeasies?"

"Not usually. Ed turned out all the lights and locked the door. He didn't want anyone pushing the buzzer and saying the code words, 'Mike sent me.' Then Ed telephoned his newspaper's city desk and relayed all the gory details."

Kathleen's cheeks now brimmed with blush, and her voice held the excitement of the moment.

"Ed and the bartender sat there with the dead body way into the wee, early morning. Can you guess why?"

"Because the drinks were on the house, he didn't call the police?"

"He waited until after the oppositions' newspapers had gone to press. When it was too late for the final edition to be rewritten, only then did Ed phone the police."

"Your stories used to feel like—well, *stories*. Now they feel almost real and a bit scary." Beth loved when her aunt chuckled over these antics from her 1920s world. "How often were *you* in actual danger?"

"Remember, it's always in the timing, dear. Always."

The phone rang. They both stared at it. Kathleen picked it up, listened, then handed it to Beth.

"You've had some phone calls." Harold sounded huffy. "All are from that Gordy researcher. He's called every ten minutes, and he insists that he has to talk with you. Sounds like he's in a panic. What's up?"

"Don't know, but I'm headed home now." Dr. Gordon's option for dealing with *her* research certainly didn't panic him. She seethed at the thought of Hugh and Gordy discussing her protocol and then Hugh agreeing to take it over. *Bastards.*

The PCCIP [President's Commission on Critical Infrastructure Protection, 1997] consolidated all the information, statistics, and even vulnerabilities for anyone who wants to read about them.

—MAGNAN, CIA, APRIL 2007

38

Saucy yipped her greetings, and Harold announced he'd ordered pizza. Beth ought to do something thoughtful for him. She thanked him, then she rushed into their bedroom and put the contents of her purse into an oversized shoulder bag.

The phone rang. Harold answered, then called to her.

Gordy again.

"Beth, we were cut off earlier. Those forms, they need statements from scientists who've worked with me."

"We'll take care of it in the morning." She turned and looked at Harold. He watched her for a moment, then he went into the living room.

"But you have to fill them out tonight." Gordy sounded out of patience with her.

"I don't see why." She felt the same about him.

"Because they have to be in the mail tomorrow."

"Get them to me early, and you'll have them before noon."

Gordy certainly hadn't been in a hurry to complete her research. How did anyone live their life so last-minute?

"That won't work. Tomorrow I have to—"

"Gordy." She felt Harold close by. "I won't be seeing you tonight."

Harold stood in the doorway, watching.

"I'll talk to you tomorrow." She replaced the receiver and looked directly into Harold's eyes.

His face transformed into granite. He strode to his chair, picked up the evening edition of the paper, and turned to the financial section.

"What's wrong?" She sat on the arm of his chair.

"I'm not sure."

"Oh come on. You don't seriously think there's another man. You know better than that."

"Less tangible. This is more complicated." He didn't make eye contact.

She shoved the paper down, pushed her face in front of his, and stared. He didn't move.

"You've never had trouble explaining yourself." She touched the tip of his nose. "What's wrong?"

He shrugged, shook out the paper, and turned a page. She knew he wasn't reading.

"I do complicated, I do serious, and, as your wife, I do intangibles. Tell me."

"Until a few weeks ago, you never had anyone from the institute call you at home." He lowered the paper and looked at her. "Within this last month, Joe Hammer called, then Mr. Gordon, and Friday night you're at the Suds and Under with that Hugh guy's face in yours. He even gave you a piece of jewelry."

"Harold—"

He held up his hand. "You have good reasons for all of this, and it isn't about you being unfaithful. It's . . ."

"My work?" She moved to her chair and sat on the edge, facing him.

"Work?" He paused. "More about what's important to you, because some things sure don't seem to matter."

The doorbell rang. Beth grabbed Saucy by the collar.

Harold pulled out his wallet on his way to the door then carried the pizza into the kitchen.

"So much is happening right now. . . ." She needed to find the correct words for him, especially for tonight.

"Of course."

She caught his insincerity. If she could just tell him the truth about Jarrod's kennel log—but no. They'd have a hellacious fight over her safety.

Damn him. Shouldn't a marriage be a partnership? Shouldn't they be each other's helpmates? She went to the cupboard and took out plates.

"Here's something that's difficult to believe." She set the plates on the table. "Within the last few days the board not only approved a new building, but the ground work is well underway."

He opened the pizza box and removed a piece.

"They're building it out behind the kennels. It's the new IT and publication building. Someone said one whole floor will be devoted to printing. I can't believe that. Guess the production of publications such as science monographs, posters, company literature, and such will all be done in-house now." She grabbed two napkins, filled glasses with water, then joined him at the table.

"Thought you needed that promotion," he said, "because the board wouldn't put money into the institute for improvements."

"That's what baffles me." The pizza was hot and cheesy. She put a piece on her plate and used a finger to detach a string of the cheese from the box. "Orin certainly gives the impression that the institute's on an austerity kick. He worries about expenditures. What do you make of this?"

"Most companies are moving beyond dial-up Internet services. I don't know how you stand your job with such slow connections."

"Our IT guy did say he'd change my computer from dial-up to cable soon."

"There you have it." Harold put the last bite in his mouth, wiped his hands, and reached for another piece.

"Come on, that wouldn't require a huge new annex."

"This last February they passed the 1996 Telecom Act." Harold took a moment to finish chewing. "The FCC labeled Internet service for computers as 'information service.' Now computers are under totally different regulations from telephone services, leaving the computer field wide open. Seems your science institute isn't about to be left behind."

Beth opened her mouth, then, having nothing to add, she closed it. This man stored so much information in his brain. He knew about so many things. . . .

"Did you spend much time with Kathleen today?" He wiped his mouth with his napkin.

"She looked fragile when I first got there, but she seemed to enjoy our conversation."

"I couldn't seem to cheer her up." He found a slice of pepperoni at the bottom of the carton and ate it.

"I'd go back to look in on her, but I need to stop by the institute."

He didn't respond.

"I have to check on something there." She took a bite.

"Naturally."

"It's important, or I wouldn't go." *Good grief, why did he have to be this way?* She reached over and patted him on his hand. "I don't see it taking me long at the institute. Then I'll go to the hospital."

"Great. I'll go with you."

"You don't need to bother." Her brain dug for more excuses he'd believe.

"No bother. I'd enjoy seeing Kathleen. I'm up for the ride."

"I can't have you waiting while I'm at the institute." She wiped her hands. "You know this is part of my job."

"Then let's do this," he said. "You take care of whatever your institute business is, and I'll go spend some time with Kathleen."

A wave of relief washed over her. She pushed away from the table, put her plate in the dishwasher, grabbed her shoulder bag, and planted a kiss on Harold's forehead.

"I'll hurry." She winked at him. Beth hated leaving Harold the way she did tonight, but he'd never understand this.

The swiftness of the grapevine at the institute today would equal the speed of light. She felt positive that Rick had told Hugh about the logs. Her stomach churned. If only Wayne hadn't talked with Hugh. Not knowing what Hugh thought or knew made her nervous, but tonight she'd be quick and careful.

If the log in Kennel B was still there, she'd be out of luck. She couldn't think of a way to get into Jarrod's Laboratory to check the companion log. But one of Jarrod's logs would be missing tonight. She was certain.

The world is a dangerous place to live; not because of people who are evil, but because of the people who don't do anything about it.

—ALBERT EINSTEIN

39

Beth parked behind the institute where they had delivered the corncrib materials and turned off her lights. This way, Hugh wouldn't see her car in the parking lot. She got out, took the key from her pocket, slid it into the padlock, and turned it. Feeling tingles of expectations, she opened the gate.

Wayne had lent her the kennels' master key. Beth felt around in her purse, found it, slipped it onto her car keychain, and put it in her pocket, along with a small flashlight. She popped the trunk lid and pulled out a heavy-duty bolt cutter. This wouldn't turn into another night-vision-goggle fiasco. Faulty kennel locks or not, there was no way would she be locked in overnight with a deafening pack of barking dogs. Swinging her purse over her shoulder, she entered the field and pulled the gate closed behind her, leaving it unlocked.

The little jaunt ahead in the dark didn't trouble her. The night air felt pleasant and carried a hint of earthy smells mixed with wild vegetation. The goats' nattering seemed unusually loud tonight. When she got closer, she kept her eyes on the side of the main building. Its security lights glowed and were visible between the kennels.

Her shin hit something. A painful cut threw her off balance. She slammed down—hands, then elbows, then knees—on hard metal. The bolt cutter clattered somewhere off the offending object. She held her breath and listened. It was too dark to see anything except way over by the security lights.

Well crap. She must have fallen on one of her corncrib panels. Why in the hell was it way over here? She shouldn't turn her flashlight on, but she needed to see what was in front of her and retrieve her bolt cutter.

She waited, again holding her breath and listening. She watched for activity around the kennels and over by the main building. All was quiet except for the barking beagles and the goats.

A quick flick on and sweep of the light showed the bolt cutter. She snapped the light off, stood, and brushed grassy weeds from her suit.

Twice those panels weren't where they should have been. Did some animal drag them away from the building? She thought for a moment, working to remember the details from earlier today. All but one was in the stack. She had to admit the panels this afternoon were catawampus, but those men said they'd put them back.

She walked over to the kennel where the co-op guys had put them and turned her light on again. Someone had heaved them away from the kennel. Searching for something? The cell-phone?

Who would look for the phone except for the person who lost it? If the phone belonged to Rick, then either Rick came back, or whoever was here wasn't looking for the phone.

Beth leaned over and focused her light on the narrow strip of ground between the kennel and the remaining panels. A scuffle had taken place—lots of soil had been churned up. She found a stick and poked around in the soft dirt. Nothing. Confused, she turned off her light.

Too much had happened today. . . . *One step at a time.* Beth took another lung full of night air and let it slide out. Rick helped Joe until after eleven that morning. Rick said he needed to hurry and feed the goats. Then, at Joe's window, she watched Rick lope along out by the kennels. That must have been about fifteen to twenty minutes later. When she first saw his phone he had it hooked to his belt. Since she found it in the dirt out here, he must have been using it, or it would have remained in that belt case. So what did he do for the fifteen to twenty minutes after he left the macaque room? She was sure he'd called Hugh. If so, then who did he call from out here?

And what were those crows worrying over?

Crows—*collective noun: a murder of crows.* She wiped the sweat from her eyes, aimed her light at the field, again snapped it on, and swept it back and forth. Dried grasses, the bulldozer and backhoe were gone, and then the light hit something metallic. She tramped through the weeds, and there was Rick's bucket. She switched the flashlight off. Those crows must have been feasting on the special goat food. Where was Rick?

Did Rick call Hugh before Wayne told him about Beth being in his office? She shivered. Rick knew too much. Hugh couldn't afford to have Rick verify what she only suspected. The drawings, the logs—had Hugh guessed that Rick's information today was a trap? Would Hugh show it if he had? She bet that as pompous and greedy as he was, if he was still around, he would.

Had Hugh told Rick to meet him back here for some reason? The crows eating the goat food—did Hugh kill Rick? Did he kill Rick here? Wrong. There were too many people, the construction workers. Except, this happened around noon. The workers would have been off somewhere eating lunch, probably next to their trucks by the gate. From the gate, the bulldozer would have blocked the view of this kennel.

If Hugh killed Rick because he knew too much, what about her? She knew too much. Her blouse clung to her, sweaty, damp, and now clammy.

She needed to leave. Beth started toward the gate, then she stopped. She had to know. How could she quit when the kennel with the log stood only a few feet away?

Silly. She wasn't in danger. No one was back here. They would have seen her light by now. She'd check on Jarrod's log and be gone.

Beth turned the key to Kennel Building B and slipped inside the prep area. Muffled sounds from the disturbed canines started up behind the insulated prep-room door. On the other side, an aisle ran the full length of the kennel, giving access to each of the dog pens.

She flipped on her flashlight. The log on the clipboard still hung on the hook. It stuck fast with her double-sided tape to the wooden frame. She checked the log—all twenty-some pages were untouched. Dang.

Beth scanned the counter tops. There wasn't anything of note. She clicked off her light and stuck it in her pocket. Now what? She gripped the door handle and wondered if she'd missed something. Nothing was left in here but her disappointment, and Harold was waiting. She started to push the handle but caught herself. Was she still alone? She stepped to the tiny window and checked.

A large form, illuminated by the golden overhead security lights, strode toward the kennel. *Hugh.*

Where to hide? There wasn't any place in this room, and if she went back into the dog pens, she'd be trapped. But if she stayed here . . .

She jerked open the heavy inner kennel door and let it bang behind her.

The excited beagles barked and howled as they lunged at her from their inside runs. They'd slobber her to death if she had to share one of their pens. But Hugh out there . . .

She scurried down the aisle until she found a run with no dogs at the gate. Beth unlatched the gate, climbed through, and shut it. If he looked through the glass window into the kennel area, would he see her? In here the air carried smells of dog and canine food. Her nose twitched. She dropped the bolt cutter and hunkered down. She'd pay for her spying tonight with profound hearing loss. A sneeze fought to escape. She pinched the bridge of her nose.

Light flooded the window of the prep area's door. Hugh knew where the switch was thanks to Rick's floor plans. Seconds later all went dark.

She sneezed.

Amid the barking, she heard the inner kennel door open. Hugh sauntered down the aisle shining a flashlight into the corners of each pen. He knew she was here.

She grabbed the bolt cutter and scurried to the back of the pen. Cool air seeped under the flap to the outside run. She crawled through and huddled against the outside wall next to the flap.

She waited. The dogs continued to bark up a circus. Minutes later she watched Hugh, with log in hand, walk under a security light over by the main building.

He was going to make copies. That meant a trip to his office. He wouldn't have seen her car. Had he guessed she was inside? He couldn't have heard her sneeze. But the door—Hugh would have noticed it wasn't locked. That's why he had checked each kennel run.

Calm down. He probably knew the locks needed repair.

But what if he'd locked her in. No, if he knew she was here, he'd kill her like he did Rick and the DU scientist.

But even if it wasn't locked, she couldn't take the chance of leaving though the front. He'd see her.

She cursed him under her breath. Her slacks and hose were ruined, and her bloody shin throbbed.

She tossed her purse off her shoulder and positioned the bolt cutter to clamp down on one of the chain links. She squeezed. *Good grief.* She wrapped both hands around the handle and squeezed harder. Finally, she made a snip.

This could take all night.

She could call Harold. She'd dropped Rick's cell phone in her purse today, playing it safe. Gavin had shown her how to use it. But if she did call Harold, he'd come tearing up here and would scare off Hugh. She could call

Joe, but he'd call the cops, and Hugh would smooth talk his way out of this mess.

She held the cutters to the next link and squeezed again. Her crappy luck made this fence-cutting her best option.

First the corncribs out of place, then the bucket where it shouldn't be—now she needed to catch Hugh where he shouldn't be, with that log in his hand.

Some of the dogs joined her outside in their runs. They continued to howl and sing to her while she labored. Her biceps burned.

Harold would be beside himself. This was taking far too long. But if she didn't do it this way, well, no matter what, she'd still make him furious. She continued squeezing.

She snipped a little over two hand widths with her fingers spread. The vertical cut would measure over sixteen inches high. She could crawl through. She tugged and pulled each bottom corner as far to the side as she could. A sharp inverted-V opening awaited her. If a German shepherd could do it, she could. Besides, she had no more muscle left to devote to this project.

Beth grabbed her purse then wiggled and pushed her way through the dirt and the fence to freedom. Wayne could pick up the blasted tool tomorrow.

She crouched where she was and watched.

If Hugh was, in fact, making copies of these log sheets, he'd have to place each sheet onto the copier one at a time. How much time had it taken her to cut the fence?

Hugh strode around the corner of the institute carrying the log.

It would take her less than ten seconds to sprint around the four outside runs and get to the entrance door. She could see him now, but she couldn't see the front door. When he got close to the door she'd lose sight of him. She'd only have seconds before he came back out. Timing *was* critical. She inched her fingers behind her until they gripped the bolt cutter.

She waited until he disappeared from view at the front of Building B, then she dashed around the runs. He was inside with the light on.

She threw the outside lock into secure position. Her lungs burned.

"Hello? Hey." He banged on the door. "Anyone out there?"

She leaned against it and caught her breath.

He pounded and then yelled some more. He thought he was trapped because of the faulty lock. He kept banging with his fist and calling for someone to let him out.

She fumbled around in her purse, pulled out the brick-like cell phone, and dialed 9-1-1. She told the dispatcher she feared bodily harm if they didn't send help. The dispatcher told her to stay on the line. *No problem there.*

Hugh now screamed for the security guard and beat harder on the door. Beth listened for a second, then looked at the phone in her hand.

She raised her fist and banged back.

"Hugh."

Silence filled the night except for the background noise of excited beagles.

"You're a cheap con artist." It was her turn to yell. "I know you stole my research."

He slammed something against the window. Glass shattered, no longer reflecting security lights. His hand, then his whole arm, protruded through, fingers grabbing at air. The tiny window didn't have much of a purpose except for a little visibility. His large frame would not be coming through.

His hand disappeared and something cracked against the door, the demise of a perfectly good chair. He screamed a string of obscenities at her.

"Same to you, Hugh." Rivulets of sweat trickled down her forehead.

"You fucking woman. Open the door, open it or I'll—open the goddamned door!"

"You've sold our protocols to your sleazeball boss in Guatemala. I can't wait to see you behind bars."

He slammed the door with the chair again.

"You can't keep me—"

"It seems I can."

"Wait till I get my hands on you—you—"

"You're a thief."

"You're a bitch. I should have done away with you when I killed your goddamned mice."

"Like you did with Rick?" She held her breath.

"Shut up." Another loud whack at the door. Would the door hold?

"Where is Rick?"

Silence, then a piece of the chair came sailing out the window past her head.

"Right, good aim. I found Rick's phone behind Kennel Building B."

"Go to hell." Was he kicking the door? "Let me *out!*"

"You cuss me out, then want me to do something for you? Where *are* your social graces?" She paused, then in her most serious voice said, "Hugh, where is Rick?"

Silence.

"He told you about Jarrod's log this morning after Wayne mentioned I was in your lab. Bet you ordered Rich to stay behind the kennels where you two could talk."

More crashing and banging.

"He knew too much. Do you have flight tickets in your wallet? How did you kill him? He was young, Hugh. No heart problem like the DU guy. Ketamine wouldn't do the job for you this time."

"Shut the fuck up, bitch."

"Strangling is too intimate. You're too meticulous." Sweat dripped from her underarms and down her sides. "What then?"

Next a loud thud. Then another, making the door vibrate. Full-body slams? She didn't have confidence in the bolts holding the rusty hinges.

"You don't seem the gun type—besides, someone might hear." Now she felt icy cold. She hugged herself, holding the cell phone in one hand. She clutched the bolt cutter in the other.

"Okay, Beth, as one researcher to another." His words were solid and quiet. "I promise I won't hurt you, or even be mad. Open the door, okay? We'll talk." His voice reminded her of a trusted uncle suggesting they play a game of—a wave of nausea made her drop that thought.

"You're the epitome of trustworthiness." Beth felt tired of all this. "You're not leaving here except in handcuffs. You might as well tell me what you did with Rick."

No answer.

"You're nothing but slime of the worst kind." She shook all over but kept her voice strong. "You swagger around being everyone's best friend, pretending to be a competent researcher, and all the while you're cheating and stealing. I know you murdered that college kid, but I haven't figured out how."

With workmen nearby, he'd pick something quiet with no struggling. A metal dustpan flew from the window past her head.

"Bet you surprised him with an injection, something lethal. Okay, the DU scientist's death probably was a mistake. You wanted him unconscious so you could steal secrets, like you did with Wayne. You do like tidy and clean. Did you stuff Rick's body behind my corncribs around noon today? Did you cover him with soil and then the panels? I bet you came back after-hours when you had more time and hid him somewhere else."

Another startling crack sounded against the door.

"Where'd you take him?"

"Go to hell."

"You're lazy, so I know you prefer easy. He's somewhere close, I bet."

"Open this goddamned door!"

"You planned to leave tonight. Did you bury him under one of those mounds of dirt out there? No, you're smarter than that. They'd find him when they used that dirt to fill in the trenches around that basement."

A full-body slam sounded on the door again.

Dogs in the adjoining kennels raced around their outside runs, helping Hugh raise the neighborhood noise level. In between the barking and the banging, Beth heard the approaching wail of the police cars.

"The police are almost here, Hugh."

"You're dead, woman."

"Hello there," Beth said to the 9-1-1 dispatcher. "I need to know, are you getting all this?"

The thief who is harder to detect and who could cause the most damage is the insider—the employee with legitimate access. That insider may steal solely for personal gain, or that insider may be a "spy"—someone who is stealing company information or products in order to benefit another organization or country.

—FBI, NOVEMBER, 2005

40

Harold arrived at the police station. He was white-faced and veins on his neck were standing out. All he said as he guided her down the steps from the precinct station was that they'd pick up her car in the morning.

"I'm sure," Beth said, "that Hugh's voice on the 9-1-1 dispatch will seal his theft of proprietary information." She had felt giddy, but Harold made her euphoria dissipate. She hated it when their moods didn't match.

"He didn't admit to anything."

"Hugh said he murdered my mice. I wish the police would take Rick's disappearance more seriously." No use in her arguing.

Harold remained silent.

"You can't be that mad at me, Harold."

He stopped, faced her, and gripped her shoulders.

"What if he'd had a gun?"

"He didn't have a gun, and even if he had—"

"You didn't know that."

"Harold, I think I deserve a gold star here." She felt all her muscles tighten. She wanted to leave, go somewhere and be alone.

He looked away and let out a long, controlled breath.

"Aren't you proud of me?" The danger, the excitement, the questioning, and now his anger—now she had nothing left to give.

"What do you expect from me?" Harold's voice shook. "I'm to sit home and wait while you get yourself murdered?"

"First, I didn't get murdered. Second, someone had to stop him. And why aren't you congratulating me instead of bawling me out?"

"I love you, Beth, but can't you see . . . you're driving me crazy."

"And can't *you* see? Your worrying is driving *me* crazy."

They drove home in silence.

~

After a few restless hours of sleep, Beth arrived at the hospital before seven the next morning. She was still flying high on the adrenaline from the night before—adrenaline mixed with her anger, anger over Harold not being more understanding. She'd taken a Midrin, because the last thing she wanted today was a migraine. She pushed open Kathleen's door.

"Dear, you're early." Her aunt's voice sounded thin and weak.

"I am," Beth said. "Did I wake you?"

"They think they'll try that surgery again. What do you think?"

"What did the doctor say?"

"He said it's cancer, but we knew that, didn't we? He said he could try the surgery again—no, that's not what he said at all. He said he wants to do some tests. I think it's a procedure that might stop some of the bleeding. . . . Oh, never mind. Whatever he wants, he said they'll do it sometime."

"Are you in pain?" Beth's insides felt like overcooked spaghetti. She kept her voice composed.

"They said I could ask for morphine. I took some earlier. It helped, but I don't think I need it." She tried to pull her pillow up higher.

"Let me help you." Beth plumped the pillow and lifted it. "Can I bring you something?"

"A glass of wine. Harold brought me this magazine, but I can't seem to concentrate to finish this story. I'm afraid my mind may be going."

Beth picked up the magazine and looked at the article, a short one about a movie star and his divorce.

"You seem as bright as ever to me." What else could she say? "I'll stop back."

"Harold said you were at the police station. That can't be right."

"Oh, Kathleen, it's a story you'll love. I'll tell it to you when I come back later." She gave her aunt a kiss on the cheek. "I'm sorry I woke you."

For now, Kathleen needed to rest and to get a grasp on her own world.

A touch of panic crept in. Her aunt's wisdom wove tightly through Beth's life, and through her relationship with Harold. It had happened so gradually, she couldn't imagine being without it.

~

When Beth arrived at the institute, her first duty was to fill out Gordy's paper work. But his so-called emergency papers weren't in her mailbox. She couldn't get Hugh out of her mind, and the officials still labeled Rick as missing. What was wrong with everyone?

She booted up her computer, sat, and scrolled down through the requisitions for controlled substances. When she had done this once before, she'd only cared about ketamine. She hadn't looked for anything else. Did Hugh have other unauthorized drugs locked in his cabinet?

She blinked a couple of times to improve her focus. Migraines caused scotomas, known as blind spots, in some sufferers. Unfortunately, she was one of those. She closed her eyes, willing herself to see the screen clear enough to read. She opened her eyes and stared.

There sat the reality of it all. The computer screen showed an order for potassium chloride dated three months earlier. A high enough dose injected into a healthy teen would stop the heart. No fuss, no mess, no autopsy evidence, and only a body to dispose of. . . .

Wetness streamed down her cheeks. Rick's murder was her fault. She'd set him up. She reached for a tissue, dabbed her eyes, and worked to swallow the painful lump growing in her throat. The dull ache of the oncoming migraine slogged it's way up the back of her neck.

Stop it. Hugh was the murderer. No one else. And Hugh set the kid up to do all sorts of unethical activities. Hugh's the only one to blame in this.

She sniffed, blew her nose, and hated the throbbing now imbedded in her right temple. Rick had been a decent teen. She wish she'd been more pleasant to him and hadn't used him. She put her head down on the desk, stifled any possibility of her sobbing, and thought about what to do next.

Strong coffee helped migraines. She got up, started the coffeemaker, took another Midrin capsule, and waited. When the burbling coffeemaker's green light flicked on, she filled two cups, locked her door, and went to Orin's office.

[239]

Orin rose from his desk and closed the door. She handed him one of the cups and the envelope containing Hugh's requisitions for ketamine and the potassium chloride.

He smiled at the coffee, then he opened the envelope and pulled the contents out. He muttered something.

"I know this upsets you." She sipped her coffee. Orin's position was on the line now that the board knew the police were involved. Next it would be the newspapers.

"I gave the police the note you sent me." He set his cup down and rubbed his face. "I had to tell them about Wayne being drugged."

"The institute's procedures," she said, "for handling controlled substances is as effective as a sieve. It needs to be put at the top of your to-be-changed list."

"Beth, the probation thing . . ." He took a swallow of coffee. "Let's forget it."

"We need to talk about Rick." She fixed her eyes on his. "That potassium-chloride requisition should convince you he didn't run away."

A knock on the door, then Yvonne stuck her head in.

"Mr. Stamford, Detective Edwards is out here. He needs you to come upstairs and explain some papers in Mr. Wendenski's office. It would save them a lot of time."

Orin waved Beth toward the door and left the coffee cup on his desk.

"You started all of this," he said. "You might as well be there for the finish."

Detective Edwards wasn't happy about Beth's joining them. He delivered a rehearsed spiel about not contaminating evidence before he ushered them into Hugh's office.

Beth shoved her hands deep in her suit pockets to remind herself not to touch more than she already had.

Hugh's desk had documents stacked on it. A drawer stood open, empty except for paper clips, rubber bands, and a few pens. His bookshelves were empty. By the filing cabinet, two boxes stuffed with folders sat on the floor.

Orin's shoulders slumped. The detective used two gloved fingers to slip a sheet of paper out of the box so they could see—notes on Hugh's research. Then the detective showed them the layer of paper below the notes.

"It's a sketch of one of our labs," Orin said.

Underneath was a thick stack of faxes. Orin and Beth leaned in to study it. Hugh had faxed the log sheets from Joe's macaque research to an overseas number.

Beth indicated the documents on the desk. There were last night's faxes from the beagle log. Hugh probably sold research secrets long before Joe's failed opossum study a few years ago.

"Proprietary information in these faxes was sent to an overseas company." Detective Edwards pointed to the desk and the ones in the box. "We'll have to turn this over to the FBI."

"What's this?" She pointed toward another stack of papers, papers ranking the institutes' researchers.

Orin's face flushed. "He made copies of files from my office. He's into everything—running all over this place at night like a damned rat."

The beneficiary of the stolen trade secrets may be traced to an overseas entity, but obtaining evidence that proves the entity's relationship with a foreign government can be difficult.

—RANDALL COLEMAN, FBI, MAY 2014

41

"What a sweet surprise." Kathleen beckoned her over to her bedside and raised her cheek for a kiss. "I didn't expect you until later."

"I'm worried about you."

"They think they have everything under control. Would you like a piece of chocolate?"

The box held only empty brown papers.

"I think you're out."

Kathleen nudged the papers around.

"Those bastards ate it all. Now watch, no one will pay attention to me."

"Did you take more of the morphine?"

"I'm not in pain. I don't believe in medicating myself to the point of being goofy. God, I hate that feeling. Now, let me overdose on cuba libres. . . ." She wrinkled her nose. "What's happening with you and Harold?"

"Why harp on my marriage, when marriage wasn't that important to you?"

"Harold seemed troubled this morning." Kathleen played with folds in the sheet. "His new work adventure puts you on edge, but I suspect he's more worried about losing you."

"Harold worries too much." Beth sank down in the chair.

"Being alone does have advantages, dear. You never have to be there for someone, don't have to feed their emotions. You never have to listen to them when your mind's on something else." Kathleen fell quiet for a moment. "You do whatever you want—stay up all night eating sardines and crackers in bed, spend hours reading a good mystery."

"A life of hedonistic pleasures." *I could fly away to the Galapagos, watch the mating dance of the blue-footed boobies, work at the Darwin Research Center. . . .*

"You're wrong." Kathleen glowered.

Galapagos Tortoises lumbered across the meadow out of sight.

"When couples go out, you're not invited, unless you have a man around at the moment. When you drape yourself over his arm, you're relegated to the role of his lovely escort. When you go out alone, men stare at you like a piece of meat. When something wonderful happens, you have no one to listen. You have no one to share your giggles or to tell how it all happened over and over again. When you're down, depressed, and the world kicks you in the ass, you have no one to care, to wipe your tears, to put an arm around you and tell you, 'there there, my love, I'm here.'"

Beth couldn't say anything to that, because that's what Harold always did.

"Because you've been hurt, because you still grieve for your mother, because you're in turmoil about your work, you want the pain to stop. We think if we dance and sing, the party will never end. But my party is over, child." Kathleen paused. "Yours isn't."

Her words settled deep.

"Harold . . . I don't mean to, but I keep hurting him."

"Dear, the way you look at him when he plays with Saucy, the way you muse over his advice—well, some of it—the way you delight in his foolishness. You always want to call him and let him know where you are. You know as well as I do, the two of you belong together."

Everything inside stirred into a jumble. The fire, her mice, Harold, his job, Gordy, last night's adrenaline, her mother's fatal illness. She held it all back with the mental equivalent of Scotch tape and string.

Kathleen's words tore through them. Beth's heart flooded, spilling the debris of those awful things down her cheeks.

Kathleen stayed silent until Beth could tidy up her thoughts and wipe up the after flow.

"My mind splashes through a lot of muck sometimes." Beth dabbed her nose.

"We're all a bit crazy, don't you think? That's what makes the world such a wonderful circus." Kathleen's skewed smile made Beth feel better.

"Speaking of circuses . . ." Beth told her about her evening in Kennel B, the wrap-up conference at the police station, and Harold's uncompromising anger.

"What type of a man would he be, dear, if he didn't come down hard about almost losing you? The danger was real."

"But I can—"

"Shhh." Kathleen held a finger to her lips. "No *buts*. You can't take that away, that drive, a man's need to protect his family. Give him that at least."

Beth couldn't dig out a reasonable argument. And then she understood. . . . Her marriage was missing only what *she* failed to nurture.

~

Time for some control over her life, no matter how small. Beth bid her aunt good-bye, shopped for groceries, and bought fresh flowers. Harold wouldn't care, but it would make her feel better.

One light glowed through the living room window. Harold met her at the door and took a sack from her.

"Harold, we have to talk, but let me fix dinner first."

"I actually need to get something from the lumber store before it closes." He set the sack down. "I'll eat later." He started out, but she grabbed his arm.

"Stay." A sliver of fear flitted through her.

"I'll be back."

"I'll grill a steak and bake potatoes for us. " She steadied her voice.

"How long do I have before it's ready?"

"About an hour?"

"I'll be here."

"We'll talk. Have you ever had Pyrat XO Reserve rum? The man said it's extra smooth and imported from Anguilla."

"Hey, relax. Okay?"

She threw her arms around his neck. He hugged her back.

"I promise I won't be going to the institute tonight."

He gave her a peck and left. Beth stowed the perishables and arranged the flowers in water while listening to a symphony in her mind. She had to hurry, light the grill, and get the potatoes in the oven.

She paused. The answering machine's red light blinked on and off.

She pressed the button.

"'Dear, you have to come. I don't know where they're taking me. I'm on some train. All these people . . . I don't know anyone. Hurry.'"

Beth dialed the hospital and asked about Ms. McPherson.

"Your aunt's fine, but she's having some delusions." Beth hung up and grabbed her keys. At the door, she stopped. *Dinner* . . . But Kathleen was frightened, she needed her. She rushed back and scribbled a note for Harold, shoved it next to the phone, and headed to the hospital.

At the nurses' station, she announced, "I'm Ms. McPherson's niece."

The nurse opened a chart. "She's experiencing what we call *sundowning*."

"Never heard of it."

"Older hospitalized patients sometimes see and hear things that aren't there, usually in the evenings."

She headed to Kathleen's room.

The door stood ajar. A dimmed lamp glowed next to the bed. Beth flipped on the overhead light.

"Is that you?" Kathleen pulled the sheet up around her chin and scrunched up her body.

"You sounded afraid." Beth went to her.

"You see them, don't you?" Kathleen's voice dropped to a raspy whisper. "I know that woman with the big head, but I can't remember her name. Would you tell me what's written there?" Kathleen pointed to the bare wall beside her bed.

"There's nothing." Beth swallowed hard.

"I'm worried about Sophie. Remember when she ran away?" Kathleen grabbed Beth's wrist and looked at her watch. "Where's Ed? He should have been back by now. Do you think Harold's with him?"

"Kathleen—"

"He should be here by now." Kathleen sat up straight. "What does that writing say? Why can't I read?"

"Kathleen, nothing's written on the wall." Beth handed her a glass of water. "You and I are the only people here."

"What's this? They want to poison me."

"You're safe," she said. "I'm here."

Kathleen held still for a few moments, then started to cry.

"I don't know what's happened," she said. "I think I've lost my mind. I'm so sorry."

"This is perfectly normal." Beth felt like crying herself. "Sometimes people get confused when they're in the hospital, especially late in the day."

"I'm not in a train, am I?"

"No."

"I'm in a hospital."

"Yes."

"You don't get an abortion here. . . ."

"What?"

"You need a lamb special." Kathleen felt around her covers. "Never mind, I shouldn't talk about it."

"Can I get you something?"

"I can't find my damned cigarettes. . . . Where's Harold?" Kathleen pressed her nurse-call light several times.

"He's at home."

"You both need a vacation. You take the ferry to St. John and catch a ride to that lovely Trunk Bay. It's heaven. You'll love it."

Beth pulled the ugly chair over to the bed.

"What did you eat for dinner, Kathleen?"

"They brought me a cup of beef broth. I rather enjoyed that. I hate green Jell-O. Why do they always serve green Jell-O?"

A male nurse stuck his head in. "Yes, Ms. McPherson?"

"Who are you? Why are you wearing those clothes?"

"I'm the night nurse. You pressed your call light. Do you need something?"

"Well, not from you I don't. Who is he, Beth?"

"Thank you anyway." Beth waved him on. "Kathleen, he *is* a nurse."

"Oh my God, Angus. . . ." Kathleen sat up and looked toward the corner of the room. "Please don't get angry. You remember my Beth, don't you? See how she's grown." Kathleen glowed. "She's stubborn like you."

Beth stared at the corner.

"Kathleen, there's nobody there."

"Don't get testy, Pops." Kathleen flashed a look at Beth and whispered, "He hates it when I call him Angus." She turned back to the corner. "It's so good to see you . . . what?" She pouted. "I don't want to talk about it. Oh, please don't leave. . . ."

What was it they said about people close to death—a committee they knew often welcomed them. Sundowning, this had to be it. Kathleen was fine—she'd be fine in the morning.

"I'll be right back." Beth stood and went to the nurses' station.

"My aunt's upset. Isn't there anything you can do?"

"She'll be fine once she goes to sleep."

"She isn't fine now. Can't you give her something? How about Phenothiazine?"

"That requires a doctor's order." The nurse picked up the phone. "This is Nurse Collins on floor three. Ms. McPherson has delusional thoughts that frighten her. Please call me." She looked at Beth. "A doctor will get back to me in a few minutes."

When Beth returned, Kathleen was wiping tears from her cheeks with her blanket.

"I miss my Saucy. She must be starving."

"Harold fed her this evening. She's at our house until you're feeling better."

"I tried to call her, you know." Kathleen sniffed and wiped her eyes on the sheet. "She wouldn't answer the phone. She's such a stubborn girl. I'm afraid my sweet little girl has forgotten all about me."

Beth picked up Kathleen's hand and held it to her cheek.

"I'm here."

"This really isn't me, you know." Kathleen took a deep breath and closed her eyes. "I'm somewhere else."

"I know. But I'm with you."

Beth turned out the overhead light, leaving only the table lamp's soft glow. Then she sat beside her aunt and waited. After a while Kathleen's breathing, though shallow, settled into the regular rhythm of sleep.

Beth went back to the nurses' station.

"The doctor prescribed haloperidol," the nurse said. "The pharmacy should have some here in a few minutes."

"A dopamine blocker. She's asleep now," Beth said. "Call me if she's frightened." Her need to take care of Kathleen went far deeper than her perfunctory vow to her mother.

～

The house was dark when she drove into their driveway, but Harold's car was parked under the streetlight.

Beth unlocked the door and stepped into moonlight spilling through the windows. She left the drapes open and made her way to the bedroom. She heard soft sounds in the darkness, Harold's quiet motorboat snores. She felt tears about to spill. The dinner, their dinner . . . they needed time to make things right.

Beth undressed and slipped under the sheet.

The motor noise stopped. She brushed a kiss across his forehead.

He rolled over and turned his back to her. Chards of ice pierced her middle.

"What's wrong?" She touched his shoulder.

He sat up, turned on the light, and looked at the clock.

"You're home earlier than when you ended up at the police station." He snapped the light off and turned his back to her again. "I should be thankful."

"She was scared," Beth squeezed his shoulder. "You wouldn't expect me to leave her."

"Who? Kathleen?"

"I left you a note."

"You did? Is she all right?"

"I think so." She felt him turn. "I'm sorry about tonight, and last night, and—"

"Shhh." Now he pulled her close.

There, in his arms, no place to rush off to—no phone calls—she melted into his warmth.

He stroked her hair.

She nuzzled into the softness of his neck and savored the faint trace of his morning aftershave, a familiar smell, a smell that flooded her with memories from their younger years. Pinaud? What happened to the abandoned thrill of their lovemaking? When did that disappear?

She inhaled deeper and called back those delicious images. She brushed the back of her hand over his five o'clock shadow, then moved her lips up along his neck to his ear. She felt him shudder, then hold his breath. He waited.

She wouldn't make him wait any longer.

An employee at a Utah company noticed a co-worker download the recipe for manufacturing a proprietary chemical and email it to his personal email account. . . . the employee had shared the manufacturing secret with an individual associated with a foreign chemical company.

—C. FRANK FIGLIUZZE, FBI, JULY, 2012

42

Beth arrived at the institute a few minutes before seven the next morning. She checked the animals in her lab, studied Teri's well-kept log sheet, and hurried out to inspect the construction on the non-human primates' enhanced environment.

The installation of the corncrib panels seemed to be zipping along, even though the crew needed to do some jury-rigging of parts. One of the botanists at the institute located some solid, dead trees for the center of the corncribs. Beth brimmed with excitement. Soon these macaques could build social relationships and play in all this glorious sunshine.

Early-morning dust billowed from behind the kennels. The ground vibrated with deep rumblings. Trucks came down the back road. Construction on the new building must be moving along, too.

She strode behind her new, almost-finished macaque home to investigate the progress on the IT and printing building. She watched churning cement trucks drive up the road. One waited for Smithy to unlocked the gate. They must be pouring the building's basement today.

While Smithy unlocked and opened the gates, she wandered over, climbed up on top of a pile of excavated dirt, stepped over a shovel, and looked into a pit about twelve feet deep. Its bottom was lined with grids of wire-type mesh, sleeves for pipe penetrations, and other mysteries of construction. She studied the solid, tamped-hard dirt bottom. This would prevent the cured cement from cracking if the ground settled or shifted underneath.

She scanned the deep trench running around the outside of the form for foundation walls. She knew that under these walls were stabilizing stem walls with heavy supporting metal. Evidently, the stem-wall cement had cured. Today they could pour the floor and the walls and fill in the outside trench.

The building was a simple rectangle, nothing fancy like an L shape or anything more aesthetically pleasing. She sighed. The governing board kept all money clasped tightly in its frugal fists—higher dividends for the institutes' investors.

The first truck rolled up and backed into position, the driver carefully keeping its wheels away from the mound of dirt in front of the outside trench. Men with shovels stood by. The truck driver lowered the mouth of the turning cement mixer, and the first pour began. Watching this process mesmerized Beth. She forgot she was in a hurry. She studied their movements and watched the flow patterns of the thick concrete as it slugged out of the mixer, gained momentum, and moved on down the chute.

Something wasn't right. Deep in her gut, she knew it. Something she'd seen. She couldn't make her mind go there. Her gaze floated back up to the rotating barrel of the truck, but her brain no longer cared about it or its contents. Something else . . .

She pulled away and turned west toward the mountains. They always comforted her, so solid, so unchanging, always dependable. *No—*

"Stop the trucks! Stop the trucks!" She stumbled off the mound of dirt, tore over, and grabbed the foreman's arm, jerking it. The foreman looked at her, pulled his arm away, and continued giving orders to his men. Her heart lurched.

She screamed again and again, willing them to not dump more cement into the pit.

She look over at Smithy. He had to see the desperation in her eyes. Bile rose. *Oh please, I can't throw up now.* She glanced around, but no one else looked at her. Smithy trotted toward her.

She could see his pity—pity for a crazy woman—in his face.

The truck kept rotating its barrel. The cement kept slogging down the chute. Men at the bottom kept shoveling. The second truck moved into position. The third truck rolled onto the property.

"Smithy, make them shut it down. You have to—"

"What in the devil? Ms. Armstrong, they can't stop. They've got to keep it moving."

"But the missing tech is buried under that floor." Her nausea increased. "They can't cement it over until we find him."

"And why would you think that?"

"He was here, in this place. He's gone, now. No one's seen him." To her horror, the second truck started dumping cement down its chute. "They can't cover this all up. Please!"

He shook his head, like a father to a distraught child.

She felt her face grow hot. She had to make him understand. The men below worked quickly with their shovels. They were adept at spreading the cement. Was she too late?

"Smithy—"

"Ms. Armstrong, unless there were insiders working together, like the Jimmy Hoffa thing, what you're thinking can't happen."

She slowed her breathing so she could hear his reason. What would he say next? She wanted it to be true, but the panic inside her didn't quiet.

"Just look at all that stuff down there. See how hard that ground is? You could tell from up here if someone had dug it up. Believe me, one person couldn't tamp it down that hard or smooth. But the main thing is that mesh covering the whole floor. Nothing's been disturbed. We could see if someone had messed with it."

"But still . . ." His reasoning made sense. Why didn't she feel reassured. Her questioning of Rick, tricking him into tattling to Hugh, knowing Hugh would take out his anger on this college kid—

"You okay?" Smithy squinted at her.

His hand, now on her shoulder, demanded she answer him. She nodded because her words weren't there.

"You don't want to halt this project, Ms. Armstrong." He spoke low with authority as he gestured to the trucks. "All that cement would be wasted, and with no reason—it's wasted money. The institute's bosses wouldn't be happy about it."

Rick blindly followed Hugh's orders, he eagerly helped Joe, and he cared for those goats. A wave of guilt drowned her. She'd overreacted. That's all.

"You're right. I feel foolish. Thanks, Smithy." But she knew that somewhere nearby Rick would be found. She backed away, then turned toward the main building. Something hid in the back of her mind, something she'd seen, and something she knew.

Between 1987 and 1989, IBM and Texas Instruments were thought to have been targeted by French spies.

—WIKIPEDIA

It is foolish to tear one's hair in grief, as if grief could be lessened by baldness.

—CICERO

43

When Beth arrived at the hospital, she went straight to Kathleen's room.

Kathleen's bed was stripped—surely only a change of sheets, but still her breath caught. She rushed to the nurses' station.

"Could you tell me where Mrs. McPherson is?"

"She's over at the lab—more tests. She should be back in her room any minute."

Beth used the time to take the elevator down, walk to the cafeteria, buy a large coffee, and take it back to her aunt's room.

Kathleen studied the breakfast tray in front of her. She moved things around, but it didn't look as if she'd eaten anything.

"Hello, dear. Tell me, do you think these pale yellow lumps are scrambled eggs?"

"That or bird poop." She leaned over and gave her aunt a kiss.

"Hmm. They look more like—what you said." She pushed her plate away. "I didn't expect to see you this morning."

"What did the doctor say?"

"Hasn't come in yet." Kathleen sat up straight and gave a series of short, dry coughs. It took her a minute to get them under control.

Beth handed her the glass of water.

"They said they might release me from the hospital."

"Are you that well?"

"I'm better today." She sighed. "I'm embarrassed about last night. I sort of flipped out, didn't I?"

"The nurses said that happens when people stay in the hospital too long. That's probably why they think you should go home." She adjusted the blinds to let in more light. "You said lots of colorful things."

"Well, none of it's to be believed. I wasn't in my right mind." Kathleen waved it all away.

"You seem on top of things this morning."

"That's what they all said at the lab. Not to worry."

"You were obsessed about being on a train. There's a story I'd love to hear."

"Mother and Angus used to take me to Chicago from Minneapolis by train when I was quite small. I loved it." She coughed a few more times and reached for her water. "Have you eaten yet?"

"Coffee—not hungry. Would you like to take a trip on on Amtrak? I'll take some vacation time in a couple of weeks when you're stronger. We can go to Chicago, rent a car. Did you and Sophie take the train when you left home?"

"Sophie and I had been friends since grade school. We took dance, music, and drama together. We even had a class called, How to Be a Lady."

"What on earth did they teach?" Beth leaned against the windowsill.

"They taught us how to light a cigarette. You had to keep your hand on your cigarette at all times. Can you imagine anyone teaching teenagers that skill now? Oh, and how to eat at a formal dinner table—what fork to use, how to hold different wine glasses."

"Grandmother insisted I set the table for our Sunday dinners," Beth said. "As sweet as she was, she monitored my placement of every utensil. She'd lecture me on why it must be set her way." Beth loved those family dinners.

"Now everyone waves their forks around when they talk." Kathleen shook her head. "To me, gesturing with a fork that's been in your mouth is the same as chewing with your mouth open."

"And Grandmother insisted I keep one hand in my lap at all times, unless I needed to cut up something."

"There were lots of things not to do," Kathleen went on, "like walking and eating at the same time."

"You mean *talking* and eating at the same time, right?"

"Walking, dear, walking and eating. Even at the beach, if we bought a hot dog, we were to stand or sit in one place while we ate. Real ladies *never* walked around while they nibbled or sipped."

"Then all your friends and parents would have had a cow today because I carried my coffee cup up from the cafeteria?"

"You could carry it, but you'd better not sip it while you did."

"Good grief, where would McDonald's be now?"

"They had us put a book on our heads and taught us to walk with our chins up so our body parts wouldn't jiggle, and they taught us how to enter a room for the best dramatic effect. First, you pause at the doorway for at least five seconds, look all around the room without moving your head, then enter. And all those things a girl needs to know about men, of course. Speaking of which, tell me about you and Harold."

"I've a lot to learn from him." She studied the shadow patterns from sunlight filtered through leaves dancing on the wall. "We do talk more now."

"I'm so happy, dear." She took a bite of eggs and nibbled a corner off her triangle of toast.

"Kathleen, why did you call Grandfather by his first name?"

She put her fork down and put on a stern-librarian look.

"Give it up, dear. Some things I do not intend to talk about. I wish I had a cigarette. These heavy discussions excite my craving."

"What's a *lamb special*?"

Kathleen turned her head to the side and coughed, so hard it sounded like she might crack a rib. When she finished, she looked exhausted.

"Do you need something? Should I call the nurse?"

"Need to catch my breath. Where on earth did you hear that term?"

"You said it last night, Kathleen. What does it mean?"

She took the lid off her coffee and sipped.

"Warm, colored water. Ugh."

"Is this one of those things you won't tell me?" Beth said.

"Not at all, dear. Ladies never mentioned certain things. There were code words."

"We used to say *PG* for pregnant in high school. If anyone said *sex* aloud, everyone considered that crude. Was *lamb special* something like that?"

"It's a story, or it won't make sense."

"Your time is mine." Beth settled into the ugly chair. Kathleen looked pale.

"Dr. Mondragon was a doctor in Jamaica, but they took away his medical license. His wife's father had a business in Puerto Rico. That's close to

St. Thomas—a beautiful island. Well, his father-in-law died of a heart condition and left the business to Dr. Mondragon."

"I bet the business had nothing to do with medicine."

"I almost hate to tell you. It sounds awful," Kathleen said. "It was a meat market down in the old part of San Juan. When women went into the meat market and asked Mondragon for the lamb special, he'd make arrangements for them."

"Arrangements?"

"If they found themselves in a family way—without the family."

"May I come in?" A trim young woman stood in the doorway. "I'm Joan Mateer, Ms. McPherson. The hospital social worker sent me. Is this your daughter?"

"She's my niece."

"Should I come back later?"

"If you want." Kathleen's voice was toneless.

"I mean, should I wait until you're alone to talk?"

"Not necessarily, what do you want to talk about?"

"Your doctor said you agreed you're ready for our services. But we don't need to do this now if you're not up to it. I'll need to ask you some questions, because we have to be certain you understand the situation, and what we do. There are forms to sign."

"Now I remember." Kathleen's face sagged, and she shut her eyes. "I don't want to talk now." She turned her face to the wall.

"Can you tell me what this is about, Ms. . . . ." Beth shot a look at her aunt.

"Joan Mateer—Joan. I'll come back later. I'm sorry to have disturbed your visit."

She left. Kathleen's eyes were still shut.

"I guess you're tired." Beth pulled the blanket up to her aunt's shoulders. "I'll be back later."

She hurried to the nurses' station. "May I talk with you for a minute?"

The nurse moved to the front of the desk.

"Good, you're here," she said. "I need to know what your plans are for your aunt after she's dismissed."

"She'll insist on going back to her apartment."

"But she agreed to hospice care yesterday. She'll need assistance from now on."

Beth felt her heart sinking. The nurse was staring at her.

"My aunt's . . ." Beth's heart kept tumbling down. "I'd like her to come home with us, but I don't think she'll agree." Now her heart sank even farther, way down below the floor. "What do people do in cases like this?"

Beth's head was full of heavy noise.

"Your aunt could stay in the hospital's hospice unit, but that's only short term. Joan will arrange home care for her, or she'll give you a list of some assisted-living places close to your home."

"I don't even know what to expect." *Breathe.*

"We never know, but the doctor said she probably has some time."

"Could he do surgery again?"

"He's stopped the bleeding. That should help."

It cascaded down on her. Kathleen had slammed into her life and stolen pieces of her—of her heart.

"Let me buzz Joan. Perhaps she can talk to you and Ms. McPherson now."

"Please don't. She came in a few minutes ago. My aunt refused to talk." Beth patted her pocket. No tissues. She swallowed. "Maybe all the paper work will have happened when I get back."

"While you're gone—got it."

"Wait. When you talk with Joan, would you see if she can convince my aunt to come live with us?" The lump in her throat made it hurt to speak. "If there's going to be hospice service, they could come to my home, couldn't they?"

"Certainly."

Beth held her fists over her mouth. She turned, and jogged along the hallway, through the exit door, down the stairs to the landing, where she slumped against the concrete wall, and then she slowly slid down to the cold metal step. There she curled up in a soaking rain, which didn't fall from the sky. She clutched at everything, struggling to keep the million pieces of her heart from hurting as they slipped away—out into the universe.

~

An hour later, she was seated in the small conference room with the doctor and Joan.

"Bladder cancer is rarely caught in the early stages," he said. "In your aunt's case, she ignored minor symptoms and put off a diagnosis until it spread throughout her system. Our goal now is to keep her free of pain."

"But," Beth said, "she'll have medication for that, and if she'll come home with us—"

"Ms. Armstrong," Joan said, "your aunt's an independent person. This is extremely difficult for her. She's concerned about how much personal care she'll need, and she refuses to be a burden on you." Joan touched Beth's arm. "Personally, I think she wants to preserve her dignity, and not have you see her in such a dependent state."

"I want her close. I need her. I should be—"

"I understand. But Ms. McPherson is of a different generation, with different standards. To her, exposing one's personal parts to a close family member destroys decorum."

Beth fought to quiet the sounds grinding in her head.

"She knows the advantages of having loved ones around," Joan said. "I explained that we could arrange for hospice care in your home. She refused."

Beth found enough of her voice to thank her before she slogged toward the elevators.

The overall population is aging. For the first time in history, and probably for the rest of human history, people age 65 and over will outnumber children under age five.

—NIH

Step with care and great tack, and remember that life's a great balancing act.

—DR. SEUSS

44

Beth entered the kitchen. Harold looked up, then finished signing a form.

"I have to talk to you about Kathleen," Beth said. "The doctor says . . . I've started looking . . ." She closed her eyes and sucked in her breath, then said, "at places for her."

The back of her throat ached. Harold set his jaw as he squared a stack of papers. She heaved a sigh before continuing.

"I need your help. Some of these places are . . ." She couldn't manage anymore.

Harold stood, held her, and whispered, "There, there—"

"I want her with us."

"I do too." He squeezed her firmly.

"She refuses."

"We need to change her mind."

They entered Kathleen's room. She opened her eyes and stared at them.

"I tried to smuggle in a rum and Coke," Harold held his palms out and said, "but they caught me."

Kathleen closed her eyes.

"We've been talking." Beth took Harold's hand. "We want you with us."

Her aunt's head moved slowly back and forth.

"Kathleen, Beth's right. You have to be with us."

No response.

Beth looked up at Harold, wanting him to do something. He shrugged. She put her hand gently on her aunt's arm and said, "Do it for us. The hospice nurse will come to our home and give you all the medical attention you need."

"Saucy's tired of my lap," Harold took over. "She wants yours. Let's spend all the time we have as a family, together."

Beth added, "You can smoke all you want. Harold will fix you cuba libres."

Kathleen opened her eyes and turned her head to the wall.

Beth didn't have what it took to outright defy her aunt. She could tell Harold didn't either, because he was searching for more to say. Kathleen wasn't giving them much to work with.

"Dear, dear Kathleen, we love you." Beth held Kathleen's hand. "Doesn't that count?"

No response.

"We'll honor your wishes for now." Beth sighed. "But *if* we can't find the right place for you, you'll be living with us."

Kathleen looked at her and said, "Thank you, dear."

They left and neither spoke when they got back in the car.

Finally Harold said, "Do you have the addresses?"

She handed him the list.

After rejecting three assisted-living homes, they walked into a bright dayroom in a facility called Carefree Living. A woman in tailored navy slacks and a white silk blouse came around to the front of the reception desk.

"Good afternoon." Her voice was melodic. "Welcome to Carefree Living. I'm Mary Ann Hettema, the owner."

"I'm Beth Armstrong and this is my husband, Harold. My aunt needs an assisted-living home."

"Your timing's perfect. Sue can handle the desk while I show you around." Ms. Hettema looked toward the perky woman behind the counter, then took

Beth by the elbow and guided her toward the far end of the room. Harold followed.

"You can see this is an all-purpose room. We have a piano over there, tables if people want to play bridge, games, crafts, and the hardwood floor makes a great dancing area."

"Need more volunteers?" Harold plinked a few notes of Bach on the piano.

"We'd love to have you," Ms. Hettema said. "Since this isn't a medical facility, we rely on the hospice nurses assigned to residents with health needs." She opened one of the big doors at the end of the room and held it for them. "Here's our kitchen. We serve fresh fruits, vegetables, and as much lean meat and protein as our budget will allow. There's so much research out there, some of it conflicting, it's difficult to know what to do."

"Have you read the theoretical studies about telomeres?" Harold cocked his head. "The longer they are, the longer the organism lives." He glanced at Beth. "But she's the scientist. She works at the institute."

"Telomeres?" Ms. Hettema shook her head.

"It's new stuff." His enthusiasm was contagious. "In this Canadian article, they think cancer-cell growth is indefinite because of the length of telomeres."

"That is a worry—"

"Maybe, but then maybe not. . . ." Harold said, but then he stopped when Beth slid Harold her *shush* look.

Beth squeezed his arm before saying, "What you're doing here with food is great. Even people with cancer benefit from good diets."

"Why is unhealthy food cheaper?" Ms. Hettema gestured toward an open doorway. "Anyway, here's the dining room. They get a form each morning to fill out—"

"Could we see the bedrooms?" Beth's energy had disappeared.

~

Harold helped her fill out an admission form. This whole process depressed her, but having him there helped.

They took some things from Kathleen's apartment, including her bedspread and some books, to make the Carefree room look less institutionalized. Then they headed home.

"Anything else?" His voice held the weight of what was happening.

"Should I make dinner for us tonight?"

"Maybe that steak you promised."

He pulled into their driveway and turned off the engine.

"You impressed me." She touched his arm, then opened her door and started up the walk. "Most people haven't heard of telomeres. You know so much about everything. I don't think I've appreciated that in you."

He unlocked the front door and held it for her as she went in.

"Thanks for your help." Everything seemed better with him at her side. "And I think your suggestion to volunteer is a good one. We need to do more things together."

"You don't have time."

"I haven't made time. Harold, I've been thoughtless and foolish. I need to go to the hospital, then I'll be back to fix dinner. I can't—oh—I—Harold."

"Beth, what exactly did the doctor say?" He wiped a tear off her cheek.

"He thinks . . . all that's left is to keep her comfortable. We're losing her from our life, Harold." She moved into the one thing in her universe she could hold on to, clutching her fingers into his back. He wrapped her in tight.

~

A hospital staffer wheeled Kathleen down to the exit and helped her into the car. When Beth closed the door and started the engine, Kathleen held out her hand. Beth took Kathleen's cigarettes and the lighter out of her purse and handed them to her.

"I know why," Beth said, "you didn't want an ambulance."

"You're a clever one." Her voice sounded stronger, and her face showed pure bliss as she inhaled.

"Please, come home with me."

"Don't start that, child. I hate all of this."

After a few seconds Beth said, "I know."

"I've been thinking about your work."

Beth reminded herself to breathe.

"You've had so many problems," Kathleen inhaled then blew out a smoke ring. "I've taken up too much of your time."

Beth sighed. "You're a treasure in our lives. My work fell apart because the institute was mismanaged."

"But you've discovered the culprit." Kathleen's voice held no energy. "I should think your boss would be pleased."

"No one believes Hugh murdered Rick. They don't even believe Rick's dead. Who knows what can be salvaged. But at least Hugh won't be doing any more damage." She stole a look at Kathleen and a sadness swept through her. Beth could lose much of what she loved in these next few days.

Kathleen coughed. "Are you a valuable employee?"

"I am, but now that Orin's position is in jeopardy—"

"Look deep." A raspy whisper. "What does Orin need?"

Beth was having trouble hearing Kathleen's words.

"What can you do for him that no one else is doing, dear? When you figure that out, you'll know what to do."

For the rest of the drive her aunt rested her head against the seatback and silently savored her cigarette.

What did Orin value? She thought about Kathleen's comment, but her mind kept jumping from her opossum study to the food discussion at Carefree living and to all those noisy beagles. She couldn't focus on any one thing. Then Harold's telomere comment emerged from the side wings and stood front and center.

~

When she pulled up at Carefree Living the director came out to meet her, and her perky assistant brought a wheelchair for Kathleen.

"Ms. McPherson, we're pleased to have you here. Let me give you a tour of our facilities before we show you your room. You'll need to put out your cigarette while we're in the building, but you can smoke in the courtyard whenever you like."

Beth fell in step behind the assistant. They finally showed Kathleen her room.

"Will this be satisfactory?"

"I don't think it makes a goddamned bit of difference, does it?"

"Thank you." Beth waved them away. "You've both been kind."

Kathleen looked toward her glass patio doors.

"I'm sorry, Kathleen. I hoped you would like this."

"It's fine. Push me outside."

She did.

Kathleen lit a cigarette, pointed to a chair, and motioned for her to pull it close.

"If you think you're going to be treated unfairly at work . . ." Kathleen stopped and coughed. "You need to let Orin know I'm the reason you've been gone so much."

"Could we talk about you and our family?"

"Please do one more thing for me."

"*One* more?" That sounded too final.

"I need an attorney, soon. Can you arrange that?"

"I . . . if you want."

"I have some money invested, along with stocks." A series of coughs. "I have no family left but you."

"Bobby and Sarah are your nephew and niece, too, Kathleen. They'd have been here for—"

"Hush." She kept her eyes focused on Beth. "I know what I'm doing."

"I'll call Ted." Laura's husband was the only attorney she knew.

Kathleen glanced upward. "There's something else. It's been on my mind, but . . . Oh, damn. . . ." Kathleen closed her eyes; her breathing seemed nonexistent.

"Would you like a drink of water?"

"I want to go to my bed." Kathleen stubbed out her cigarette, then stuffed the pack and her lighter into the pocket of her robe. She closed her eyes and pointed toward her room.

Her aunt sat with no expression, no muscle tone, and the only movement came from her shallow breathing. Beth stood, took the handles of the wheelchair, and pushed her to her room. She helped her get from the chair into bed.

"Kathleen—"

"Shhh." Kathleen's eyes remained closed.

Beth went down the hallway, called Ted, then drove home. She told Harold all about Kathleen and explained what she planned to do. Beth brushed Saucy until her coat glistened, then she snapped on Saucy's lead and drove back to Carefree Living.

The two of them headed down the hallway to Kathleen's room. Saucy's tail wagged all the way as residents stopped to pet and coo over her. Beth didn't care if the home allowed pets or not. Kathleen's name was now on the wall next to her door.

She went in. Saucy's tail drooped. The dog crept over to the bed and whimpered. Beth picked her up and placed her at the foot. Saucy picked her way up to Kathleen's face, and then she lay down on top of Kathleen's chest and sniffed. Her feathery tail slowly swept back and forth.

"My baby girl." Kathleen reached to caress Saucy's ear. There were tears in the corners of her eyes. She looked up at Beth.

"Thank you, child."

On the bed were some legal papers and a box of cookies with the lid off.

"Ted's been here already?"

"Take them. I can't eat."

She looked terrible . . . no substance to her at all. Eyes sunken, lips cracked, and her white hair fell every which way.

"Would you like me to brush your hair?"

Silence.

Beth stood still, watching her. Only Kathleen's hands moved, playing with the dog's ears.

"Dear, those papers . . . my will—keep them safe."

She couldn't move. She didn't want those papers; she wanted to keep *Kathleen* safe.

"Go on, dear. Bring me my robe."

Beth slid the folded sheaf of papers into her purse without looking at them. She held out the robe.

"Put it over the chair arm."

"Your cigarettes are in the pocket." Beth's throat ached. "I'll take you out on the patio when I come back after dinner." She went over to scoop up Saucy, but she waited while Kathleen rested her cheek on the dog's head.

The drive home was a blur. Beth walked into the house and crumpled into her favorite chair. Saucy climbed in her lap, whimpered, and tried to lick her face. She curled her arms around the dog.

"Oh, no—did she . . . Harold stood in front of the chair.

She shook her head, released Saucy, took a huge breath, sniffed, and looked for something to wipe her nose. Harold handed her a box of tissues.

She used two of them, looked around, then tossed them on the table.

Beth took another tissue. "She doesn't like that place."

"I know." Harold disposed of the tissues.

"She misses Saucy."

"I know."

They sat in silence. Beth couldn't figure out what to do.

Harold stared at the floor.

The phone rang.

Harold pulled himself up, went to the desk, and answered it.

He put his hand over the receiver and whispered, "Carefree Living."

"What's wrong?" Beth's insides flipped.

He held up one finger for her to wait. She clutched his arm and studied his expression.

"Of course . . ." He looked at Beth and grinned. "We do understand."

He hung up, let out a skull-rattling whoop, grabbed Beth, and jigged around the room.

"What is it? What?"

It took him a minute before he could answer.

"You left her cigarettes with her. They told her she couldn't smoke inside, and she told them where to go." His strange yips and cheers kept bubbling all over. "She's gotten herself kicked out."

Beth burst into giggles and grabbed her keys.

~

"Their expectations—totally unreasonable." Kathleen brandished her hands as Harold wheeled her through the garage and into the kitchen. "You'd think they'd want their guests to be comfortable."

Beth suppressed a grin.

"You do understand I'm only staying here until you find a place that will let me keep my cigarettes and my dog?"

Harold helped Kathleen into her bed.

"I'm about to fix dinner." Beth fluffed the pillow. "I'll bring you some."

"Maybe a little Coke with some lime and—"

"I'm on it." Harold rushed out.

Beth offered her the cigarettes and a clean ashtray.

"Thank you, dear, but for some reason they don't taste that good anymore."

One unique aspect of the private-sector survey . . . was the magnitude of the estimated dollar loss from economic spying—potentially $2 billion a month for all US businesses.

—REPORT TO CONGRESS ON FOREIGN ECONOMIC COLLECTION AND INDUSTRIAL ESPIONAGE: 1996

45

Beth dropped a leave-of-absence request on Nancy's desk, unlocked her door, and turned on her computer. As soon as it was ready, she clicked to connect it to the Internet. Wow, what a difference. The IT guy must have changed her Internet access from dial-up to cable.

Well, of all days, hugs to that IT guy. Gavin mentioned some big changes ahead. No wonder IT needed its own building. That building . . . she kept thinking about something she saw out there, or something left on the ground, or . . . Hugh wouldn't have moved Rick's body far. He stayed away from all physical work. When she'd climbed up on that mound of dirt, she'd stepped over a . . . a discarded *shovel*—She grabbed her phone.

"Nancy, put me through to Orin." Her breathing sounded like she'd been running. She heard his phone pick up.

"Good morning, Beth."

"Orin, I know where Rick is. Meet me at the new IT building." She hung up, not waiting for an answer.

She didn't bother to lock her door or grab her purse. She bolted out the atrium doors and across the grass. *Please don't let me be too late, please.*

She charged out from between the kennels. The bobcat driver pushed mounded soil down into the outside trench at the far corner of the basement.

She studied the mound of dirt encircling the work. There lay the shovel. No other tools were scattered about. She climbed to the top of the pile and stared down into the trench. Someone *had* shoveled lots of soil into it. She looked beyond the lose dirt. The rest of the deep ditch still appeared nicely chiseled out. Then something else caught her eye. An edge of a coin protruded from a clod of dirt near her foot. She picked it up—a brass button—like the ones from Rick's shirt.

She heard sirens in the distance and saw Orin between the kennels huffing toward her. Hugh was a lazy, murdering bastard.

Her only gratification came from knowing that Orin now trusted her knowledge. He'd called the police before anyone had even verified that Rick's body was dumped in that trench.

The police uncovered Rick's body and did what they had to do. Then they dismissed her. Beth went back to her office, but Orin stayed longer.

She couldn't concentrate on today's project. Everything seemed impossible. What would this world be like if everyone could have at least one do-over? She shut out the noise in her head, steadied her breath, forced her hand to control the mouse, and clicked on the Internet server. Bingo. No dial-up waiting. She was mesmerized and became lost in her own researching. Then her phone rang.

"Ms. Armstrong, your husband's on the line. He said it's an emergency."

～

When Beth entered Kathleen's bedroom, the hospice nurse was standing over her.

"She seems to have a good deal of mucus that plugs her windpipe." The nurse checked Kathleen's vital signs then moved the suction tube into her mouth.

"Is this serious?" Beth couldn't breathe, either.

"If I can't get her airway cleared."

Harold stood silent, shifting his weight from one foot to the other.

After a few seconds Beth couldn't stand it. "Should I call 9-1-1?"

"Hospice services don't permit that."

Kathleen was gray.

Beth's stomach churned. She lunged for the phone anyway.

"There." The nurse straightened.

Color returned to her aunt's face.

"Page me if it happens again." The nurse removed the blood-pressure cuff. "Please don't call 9-1-1. They're required to transport the patient to the hospital and take proactive measures, which could be painful to her. We only focus on palliative care now."

"Is she going to be all right?"

"Mrs. McPherson's exhausted, but I suspect she'll feel better after she sleeps. She's probably not uncomfortable now, but if she's in any pain, give her this." She placed the medicine on the table next to the bed. "Here are the instructions."

When Kathleen faded into sleep, Beth returned to the institute. She had one last piece of unfinished business before she took her leave of absence.

She went straight to the front desk and gave Nancy a hug.

"I hear your son's in remission. This may sound crazy, but tell your husband to get his license fast. This institute needs extensive renovation, and when I have that administrator's position, he'll be first on my list for inside carpentry projects. Now, I'm locking my door. I'm not to be disturbed unless it's an emergency from my home."

She spent the day in her office. At half past four, she pressed the print button. *Kathleen, I wish you were here to watch. I can be as feisty as someone else I know.*

Then she gathered up the pages, clipped them together, and went down the hallway to Orin's office.

Yvonne gave a start when she saw her.

"Hi, Yvonne. Everything's fine." Beth opened Orin's door and walked in.

He was on the phone, pacing. When he saw her, he mumbled something and replaced the receiver.

"Aw, Beth." His face showed the strain of this morning.

"You're a good person, Orin. I'm going to make you a little happier." She held up the papers printed from her copier. "Here's something I've devised."

He looked toward the clock on the wall.

"I know . . . it's five o'clock on a long day. But this will only take a few minutes. She strode to his desk. Do you remember what you said to me the day I came in to talk about my dead mice?"

He closed the door. "We talked about a lot of things."

"Orin, you said finance is the lifeblood of this institution, and you were right. We need creative ways to get our name on the lips of all the major pharmaceutical companies."

He studied her like he didn't know whether he should fight or flee.

"Look at this." Beth handed him the top four sheets. "Do you know what the fastest growing population in our society today is?"

"Baby boomers, almost senior citizens." Orin flipped through the pages she handed him. Something caught his interest, and he sank into his chair.

"That huge bubble of population," she said, "is moving into the age where medical issues can dominate their lives."

He studied her information for a few minutes. Then he looked up.

"You're talking here," he said, "about diabetes, cataracts, gastrointestinal diseases, aging of the skin, Alzheimer's, cancer. . . ."

"This is our opportunity, Orin."

"'Normal chromosome division,'" he read aloud, "'creates destruction of some of the DNA information.' . . . All right, quick—summarize what I'm looking at here."

"It's about cells that stop dividing and cells that continue to divide indefinitely—like cancers."

"And that's because . . ." He looked at the paper. "Telomeres limit cell division?"

"During somatic cell division there's a shortening of the telomeres that cap the ends of chromosomes. Unfortunately, each time our human or animal cells divide, telomeres lose DNA information." She looked up to be sure he was listening. "In other words, telomere shrinkage could be life's ticking clock. It might determine cellular aging for humans and animals."

Orin pointed to a paragraph. "Telomere shortening may be a consequence of aging. Sounds like the chicken or egg thing."

"But look, this enzyme promotes telomere repair. Malignant cells are immortal because *telomerase* keeps them going."

"Interesting," he said. "But I think we may be jumping on this too late." Orin walked to his bookcase and ran his finger over a series of journals.

"To me," she said, "this dichotomy of telomerase's role in cancer growth and our own mortality from noncancerous, unrepaired telomeres, is wide open for research."

Orin mumbled something to himself.

"Merck, Lilly, Abbott, Wyeth, and a few other pharmaceuticals I've spoken with this afternoon are all interested in reviewing possible research protocols from our scientists on anti-aging studies."

"I don't know, Beth."

"Here." She stood and handed him another page. "This is a major dog-food company *eager* for us to do a double-blind study using their dog food *and* using their dog food with additives—special supplements."

Orin scanned the paper and handed it back to Beth. "This all has merit, but everyone's busy with their own research. And to get the types of animals ordered—"

"We have fourteen beagles in our senior-retirement colony. I could talk with Liz or one of the other researchers who has a light schedule this next month, write the protocol, then present it at the next IACUC meeting."

His face relaxed for a moment. "I like that. Simple and the dogs would enjoy it. This has human implications too."

"Look at this last page." She walked over and handed it to him.

His eyebrows seemed uncontrolled; they went up and down as he read. He put the paper down.

"What's this? Looks like you've organized the available researchers' schedules, assigned them to the open laboratories, matched possible proposed protocols with different types of animals that are here at the institute, and given a proposed timeline." Now he grinned.

"And here's a detailed plan for securing our controlled substances. Orin, you know I'm good at this." It was five-thirty. Good grief, he'd taken her off probation, and there she was demanding a promotion.

He stared at the carpet and pursed his lips.

"Orin?" His ticks and silence drove her nuts.

"Go to the RRC, pick up your personal items, come back here, and sign your leave-of-absence request."

Her breath caught.

"I'll call a joint meeting of the board and foundation. We'll have more strength if I include the foundation members."

She relaxed.

"I'm putting you down for as many weeks as you want, Beth. I've thought you needed a vacation for months now." His eyes seemed brighter. "Check in whenever. Your opossum study's about finalized, and I suspect you'll want to put in a few hours to help train lab techs to put new life into those old beagles."

"Orin, a—a favor, please." The back of her throat ached and caused her voice to catch. She took a moment before she forced herself to say, "Would you tell Joe to move the nonhuman primates into their new corncrib-kennel homes?"

"Beth, you should be the one who does that." He rested his hand on her shoulder. His eyes reflected her own disappointment.

"The macaques, I—they've waited too long." Moisture blurred her vision.

Orin gave her shoulder a couple of pats, then he cleared his throat. "We all know about your family medical situation. My best wishes to you and your aunt."

Only in quiet waters things mirror themselves undistorted.
Only in a quiet mind is adequate perception of the world.

—HANS MARGOLIUS

46

"You still don't know if you'll get the promotion?" Harold took the lime slice Beth had put on the edge of his glass and squeezed the juice into his drink.

Beth passed the dish of cashews to him.

"It all depends. I know he'll lobby for me. There's so much that needs to be fixed, but I'm encouraged."

Saucy trotted into the living room with Meaty Dog bits on her whiskers. She stopped in front of Harold and sat up on her haunches. He tossed her a cashew, which she caught.

"I've left you two alone too much." Beth sipped her chardonnay. "He's taught you bad habits, young lady."

"Wait till you see her other tricks." He grinned. "You say Orin's given you time off until the first of next month?"

"He did. You keep your life fun, don't you?" She tucked her feet under her.

"I do my best." He handed her an envelope from under a magazine. "This came for you from the insurance company a couple of days ago. Sorry, I forgot."

"I'm sick of filling out questionnaires."

Some time ago he'd handed her another envelope. Where had she put it? She opened the insurance letter, then passed it back to Harold.

"I'll be damned." He slapped it against his knee. "Faulty wiring."

She glanced toward the guest room.

He did too. "Kathleen—we talked a little this afternoon." He took another cashew but held it. "She does sleep a lot."

Saucy perked up and watched.

Beth watched him hand Saucy the cashew and knead the dog's floppy ears.

"Kathleen . . . she and I . . ." Harold stopped.

"I know."

He nuzzled Saucy's neck.

"I'll be right back." Beth stood. Harold had given her an envelope right before the house fire. She scooted to the bedroom and searched through her closet. She found her hooded sweatshirt and put her hand in the pocket. She felt a familiar tingle of expectation when she touched the envelope and pulled it out.

She slid her fingernail under the flap and took out the pages. On the first page he'd created a pen-and-watercolor drawing of different things they did together when they were dating. She adored the picture of them ice-skating. On the second page were illustrations of the Broadmoor Hotel dinner and their engagement. On the third page he'd captured her descent of her home's grand staircase to take his hand in marriage. Underneath this drawing he'd written, *On this, the anniversary of our engagement, I renew my pledge to forever stand by your side.*

She carried the envelope to the living room. Harold smiled—he always did, a fleeting one, whenever she entered a room.

"Until Kathleen came," she said, "I'd turned our life into drudgery. Tonight, you with Saucy, the both of us in each other's company—neither of us should ever have to slog through our lives. You're a genius, Harold."

She handed him the envelope. He looked at it, then stood.

"We both need to do what we love." She hugged him.

"Beth, I know how important your work is to you."

She crumpled into his chest.

"You're more important to me than I could ever let you know." She closed her eyes. "I love the way you love me."

He fastened his arms around her like he would never let her go.

"From now on we're a team." She felt energized. "I'll be your business manager. I can do it nights and weekends."

"Your job doesn't keep you busy enough?"

"It does, but this way I can keep track of all the Rachels in your life."

"Sorry, my lady, Rachel needed me. She had her hands full with all those cute, exuberant blondes."

"You're not fooling me."

"She has orange-red hair, a cane, and she's about eighty something. I installed a doggie door for her six blonde poodle princesses."

"I love you, Harold."

"I know."

They fell silent. She stared at Harold. Their teasing didn't erase their dread.

He motioned toward the guest room. "Does Kathleen know about your day?"

"It's probably not important to her at this point. I'll go see her."

"The hospice nurse should be finished now. Want me to go with you?"

"I need some alone time with her." She rubbed her temples.

She went to the bedroom and tapped on Kathleen's door before pushing it open.

The hospice nurse closed her bag and looked up. "I like to check the vital signs before I go home. She's had a good afternoon, but I've put her back on oxygen. She'll rest better."

The nurse scribbled something on her pad, tore it off, and handed the white square to Beth. "This is the medication I've given her tonight."

A chill went through Beth. The torn note . . .

Kathleen had said Beth was her only living relative, her only close relative.

She glanced at her watch—the inscription.

She heard the nurse's good-night and the door closing.

That paper, that little white square, like the one many years ago. She'd never seen her mother so upset.

She walked to the edge of the bed, pulled the chair close, then collected her thoughts.

"Kathleen, I don't know if you can hear me or not."

Kathleen opened her eyes, then closed them.

Beth held one of her hands, placed it to her cheek, and then released it carefully back down to the blanket.

"Are you in pain?" Her aunt's cheeks held more color. It must be the oxygen.

"No." The whisper hit her right in the heart. Beth hadn't expected any response.

"I have some things to tell you," Beth said. "The fire was caused by faulty wiring. I wish I could go back and redo how I treated you."

Kathleen opened her eyes.

"You can't know . . ." Beth's voice quivered. "You mean so much to me."

"Cancel our Amtrak trip, dear," she whispered. "I've worried about that."

"You've been right about Harold, about everything. Tonight I fixed him a cuba libre with limes and gave him cashews. He feeds them to Saucy."

"Good little girl," Kathleen's whisper sounded hoarse.

Beth's words stuck deep inside her for a moment. She swallowed.

"Kathleen, I've always wondered why my mother and I seemed different. I honestly tried to be what she expected."

The rise and fall of Kathleen's chest was shallow and out of rhythm. Her eyes stayed closed.

"Mother couldn't understand why I didn't act more like Bobby and Sarah. I always felt out of tune. We never found a special closeness." Beth's voice caught. "That note I thought mother wrote? She didn't. You wrote the note, didn't you? You were asking *her* a personal favor."

Kathleen opened her eyes.

"And my mother's watch. I figured Grandfather gave it to her, because of the inscription. *For where thou art, there is the world itself.*"

Beth leaned close, wiped her eye with the back of her hand, then brushed a white wisp of hair from Kathleen's.

Please, we need more time.

"You gave my mother—your younger sister—much more than that watch. Your voice is always in my head, guiding me, pushing me, scolding me, laughing with me. You've wrapped yourself so tightly in my heart. Kathleen, I love you, and . . ."

She took one of the frail hands back in hers.

"And I know who you *are*." Beth struggled to bring these words to the surface.

Kathleen's mouth opened, then closed. Beth felt Kathleen's hand give hers a slight squeeze. A flicker of a smile appeared before her *mother* slipped into sleep.

Beth wanted to wake her, to ask her the thousand questions racing through her mind. Instead, she watched her mother's respiration change from shallow and sporadic to slow and rhythmic. Kathleen would enjoy a much needed and restful sleep tonight.

They'd talk in the morning. Beth's mind filled with melodies from

Boccherini's String Quintet tended by a field of wildflowers. A flood of glowing warmth with echoes of her grandfather's voice spread through her.

We are such stuff as dreams are made on. . . .

DISCUSSION QUESTIONS

1. In the first part of the story, Kathleen and Beth are at personal odds. What interactions seemed to cause them to distance themselves from each other, and then what interactions seemed to bring them closer together?

2. Harold added to Beth's stress level and anger in the beginning. What was Beth's attitude about Harold and Kathleen's relationship? What helped Beth's attitude change?

3. In what way did Beth's work and her home life required different types of management skills? How successful did Beth handle this?

4. How did the science research institute setting add to or take away from this reading experience?

5. What were your thoughts about Harold and Kathleen's friendship?

6. Why do you think Orin (Beth's boss) treated Beth the way he did?

7. Kathleen freely gave Beth more advice than she cared to receive. How wise was Beth to follow Kathleen's advice?

8. Harold gave Beth advice, too. Would she have been better off following Harold's advice?

9. Was Harold overly protective? How might Beth have handled Harold's concerns more considerately?

10. Kathleen loved telling stories from her Chicago/Detroit Roaring Twenties years. Some were to help Beth get successfully down her troubled path. Did you find these stories engaging or distracting? Why?

11. When Beth and Kathleen began to trust each other, they fell into discussions about family and life. What did you think about these?

12. If you could ask Beth, Kathleen, or Harold one question, what would it be?